The Magic Goes Away

LARRY NIVEN, JERRY POURNELLE, & MICHAEL FLYNN

Fallen Angels

JERRY POURNELLE & ROLAND GREEN

Tran

JERRY POURNELLE & S. M. STIRLING

Go Tell the Spartans
Prince of Sparta

JERRY POURNELLE & CHARLES SHEFFIELD

Higher Education

The Magic Goes Away

C O L L E C T I O N

The Magic Goes Away
By Larry Niven

The Magic May Return
Edited by Larry Niven

More Magic
Edited by Larry Niven

POCKET BOOKS

NEW YORK   LONDON   TORONTO   SYDNEY

POCKET BOOKS, a division of Simon & Schuster, Inc.
1230 Avenue of the Americas, New York, NY 10020

ISBN: 0-7434-1693-7

First Pocket Books trade paperback edition February 2005

10 9 8 7 6 5 4 3 2 1

POCKET and colophon are registered trademarks of
Simon & Schuster, Inc.

For information regarding special discounts for bulk purchases,
please contact Simon & Schuster Special Sales at 1-800-456-6798
or business@simonandschuster.com

TABLE OF CONTENTS

Ψ

Ψ

INTRODUCTION

4

BEFORE THERE WAS science fiction there were fairy tales. They had the same purpose as the science fiction shaped by Dante and later generations: to entertain and to teach truths. (It's not Dante's fault that his science has all turned to fantasy.) What I noticed as a kid was that the further back in time the stories reached, the more powerful the magic was.

In 1967 or so, a great truth dawned on me. If magic were a nonrenewable resource, the great days of magic and wizards and gods would have evolved into the present day.

I saw other truths by their contrast with traditional fantasy fiction. A wizard who can't beat a swordsman isn't much of a wizard. If magic is anything like dependable, it will form the basis of the civilization, not exist as some anomaly to be ferreted out by Conan the Cimmerian. Laws and guilds will form to restrict the use of spells. Mer-folk will run the fishing industry, trading for fire-worked tools.

So there was a short story, "Not Long Before the End," here included. Later I designed cities and cultures. A novelette evolved, "What Good Is a Glass Dagger?", and then a novel, *The Magic Goes Away*.

The flavor of these stories is melancholy. Civilizations are dying. Everything is turning mundane. Humans are learning to fish. Dragons are mutating, turning strange. Yet there are still wonders.

My cloud walking scenes derive from many hours of looking down on clouds from airplanes. It always looks like you could walk on them.

When I'd turned in *The Magic Goes Away*, Jim Baen, then at Ace Books, suggested we open up the Warlock's world to other writers.

The Magic May Return and *More Magic* are all very different stories. A couple of them are mine, one written with Dian Girard: I was hoping these new stories would reinspire me, and they did.

The latest developments in this universe are three novels, collaborations with Jerry Pournelle.

The Burning City reached print in 2001. I owe thanks to John Ordover, our editor at Simon & Schuster, who says he was inspired by *The Magic Goes Away* when he was a kid. He offered some notable inspirations. It was his suggestion that our characters negotiate with bees.

Burning Tower should reach the bookstores in January 2005.

Burning Mountain is barely begun.

—Larry Niven

The Magic
Goes Away

ψ

Table of Contents

ᛉ

Ψ

OROLANDES

♉

THE WAVES WASHED him ashore aboard a section of the wooden roof from an Atlantean winery. He was half dead, and mad. There was a corpse on the makeshift raft with him, a centaur girl, three days dead of no obvious cause.

The fisherfolk were awed. They knew the workmanship of the winery roof, and they knew that the stranger must have survived the greatest disaster in human history. Perhaps they considered him a good luck charm.

He *was* lucky. The fisherfolk did not steal the golden arm bands he wore. They fed him by hand until he could feed himself. When he grew strong they put him to work. He could not or would not speak, but he could follow orders. He was a big man. When his weight came back he could lift as much as any two fishermen.

By day he worked like a golem, tirelessly: they had to remember to tell him when to stop. By night he would pull his broken sword from its scabbard—the blade was broken to within two thumbs of the hilt—and turn it in his hands as if studying it.

He stayed in the bachelors' longhouse. Women who approached him found him unresponsive. They attributed it to his sickness.

Four months after his arrival he spoke his first words.

The boy Hatchap was moving down the line of sleeping bachelors, waking them for the day's fishing. He found the stranger staring at the ceiling in grief and anguish. "Like magic. Like magic," he mumbled—in Greek. Suddenly he smiled, for the first time Hatchap could remember. "Magician," he said.

That night, after the boats were in, he went to the oldest man in the village and said, "I have to talk to a magician."

The old man was patient. He explained that a witch lived in the nearest village, but that this Mirandee had departed months ago. By now she would be meeting colleagues in Prissthil. There would be no competent magician nearer than Prissthil, which was many days' journey.

Mad Orolandes nodded as if he understood.

He was gone the next morning. He had left one of his bracelets in the headman's house.

ψ

THE WARLOCK

♃

PRISSTHIL AND THE village called Warlock's Cave were six hundred miles apart. Once the Warlock would have flown the distance in a single night. Even today, they might have taken riding dragons, intelligent allies . . . and in one or another region where too much use of magic had leeched *mana* from the earth, they might have left dragon bones to merge with the rocks. Dragon metabolism was partly magical.

It annoyed the Warlock to be leaving Warlock's Cave on muleback; but he and Clubfoot considered this prudent.

It was worse than they had thought. The *mana*-rich places they expected to cross by magic, were not there. Three of their mules died in the desert when Clubfoot ran out of the ability to make rain.

The situation was just this desperate: Clubfoot and the Warlock, two of the most powerful magicians left in the world, came to the conference at Prissthil on foot, leading a pack mule.

Clubfoot was an American, with red skin and straight black hair and an arched beak of a nose. His ancestors had fled an Asian infestation of vampires, had crossed the sea by magic in the company of a tribe of the wolf people. He limped because of a handicap he might have cured decades ago, except that it would have cost him half his power.

And the Warlock limped because of his age.

Limping, they came to the crest of a hill overlooking Prissthil.

It was late afternoon. Already the tremendous shadow of Mount Valhalla, last home of a quarrelsome pantheon of gods now gone mythical, sprawled eastward across Prissthil. The village had grown since the Warlock had last seen it, one hundred and ten years ago. The newer houses were lower, sturdier . . . held up not by spells spoken over a cornerstone, but by their own strength.

"Prissthil was founded on magic," the Warlock said half to himself.

Clubfoot heard. "Was it?"

The Warlock pointed to a dish-shaped depression north of the city wall. "That crater is old, but you can still see the shape of it, can't you? That's Fistfall. This village started as a trading center for talismans: fragments of the boulder of starstone that made that crater. The merchants ran out of starstone long ago, but the village keeps growing. Don't you wonder how?"

Clubfoot shrugged. "They must be trading something else."

"Look, Clubfoot, there are *guards* under Llon! Llon used to be all the guard Prissthil needed!"

"What are you talking about? The big stone statue?"

The Warlock looked at him oddly. "Yes. Yes, the big stone statue."

Winds off the desert had etched away the fine details, but the stone statue was still a work of art. Half human, half big gentle guard dog, it squatted on its haunches before the gate, looking endlessly patient. Guards leaned against it forepaws. They straightened and hailed the magicians as they came within shouting distance.

"Ho, travelers! What would you in Prissthil?"

Clubfoot cried, "We intend Prissthil's salvation, and the world's!"

"Oh, magicians! Well, you're welcome." The head guard grinned. He was a burly, earthy man in armor dented by war. "Though I don't trust your salvation. What have you come to do for us? Make more starstone?"

Clubfoot turned huffy. "It was for no trivial purpose that we traveled six hundred miles."

"Your pardon, but my grandfather used to fly half around the world to attend a banquet," said the head guard. "Poor old man. None of his spells worked, there at the end. He kept going over and over the same rejuvenation spell until he died. Wanted to train me for magic too. I had more sense."

A grating voice said, "Waaarrl . . . lock."

The blood drained from the head guard's face. Slowly he turned. The other guard was backing toward the gate.

The statue's rough-carved stone face, a dog's face with a scholar's thoughtful look, stared down at the magicians. "I know you," said the rusty, almost subsonic voice. "Waarrllock. You made me."

"Llon!" the Warlock cried joyfully. "I thought you must be dead!"

"Almost. I sleep for years, for tens of years. Sometimes I wake for a few hours. The life goes out of me," said the statue. "I wish it were not so. How can I do my duty? One day an enemy will slip past me, into the city."

"We'll see if we can do something about that."

"I wish you luck."

Clubfoot spoke confidently. "The best brains in the world are gathering here. How can we fail?"

"You're young," said Llon.

They passed on. Behind them the statue froze in place.

ψ

OROLANDES II

♃

IT WAS LUCK for Orolandes that Prissthil was no farther. Else he would have died on the way. He made for a place he knew only by name, stopping sometimes to ask directions, or to ask for work and food. He was gaunt again by the time he reached Prissthil.

He circled a wide, barren dish-shaped depression. It was too circular, too regular; it smacked uneasily of sorcery. There was a great stone statue before the city gate, and guards who straightened as he came up.

"We have little need for swordsmen here," one greeted him.

"I want to talk to a magician," said Orolandes.

"You're in luck." The guard looked over his shoulder, quickly, nervously; then turned back fast, as if hoping the swordsman wouldn't notice. "Two magicians came today. But what if they don't want to talk to you?"

"I have to talk to a magician," Orolandes said stubbornly. His hand hung near his sword hilt. He was big, and scarred, and armed. Perhaps he was no longer an obvious madman, but the ghost of some recent horror was plain in his face.

The guard forebore to push the matter. The stranger was no pauper; his gold arm band was a form of money. "If you're rude to a magician, you'll get what you deserve. Welcome to Prissthil. Go on in."

Ψ

THE WARLOCK II

♃

THE INN THE Warlock loved best was gone, replaced by a leather worker's shop. They sought another.

At the Inn of the Mating Phoenixes they saw their mule stabled, then moved baggage to their rooms. Clubfoot flopped on the feather mattress. The Warlock dug in a saddlebag. He pulled out spare clothing, then a copper disk with markings around the rim. He moved to set it aside; then, still holding it, he seemed to drift off into reverie.

Hundreds of years ago, and far east of Prissthil, there had been a proud and powerful magician. He was barely past his brilliant apprenticeship; but he had the temerity to forbid the waging of war throughout the Fertile Crescent, and the power to make it stick. He consistently hired himself out to battle whichever nation he considered the aggressor.

Oh, his magic had been big and showy in those days! Floating castles, armies destroyed by lightning, phantom cities built and destroyed in a night.

In his pride he nicknamed himself Warlock. Had he known that his nickname would become a generic term for magicians, he would not have shown surprise.

But over the decades his spells stopped working. It happened to all magicians. He moved away, and his power returned, to some extent . . . then gradually dwindled, until he moved again.

It happened to nations too. Bound together by its own gods and traditions and laws and trade networks, a nation like Acheron might come to seem as old and stable as the mountains themselves . . . until treaties sealed by oaths and magic lost their power . . . until barbarians with swords come swarming over the borders. All knew that it was so. But the Warlock was the first to learn why, via an experiment he performed with an enchanted copper disk.

If he kept his discovery secret through succeeding decades, his motive was compassion. His terrible truth spelled the end of civilization, yet it was of no earthly use to anyone. Fifty years ago his secret had finally escaped him, for good or evil; it was hard to know which.

"Never mind that," said Clubfoot. "Let's get dinner."

The Warlock shook himself. "Shortly," he said. He set the Wheel aside and reached again into the saddlebag.

Clubfoot snorted. He gathered up spilled clothing and began hanging it.

The Warlock set a wooden box on the table. Inside, within soft fox skins, was a human skull. The Warlock handled it carefully. One hinge of its jaw was broken, and there were tooth marks on the jaw and cheekbones and around both earholes.

Clubfoot said, "I still think we should have contrived to lose that."

"I disagree. *Now* let's get dinner."

The inn was crowded. The dining hall was filled with long wooden tables, too close together, with wooden benches down both sides. The magicians fitted themselves into space on one of the benches. Citizens to either side gradually realised who and what they were and gave them plenty of room.

"Look at this logically," Clubfoot said. "You've carried Wavyhill's skull six hundred miles, when we had to throw away baggage we needed more. It's just a skull. It's not even in good condition. But if there's enough local *mana* to power your spells, and if you work your spells exactly right, you just might be able to bring Wavyhill back to life so he can kill you!"

The Warlock stopped eating long enough to say, "Even if I revive it, it's still just a skull. You'll be all right if you don't stick your fingers in its mouth."

"He's got every reason to want your life! And mine too, because I'm the one who led you to Shiskabil and Hathzoril. If I hadn't found the gutted villages, you'd never have tracked him down."

"He may not have known that."

"I'd rather he did. Hellspawn! He's branded my memory. I'll never forget Shiskabil. Dead empty, and dried blood everywhere, as if it had rained blood. We may never know how many villages he gutted that way."

"I'm going to revive him tonight. Want to help?"

Clubfoot gnawed at the rich dark meat on an antelope's thighbone. Presently he said, "Would I let you try it alone?"

The Warlock smiled. Clubfoot was near fifty; he thought himself experienced in magic. At five times his age the Warlock might have laughed at Clubfoot's solicitude. But the Warlock wasn't stupid. He knew that most of his dangerously won knowledge was obsolete.

The *mana* had been richer, magic had been both easier and more dangerous, when the Warlock was raising his floating castles. Clubfoot was probably more in tune with the real world. So the Warlock only smiled and began moving his fingers in an intricate pattern.

Primary colors streamed up from between the Warlock's fingers, roiled and expanded beneath the beamed roof. Heads turned at the other tables. The clattering of table knives stopped. Then came sounds of delight and appreciative fingersnapping, for a spell the Warlock had last used to blind an enemy army.

Now a lean, scarred swordsman watched the Warlock with haunted eyes. The Warlock did not notice. As he left the dining hall he took with him a bunch of big purple grapes.

Ψ

THE SKULL OF WAVYHILL

4

THE WARLOCK COULD remember a time when murder was very dangerous; when the mystical backlash from a careless killing could reverberate for generations. But that was long ago.

The magician nicknamed Wavyhill—as all magicians carried nicknames, being wary of having their true names used against them—had learned his trade in an age when all spells were less powerful. There was still strong *mana* in murder, but Wavyhill had learned to control it. He had based a slave industry on the zombies of murder victims, and sold the zombies as servants, then set them to killing their masters to make more zombies . . .

He had also used magic to make himself unkillable. For these past twenty years he must have been regretting that terribly.

Wavyhill's skull sat grinning on the table. Clubfoot regarded it uneasily. "It may be we've had too much wine to try this sort of thing tonight."

"Would you rather try it tomorrow, before dawn, with hangovers? Because I want Wavyhill with me when we meet Mirandee and Piranther."

"*All* right, go ahead." Clubfoot bolted the door, then worked spells against magical intrusion. Reviving a murderous dead man was chancy enough without risk of some outsider interfering—and there were amateur magicians everywhere in Prissthil. Magic was an old tradition here, dating from a time when starstone was plentiful.

The Warlock sang as he worked. He was an old man, tall and lean, his head bald as an egg, his voice thin and reedy. But he could hold a tune. The words he sang belonged to a language no longer used except by members of the Sorcerers' Guild.

He knotted a loop of thin leather thong to mend the broken jaw hinge. Other strips of thong went along the cheekbones, the jaw hinges, the ears. Many overlapped. When he finished they formed a crude diagram of the muscles of a human face.

The Warlock stepped back, considering. He cut up a sheet of felt and glued two round pads behind the ear holes. A longer strip went inside the jaws, the back end glued to the table between the jaw hinges.

He looked at Clubfoot, who had been watching intently. Clubfoot said, "Eyes?"

"Maybe later." The Warlock said in the old language, "Kranthkorpool, speak to me."

The skull opened its jaws wide and screamed.

Clubfoot and the Warlock covered their ears. It didn't help. The skull's voice was not troubling the air, and it did not reach the ears. At least it would not bother the other guests.

"He's insane! Shut him off!" Clubfoot cried.

"Not yet!"

The skull screamed its agony. Minutes passed before it paused as if drawing breath. Into the pause the Warlock shouted, "Kranthkorpool, stop! It's over! It's been over for twenty years!"

The skull gaped. It said, "Twenty years?"

"It took me almost that long to find your true name, Kranthkorpool."

"Call me Wavyhill. Who are you? I can't see."

"Just a minute." The Warlock plucked two of what was left of the grapes. He picked up the skull and inserted them into the eye sockets from inside. He inked in two black dots where they showed through the sockets.

"Ah," said the skull. The black dots moved, focussed. They studied Clubfoot, then moved on. "Warlock?"

The Warlock nodded.

"I thought I'd killed you. You were two hundred years old when I cancelled your longevity spells."

"I was able to renew them. Partly. I give you a technical victory, Wavyhill. It was my ally who defeated you."

"Technical victory!" There was hysteria in the skull's falsetto laughter. "That werewolf rug merchant kept tearing and tearing at me! It went on forever and ever, and I couldn't die! I couldn't die!"

"It's over."

"I thought it wouldn't ever be over. It went on and on, a piece of me gone every time he got close enough—"

The skull stopped, seemed to consider. Its expression was unreadable, of course. "I don't hurt. In fact, I can't feel much of anything. There was a long time when I couldn't feel or see or hear or smell or . . . Did you say twenty years? Warlock, what do I look like?"

The Warlock detached a mirror from the wall, brought it and held it. Wavyhill's skull studied itself for a time. It said, "You just had to do that, didn't you?"

"I owed you one. Now you have a decision to make. Do you want to die? I can cancel the spell of immortality you put on yourself."

"I don't know. Let me think about it. What do you want of me, Warlock?"

"Some technical help."

The skull laughed. "From me?"

"You were the world's first necromancer. You were powerful enough to defeat *me*," said the Warlock. "I'd be dead if I hadn't brought help. You used your power for evil, but nobody doubts your skill. Tomorrow I meet two powerful magicians. We'll want your advice."

"Do I know of them?"

"Piranther. Mirandee."

"Piranther!" The skull chuckled. "I'd like to see that meeting. Piranther walked out on your conference, didn't he? After you called him a shortsighted fool. I heard that he took a whole colony of his people to the South Land Mass and swore never to come back."

"You heard right. And he never did come back, but he's coming now."

The skull was silent for a time. Then it said, "You've roused my interest. I don't care to die just now. Under the circumstances that may be silly, but I can't help it. Can you make me a whole man again?"

"Look at me."

The Warlock's back was festive with colored inks: a five-sided tattoo, hypnotic in its complexity. The famous demon trap, once a housing for the Warlock's guardian demon, was empty now; but he still preferred to wear nothing above the waist. Its purpose had been lost, but the habit remained.

It showed him to disadvantage. The Warlock's ribs protruded. His small pot belly protruded. Pouchy, wrinkled, unflexible skin masked the strong lines of his face and showed the shrinkage of his musculature. Vertebrae marched like a tiny mountain range across the fading inks of the empty demon trap.

The skull sighed mournfully.

"Look at me! I wish my youth back, if wishing were all it took," the Warlock said. "I was young for two hundred years. Now the spells are failing. All spells are failing."

"So you need a necromancer." The dots on the grapes turned to the red man. "Are you involved in this madness too?"

"Of course."

The Warlock said, "This is Clubfoot, our ally."

"A pleasure. I'd take hands, but you see how it is," said Wavyhill.

Clubfoot was not amused. "One day you may have hands again, but you will never take my hand. I've seen the villages you gutted. I helped kill you, Wavyhill."

The dots on the grapes turned back to the Warlock. "And this tactless boor is to be our ally? Well, what is your project?"

"We're going to discuss means of restoring the world's *mana*."

The skull's laugh was high and shrill. The Warlock waited it out. Presently he said, "Are you finished?"

"Possibly. Will it take all five of us?"

"I tried to call a full meeting of the Guild. Only ten answered the call. Of the ten, three felt able to travel."

"Has it occurred to you that magic can only use up *mana*? Never restore it?"

"We're not fools. What about an outside source?"

"Such as?"

"The Moon."

The Warlock expected more laughter. It did not come. "*Mana* from the Moon? I never would have thought of that in a thousand years. Still . . . why not? Starstones are rich in *mana*. Why not the Moon?"

"With enough *mana*, and the right spells, you could be human again."

The skull laughed. "And so could you, Warlock. But where would we find magic powerful enough to reach the Moon?"

The door rocked to thunderous knocking.

The magicians froze. Then Clubfoot stripped a bracelet from his upper arm. He looked through it at the door. "No magic involved," he said. "A mundane."

"What would a mundane want with us?"

"Maybe the building's on fire." Clubfoot raised his voice. "You, there—"

Neither the old spells, nor the old bar across the door, were strong enough. The door exploded inward behind a tremendous kick. An armed man stepped into the room and looked about him.

"I have to talk to a magician," he told them.

"You are interrupting magicians engaged in private business," said the Warlock. No sane man would have needed more warning.

The intruder was raggedly shaved, his long black hair raggedly chopped at shoulder length. His dark eyes studied two men and a skull decorated with macabre humor. "You *are* magicians," he said wonderingly. In the next instant he almost died; for he drew his sword, and Clubfoot raised his arms.

The Warlock shook Clubfoot's shoulder. "Stop! It's broken!"

"Yes. I broke it," said the intruder. He looked at the bladeless hilt, then suddenly threw it into a corner of the room. He took two steps forward and closed hands like bronze clamps on the Warlock's thin shoulders. He looked searchingly into the Warlock's face. He said, "Why did it happen?"

Clubfoot's arms were raised again.

Human beings are fragile, watery things. Death spells are the easiest magic there is.

"Back up and start over," said the Warlock. "I don't know what you're talking about. Who are you?"

"Orolandes. Greek soldier."

"Why did you break your sword?"

"I hated it. I thought maybe it happened because of the people I killed. Not the other soldiers. The priests."

Clubfoot exclaimed, "You were in the Atlantis invasion!"

"Yes. We finally invaded Atlantis. First time Greeks ever got that far." Orolandes released the Warlock. He looked like a sleepwalker; he wasn't seeing anything here in the room. "We came for slaves and treasure. That's all."

"And trade advantage," said the Warlock.

"Uh? Maybe. Nobody told me anything like that. Anyway, we won. The armies of Atlantis must have gotten soft. We went through them like they were nothing. But the priests were something else. They stood in a long line on the steps of the big temple and waved their arms. We got sick. Some of us died. But we kept coming, crawling—I was crawling, anyway—and we got to them and killed them. And then Atlantis was ours."

He looked with haunted eyes at the magicians. "Ours. At last. Hundreds of years we'd dreamed of conquering Atlantis. We'd take their treasure. We'd take away their weapons. We'd make them pay tribute. But we never, we never wanted to kill them all. Old men, women, children, everyone. Nobody ever thought of that."

"You son of a troll. I had friends in Atlantis," said Clubfoot. "How did you live through it? Why didn't you die with the rest?"

"Uh? There was a big gold Tau symbol at the top of the steps. We were laughing and bragging and binding up our wounds when the land started to shake. Everybody fell over. The Tau thing cracked at the base and fell on the steps. Then someone pointed west, and the horizon was going up. It didn't look like water. It was too misty, too big. It looked like the horizon was getting higher and higher.

"I crawled under the Tau thing with my back against the step. Captain Iason was shouting that it wasn't real, it was just an illusion, we must have missed some of the priests. The water came down like the end of the world. I guess the Tau thing saved my life—even the water couldn't move it, it was so heavy—but it almost killed me too. I had to get out from under it and try to swim up.

"I grabbed something that was floating up with me. It turned out to be part of a wooden roof. I got on it. A centaur girl came swimming by and I hauled her up on the roof. I thought, well, at least I saved one of them. And then she just fell over."

Clubfoot said, "There's magic in centaur metabolism. Without *mana* she died."

"But what happened? Did we do it?"

"You did it," said Clubfoot.

"I thought . . . maybe . . . you'd say . . ."

"You did it. You killed them all."

The Warlock said, "Atlantis should have been under the ocean hundreds of years ago. Only the spells of the priest-kings kept that land above the waves."

Orolandes nodded dumbly. He turned to the door.

"Stop him," said Wavyhill. As Orolandes turned to the new voice, the skull snapped, "You. Swordsman. How would you like a chance to make amends?"

Orolandes gaped at the talking skull.

"Well? You wiped out a whole continent, people and centaurs and mer-people and all. You broke your sword, you were so disgusted at yourself. How would you like to do something good for a change? Keep it from happening to others."

"Yes."

Clubfoot asked, "What *is* this?"

"We may need him. I may know of a source of very powerful *mana*."

"*Where?*"

"I'll reserve that. Do the words 'god within a god' mean anything to you?"

"No."

"Good." The skull chuckled. "We'll see what develops tomorrow. See to it that this . . . Orolandes is with us when we meet your friends. You, Orolandes, have you got a room here?"

"I can get one."

"Meet us at dawn, for breakfast."

Orolandes nodded and walked out. There was no spring in his walk. His sword hilt he left lying in a corner.

♆

FISTFALL

♃

FROM PRISSTHIL'S GATE one could make out an elliptical depression, oddly regular, in the background of low green hills. Time had eroded Fistfall's borders; they disappeared as one came near. Greenery had covered the pits and dirt piles where earlier men had dug for starstone. From what must be the rim, Orolandes could see only that the land sloped gradually down, then gradually up again.

It was just past sunrise; there was still shadow in the hollow. Orolandes shivered in the morning chill.

The old man did not shiver, though he walked naked to the waist. A talking skull sat on his shoulder, fastened by straps over the lower jaw. He and the skull and the younger man chatted as they walked: trivia mixed with incomprehensible shop talk mixed with reminiscence from many lifetimes.

Orolandes shivered. He had fallen among magicians, willingly and by design, and he was not sure of his sanity. Before that terrible day in Atlantis he would never have considered a magician to be anything but an enemy.

In the village of the fisherfolk Orolandes had waited for the images to go away. Don't speak of it, don't think of it; the vivid memories would fade.

But in the dark of sleep the sea would rise up and up and over to swallow the world, with his spoils and his men and the people he'd conquered. He would snap awake then, to stare into the dark until it turned light.

Or on a bright afternoon he would heave at the awkward weight of a net filled with fish . . . and he would remember pulling at the limp, awkwardly right-angled centaur girl, trying to get her up on the broken roof. She'd *had* to lie on her side; he'd felt unspeakably clumsy trying to give her artificial respiration. But he'd seen her breath at last! He'd seen her eyelids flicker open, seen her head lift and look at him . . . seen the life go out of her then, draining away to somewhere else.

What had happened that day? If he knew *why*, then the horror would leave him, and the guilt . . . He had clung to that notion until last night. Now he knew. What the magicians had told him was worse than he had imagined.

The notion he clung to now might be the silliest of all. Orolandes could read nothing in the white bone face of the dead magician. Even to its friends it was a tolerated evil. But nobody else had offered Orolandes any breath of comfort.

On the strength of a skull's vague promise, he was here. He would wait and see.

* * *

The Warlock felt uncommonly alive. As they moved into Fistfall his vision and his hearing sharpened, his normal dyspepsia eased. Over the centuries the townspeople had removed every tiniest fragment of the boulder that had come flaming down from the skies; but vaporised rock had condensed and sifted down all over this region, and there was no removing it. Old spells took new strength.

Down there in the shadow, two walked uphill toward them.

"I recognise Mirandee," said Clubfoot. "Would that be Piranther?"

"I think so. I only met him once."

Clubfoot laughed. "Once was enough?"

"I'm surprised he came. We didn't part as friends. I was so sure I was right, I got a little carried away. Well, but that was fifty years ago." The Warlock turned to the swordsman. "Orolandes, I should have said it before. You can still turn back."

The big man's hand kept brushing his empty scabbard. He looked at the Warlock with too-wide eyes and said, "No."

"You are about to learn the secrets of magicians. It isn't likely you'll learn too much, but if you do, we may have to tamper with your memory."

It was the fist time the Warlock had seen him smile. The swordsman said, "There are parts you can cut out while you're about it."

"Do you mean that?"

"I'm not sure. What kind of man is that? Or is it the woman's familiar?"

The man approaching them was small and dark-skinned and naked in the autumn chill. His hair was white and puffy as a ripe dandelion. A skin bag hung on a thong around his neck.

"His people come from the South Land Mass," said Clubfoot. "They're powerful and touchy. Be polite."

Piranther's companion was a head taller than he was, a slender woman in a vivid blue robe. Snow-white hair fell to her waist and bobbed with her walk. Mirandee and the Warlock had dwelt together in a year long past, sharing knowledge and other things, experimenting with sex magic in a way that was only partly professional.

But now her eyes only brushed the Warlock and moved on. "Clubfoot, a pleasure to see you again! And your friends." Visibly she wondered what the scarred, brawny, bewildered man was doing here. Then she turned back to the Warlock, and the blood drained from her face.

What was this? Was she reacting to the bizarre decorated skull on his shoulder? No. She took a half-step forward and said, "Oh my gods! Warlock!"

So that was it. "The magic goes away," he told her gently. "I wish I'd thought to send you some warning. I see that your own youth spells have held better."

"Well, but I'm younger. But you are all right?"

"I live. I walk. My mind is intact. I'm two hundred and forty years old, Mirandee."

Wavyhill spoke from the Warlock's shoulder. "He's in better shape than I am."

The woman's eyes shifted, her brow lifted in enquiry.

"I am Wavyhill. Mirandee, I know you by reputation."

"And I you." Her voice turned winter-cold. "Warlock, is it proper that we deal with this . . . murderer?"

"For his skill and his knowledge, I think so."

The skull cackled. "I know too much to be absent, my dear. Trust me, Mirandee, and forgive me the lives of a few dozens of mundanes. We're here to restore the magic that once infused the world. I want that more than you do. Obviously."

But Mirandee was looking at the Warlock when she answered Wavyhill. "No. You don't."

The age-withered black man spoke for the first time. "Skull, I sense the ambition in you. Otherwise you conceal your thoughts. What is it you hide?"

"I would bow if I could. Piranther, I am honored to meet you," said Wavyhill. "Do you know of the god within a god?"

Piranther's brow wrinkled. "These words mean nothing to me."

"Then I have knowledge you need. A point for bargaining. Please notice that I am more helpless than any infant. On that basis, will you let me stay? I won't ask you to trust me."

Piranther's eyes shifted. His face was as blank as his mind, and his mind was as dark and hidden as the floor of the ocean. "Warlock, I should be gratified that you still live. And you must be Clubfoot; I know you by reputation. But who are you, sir?"

"Orolandes. I, I was asked to come."

Wavyhill said, "I asked him. His motives are good. Let him stay."

Piranther half-smiled. "On trust?"

Wavyhill snorted. "You're a magician, they say. Read his mind. He hasn't the defenses of a turtle."

That, and Piranther's slow impassive nod . . . "No!" cried Orolandes, and his hand spasmed above the empty scabbard. He backed away.

The skull said, "Stop it, Greek. What have you to hide?"

Orolandes moaned. His guilt was agony; he wanted to burrow in the ground. One flash of hate he felt for these who would judge him: for the Warlock's sympathy, the woman's cool curiosity, the black demon's indifference, the red magician's irritation at time-wasting preliminaries. But Orolandes had already judged himself. He stood fast.

Corpses floated in shoals around his raft. They covered the sea as far as the horizon. Sharks and killer whales leapt among them . . .

Piranther made a grimace of distaste. "You might have warned me. Oh, very well, Wavyhill, he's certainly harmless. But he trusts you no more than I do."

"And why should he?"

Piranther shrugged. He settled gracefully onto a small grassy hillock. "I had hoped to be addressing thirty or forty trained magicians. It bodes ill for us that no more than five could come. But here we are. Who speaks?"

There was an awkward pause. Clubfoot said, "If nobody else wants to . . ."

"Proceed."

Mirandee and the Warlock settled cross-legged on the ground.

Clubfoot looked toward Mount Valhalla, collecting his thoughts. He may have been regretting his temerity. After all, he was the youngest of the magicians present. Well—

"First there were the gods," he said. "Earth sparkled with magic in those days, and nothing was impossible. The first god almost certainly created himself. Later gods may not have been *that* powerful, but there are tales of mountains piled one on another to reach sky-dwelling gods and overthrow them, of a god torn to pieces and the fragments forming whole pantheons, of the sun being stopped in its track for trivial purposes. The gods' lives were fueled by magic, not fire. Eventually the *mana* level dropped too low, and the gods went mythical . . . as I suppose we'd die if fires stopped burning.

"We still have the habit of thanking the gods, mundanes and sorcerers alike. With reason. Before they died, some of the gods played at making other forms of life. Their creations were their survivors. Some live by what seems to be slow-burning fire . . . men, foxes, rabbits . . . and most plants use fire from the sun. Other plants and beasts use fire and *mana* both. We find unicorns surviving in *mana*-poor regions, though the colts are born with stunted horns, or none. But many *mana*-dependent peoples are going mythical: merpeople, dragons, centaurs, elves. Hey—"

Clubfoot did a strange thing for a man making a speech. He darted over to a boulder, heaved at it and turned it over. Underneath was a blob of grayish jelly two feet across.

In his youth the Warlock had killed carnivorous *goo* the size of houses. To a mere warrior they were more dangerous than dragons: a sword was generally too short to reach the beast's nucleus. By contrast this *goo* was tiny. It was formless and translucent, with darker organs and vacuoles of food showing within its body. It arched itself in the morning sunlight and tried to flow into Clubfoot's shadow.

"There! That's what I'm talking about!" Clubfoot cried. "The *goo* are surviving, but *look* at it. *Goo* are named for the first word spoken by a baby. They're said to be children of the first god: formless, adaptable, created in the image of the Crawling Chaos. We saw them smaller than a man's fist in the desert, where the *mana* is poor. Do you see how small it's gotten? *Goo* live by fire and magic, but they can use fire alone. When the world is barren of magic the *goo* will remain, but they'll probably be too small to see.

"And we'll survive, because we live by fire alone. But we'll be farmers or merchants or entertainers, and the swordsmen will rule the world. That's why we're here. Not to save the centaurs or the dragons or the *goo*. To save ourselves."

"Thank you. You're very eloquent," said Piranther. He seemed to have taken charge, with little challenge from anyone. He looked about at the rest. "Suggestions?"

Mirandee said, "What about your project, Piranther? Fifty years ago you were going to map the *mana*-rich regions of the world."

"And I said that was self-limiting," said the Warlock.

"And you called me a short-sighted fool," Piranther said without heat. "But we carried through in spite of you. As you know, there are places human magicians never reached or settled, where the *mana* remains strong. I need hardly point out that they are the least desirable living places in the world. The land beneath the ice of the South Pole. In the north, the ice itself. The clouds. Any fool who watches clouds can tell you they're magic. I know spells to render cloud-stuff solid and to shape it into castles and the like."

"So do I," said the Warlock.

"So did Sheefyre," Mirandee said dryly. "The witch Sheefyre will not be joining us. She took a fall. Where are you on a cloudscape when the *mana* runs out?"

"Precisely. It was our major problem," Piranther said. "There are places one can practice magic, but when the spells stop working, where are you? A desert, or an inaccessible mountaintop, or the terrible cold of the South Pole. But our search turned up one place of refuge, an unknown body of land in the southern hemisphere.

"Australia was probably infested with demons until recently. They're gone now. All we have of them is the myth of a Hell under the world. But why else should the fifth largest land mass in the world have been unin-habited until we came? You know that when we finished our mapping proj-ect," said Piranther, "I took my people there, all who would go. The *mana* is rich. There are new fruits and roots and meat animals. On a nearby island we found a giant bird, the moa, the finest meat animal in the world—"

The Warlock grinned. "Do I hear an invitation to emigrate?"

For a moment Piranther looked like a trapped thing. Then the bland, expressionless mask was back. He said, "I'm afraid we have no room for you."

"What, in the world's fifth largest land mass?"

"At the conference fifty years ago you said . . . what was it you said? You said that mapping *mana*-rich places only brings magicians to use up the *mana*. So—" Piranther shrugged delicately. "I take you at your word."

They looked at him. He was hiding something . . . and he knew they knew . . . "I must," he said. "The castles we raised by magic along the coast are falling down. The ambrosia is dying. We must migrate inland. I fear the results if my students can't learn to use less powerful spells."

"They'll go further and further inland," Mirandee said in a dreamy voice, "using the *mana* as they go." Her face was blank, her eyes blind. Sometimes the gift of prophecy came on her thus, without warning. "Thousands of years from now the swordsmen will come, to find small black people in the barren center of the continent, starving and powerless, making magic with pointing-bones that no longer work."

"There is no need to be so vivid," Piranther said coldly.

Mirandee started. Her eyes focussed. "Was I talking? What did I say?"

But nobody thought it tactful to tell her. Clubfoot cleared his throat and said, "Undersea?"

The Warlock shook his head. "No good. There's nothing to breath in the water, and the *mana* is in the sea floor. When the spells fail, where are you?" He looked around him. "Shall we face facts? There's no place to hide. If we can't bring the magic back to the world, we might as well give it to the swordsmen."

Piranther asked, "Do you have something in mind?"

"An outside source. The Moon."

Nobody laughed. Even the Greek swordsman only gaped at him. Piranther's wrinkled face remained immobile as he said, "You must have been thinking this through for hundreds of years. Is this really your best suggestion?"

"Yes. Silly as it sounds. May I expound?"

"Of course."

"I don't have to say anything that isn't obvious. Stones and iron fall from the sky every night. They burn out before they touch earth. Their power for magic is low; it has to be used fast, while they still burn.

"Some starstones do reach earth. The bigger they are, the more power they carry. Correct?" The Warlock did not wait for an answer. "The Moon is huge. Watch it at moonrise and you'll know. It should carry enormous power—far more than the Fist carried, for instance. In fact, it must. What else but magic could hold it up? I suggest that the Moon carries more *mana* than the world has seen since the gods died.

"But you don't need me to tell you that, do you?—Orolandes, is there magic in the Moon?"

The ex-soldier started. "Why ask me? I know no magic." He shrugged uncomfortably. "All right, yes, there's magic in the Moon. Anyone can feel it."

"We all know that," said Piranther. "How do you propose to use it?"

"I don't know. If our spells could reach the Moon at all, it's own *mana* would let us land it."

"This all seems very . . . hypothetical," Mirandee said delicately. "I don't know what holds the Moon up. Do you? Does anyone?"

There were blank looks. Wavyhill's skull cackled. "We could pull the Moon down and find we'd used up all the *mana* doing it."

Mirandee was exasperated. "Well, then, does anyone know how *big* the Moon is? Because the bigger it is, the higher it must be, and the harder it's going to hit! It could be thousands of miles up!"

"It must be tremendous," Piranther said. "From Iceland and from Australia, it looks exactly the same. Nothing remotely as large has ever struck earth. Otherwise we'd find old records of it in the sky, records of a time when there were two moons."

"We'll have to give it plenty of room, if we solve the other problems." The Warlock hesitated. "I'd thought of the Gobi Desert."

Wavyhill said, "There's even more room in the Pacific."

Clubfoot made a rude noise. "Tidal waves. And we couldn't get to it after it sank." He tugged thoughtfully at a single braid of straight black hair. "Why not the South Pole? No, forget I said that. The Moon never gets over the Poles."

Piranther wore an irritating half-smile. "Basics, brothers, basics. We don't know how big the Moon is. We don't know what it weighs, or what holds it up. We don't have magic powerful enough to reach it. You're all thinking like novices, trying to do it all in one crackling powerful ceremony of enchantment, whereas in fact we need spells and power to *reach* the Moon, and *study* it, and *learn* enough to tell us what to do next, and finally to *use* that magic to tap the Moon's power." His smile deepened. "There is nothing in the world today that is sufficiently sacred to do all that. Warlock, you once called me a short-sighted fool. I will not call you short-sighted. Your daydream would be work for generations, if it could be done at all."

The Warlock was not pleased.

"What exactly are you gloating about? We had the big conference fifty years ago. The power existed, *then*. But you and your group wanted to make maps."

Piranther's half-smile disappeared. His small black hand stroked the skin bag at his chest—and forces could be felt gathering.

"I know of a *mana* source," said the skull on the Warlock's shoulder.

Wavyhill saw that he had everyone's attention. "I thought I had better interrupt while we still had a conference. I wish I could give guarantees, but I can't. I may know of a living god, the last in the world. I'll lead you to it."

"I find this hard to believe," Piranther said slowly. "A remaining god? When even the dragons are nearly gone? When half the world's fishing industries are run by men, from boats, because the merpeople have died off?"

"It seems more believable when you know the details. I'll tell you the details, and I'll lead you to it," said Wavyhill. "But I want oaths sworn. To the best of your abilities, when we have gained sufficient *mana* for the spells to work, will each of you do your best to return me to my human form?"

Nobody hurried to answer.

"Remember, your oaths will be binding. A *geas* is more powerful than any natural law, in a high-*mana* environment. Well?"

"I had other projects in mind," Piranther said easily. "Your oath would claim too much of my time. Also, you have a much greater interest in the Warlock's project than any of us."

"Your interest isn't slight," said Wavyhill. "We who pull down the power of the Moon will rule the world."

"True enough. But why should you have a head start on the rest of us while we fulfill your *geas*? Swear us the same oath, Wavyhill. Then we can *all* scurry about for ways to put you back together again. Otherwise we'll wake to find you ruling us."

"Willingly," said Wavyhill, and he swore.

Piranther listened with his half-smile showing, while Mirandee and the Warlock and, reluctantly, Clubfoot swore Wavyhill's oath.

Then, "I will not swear," said Piranther. "Thus I presume you will not guide me?" He stood, lithely, and walked away. If he expected voices calling him back, there were none, and he walked away toward Prissthil.

"That means trouble," said Wavyhill.

"We can do it without him," said Clubfoot.

"You don't follow me," said Wavyhill. "I meant what I said. If we fail, there is no world. If we draw the power of the Moon, we rule the world. If Piranther follows us and learns what we learn, and if Piranther is there when we pull down the Moon or whatever, he's the only one of us who can concentrate purely on controlling it."

Clubfoot saw it now. "You and your stupid oath."

"He'll have serious trouble following us," said the Warlock.

ψ

THE MOUNTAIN

♃

THEY CLIMBED MOUNT Valhalla on foot: three magicians, two porters hired in Prissthil, Orolandes carrying a porter's load, and the skull of Wavyhill still moored to the Warlock's shoulder. Wavyhill's eyes had been replaced with rubies.

He had hired the porters, he had chosen their equipment, but Orolandes had no idea why he was going up a mountain. He had asked Wavyhill, "Is the last god at the peak, then?"

"Gear us for the peak," Wavyhill had told him, "and don't think too much. Piranther can read your mind. He'll be getting your surface thoughts until we can break you loose."

The porters were small, agile, cheerful men. They did better than Orolandes at teaching the magicians elementary climbing techniques. They showed neither awe of the magicians' power nor scorn for their clumsiness. To natives of Prissthil a magician was a fellow-professional, worthy of respect.

Clubfoot was a careful climber, little hampered by his twisted foot. But they were all aging, even Mirandee of the smooth pale skin and the white hair. On the first night they hurt everywhere. They couldn't eat. They moaned in their sleep. In the morning they were too tired and stiff to move, until hunger and the smell of breakfast brought them groaning from their blankets.

It was good for Orolandes' self-confidence, to see these powerful beings so far out of their element. He became marginally less afraid of them. But he wondered if they had the stamina to continue.

As the ascent grew steeper the packs grew lighter. Food was eaten. Heavy cloaks were taken from the packs and worn. But the air grew lean, and Orolandes and the porters panted as they climbed.

Not so the magicians. With altitude they seemed to gain strength. Here above the frost line there were even times when the rich creamy fall of Mirandee's hair would darken momentarily, then grow white again.

It usually happened when they were passing one of the old fallen structures.

They had passed the first of these on the third day. No question about what it was. It was an altar, a broad slab of cut rock richly stained with old blood. "This was why the gods survived so long here," the Warlock told Orolandes. "Sacrifice in return for miracles. But when the gods' power waned in the lands below the mountain, the miracles weren't always granted. The natives didn't know why, of course. Eventually they stopped sacrificing."

Higher structures were stranger, and not built by men. They passed a cluster of polished spheres of assorted sizes, fallen in a heap in a patch of snow. They glowed by their own light: four big spheres banded in orange and white, one with a broad ring around it; three much smaller, one mottled ochre and one mottled blue-and-white and one shining white; and two, the smallest, the yellow-white of old bone. Further on was a peaked circular structure sitting on the ground. It looked like a discarded roof.

Though Orolandes was still the master climber, this was evidently magicians' territory.

There was no firewood on the third night. It was not needed. After they made camp the magicians—tired but cheerful, no longer bothered by strained muscles—sang songs in a ring around a sizeable boulder, until the boulder caught fire. Another song brought a unicorn to be slaughtered and butchered by the porters. Orolandes could only admire the porters' aplomb. They roasted the meat and boiled water for herb tea on a burning rock, as if they had been doing it all their lives.

After dinner, as they were basking around the fire, Clubfoot said to Mirandee, "You know that I've admired you for a long time. Will you be my wife while our mission lasts?"

Orolandes was jolted. Never would he have asked a woman such a question except in privacy. But Clubfoot did not expect to be turned down . . . and it showed in his face when Mirandee smiled and shook her head. "I gave up such things long ago," she said. "Being in love ruins my judgement. It takes my mind off what I'm doing, and I ruin spells. But I thank you."

On the morning of the fourth day they came on a flight of stairs leading up from the lip of a sheer cliff. Aided by climbing ropes, they crawled sideways along an icy slope to reach the stairs: broad slabs of unflawed marble that narrowed as they rose, but that rose out of sight into the clouds.

Placed on random steps were statues, human, half-human, not at all human. Orolandes tried to forget, and could not, a half-melted thing equipped with tentacles and broad clawed flippers and a single eye. But there was a hardwood statue of a handsome, smiling man that Orolandes found equally disturbing, and for no reason at all. Magic. Here where men could not live because they could not grow food, magic still lived.

Snow and ice covered the rocks to either side, but no ice had formed on the marble. The stairway rose past strange things. Here was something shattered, a hollow flowing shape that must have looked like a teardrop flowing upward before it broke at the base and toppled. There, a single tree bore a dozen kinds of ripe fruit; but it withered as the magicians came near, until nothing was left but a dry stick.

And there, a section seemed to have been bitten out of the mountainside to leave a broad flat place. An arena, it was, where two sets of metal-and-leather armor stood facing each other in attack position, weapons raised, each piece of armor suspended in air. As the little party climbed past, the armor dropped in two heaps.

The Warlock stopped. "Orolandes, climb down there and get one of those swords."

"I gave up swords," said Orolandes.

"Maybe you won't use it, but you should have it. Magic can't do everything. None of us has ever used a sword . . . except Wavyhill."

The skull laughed on his shoulder. "Much good it did me, then and now. Get the sword, Greek."

Orolandes shucked his pack and clambered down and across the icy slope. At his approach the fallen armor stirred, then slumped. He chose the straight-bladed sword over the scimitar. It would fit his scabbard. It felt natural in his hand, but it roused unpleasant memories.

He was turning to go when he saw what had been hidden from the stair by a shoulder of rock.

Rows of thrones carved into the slanted rock face. Stands for the battle's audience. On each of the scores of thrones a wisp of fog shifted restlessly.

Orolandes retreated behind his sword. Nothing followed.

Now the marble stairs above them were hidden by cloud, the banner of cloud that always streamed from the mountain's peak.

The Warlock dismissed the porters, paying them in gold. Orolandes piled what was left in the packs into one pack, and they went on, up into the cloud.

The cold became wet cold. Ice crystals blew around them. The magicians below were half-hidden. Orolandes climbed with one hand on the rock wall. The other side was empty space.

The snow-fog thinned. They were climbing out of the cloud.

They emerged, and it was glorious. The cloud bank stretched away like a clean white landscape, under a brilliant sun and dark blue sky. The Warlock rubbed his hands in satisfaction. "We're here! Orolandes, let me get into that pack."

The others watched as he chose his tools. If the Warlock had told them what he was about, Orolandes hadn't heard it. He did not speculate. He waited to know what was expected of him.

The attitude came easily to him. He had risen through the ranks of the Greek army; he could follow orders. He had given orders, too, before Atlantis sank beneath him. Since then Orolandes had given over control of his own fate.

"Good," muttered the Warlock. He opened a wax-stoppered phial and poured dust into his hand and scattered it like seeds into the cloudscape. He sang words unfamiliar to Orolandes.

Mirandee and Clubfoot joined in, clear soprano and awkward bass, at chorus points that were not obvious. The song trailed off in harmony, and the Warlock scattered another handful of dust.

"All right. Better let me go first," he said. He stepped off the stairs into feathery emptiness.

He bounced gently. The cloud held him.

Clubfoot followed, in a ludicrous bouncing stride that sank him calves-deep into the fog. Mirandee walked out after him. They turned to look back at Orolandes.

Clubfoot started to choke. He sat down in the shifting white mist and bellowed with a laughter that threatened to strangle him. Mirandee fought it, then joined in in a silvery giggle. There was the not-quite-sound of Wavyhill's chortling.

The laughter seemed to fade, and the world went dim and blurry. Orolandes felt his knees turn to water. His jaw was sagging. He had climbed up through this cloud. It was cold and wet and without substance. It would not hold a feather from falling, let alone a man.

The witch's silver laughter burned him like acid. For the lack of the Warlock's laughter, for the Warlock's exasperated frown, Orolandes was grateful. When the Warlock swept his arm in an impatient beckoning half circle, Orolandes stepped out into space in a soldier's march.

His foot sank deep into what felt like feather bedding, and bounced. He was off balance at the second step, and the recoil threw him further off. He kicked out frantically. His leg sank deep and recoiled and threw him high. He landed on his side and bounced.

Mirandee watched with her hands covering her mouth. Clubfoot's laugh was a choking whimper now.

Orolandes got up slowly, damp all over. He waded rather than walked toward the magicians.

"Good enough. We don't have a lot of time," said the Warlock. "Take a little practice—we all need that—then go back for the pack."

Ψ

CLOUDSCAPES

♃

THE LAYER OF cloud stirred uneasily around them. It was not flat. There were knolls of billowing white that they had to circle round. It was like walking through a storehouse full of damp goose down. The cloud-stuff gave underfoot, and pulled as the foot came forward.

Orolandes found a stride that let him walk with the top-heavy pack, but it was hard on the legs. Half-exhausted and growing careless, he nearly walked into a hidden rift. He stared straight down through a feathery canyon at small drifting patches of farm. A tiny plume of dust led his eye to a moving speck, a barely visible horse and rider.

He turned left along the rift, while his heart thundered irregularly in his ears.

Clubfoot looked back. Mount Valhalla rose behind them, a mile or so higher than they'd climbed, blazing snow-white in the sunlight. "Far enough, I guess. Now, the crucial thing is to keep moving," he said, "because if the magic fails where we're standing it's all over. Luckily we don't have to do our own moving."

He helped Orolandes doff the pack. He rummaged through it and removed a pair of water-tumbled pebbles, a handful of clean snow, and a small pouch of gray powder. "Now, Kranthkorpool, would you be so kind as to tell us where we're going?"

"No need to coerce me," said Wavyhill. "We go east and north. To the northernmost point of the Alps."

"And we've got food for four days. Well, I guess we're in a hurry." Clubfoot began to make magic.

The Warlock did not take part. He knew that Clubfoot was a past master at weather magic. Instead he watched Mirandee's hair.

Yes, her youth had held well. She had the clear skin and unwrinkled brow of a serene thirty-year-old noblewoman. Her wealth of hair was now raven black, with a streak of pure white that ran from her brow all the way back. As she helped Clubfoot sing the choruses, the white band thickened and thinned and thickened.

The Warlock spoke low to Orolandes. "If you see her hair turn sheer white, run like hell. You're overloaded with that pack. Just get to safety and let me get the others out." The Greek nodded.

Now the clouds stirred about them. The fitful breeze increased slightly, but not enough to account for the way the mountain was receding. Now the clouds to either side churned, fading or thickening at the edges. Through a sudden rift they watched the farmlands drift away.

"Down there they'll call this a hurricane. What they'll call us doesn't bear mentioning," Clubfoot chuckled. He walked back to where Orolandes was standing and settled himself in the luxurious softness of a cloud billow. In a lowered voice he said, "I've been wrestling with my conscience. May I tell you a story?"

Orolandes said, "All right." He saw that the others were beyond earshot.

"I'm a plainsman," said Clubfoot. "My master was a lean old man a lot like the Warlock, but darker, of course. He taught half a dozen kids at a time, and of course he was the tribe's medicine man. One day when I was about twelve, old White Eagle took us on a hike up the only mountain any-where around.

"He took us up the easy side. There were clouds streaming away from the top. White Eagle did some singing and dancing, and then he had us walk out on the cloud. I ran out ahead of the rest. It looked like so much fun."

"Fun," Orolandes said without expression.

"Well, yes. I'd never been on a cloud. How was a plains kid to know clouds aren't solid?"

"You mean you never . . . realised . . ." Orolandes started laughing.

Clubfoot was laughing too. "I'd seen clouds, but way up in the sky. They looked solid enough. *I* didn't know why White Eagle was doing all that howling and stamping."

"And the next time you went for a stroll on a cloud—"

"*Oh,* no. White Eagle explained that. But it must have been a fine way to get rid of slow learners."

* * *

Mirandee was saying, "Do you really think Piranther can't follow us?"

"There's no way he can travel this fast on the ground," said the Warlock. "If he's in the clouds, we'll know it. Just as our weather pattern must be fairly obvious to him. Do you see any stable spots in this cloud canopy?"

"No . . . but there used to be other ways to fly."

The Warlock snorted. "Used to be, yes."

Mirandee seemed really worried. "I wonder if you aren't underestimating Piranther. Warlock, I had occasion to visit Australia not long ago."

"Mending fences for me?"

"If you like. I thought he might be ready to forget heated words long cooled. He wasn't." She gestured nervously. "Never mind that. I saw *power*. There are roc chicks in that place, baby birds eight feet tall, that breed as chicks and never grow up. Piranther's people raise them for the eggs! And let children ride on their backs! I watched apprentice magicians duel for sport, with adepts standing by to throw ward-spells. It was like stepping two hundred years into the past. I watched a castle shape itself out of solid rock—"

"And now all the castles are falling down, or so says Piranther. The *mana* can't be *that* high, not if the rocs have turned neotenous. Piranther can't be as powerful as all of us put together."

"He's their leader. The most powerful of them all."

The Warlock settled his back against a soft billow of cloud. "This place is paradise for a lazy man. Orolandes!" he called.

Orolandes and Clubfoot came chuckling about something. The swordsman let the Warlock put his hands on his head and mutter an ancient spell.

"That should break the link between you and Piranther. Now, Wavyhill, tell us about the last god."

Orolandes settled himself cross-legged. He felt no different . . . and he was never going to relax here, despite the infinity of feather bed. But he would not show it either.

"Roze-Kattee was male and female," said the skull on the Warlock's shoulder, "and his attributes were love and madness. He was god to the Frost Giants, way north of here, where we're going. He hasn't been heard of in half a thousand years, not since the Nordiks conquered the Frost Giants. But he's said to be dormant, not dead."

"Said by whom?" Mirandee asked. "The Frost Giants are nearly mythical."

"Oh, the Nordiks still have a few Frost Giant slaves. But the Frost Giants never talked about Roze-Kattee. All I've got is the old Nordik epic, the Hometaking Wars Cycle, which is certainly slanted and possibly garbled."

Mirandee was shaking her head. "I've heard other tales of sleeping gods."

"This one's different. Mirandee, when I was still an apprentice, my master Harper was interested in the Hometaking Wars. He didn't see how the Nordik gods beat the Frost Giant gods on their home ground. In fact they won every war except the last one."

"But we know that," the Warlock said. "The Nordik gods were destroyed when the Nordiks were driven out of the Fertile Crescent. They had no gods. So they fought with swords, and the Frost Giants used magic, and over three generations they used up the magic."

"Right, and the Nordiks came swarming in before the Frost Giants could learn swordsmanship. But Harper never learned about *mana* depletion. That was left to you, Warlock. You and your damned Wheel. Harper and I spent some time trying to learn why Roze-Kattee failed his and her people."

"Well?"

"It's an unusual story," said Wavyhill's skull. "According to the Hometaking Wars Cycle, the Frost Giants took it on themselves to protect their god, instead of the other way around. When the Nordiks beat their army, three of the Frost Giant hero-priests were taking Roze-Kattee to safety. The god had lost all his power. He could barely move."

Clubfoot said, "That's not the kind of tale someone makes up about his enemies. But, look: why didn't the Nordiks just find out where the god was and dig him up?"

"Oh, they probably tortured a few Frost Giants. Maybe they got the wrong ones. Maybe the hero-priests migrated afterward, or cut their own throats. But maybe the Nordiks didn't try too hard. Why should they? Roze-Kattee did *not* save the Frost Giants. He went peacefully to sleep, somewhere. The poor time-weakened thing might be barely capable of killing any Nordik who found him."

The setting sun was still brilliant, under a higher cloud canopy that thickened as night came on. Mount Valhalla was a mere point of splendor far to the southeast. The clouds were soft against Orolandes' back. He was relaxing in spite of himself. It was all so unreal. Could one die in a dream?

"The magic went away and the gods died," the Warlock said. "What makes you think Roze-Kattee didn't? What would a Frost Giant consider a place of safety?"

"The cycle speaks of a 'god within a god.'"

"You've already said Roze-Kattee had a dual nature."

"Harper and I found another interpretation. We have to stretch the definition a little, but . . . if we're right, then Roze-Kattee could still be alive. And the Nordiks had plenty of reason not to go looking for him."

"And we don't?"

"Time has passed. We know more than those barbarians did. We have more to gain. And less to lose," said Wavyhill.

An upper cloud layer covered the stars. It had not been cold during the day, when sunlight was bouncing back at them from all of the reflecting white landscape; but it was cold now. Orolandes lay in the dark, afraid to move, hoping that a rift would not form where he was lying. When the silence had become unbearable he said, "I wish I could see your hair."

Mirandee was nearby. She said, "Why, swordsman! Is that a compliment?" as if she didn't much care for it.

"If your hair turns white, we're about to fall."

After a time she said, "Magicians and swordsmen go together like foxes and rabbits. What are you doing among us?"

"Ask Wavyhill."

"But you didn't have to come."

"I did a terrible thing. I don't want to talk about it."

She laughed, invisible silver. "Tell me now, or I'll read your mind. Wavyhill said you had no defenses."

Out of the need to confess; out of his sure knowledge that the words would block his throat, rendering him mute, as he had been mute among the fishermen; out of some obscure need to be punished . . . Orolandes said, "Go ahead. Piranther did."

There was a long dark silence. Then the witch woman said, "Oh, Orolandes!" in a voice filled with tears.

"I'm sorry."

"I know. I can see it. All charged up with the need to prove you were a man. Running into death waving that big damned sword. Crawling to kill the priests because they were killing your friends."

"Yes."

"I shouldn't have looked. That's usually the way of it. I find out I shouldn't have looked."

"I can't do anything about the people that drowned. Maybe I can help put the magic back in the world. What does Wavyhill have in mind for me? Do you know?"

"No. His mind's locked tight. I trust the Warlock, though. He'll control Wavyhill. Go to sleep, swordsman."

Little chance of that, Orolandes thought. He looked toward where her voice had been. Was there a pale spot in the enveloping darkness? Long hair turning white?

"There's circulation in the clouds around and beneath us. The *mana* circulates. We won't fall. Go to sleep," she said.

Something touched his sword arm and he woke and rolled hard to the left and came up on his feet, sword in hand. It was black as the inside of a mole's belly. The footing was unfamiliar, treacherous. A woman's voice cried, "Don't!"

And he remembered.

"Mirandee? Did you wake me up?"

"You were having nightmares."

"Sorry. Was I screaming or something?"

"No. Just the nightmares. I wish I'd stayed out of your mind. I've never met anyone so unhappy."

"Can you blame me?" He sank down in unseen softness.

"Yes. You've killed a dozen men at least with your sword. Why be so upset about Atlantis? You killed more people, but it's the same thing, isn't it?"

"When I kill a man with a sword, it's because he's a soldier. He's trying to kill me."

"If you weren't on his territory—"

"Then he'd be on mine! If Greece didn't have an experienced army she'd be meat for the first wolf that came at the head of an experienced army. Magic didn't help the Frost Giants, and that was a long time ago. These days magic doesn't even slow down an army. So everyone needs armies."

"Wars of magic aren't much prettier. Get the Warlock to tell you about his duel with Wavyhill. Or get Wavyhill to tell you."

"All right." Orolandes was sliding back into sleep. But the nightmare waited for him . . .

The touch of her hand on his arm startled him. "You're still unhappy."

"I can't do anything about it."

"I can." Her hand moved up into his sleeve, caressingly.

He laughed. "Does the fox bed with the rabbit?"

"We are two human beings. How long has it been since you were with a woman?"

"A long time. I—" He hadn't wanted one. He would have thought: she is sharing love, all unknowing, with a man who murdered thousands. When the women of the fishing village came, he had turned them away without speaking, as if his voice alone would tell them what he was.

This Mirandee: he had never seen her as a woman. A figure of power she had been, a dangerous being who tolerated him, whose presence was necessary to his goal. Her mockery had hurt—

"Well, but you were so frightened! You should have seen yourself. I was frightened myself," she confessed. "I've never been on a cloud before."

Her hand felt good on his arm. It was so cold and so lonely here. He found her face with his fingers. He traced the contours gently; he stroked her temples, and scratched her behind the ears, as he would with a Greek woman. They lay against each other now, but he felt only a double thickness of fur, and the cold of a mountain night on his face . . . and then her cheek against his, barely warmer.

This was better than going back to the nightmare. And she knew; he was hiding nothing from her. She knew, yet she was willing to touch him. He was grateful.

He was half asleep when the lust rose up in him, burning. She sensed it. They began opening each other's robes, leaving them on to protect their backs against the cold. Even now his urgency was tempered by that uncharacteristic gratitude. He wanted to make her feel good.

He succeeded. In climax she was wildcat and python combined: her arms and legs clasped him hard, pulling him into her.

They lay against each other with their robes overlapping. Orolandes was pleased and proud.

A thought crossed his mind . . . and she laughed softly in his ear. "No, I did not falsify my pleasure to give you confidence. And no, you have not become a lover fit for a queen's harem. Your mind is in mine. I feel what you feel. It's . . . exciting."

Ruefully, but not very, he said, "What joy you would have had of another mind reader!"

She laughed more loudly. "If I were ready to die, yes, that would be a fine way to leave the world!"

"Oh."

"You've found your voice. When we shared love you didn't speak at all."

His mind flashed back to the fishing village.

"Never mind," she said quickly. "Shall we sleep like this?"

He nestled against her and slept without dreams.

The Warlock woke blinking in the sudden dawn. He was hungry. His face was sharply cold where it poked through the robes. The rest of him was warm and comfortable in the robes and the cloud-stuff.

Clubfoot was on his back, sprawled out like a starfish in the clouds, looking indecently comfortable. Wavyhill's skull was where the Warlock had mounted it last night, on a billowing knoll of cloud.

The Warlock called up to Wavyhill. "Anything?"

"Nothing attacked. The *mana* level stayed high. It's still high; all my senses, such as they are, are razor sharp. I think I heard something that wasn't just the wind, around midnight. I couldn't tell what. It might have been wings, big wings."

"Something big enough to carry Piranther?"

"I don't know. That's the trouble: you think some beast has gone mythical, and then you get into a place of high magic and it swoops down at you.

There might be all kinds of survivals, here in the sky . . . Warlock, had you thought of probing the Moon from here?"

"No raw materials. No food sources either." The Warlock grinned. "That might not bother you, but you can't work alone."

"Right. Someone has to make the gestures."

During the night much of the cloudscape had melted away. The mass they still occupied was pushing upward in the center. For some hours it must have blocked Wavyhill's view forward.

Wavyhill asked, "Are you sure we've lost Piranther?"

"I . . . no."

"All right. Neither am I."

"I don't see how he could be following us. But that's no guarantee at all. Piranther and his people have had most of fifty years to explore the South Land Mass. What could he have found in the way of talismans?"

"Another Fistfall?"

"Or more than one. He could be pacing us on dragonback." The sky burned deep blue, nearly cloudless, but the Warlock said, "Behind that one cloud, maybe, watching us. I was overconfident."

"Did you have a choice? Relax. This is a fun way to travel. By the way, there has been another development. Tiptoe around this knob of cloud and you'll see."

Tiptoe? The clumsiest giant would not make an audible footfall here. The Warlock waded around, and saw Mirandee and Orolandes wrapped in each other's arms in the cloud shadow.

Perhaps he lied, to Wavyhill or to himself. "Good. I was afraid they wouldn't get along."

The air mass rushed steadily north and east. The center continued to push upward. By noon they were high on the slope of a billowing mountain, a storm thunderhead.

Clubfoot trekked up to the peak. "It's steeper on the forward face," he reported when he came back. "I don't like the footing much, but the view is terrific. Wavyhill, let's set you up there as lookout."

"Lookout and figurehead. Why not?"

In the end they stayed up there, Clubfoot and Wavyhill and the Warlock. Orolandes and Mirandee declined to join them.

It was a heady view. The crackle of lightning sounded constantly from underneath them. Flights of birds passed far away, flying south. Once an eagle came screaming down to challenge their invasion of its territory. That was worrying. They had nothing to throw at the bird, and any magic might melt the cloud beneath them. Fortunately the eagle saw the size of them and reconsidered.

Wavyhill said, "We might be the last human beings ever to see this, for thousands of years, maybe forever."

They were passing over an endless forest. To their right the cloud-shadow brushed the treetops; on the left a behemoth waded through crackling tree trunks, stopped, looked up at them with intelligent eyes. The cloudscape sloped steeply down from here, dazzling white, with shadowed valleys and rifts in it.

"We couldn't ask for a better vantage point," said the Warlock. "Or more comfortable seating." And he glanced at Clubfoot. "What's wrong with you? You look like your last friend just died."

"Orolandes is a fine young man," Clubfoot stated. "He is brave and loyal, and unlike many swordsmen, he has a conscience. Bearing all that in mind, would you tell me what the hell Mirandee sees in that bloody-handed mundane?"

"You could ask Mirandee."

"I'd rather not."

"Would it help if I told you why Mirandee turned down your offer? I think she was being polite. To me. We shared a bed once. She didn't want to remind me of what I've lost."

"All right. That was nice of her. But *why—*"

"Nobody can tell you." The Warlock looked at him. "I'd have thought you were too old for this kind of acidic jealousy."

"So would I," said Clubfoot.

At sunset the winds around the peak turned chilly. The two magicians climbed down the back slope of the thunderhead. The cloud surface was uneasy, in constant slow-flowing motion. They ate their cold rations and went to sleep.

But Wavyhill remained on the peak, on duty.

★ ★ ★

The third day was very like the second. Orolandes and Mirandee kept their own company, finding privacy in one of the shadowed valleys well aft of the thunderhead peak. Clubfoot and the Warlock lolled on the peak.

Clubfoot seemed to have come to terms with himself. He had been stiffly polite to Mirandee at breakfast, but here he could relax. "This is the way to travel. We should have gone to Prissthil this way, Warlock."

The Warlock chuckled. "That would have been nice, wouldn't it? We couldn't. No mountains to climb near Warlock's Cave. And the only place to get off would have been high on Mount Valhalla. Without porters. Come to that, we'll have a problem when we get to where we're going. Just where are we going, Wavyhill?"

"It'll be part of a mountain range, and our weather magic should work," said Wavyhill, "unless I'm wrong from the start. At this speed we'll get there late tomorrow. We will have to do some climbing."

Clubfoot shifted in the cloud-stuff. "So we'll rest up for it."

Wavyhill studied him. "Comfortable, isn't it? You complacent troll, you. You've all been sleeping like the dead. And Mirandee and the swordsman, I guess they earned it, mating like mad minks all day. I wish I could *sleep!*"

Clubfoot's anger left him as suddenly as it had come. "We could block your senses."

"It's not the same. It's not the same as sleeping, or blinking, or—or crying. I want *eyelids.*"

"Let's try something," said Clubfoot.

They tied a line to his jawbone, for a marker, and pushed Wavyhill a foot deep into cloud. They pulled him up a minute later, and then half an hour later. He said he was comfortable. It was not like sleeping, Wavyhill said, but it was like resting with his eyes closed.

They left him there until sunset.

In a shadowed valley, enclosed in cottony wisps of fog that resisted motion, Orolandes lay with his cheek on Mirandee's belly. The sunlight filtered through the cloud walls to bathe them in pearly light.

"Love and madness," he mused. "They go together, don't they?"

"You feel your sanity returning?"

"Why, no, not at all."

"Good." She chuckled. The flat abdominal muscles jumped pleasantly under his ear.

"I wonder," he said. "What makes this Roze-Kattee a god of love and madness? The gods came before men, didn't they? Did gods fall in love? And go mad?"

Troubled, she shifted position. "Good question. We'll have to know the answers before we do anything drastic. I'd guess that one day an anonymous god looked around itself and decided it would die without worship. There were men around. What did they need that Roze-Kattee could supply? Some gods were more versatile than others. Roze-Kattee probably wasn't."

"What would a god of love and madness *do?*"

"Oh . . . bestow madness on enemies. Ward it from friends. Love? Hmmm."

"The same thing? Make the Frost Giants' enemies love them?"

"Why not? And arrange good political alliances by fiddling with the emotions of the king or queen. Priests learn to be practical, if their gods don't."

"Do you think this god will fight us?"

She shifted again. "It needs us as much as we need it. We'll know better when we see this dormant god." Her long fingernails tickled his chest hairs. "Don't think about it now. Think about sharing love on a cloud. Few mundanes have that chance."

"It does take practice."

"We've had practice."

"I'm the only fighter among you. Magicians wouldn't break their backs to protect a swordsman."

"But I would."

In the night something woke the Warlock. He stirred in seductive comfort while his eyes searched the vivid starscape. Nothing, only stars . . . He was dropping off to sleep when it came again: a surging beneath him, like a cloud-muffled *bump.*

Clubfoot's sleepy voice said, "What?"

"Don't know."

There was a more emphatic *bump.*

* * *

Orolandes felt it too: a surging beneath him. He stirred and felt momentary panic.

"Cloud. You're on a cloud," Mirandee said reassuringly. Her eyes were inches away; her breath tickled his growing beard.

"All right. But what was that—"

The cloud surged again.

Orolandes ran his fingers through her hair—it was raven black by starlight—rolled away and stood up. The others would be around the side of the puffy thunderhead peak. He walked that way, aware that Mirandee was following him.

Clubfoot and the Warlock were on their feet. Clubfoot called, "Did you see anything?"

"No, but I felt—"

Beyond the two sorcerers, beyond the edge of the cloudscape, a shadow rose up and blotted out the stars. Starlight reflected faintly from huge wide-set eyes.

Mirandee was behind him, her hand on his hip.

"Don't make magic," the Warlock called. "Not yet. It's a roc."

The great bird was treading air, holding itself in position with an occasional flap of its wings. It cocked first one eye, then the other, to study the people on the cloud. Then it spoke to them in a basso profundo thunderclap.

"CAW!"

"Caw yourself!" Orolandes snarled, and he stamped toward it. His sword was longer than the bird's beak, he thought. It would reach an eye. This would be a wild way to die. But Mirandee would be safe, if he could put out an eye.

"CAW!" bellowed the bird. Its wings rose and snapped down.

A hurricane gust threw Orolandes backward. He curled protectively around the sword blade, somersaulted twice and came up crouched. Another blast beat straight down on his head and shoulders.

The bird was overhead, swooping down on Mirandee.

Orolandes tried to run toward her. The cloud-stuff tangled his feet, slowing him.

Mirandee shouted something complex in nonsense syllables.

Soft blue radiance jumped between her outspread arms and the bird's descending beak. Her hair flashed white, and she dropped.

Orolandes howled.

The bird fluttered ineffectually and fell into the cloudscape in a disorganized tangle.

Orolandes attacked. His blade's edge buried itself in feathers. He set his feet, yelled and slashed again at the neck. He cut only feathers.

The bird's wings stirred feebly. It lifted its head with great effort, said, "CAW?" and died.

Mirandee cried, "Help!"

Her hair was a black cloud spilled across white. She was buried to the armpits. "I stole its power. Gods, I feel all charged up! Lucky I remembered that vampire spell or I'd be trying to fly myself." She was babbling in the shock of her brush with death. "Clubfoot, can you get me out of here?"

Orolandes went to her, treading carefully, knee-deep in viscous cloud. He lifted her by the elbows, pulled her out of the pit and set her down.

"Oh! Thank you. That vampire spell, old Santer taught it to me a hundred years ago, and I just knew I'd never use it. I thought I'd forgotten it. It wouldn't even work anymore, most places. Oh, 'Landes, I was so *scared*."

Clubfoot said, "You sucked that bird dry, all right. Look."

The bird was deep in cloud and sinking deeper. As they watched it vanished under the surface.

"We can't stay here," said Clubfoot. "We don't want anyone walking into that patch. It wouldn't hold a feather, and you can't tell it from the rest of the cloud."

They moved far around the steeper northern face of the travelling storm.

Ψ

THE NORDIKS

4

ON THE THIRD morning black-and-white mountains reared their tremendous peaks to east and north. "Aim for the northernmost peak in the range," Wavyhill ordered.

Clubfoot began his weather magic. The Warlock pulled a band of silver from his upper arm and peered through it for a time. One distant rounded peak glowed a faint blue-white. "That's it. There's magic in that mountain," he said. "Wavyhill . . ."

"Well?"

Slowly the Warlock said, "I'm only just starting to grasp the *audacity* of what we're doing. I never tried anything this big, even when I was young."

"What have we got to lose?" Wavyhill chuckled.

"I wish you'd stop saying that. Clubfoot, how are you doing?"

"Having some trouble."

The cloudscape drifted east. Clubfoot continued to try to swing them north. By noon the clouds were sweeping across the foothills, and surging like a sluggish sea. It was no use trying to stand. Even Clubfoot gave up the effort.

At first it wasn't bad, riding a continual earthquake on an infinity of damp featherbed. Then Orolandes grew seasick. Twice in his life he had ridden out a storm aboard a warship; but in a way this was worse. They were trying to steer the storm itself. Clubfoot wore a grim look Orolandes didn't like at all. Sections of cloudscape roiled into sudden ridges and hills; others tore away and drifted off in white puffs. Once the limping magician tried to stand and gesture, and a hill of cloud-stuff surged up under him and sent him spinning downslope. After that he stayed down.

The spell-hardened cloud deformed like taffy as it surged against the dark mountain slopes. Orolandes clenched his teeth against the tumbling of his belly. Ships didn't do that! He was flat on the cloud now, like all the others, with his arms and legs spread wide.

The cloudscape slid up the mountain face; slowed and finally, balked from crossing the range, the mass slid north instead. The ride became less chaotic. Orolandes began to relax.

"At least we're going in the right direction," Clubfoot muttered. He stood up. "Now let's see if I can—" And he stopped, astonished. He was hip deep in cloud.

And Orolandes was sinking deeper, deeper in cloud. He couldn't see the others.

Clubfoot bellowed, "Stay down! Flatten out!" He began to sing in the

Guild tongue, unfamiliar words in a tone of desperation. He was chest deep and sinking, like a captain going down with his ship, as the clouds converged over Orolandes' head.

He sank through white blindness. He held his breath and readied himself—he thought he was ready—for the moment when he would drop out of the cloud.

Too long. He gasped for breath, and found he could breathe cloudstuff.

Somewhere above his head Clubfoot was still singing. If Orolandes yelled for Mirandee he might interrupt that spell; but it was very lonely to die like this. The white had turned light gray. The seconds stretched excruciatingly . . . then rough ground brushed against him and spun him head over heels.

He was on his back on solid, solid ground, with dirt and small stones beneath him and gray cloud all around. He stayed there and shouted. "Mirandee!"

Nothing.

"Clubfoot! Warlock!" He was afraid to move. To find solid ground in a cloud was too much of sorcery with too little warning. And he was still blinded by cloud!

Then a shape formed in the cloud, and resolved. He saw a pale, blond, very hairy warrior. The armored man walked in a furtive, silent crouch, his eyes shifting nervously, trying to see in all directions at once. His spear was poised to kill. But he didn't look down.

This, at least, was in Orolandes' field of experience.

The stranger's first glimpse of Orolandes showed him much too close, in the air, with sword drawn. The stranger's jaw dropped; then he tried to scream and thrust at the same time. Orolandes batted the spearhead aside and stabbed him through the open mouth.

He waited. No more blond warriors came. Presently Orolandes allowed himself to look down.

The dead man was armored in leather reinforced by brass strips. He carried sword and dirk in addition to the spear. He looked to be just past twenty, and well fed; and none of that was good. A well fed populace could support many soldiers, and a young man wouldn't be wearing the best of the armor. A good-size, well-equipped band could be moving out there in the . . . fog.

Of course, fog! Orolandes grinned at himself. A cloud on the ground must be fog! Clubfoot must have managed to land the cloud while it was still viscous enough to hold them. That must have shaken the soldiers: sticky fog, and a hillside seeded with magicians.

Orolandes walked into the fog. He was painfully alert. In this white blindness you could kill friend as easily as foe. He spent some time stalking a small tree. Later two man-shaped shadows formed faintly in the mist, standing motionless above . . . a seated man? Orolandes charged in silence, and killed one of them before they knew they were threatened. The other fended Orolandes off long enough to scream for help. He fought badly . . . and lost.

The Warlock did not get up. He looked bad; as if he had collapsed in upon himself. He blinked and spoke in a feeble whisper. "Orolandes?"

"Yes. They'll be coming, we've got to move. Are you hurt?"

"Youth spell's worn off. No *mana* here. Take—"

"Where are the others?"

"Don't know. You can't find them. Take Wavyhill. Go up."

"But—"

"Uphill till Wavyhill talks. Go." The Warlock slumped back. His breathing was an ugly sound.

Orolandes bent quickly and detached the skull and its harness from the Warlock's bony shoulder. The decorated skull seemed a pathetic toy; there was no life in it. He tucked it under his arm and moved into the fog in a crouched and silent run. Nordik warriors would be answering that scream.

He had to find Mirandee.

The Warlock rested with his eyes closed. There were bruises and a wrenched shoulder, but it was years that crippled him now. Cold seeped into his bones.

Metal clinked. He opened his eyes.

Large magics had deserted him in this dead place, but at least one small magic remained. The gift of tongues was no big, showy sorcery. Some could learn languages with no magic at all. But the gift could be useful.

The Warlock spoke in Nordik. "Don't kill me."

The man in beaten bronze armor said, "I make no such promise. Are you such a weakling as you seem? How did you slay these my men?"

"The swordsman we hired to guide us slew them, then fled."

"Describe him."

If Orolandes was caught he would be killed anyway, the Warlock told himself. He described Orolandes accurately, and added, "He was the only one of us who knew how to find the treasure."

"What treasure was that?"

"The god within a god," the Warlock said. If they wanted the treasure they would capture Orolandes alive . . . maybe. It was worth a try. "Such a thing would be immensely valuable to us. We were all magicians save him."

"How many are you?"

"Me, and a cripple named Clubfoot, and a woman named Mirandee." And a skull. Pitiful, thought the Warlock. "We can't harm you here."

"I know. Stand up or I'll cut your throat."

It was a long and painful process, but the Warlock got to his feet. The man in bronze watched in disgust. "You'll never walk alone," he said.

He called, and two soldiers came out of the fog with Clubfoot between them. Clubfoot had a nosebleed. It seemed his only injury, save that he shambled like a man who had lost all hope.

"You may carry each other," the man in bronze instructed them. "Do not delay me. You still live because you've not become a nuisance. Your swordsman is a thorough nuisance, and he will die."

The white mist enclosed them still as they made their way downslope. The Nordiks seemed unsure of their path. Perhaps they were lost. It slowed them, and that was good, for the magicians were nearly killing themselves keeping up. Clubfoot was carrying half the Warlock's weight. He limped heavily on his birth-mangled foot.

The first time the Warlock tried to speak to him, a spear shaft rapped his funnybone. It hurt like hell. The man in bronze armor said, "You must speak only in our tongue. We have no wish to be cursed."

"Curses won't work here," Clubfoot said.

"We know that. We're so certain that we won't even bother to test it. Right?"

Clubfoot nodded. He was morose, tired, defeated.

The Warlock spoke to him in Nordik. "Good landing. I never thought we'd live through that."

It seemed he wouldn't answer. Then, "I just got us down where I could. I thought I'd done a good job till *they* showed up."

"It's still better than failing to fly down. Where are you on a cloud when the magic runs out?"

The leader was a big man, strong enough to wear bronze armor without noticing the weight. White showed in his beard, and an old scar above one eye. He hadn't seemed to care if his prisoners lived or died . . . until now. Now he stared openly. "Were you actually riding on a cloud?"

"We traveled almost a thousand miles on that moving storm, thanks to Clubfoot's weather magic."

"What's it like?"

The Warlock suppressed a sigh of relief.

Mirandee could stay free. Her special talent would protect her, even here. Orolandes? They'd have to hope, and hope hard, because the swordsman was carrying Wavyhill. But Clubfoot and the Warlock could only expect to be questioned, then killed. Unless they could trade on their novelty value.

"Picture the most luxurious bed you've ever heard of," he said. "Not beds you've slept in, but beds from legend. Cloud-stuff is softer than that . . ."

Close behind him in the fog, a voice spoke to him. "Orolandes."

He jumped violently. He kept his sword high as he said, "Mirandee?" They might have captured her already—

"No, I stayed clear of them. Barely. There's a fog on my mind that's worse than this around us. Which way is the nearest mountain?"

"What about the others?"

She shook her head. Her leather garments had suffered, but Mirandee wasn't hurt; she didn't even seem rumpled. "We can't do magic here," she said. "For miles and miles around it must be nothing but old battlefields. Were you thinking of rescuing them singlehanded? Or teaching me to use a sword?"

"What do we do, then?"

"We get out of this dead area. Uphill. If Wavyhill can lead us to the 'god within a god,' we'll just summon the others." She took the skull in both hands; her hair brushed Orolandes' cheek. "He doesn't look good."

"Was that a joke?"

She laughed. "Poor Wavyhill. Strap him to my shoulder, will you? Leave your arms free. No, I meant that he could be really dead. I'll have to do the spells all over again . . . Orolandes? Do you remember Wavyhill's true name?"

"Not offhand."

That bothered her badly. "Try to remember. We can't do a revival without Wavyhill's true name."

"All right. The wind's that way," Orolandes said, "and that was the way the cloud was moving along the mountains. North. So we go east."

Orolandes didn't like the touch of Wavyhill: dry, dead bone, and just a trace of the smell of death. He emphatically didn't like strapping the skull next to the witch's ear. "Why can't we stow it in the pack? It'll be safe enough."

"Think of it as Wavyhill, our ally. The attitude is a large part of magic, love. He'll live more readily if I'm here waiting for him to advise me." She smiled at him, lovingly, and the skull grinned on her shoulder.

It became too dark to climb before they were barely started. They camped among half-seen trees. Mirandee's small crystal ball had shattered in the fall, and they spent some time shaking shards and slivers of crystal out of the blankets and the pack.

In the night the fog turned to powdery snow. They wakened chilled despite blankets and bruised by the hard ground.

The chill dissipated as they climbed, but Mirandee tired easily. Her hair was white again. She drove herself hard. By noon they had climbed above the fog.

Mirandee argued for going straight up the nearest peak. But even if Wavyhill revived, they'd only have to go down again; it was not on their path to the hump-shouldered magical mountain. Mirandee gave in to his arguments, possibly with relief.

They went north and upward. They would stick to the ridges.

They had clean snow for water. They saw food, always receding at a good clip: a mountain goat, a small bear that shambled off although Orolandes shouted scathing insults at it. Orolandes wished for a bow and arrow, and settled for a stabbing spear made by using some of their rope to bind his sword to a straight sapling.

They didn't talk much. Each had private woes which they suffered in silence . . . but Mirandee sensed her lover's shame at abandoning companions. What with the closing in of her own mind, the loss of youth and magic, she suffered for two. Orolandes wanted to comfort her. He had no skill at it, but her empathy spoke for him.

So it went until, at sunset of the third day, Orolandes saw an elk. It would have been enough meat to feed a village, but to Orolandes it looked just right for two. He started toward it, prowling, trying to determine windage. The elk cropped the sparse mountain grass with an eye constantly lifted toward danger.

Then, casually, it turned toward Orolandes and walked toward him, ignoring the grass, looking straight ahead . . .

To a hunter Mirandee's voice was shockingly loud. "I've summoned it. Can you butcher it?"

The elk stood waiting for him to slash its throat. He did, feeling like a murderer. The sword cut through throat and spine with startling ease. The magic sword—

"I wish we knew its name," Mirandee said. "As it is, we're trusting someone else's magic whenever we use that sword."

She had a boulder blazing before he finished the gory job of butchery. Her hair was half black, half white.

And the decorated skull on her shoulder talked to them as they ate. "Magicians spend decades searching out each others' true names, Greek. It numbs my mind that you could hear mine twice, and forget! No, Mirandee, I'm not going to tell you. Enough that the Warlock and Clubfoot can move me like a puppet. You would be one too many."

". . . biggest bird that ever lived. We thought they'd all gone mythical. Suddenly there it was, diving down on Mirandee." The Warlock's voice was thin and reedy, and he had to pause for breath . . . for air hotter than the atmosphere of Hell, that scalded his throat. It didn't matter. They listened. "Claws like eight curved sword blades. Eyes the size of your shield, Poul . . ."

The sauna was a big underground room with a wood stove glowing in the middle. There were benches along all four walls, on two levels; and thank the gods for that, for the Warlock was on the lower, cooler level. He'd have been on the floor except that it would violate Nordik custom. The village held more than two hundred, and half of them were in this incandescent room, sweating enough to fill a respectable river. They were all stark naked: men and women, older children and people so old they couldn't walk without assistance, and even some Frost Giant slaves, seven and eight feet tall, sitting on the lower benches with their heads near the ceiling.

The Warlock had seen strange peoples in his day. He knew how various were the ways of being human. He hid his surprise at sauna customs, and showed only the diffidence of a stranger who must be shown the rules. When Poul explained that they roasted themselves in this fashion to keep themselves healthy, he only nodded.

Clubfoot had guffawed when the Warlock told him that. (But they were alone then.) To the Warlock it was a disturbing sign of the times. Medicine was a branch of magic. Take the magic out of medicine, and what was left? *This?*

He wouldn't have been human if he hadn't shown some discomfort. And it was stranger than strange, to see this many naked men and women crowded this close together, pouring sweat, and none of them so much as flirting! And every so often someone would bolt and run for the river downslope. Ten minutes later he'd be back, and if he brushed you in passing his skin was icy, as if he'd been dead for days.

Yet they were paying him a signal honor, and it behooved him to take advantage of it.

"Oh, Wavyhill was as evil a man as I've ever known. He killed whole villages, and not by coming on them with swords, but by stealth, by gaining their trust. He sold them zombie servants that were dead men from the last village he'd gutted, revived and hidden under the seeming of good troll slaves. One night the trolls would take up knives and . . ."

It had been very different three nights ago, when Harric reached
Vendhabn Village with magicians as his prisoners.

Vendhabn was a place of stone houses with steeply peaked roofs and tiny
windows lining both sides of a street of trampled dirt that curved like the
cowpath it had once been. Houses of human scale, until you came to the
great hall in the middle of town.

The Warlock was dopy with fatigue and sudden senility, and Clubfoot
wasn't exactly alert, but they noticed the hall. It was tremendous. The stone
blocks that made it were tremendous. The door was eighteen feet tall, and
built of whole trees . . . and it was old. He wondered if it had been built by
Frost Giants.

The night was dark and still foggy. Nobody was about. That was good;
the Warlock had dreaded being put on show for a japing mob. The bronze-
armored man named Harric led them past the great hall and into what had
to be a jail: a hut built to the same colossal scale as the great hall, a single
room with a roof eighteen feet high, and more recent stone partitions dividing it.

Their tiny room had a small window in the door. The guard outside was
a tall, gangling warrior with big knobby hands. The Warlock was too
exhausted to speak, to do anything but flop on the straw bedding and try to
keep breathing. As Clubfoot bent over him, hurting with the need and the
impossibility of curing him by magic, the Warlock had gasped three words.

"Keep them entertained."

Later that night he had awakened; but Clubfoot still didn't know that. The
guard and Clubfoot had been pressed close to the window in the door. Clubfoot had been telling the guard about lovemaking on a solidified cloud, exactly
as if he had done it himself . . . exactly as his jealousy-fired imagination must
have painted it. Certainly the Warlock had not been meant to hear.

In the morning he had felt stronger. He'd been able to eat some bread
and drink some mead. Last night's guard had seemed friendly enough, and
a bit awed by his prisoners. Clubfoot had introduced him as Poul
Cloudscraper.

The magicians talked quietly on the straw bedding. "We'd rather be
guests than prisoners," the Warlock said. "What are the chances?"

"Maybe. I talked to Poul last night. Blamed the killings on Orolandes. If they get him I'll have to say I lied. I made out that we were kind of his prisoners."

"If they get Orolandes we can cut our throats. I'd like to give the impression we're taking their hospitality for granted. It just hasn't occurred to us that they might cut a wandering magician's throat—"

"Too late. I asked Poul about that. He can't protect us. He's a householder, but he only gets one vote in council."

"Oh."

"How's this? You're a lovable, trusting old man, and I'm your ex-apprentice who lives only to take care of you. It might stop your heart if you thought you'd been threatened by our hosts. Should anyone be so boorish as to raise the subject—"

"You insist that I mustn't find out. Good. Help me up."

Leaning heavily on the red man's shoulder, he peered out the small window. There were men and women dressed too lightly against the cold, moving to avoid puddles and patches of half-melted snow. Two giant women went past with a dressed ox carcass slung from a pole. They were both very pale of skin, and white-haired, though they seemed young, and they stood seven feet tall or taller. The Warlock glanced at Poul, their big Nordik guard, and caught Clubfoot's warning headshake; there was no good reason whatever to speculate on whether Poul was part Frost Giant.

"We need not mention our ally Wavyhill. Too macabre," said the Warlock.

"Right. But tell 'em about the duel, it's a good story."

"Fine. So you're the old man's loyal apprentice, and you wouldn't dream of deserting him in these his remaining years. Once they're convinced of that they may loosen your tether. If you get the chance, you run."

"No way."

"I mean it. I'm out of the game. Here—" The Warlock slipped the silver bracelet from his upper arm. "This'll point out the mountain. Mirandee will head there, and she'll have Orolandes and Wavyhill."

"Sure," said Clubfoot. He was certainly lying. He helped the Warlock back to the straw to rest.

* * *

"We use the sauna once in ten days," Poul Cloudscraper said. Poul was on an upper rack of benches. His impressively big feet were propped higher than his head, on a row of rails for that purpose. "We keep it only warm all the time. If one comes dying of the cold, we can warm him quick."

"You certainly can."

"Then again, the sauna brings on a quick childbirth. You would be surprised at how many children are born in the sauna."

"Not at all. I'm about to give birth myself."

Poul was concerned. "Shall we dip in the river again, or have you had enough?"

The river had been icy; he had thought it would stop his heart. And now he was pouring sweat again. "I've had as much ecstasy as I can stand," he assured the guard.

The cooling-off room was next to the sauna itself. It was crowded. The Nordiks would rest in here for half an hour, then leave . . . but today they weren't leaving. As the Warlock washed himself he tried to hear what Clubfoot was telling them.

"None of us is old enough to remember what the gods are like," the lame magician was saying. "Not even my friend the Warlock here. How did you like the sauna, Warlock?"

The Warlock smiled back. "A unique experience." He accepted a towel from a silent Frost Giant woman. She used another towel to dry his back.

"There are some interesting legends, though," Clubfoot said. "The god Dyaus-pita took a number of human women as lovers. Most of them came to grief. There was one who insisted that he show himself in his true form . . . which was probably a mistake." The pleasantly shaped young woman next to Clubfoot was one the Warlock remembered: Harric's younger sister. Good. If Clubfoot could pacify the bronze-armored warrior . . .

The time of the japing mob had come, of course. At midmorning Harric led them out. It was funny in a way, to see the villagers' embarrassed reactions to Harric's conquest: a cripple and a feeble old man. The magicians answered politely to some of the gibing questions put to them; they attempted to act like guests rather than captured freaks, and hoped that they would not therefore be taken for madmen. Harric put them back in their cell and went away angry, and the villagers went back to their tasks. The children remained.

There must have been a hundred children of all ages, maybe more. At first they only stared. The magicians began to talk to them. They gathered closer. Here and there you would see a younger one sitting on a teenager's shoulders. At the back, a few white-haired, white-skinned boys and girls stood like trees among saplings, straining to hear. Clubfoot and the Warlock took turns at the window to tell tales of dragon fights, wars of magic, ancient kingdoms, strange half-human peoples . . .

Evening came, and most of them disappeared to their dinners. For those who stayed, the Warlock tried the spell he had used at the inn in Prissthil for the diners' entertainment. In the darkness the colors were dimmer yet, like the Northern Lights brought to earth. The children loved it.

The next morning brought a cluster of angry parents.

The Warlock was exhausted. He had to let Clubfoot deal with them. He lay on the straw with his eyes closed, listening to Nordik anger and Clubfoot's tones of bewildered hurt. He wondered what had gone wrong.

". . . turn them into *magicians?* My son will grow up to be . . ."

". . . corrupting our children . . ."

". . . wiser to learn *our* customs before you . . ."

". . . too dazzled to do their work, now you've filled their heads with . . ."

Came the noon meal, and they were left alone. "I wasn't a lot of help, was I?" the Warlock said miserably. "How much trouble are we in?"

But Clubfoot seemed thoughtful rather than worried. "Not as much as you'd think. I got one old woman talking for the rest of 'em. She's the ring-bearer's mother." The gift of tongues informed the Warlock that the ring-bearer was the lord of the hall, effectively the mayor. "Her name's Olganna. Warlock, a lot of the parents are delighted we've got the kids interested in something. And the children are all on our side, of course."

"What in the gods' names was *bothering* those people?"

Clubfoot's grin flashed. "Magic was always used against the Nordiks, never for them. They didn't have any. The tales they tell their children today are all about brawny Nordik warriors against evil magicians. Justice triumphed, and now there's no more magic."

"Oh."

"So now the kids are constantly bothering the Frost Giant servants at their work, and they don't do their own chores either. They want magic. Only Frost Giants make magic." Clubfoot dipped bread into stew, and said, "I learned some things. The Frost Giants really did have a god named Roze-Kattee, and his powers did hold off the Nordiks for a hundred years or so. Then the god's powers waned, and the Nordik berserkers swarmed all over the Frost Giant warriors."

"So that much was true, at least. What else did you find out about Roze-Kattee?"

"Olganna couldn't seem to tell me what the god was *doing* to the Nordik armies. I think it's been forgotten. Maybe they never knew. One thing, though. Do you know what a berserker is?"

"Not by that name."

"A berserker sort of goes insane before battle. He froths at the mouth, he chews his shield, he charges the enemy and keeps going until he's actually hacked apart. He doesn't notice wounds, even lethal wounds. What I want to know is, did the Nordiks have berserkers when they were driven out of the Fertile Crescent?"

"Yes. A lot of tribes developed that technique when it got to be so difficult to raise actual zombies."

"Well, the Nordiks didn't use berserkers until the actual last battle. Olganna said so and they all backed her up."

"That's funny. I wonder why . . . god of love and madness?"

Clubfoot nodded vigorously. "That's what I thought. The Nordiks couldn't fight because Roze-Kattee kept bringing the Nordik berserkers to their senses. One more thing. The Frost Giants still worship Roze-Kattee."

"What? But they're slaves!"

"Interesting, isn't it?"

They emptied their stew bowls and set them aside. Presently the Warlock said, "Have you thought what will happen to these people if Wavyhill and Mirandee can bring back magic to the world?"

Clubfoot shrugged. "They're swordsmen."

"Well, yes . . . Meanwhile we've got to cool off the irate parents somehow."

"We can change our tune. There are tales where magic really was used for evil. Wavyhill's zombie servants, and the demon-sword Glirendree, and the raising of the dead in the war against Acheron."

"That'll help. What about a magic show?"

"What?"

"Let the kids get it out of their systems. The adults too. I'm sure we can work something up."

"Maybe. I'll ask Olganna what she thinks."

The magic show had been a huge success. The Warlock had pretended to call up the dead: phantasms that Clubfoot animated with his thoughts. Clubfoot had read minds, discreetly, and told the contents of locked boxes. The Warlock had told futures, again using some discretion.

But they were still in the cell when the day of the public sauna dawned.

He drowsed facedown on the wooden bench while talk floated around him . . . *sent a plague that killed most of his worshippers . . .* His knuckles brushed dry earth. *Why? Stingy with their sacrifices . . . understandable. Baal took every first-born child . . .* The bench was harder than cloud and he was naked, but the air was warm and dry and pleasantly scented with wood and woodsmoke. *Started as a war between men . . . eventually split the whole pantheon, with gods fighting on both sides . . . boredom. Sure, the gods had their squabbles, but it was boredom . . . flattened both cities before . . .* Clubfoot was still talking about gods. The Warlock dozed. *Mostly they worshipped out of fear. Why else would the . . .*

Some phrase caught the Warlock's attention and pulled him awake. He sat up. He felt good, better than he'd felt in days.

"There's no mystery to it," Olganna was telling Clubfoot. Her hair was white and whispy-thin, she was small and withered and wrinkled, but she still looked like she could climb a mountain. Deep stretch marks on her belly told of her eight sons and eleven daughters. "They simply wouldn't surrender unless they were allowed to serve their god. Our forefathers could have killed them all, of course, but what for? This Roze-Kattee hadn't helped them. We let them have their way."

The Warlock sat up. Nobody seemed to think it strange that he had dozed off here.

"I wonder what makes them so loyal," Clubfoot said.

"Why, they just . . . are. Or stubborn," said Olganna. She seemed unaware that two Frost Giants, man and woman, were drying themselves on the far side of the room. "Once in my life and once before I was born, we got tired of their taking so much time off for their ceremonies. In my time it was a crop that had to be got in. We postponed the ceremonies. They stopped work, all work, till we gave in. It was a hungry winter."

"But don't you find that strange? All the old tales tell of gods striking mortals down for some casual mistake, or as part of some godlike game, or just for being proud of their own accomplishments. Sometimes the prayers and sacrifices were bribes for service, but usually they were just to get the god to let them alone: no more floods, no more plague, no more lightning, please. What did Roze-Kattee *do* for the Frost Giants?"

"I've wondered." Olganna frowned. She looked about her . . .

They might have been father and daughter, or uncle and niece, or man and wife; their ages weren't *that* different. White hair, pale skin, eyes the color of ice, spare frames seven feet tall: they looked very much alike. They sat together, with Nordiks comfortably close on both sides of them, in the egalitarian style of the sauna, and they rested in the peace that follows the heat.

Olganna called across the room, and the entire village must have heard her. "Gannik, Wilf, just why *do* you still serve a god nobody's seen in a hundred years?"

The old man flinched. Certainly he had not come to the sauna to be cross-examined. But some are more equal than others, and Olganna's son was the ring-bearer, the lord of the Hall. The pale young woman beside him didn't help matters; she was looking at Gannik as if she too expected an answer.

He shrugged and answered. "Those who do not worship do not marry, do not love, are not loved. It was always that way. If one loses faith after a long and successful life, his wife will desert him, his children will not speak to him, none will help him when he is sick and aged. If Roze-Kattee frowns on a man, he is impotent; on a woman, her lovers are impotent. We knew this long before you came to live in our land."

Clubfoot had been clever, telling his tales of gods. So now we have our answer, the Warlock thought. Roze-Kattee's power lay in the taking. He took the madness from a berserker, and the power of love from an apostate. But if the god himself had been impotent for hundreds of years . . .

With a thrill of horror the Warlock saw that it didn't matter. For thousands of years only the devout had had children. Roze-Kattee had bred the Frost Giants for loyalty to Roze-Kattee.

And while this flashed through his mind Olganna was nodding dismissal to Gannik. She was satisfied. To Clubfoot she said, "My nephew tells me that you came here to search out Roze-Kattee."

The Warlock flinched. Clubfoot said, "We came searching knowledge of Roze-Kattee. How could we not? Roze-Kattee may be the last living god, and knowledge is power to a magician. Usually." Ruefully, "This time it was a mistake. We have lost power."

The pair of Frost Giants seemed to have lost interest. But slaves had always been good at that.

$$\psi$$

THE CAVERN OF THE LAST GOD

$$4$$

THE RIDGED BACK of the mountain chain was an easier path than Orolandes had expected. These mountains were old, worn to smooth rock and rotted to soil that could hold the occasional grimly determined tuft of grass; and the towering peaks were all to the south, behind them. Mirandee's hair remained white, but she was strong.

Yet the journey had its difficulties. Their boots wore out, and they lost half a day summoning rabbits and skinning them for new boots. Always as they walked, they had Wavyhill for their entertainment. Unhampered by the need to draw breath, Wavyhill talked constantly of the ease with which magicians used to travel, and the precautions they could and should have taken to save this grueling walk. His life story was a chain of enemies made and defeated, and they had it all in detail, until Mirandee threatened to move his felt tongue to the backpack. "What makes you so garrulous?" she demanded. "You never needed company when you were living all alone in those fortified castles."

"Oh, blame it on the Warlock, dear. I was deaf and dumb and blind for thirty years. You'd want to talk too."

"He could have revived you earlier, if you'd told him your true name before the battle," she said, and Wavyhill chortled hollowly.

But he woke her that night by saying, "Kranthkorpool. It's Kranthkorpool. Just in case."

It took them six days.

The last few miles were the easiest, a wide, rounded ridge of smooth rock sloping gently downhill. Mirandee's hair went dark and light as if cloud-shadows were passing. It was late afternoon.

The slope dipped more drastically there at the end, until it was a vertical drop. "Wavyhill? This way?"

"Yes! Get us down there, Greek!" Wavyhill was almost indecently eager.

Orolandes motioned Mirandee back. He stood at the edge of the drop, looking around, taking his time.

From the lip it was thirty feet to flat dirt. The rock face must slant inward; he couldn't see it.

The drop could be made in two stages, by way of what looked to be a congealed river of lava. It was twenty feet high and thirty-odd feet wide, a rounded ridge of smooth gray rock with big potholes all over it, and it ran beneath Orolandes' feet. Ten feet down, then another twenty feet to dirt. But the lava river itself was rounded to vertical all along its length, and it ran further than he could see, twisting into the broken foothills.

"It'll be easier just to moor the line and climb down here. Here—" He showed Mirandee how to slide with the line around one ankle and clutched between the feet. He slid down first, then stood underneath, ready to break a witch's fall. She did fine. He caught her anyway, for pleasure.

They stood before the mouth of an enormous cavern, under the edge of the roof.

"In there," Wavyhill whispered. "I was right. I wasn't sure until now."

Orolandes dropped the pack and drew his sword. "Stay behind me, love."

Wavyhill laughed. "Do you have any idea what to expect?"

Orolandes boosted himself to the top of a chest-high buttress of stone. "Tell me."

Wavyhill didn't answer.

Orolandes pulled Mirandee up. They looked into the cavern.

"Don't go any further," said the skull.

The entrance was big, but it widened even further beyond the opening. In the darkness they could see vertical bars, stalactites and stalagmites of prize-winning size. The twenty-foot high river of gray stone ran deep into the darkness . . . or it had run out of there, glowing, long ago.

"It's big," Orolandes said. "Do you know what this dormant god looks like? How big it is?"

"Don't go any further. I mean it."

True, he'd been edging in. Mirandee asked, "Why not?"

"We have a decision to make," Wavyhill said. "Do we risk this without Clubfoot and the Warlock? Or shall we try a Great Summoning now?"

"That's no decision at all. We don't have the power."

"I think there might be enough to—"

"Wavyhill, I'm surprised at you! The *mana* is here, but it's too diffuse. We need the last god first. You know what would happen if we tried a Great Summoning and failed."

Orolandes waited. He didn't have to trust Wavyhill. In one second his sword could split that skull, and without scratching Mirandee's shoulder.

"Mirandee, it only strikes me that we might not *know* enough between us to—"

"I will *not* try any Great Summoning until we have the power to do it. And you can't make the gestures."

Wavyhill gave a barking laugh. "You win. All right, Greek, put the sword down and go in and find the dormant god."

Mirandee said, "Alone?"

Orolandes said, "Put down the sword?"

"I said that, yes. Of course, neither of you *has* to take any orders."

It was dark in there. Menacing. The sword's weight felt comfortably normal in his hand.

"Leave it here. Otherwise it'll kill you. Snap out of it, Greek, this is your big moment!"

He didn't like Wavyhill's obscene grin; but Orolandes had made his decision long since. He set the sword on a boulder. He turned and walked into the darkness.

Stalagmites stood thicker and taller than he was. He had to duck the points of the longer stalactites at first, but then the cavern's roof became too high for that.

Wavyhill's echoless voice followed him. "I don't know the size or shape of what you're looking for. You'll find it on the other side of that stream of smooth rock, probably far back."

He turned and called, "All right."

It happened while his head was turned. Motion exploded around him. Things swatted his head from two directions. Orolandes threw himself flat and rolled over clutching for his sword. Things screamed all around him, their voices excruciatingly high-pitched.

Still fluttering, still screaming, they wheeled away from him. Dark shapes swarming around the roof. Bats. Orolandes got up and moved on, breathing heavily.

The lava flow ran along the side of the cavern. It ran the full length, back to a deeper blackness at the end. Orolandes' exploring hands found smooth rock marred with potholes. Strange to find potholes here where there was no rain. And in the sides, too.

Strange but convenient. He climbed the potholes, up the rounded side of the rock. Stalactites hung low over the top.

Between the back side and the cavern's wall was a three-foot gap. Orolandes walked toward the back, ducking stalactites, looking into the gap.

The deeper blackness at the back: could it be another cavern? He might have to search that too. Should have brought a torch. But there was a shadow far back along the gap, a big shadow. If that was the god, it was too big to be moved. Even if it wanted to be moved.

From the beginning he had wondered if it would fight him.

Wavyhill's shout came jarringly. "Orolandes! Come back! Come back *now!*"

"What for?" Orolandes' own shout echoed around him.

"Now! Obey me!"

He didn't trust Wavyhill worth a troll's curse. But he trusted the panic and anger in that command. He dropped lightly from the lava flow, caught himself in a controlled roll, stood up and jogged toward the entrance.

The entrance flamed with daylight. Orolandes jogged around stalagmites with his eyes on the chancy footing and his head lowered to avoid the down-pointing spires.

Mirandee leaned casually against a smooth rock wall, seemingly watching him. It was hardly a scene of panic. Orolandes called, "What's the trouble?"

He knew that when his muscles locked. He teetered on a rigid forward leg, then toppled on his right side in running position. He tried to cry out, but his voice was locked too.

Mirandee didn't move, didn't speak, didn't blink.

The sword was on the boulder where he had left it, a tantalizing arm's reach away.

The skull on Mirandee's shoulder said, "I'm sorry. My mistake, and it was made right at the beginning." He raised his voice. "Piranther! Where are you?"

"I'm just over your heads."

Piranther floated like an autumn leaf into the bright entrance.

$$\Psi$$

THE FROST GIANTS

$$\text{♃}$$

THEY SHOULD HAVE thought of it. Granted that the Warlock was sick with age and Clubfoot was trying to keep them both alive with old stories; there was more to it. Sorcerers have a blind spot, and that blind spot is—

"—swords. They keep appearing in your old tales," said Harric. The burly redhead was dressed casually now, in leather and flaxen cloth. "Are these magic swords all a thing of the past?"

Harric's invitation to dine at his table had surprised the Warlock. Less surprising was the presence of another guest, their young guard, Poul. Two other men struck the Warlock as fighting men; their arms were thick with muscle, they bore healed scars, and they walked as if they didn't expect anyone to be standing in their way. Now he began to understand.

"Wavyhill had a magic sword," Clubfoot was saying. "It didn't help against the Warlock. And there was a demon forced to the form of a sword: Glirendree. The Warlock killed it. In fact . . . Warlock, I guess you're our expert on magic swords."

The Warlock smiled. Oh, yes, he should have made this happen earlier. "What would you like to know?"

"Where do they come from? What do they do?"

"Hmm . . . Glirendree doesn't count. He was an actual demon. Wavyhill's sword was enchanted to strike always at the vitals of an enemy. You can do that, or set it to block another's weapon, or make it sharp enough to cut boulders, or all three."

"Can you do that to any sword?" Harric leaned across the table.

"Mmm . . . I can, or could, if I were in a place where magic works."

"All right, you've said that murder carries this magical power. There were battles fought all through here—"

"No, no. Murder and war are not the same. The intent is different, and the intent counts for a good deal."

Harric settled back. The Warlock sipped mead and waited. Presently Poul said, "Kinawulf's barrow?"

"Yes, by the gods! Warlock, Kinawulf was a ring-bearer of our people who tried to practice sorcery himself. He had some success until Roze-Kattee turned his followers against him. They slew him after torture. His barrow is a place of ill fame, but with swords and magic to guard us we should be safe enough."

"It sounds perfect. How far is it?"

"Most of a day's walk . . . uphill. Mpf, we had best make you a litter. Are there materials you need?"

The Warlock asked for parchment and colored inks. "I'll send Clubfoot scouting for herbs. And bring the swords, of course."

They set out on the morning of the sixth day. The swordsmen were heavily laden: two to carry the Warlock, the others carrying half a dozen extra weapons in addition to the magicians' materials. In his present condition the Warlock wondered if he could pick up any one of those great metal killing-things, built heavy enough to slice through armor.

He was mildly disappointed, and mildly relieved, that Clubfoot had come back with the herbs. Hell, Clubfoot hadn't promised to run. Maybe there had been a guard. He didn't ask.

The trees thickened as they went, until Poul and the Nordik named Hathsson had to slide sideways to move the Warlock's chair between the trunks. The Warlock sighed and said, "I'll walk from here."

"It's not much farther. Bring the chair anyway," Harric ordered.

The forest smells were pleasant. Harric passed a fat skin of mead around, then discarded it. Clubfoot said, "I've been wondering what happened to this Kinawulf. We seem to have worked out that Roze-Kattee drove people *sane*."

"Selectively," said the Warlock. "Who attacked Kinawulf? Someone who had reason for hatred or jealousy?"

"His younger brother and a few followers, helped by Kinawulf's wife."

"I expect Kinawulf's problem was that none of his own followers were mad enough to stand in the way of a sword. That was Roze-Kattee's doing. The god wouldn't have touched Kinawulf himself; he might have surrendered. We may well find magic operating around the barrow."

"There—" Harric pointed.

The barrow was the peak of a small hill covered in green grass. It was clear of trees. "We want the top," said the Warlock.

He was behind the others as he climbed, puffing, leaning on Poul's arm. Why didn't he feel stronger, if this place was so rich in *mana?* There was *mana,* but not enough to power a youth spell, or to work a loyalty spell or a death spell on swordsmen. Or to do much to a metal sword. Now, how does one explain to a known berserker that one can't give him a dozen magic swords after all?

They heard Hathsson shout. Poul sprinted for the top of the hill, sword in hand. The Warlock struggled after him.

Even in this northern cold, Piranther went naked. His bright eyes searched for motion, for any sign that his spell of paralysis had failed. Nobody moved.

Piranther relaxed his grip on the leather bag at his throat. He walked nonchalantly past Mirandee, inspecting her; then turned his attention to the skull.

"Kranthkorpool, speak to me. Did you find the dormant god?"

"Maybe." It was no more than the truth, but Wavyhill's voice was strained.

Piranther slit the straps that held the skull to Mirandee's shoulder. He lifted it down and looked at it, his fingers avoiding the gnashing jaws. "I could smash you," he said. "Or I could take away your senses and bury you here. Who would ever find you? Don't make me dig for information, Kranthkorpool."

Wavyhill said, "I think the Frost Giant priests must have put it behind that long, rounded wall of rock, far back. The Greek knows."

"Thank you. Why did you want him? You could have fetched it for your-selves."

"He's the only strong one among us. The god is bound to be heavy. Too heavy for you, too, Piranther. Can we deal on that basis?"

Piranther looked thoughtfully into the cavern. "But with the *mana* inherent in it, you could float it out. Why—?"

"Curse it, we can't afford the loss! We need all the *mana* the god has left to it. Don't you understand, this is the biggest thing anyone ever dreamed of!"

Piranther laughed. "Your big and foolish project. Your one solution to all the world's problems. Never trust such solutions, Kranthkorpool. I will take the dormant god back to the South Land Mass for our own use. It will serve our needs for some time to come." He set the skull down fac-ing him. "I can leave it dormant for now. I do not need its *mana*. I have these."

Orolandes tried to make out what Piranther was holding. He saw intri-cate flashes of colored fire against the dark pink of Piranther's palm.

"Black opals. See how beautiful they are. Sense their power. There are more black opals in the South Land Mass than in all the rest of the world. Even so . . . our numbers increase. These will not last forever. We must have the dormant god."

"You think small."

"Perhaps. Where are the others?"

"I don't know." Again Wavyhill's voice was strained.

"Must I dig for information?"

"Dig . . . then. You say my . . . name badly." Was Wavyhill *gloating?*

Piranther shrugged. He turned to Orolandes' backpack. "Certainly Mirandee carried a crystal ball. True, my dear? Let us look in on them." He upended the pack, and things spilled out: blankets, a smoked joint of elk, rope, pouches of dusts, the copper Warlock's Wheel, a few sharp slivers of crystal. "Could I be wrong? Kranthkorpool!"

"She smashed it falling out of a cloud." No mistake now, Wavyhill was gloating.

"Then we'll do it the hard way. After all, I have the power. If Clubfoot and the Warlock are trying to harm me . . ." Piranther selected a fine, polished bit of many-colored fire as big as his toenail. ". . . we'll just interrupt them."

The Nordiks had armed themselves. They were looking downslope to where three Frost Giants waited on the hidden side of the barrow hill.

A patch of snow behind them made them hard to see. Gannik and Wilf stood tall with a dignity they hadn't worn in the sauna. The third Giant was getting to his feet, taking his time.

It was worth the wait. The third Frost Giant stood seventeen or eighteen feet tall. He wore a fur about his hips, the skin of a white bear, and nothing else. His wild white hair and beard flared about his head; he was all white, even to the small tree that hung casually from one hand, with a knob of roots at the end to make an impressive cudgel.

Sword conspicuously in hand, Harric strode forward to call down the hill. "What do you want here?"

"Give us the magicians," the big one boomed.

"They are our guests. We hold the high ground."

The Warlock whispered to Hathsson, "What does he mean?"

"They have to come at us uphill," the blond Nordik whispered back. "Can you enchant our swords before they decide to charge?"

"No."

Meanwhile the big Frost Giant laughed boomingly and cried, "We are the high ground! And we must have the magicians. May Wilf come to speak to you without being hurt?"

"Yes."

If the Frost Giant woman was afraid, she showed none of it. She walked up without haste to join them. Harric opened conversation by saying, "Nordiks have fought Frost Giants before."

"We must have the magicians. Why must any of us die? You argued whether to kill them yourselves."

Interestingly, Harric did not deny it. "They are to do us a service. But even that is less important than this: Nordiks do not take orders from Frost Giants."

The Frost Giant woman looked down at Harric. "Have we not worked willingly for all of our lives? Have we refused you anything but one thing? These men threaten our god."

Clubfoot tried to interrupt, but Harric gestured him to silence, and answered her himself. "Your god had lost nearly all its power when you buried it."

"He kept enough," Wilf said wistfully. "I've heard the old ones talking. Even today, while the god within a god sleeps . . . first love always fades. Marriage goes from adoration to companionship. My own lover turned to another woman for mere variety. If the god truly died—"

"We do not threaten your Roze-Kattee!" Clubfoot shouted. "Tell the big one that we want to bring the god back to life."

The Warlock saw sidelong glances between the Nordiks. *Curse!* But Wilf's reaction was stranger. The woman was blushing: pink blood beneath the white of cheek and throat. She wouldn't look at the magicians. It was suddenly obvious that the Frost Giants preferred their god dormant.

Harric asked, "Who is this tall Frost Giant who threatens us?"

"Tolerik is my father's cousin. He ran away when he was eleven; you may remember. He's lived here ever since. Sometimes we bring him things he can't get here." All in a rush she said, "We must have the magicians. If you give them to us, Tolerik will work for you for a year."

The local *mana* had allowed a Frost Giant to reach his full height, but it was too low to let a magician defend himself. They could only wait.

Poul said, "But by law he is already—"

Harric's voice easily drowned him out. "Very well. Take them."

Clubfoot dived for the pile of swords. Hathsson's foot hooked Clubfoot's twisted ankle. As Clubfoot sprawled headlong he felt a sword's point pressing the small of his back. Clubfoot froze.

Poul said, "But the swords! Wilf, will Tolerik let the magicians enchant our swords first?"

"Don't be a fool. We can't trust them now," Harric said.

Wilf gestured downslope. Her father and his huge cousin started up. The Warlock was cursing himself for that moment of stunned surprise. Surprise, that warriors would betray a magician!

What kind of threat would cow an armed man the size of a big tree? The Warlock raised his arms. A fantasm, a great red-and-gold dragon stooping, slashing . . . if the Giant dodged, if he fell downslope, his height alone might break his neck . . .

The Giant's hand closed around Clubfoot's ankles and lifted him.

Colors formed in the air, tinges of red and gold. Harric frowned and rapped the Warlock's skull with his spear haft. The Warlock sank to his knees with the pain. He saw Clubfoot writhing in the Giant's hand as the Giant prepared to dash his brains out against a rock.

Darkness rippled around Clubfoot, swallowed him, swallowed the Giant's hand to the wrist. The Giant yelled and tried to pull away.

The Warlock sagged on the grass. It was all right. He saw the darkness closing around him and knew it for what it was: a Great Summoning. Mirandee must have found the god-within-a-god.

The hillside disappeared, and he was on dusty stone. Strength flowed into him, the strength of youth spells reviving. The Warlock stood up, saying, "W—"

And every muscle locked in place, locked him standing with his hand extended, his eyes smiling, his lips pursed on a W.

Clubfoot was on a rock floor with a great severed hand holding his ankles. Beyond him, Orolandes lay awkwardly, like a toppled statue. Mirandee leaned casually against a wall. Piranther—

Piranther returned the Warlock's smile. "I must remember to ask Clubfoot about that hand. What kind of allies were you gathering against me?" He dusted his hands together; the dust fell like motes of colored fire. He turned to the decorated skull sitting on a rock behind him. "Or did you trick me? Did I rescue them from a greater danger?"

"Revive them and ask," Wavyhill suggested.

"I like them better the way they are. Well, let us see your dormant god," said Piranther. He stepped delicately across Orolandes.

"If—"

Piranther turned.

"Nothing," said the skull. "Just a thought."

"Well?"

"You still can't move him."

"I'll decide that." Piranther turned and walked into the cavern.

Orolandes lay frozen in a frozen world. Behind him Piranther's footsteps were casually erratic, growing faint and blurred with echoes.

Wavyhill spoke low. "I hope you're not dead. If you're all dead, then I'm in serious trouble."

The skull chuckled softly. "He's deep in the cavern now. Warlock, if you can hear me, I claim a vengeance foregone. I could have suggested that he take you with him, for advice. He could have bound you with a loyalty spell, and you would have walked in with him. Warlock, Clubfoot, do you remember what you did to me, do you see what I am now? Mirandee, do you remember suggesting that I wasn't worthy to join you?"

The rock softened under Orolandes' rigid elbow. The light grew pink; or was the rock itself changing color?

The roof of the entrance descended.

Behind Orolandes came Piranther's echoing scream. Wavyhill laughed shrilly, madly. A warm wet wind blew against Orolandes' back. It stank like the breath of a thousand wolves. Piranther's scream ended as if muffled.

The roof above him had dropped low enough to touch the Warlock's head.

Wavyhill ended his cackling. "Well? Am I right? Did I have your lives in my grasp? Isn't it a *marvelous* hiding place for the last god? Greek, you probably still don't understand. Have you heard of the World-Worm, the snake that circles the world and swallows its own tail? The Alps and the Andes and the Rocky Mountains all form a part of its body. And you lie within its mouth."

Orolandes said, "Uhn!"

"Oh, ho! You're alive, are you? That paralysis won't last. I could free you now, if I could make the gestures. I don't think Piranther did anything fancy; he just bulled through our ward-spells with the power in his black opals.

"Marvelous, isn't it? The World-Worm is a strange beast. Of course it couldn't possibly live by eating its own flesh. The tail used to have flanges of bone behind those huge pores. It sweeps up all kinds of things: turf birds' nests, the dens of animals that lair in the pores, even full grown trees growing in the dirt the flanges sweep up. It grows very slowly this tail. And of course anything that wanders into the mouth gets eaten. I should be talking in the past tense, really," said the skull. "The fins are all weathered away. The World-Worm is like all magical forms of life; it turns to stone when the *mana* runs low. Like dragon bones. Like that statue in front of the Prissthil gates. What fooled Piranther was the tail. Running back into the mouth like that, it changes the shape so the cavern isn't mouth-shaped any more."

Teeth, thought Orolandes. I was jogging through a forest of spike teeth. He said, "Uhn!" The calf of his leg kicked suddenly, painfully.

The roof of the cavern was rising . . . and changing in color, greying to the look of stone.

"Can talk," Clubfoot said. "Can't move yet. Anyone?"

The Warlock grunted. "Spell should wear off soon."

"Got us with those black opals," said Clubfoot. "We couldn't know. Wavyhill. Why here?"

"Why, it's obvious! Look: nobody who knows what this place is would come here. The World-Worm must have been nearly dead for centuries, but who'd risk it? If a mundane wandered in here all unknowing, nothing would happen. But if a magician came here looking for the dormant god—" Wavyhill chuckled. "There's *mana* in magic. The power of their spells hovers around magicians. Put a *mana* source in the World-Worm's mouth and what happens?"

"Poor Piranther," said Mirandee.

"It wakes up for a snack," Clubfoot said callously.

"I think it would have done that even without the opals. Any time a magician comes calling . . . or a swordsman carrying a sword stolen from a place where gods once lived. In the meantime, whatever *mana* is still with the World-Worm is there to keep the dormant god alive. If our luck holds."

Clubfoot had called up a pair of hares: an old and simple magic, still potent almost everywhere. He had started a fire and cleaned the hares and was now roasting them. In his stiff back there was a rejection of the quarrel now going on in the cavern entrance.

"I won't let him go," Mirandee said. She sat with her back to them, her legs dangling over the stone buttress . . . over what must be the World-Worm's lower lip.

Orolandes came up behind Mirandee. He moved stiffly. They were all sore from the cramps that had followed their paralysis. He put his hands on her shoulders, ignored their angry shrug. "It is what we came for."

"Idiot! It's eaten a powerful magician *and* his black opals. It may not sleep again for years! Wavyhill, tell him! It eats things that wander into its mouth!"

"It may have gone dormant again," the skull said comfortably. "It was *mana*-starved for generations. It's a big beast; it needs nourishment."

"Father of trolls!" she spat.

"Retired."

"Mountain goat," the Warlock said without turning. He stood at the corner of the cavern's mouth, a little apart.

He was ignored. The skull on the rock said, "Listen, girl. I gave up my vengeance against these, my murderers. I am willing to risk a swordsman to the same high purpose."

The Warlock began singing to himself.

"Well, 'Landes? You heard him. You can't throw away your life after that. What about me?" Mirandee demanded.

Floating bodies, myriads of bodies, shoals of bloated human bodies turned in the waves, bumping gently against each other and against the wooden raft on which Orolandes lay dying of thirst beside the decaying body of a centaur girl. Did they thirst for vengeance? They had the right . . .

and if Orolandes walked out of the cavern alive, there were lives still to be saved. There were centaur and satyr tribes in Greece. He said, "I have to."

"If you die I'll die!"

He was startled. "You'll die? Because you read my mind?"

"Yes!"

Wavyhill said, "She's lying. Think it through. Piranther read your mind too. Would he have taken that risk?"

Orolandes looked at her. Her eyes did not drop. "I mean it. I won't live without you."

A clattering of hooves startled them. They turned as a mountain goat bounded up on the World-Worm's lip and stood gazing up at the Warlock.

"Any of you idiots could have thought of this," the Warlock told them. He turned back to give the goat its orders.

Stiff-legged and blank of eye, the goat walked into the cavern. They watched it blunder into stalagmites and stumble on until it had reached the entrance to the inner cave . . . the World-Worm's gullet.

Clubfoot spoke grudgingly, it seemed. "You can wait till morning. Have some dinner."

"No."

Mirandee sat stony-eyed. She did not look up as Orolandes stroked her hair, turned and walked after the goat.

The smell of broiling meat followed him and made it hard to go on. He circled teeth taller than himself. He climbed the soil-gathering potholes in the side of the long, long tail. He walked along the top of the tail with his torch casting yellow light into the gap.

He heard only his own footsteps. The bats . . . the bats must have been eaten along with Piranther. The flickering flame made motion everywhere. How would he know when the roof began to descend?

Far at the back, the tip of a stalagmite tooth showed above a whitish mass that enclosed it.

The last god was no bigger than Piranther, made of nearly translucent marble. It sat with its arms and legs wrapped tight around the base of a tooth. Its slanted eyes glowed yellow-white by torchlight. Its face and ears were covered with fur. In the triangular shape of its face there was something cat-feminine.

It took some nerve to wrap his arms around the stalagmite and, throwing all of his weight into it, try to move the tooth. It was solidly fixed.

"There's no way to get it loose from there," he told the magicians. "Your Roze-Kattee was a coward, Wavyhill. It's got a death-grip on that tooth." And he sat down to eat hot disjointed hare, one-handed, with his other arm around a weeping Mirandee. He had been ready to die in there; he had come out alive, and he was famished.

When there was nothing left but bones, Wavyhill said, "It sounds bad."

Orolandes grunted. "Would you consider chopping through one of the god's arms?"

"No."

"Then we'd have to chop through the tooth at the base, then have a team of men pull out tooth and statue together. Work for an army. Can we hire some of the Nordiks? They live close enough to—"

The Warlock chopped at the air. "The Nordiks won't help us. Even the Frost Giants seem to prefer their god dormant. Curse them and their coward god."

"And my lost vengeance," said Wavyhill.

Clubfoot sat hugging his knees. "I don't believe it. We came all this way, and now . . . No. There's an answer. We've got meat to be called and snow for water. We'll stay here until we find an answer."

ψ

THE GOD OF LOVE AND MADNESS

4

FOURTEEN THOUSAND YEARS have garbled all the details.

The last god is remembered in diverse legends. Roze became Eros, Kattee become Kali and Hecate, their qualities radically changed. Now only children hear of the Warlock's great project. They learn of a foolish frightened hen who ran screaming to tell the world that the world was ending. Some she convinced. In a desperate effort to salvage something, she led them into a cave.

The solution was in the cave. So close . . .

"We *can* get close!" A bellowing voice cut deep into the Warlock's dreams.

He rolled over, blinking. He heard rustlings and grunts of annoyance around him, and saw Clubfoot looming over him in gray pre-dawn light. Half asleep, he struggled to sit up.

Clubfoot was shivering with excitement. "Wavyhill, do you remember that gesture-spell, the variant on the Warlock's Wheel? The one that cancels *mana*."

"Remember it? Sure. I designed it. Nearly killed the Warlock with it, too. Shall I teach you the gestures?"

The Warlock said, "Wait a minute. I'm still trying to wake up. Clubfoot, have you really got something?"

"Yes! We can't get into the cavern, right? But we can get close! Roze-Kattee is just inside the World-Worm's cheek!"

Orolandes woke later, to the smell of roasting rabbit and the pleasant sound of Mirandee's humming. "Eat," she said gaily. "We've got work to do."

"Work? That's good. Yesterday it was all a dead end. Where are the others?"

"Already at work. Today it's different. I had a dream."

"So? Or do you dream the future? You're so much a man's ideal woman, I keep forgetting what else you are."

She kissed him. "Sometimes I dream the future. It's not dependable." Her brow wrinkled. "This one was funny. I guess it means success. I dreamed the sky was falling."

Orolandes laughed. "That sounds scary."

"No, I wasn't frightened at all. And it is what we're after, isn't it?"

"Maybe, but it sounds scary as Hell when you put it like that. What *did* you feel, watching the sky fall?"

"Nothing."

* * *

After breakfast they walked on bare earth, swinging their linked hands. On their left a sloping wall of stone rose out of the earth, higher and higher above them as they walked on. The stone was smooth, worn by the wind, until only a suggestion of scales was left to show that this was the side of the World-Worm's head.

They came to where a patch of the smooth rock turned to crumbly sandstone. Here was a hole in the rock, head-high, and sand spilled beneath it. Orolandes paused to look, but Mirandee pulled him on.

The second hole was higher and larger, big enough for a man to crawl through. Clubfoot and the Warlock waited as they came up. The magicians had piled rocks as stepping-stones to reach the hole. Orolandes climbed the pile and looked through.

It was black as a stomach in there. Clubfoot coaxed the end of a branch into flame and handed it up to him. By firelight Orolandes saw that he was ten feet away from the marble statue of Roze-Kattee.

"How did you break through? We don't have so much as an ax."

"We cursed it," said the Warlock. "Wavyhill evolved a gesture-spell that uses up the *mana* in whatever he aims it at. He used it on me once. We don't use it much these days. It's wasteful."

Wavyhill spoke from his accustomed perch on the Warlock's shoulder. "This isn't just rock, after all. It's a great brute of a dying god."

Orolandes nodded. "What's the next step? Can you revive Roze-Kattee through that hole?"

"We think so. The next step is tricky, and it involves climbing," said the Warlock. "That leaves it up to you and Clubfoot."

Clubfoot nodded, but he didn't look happy.

And Mirandee was frowning. "Why, no. I climb better than you, don't I, Clubfoot?"

"Well, there's more to this than—"

"And I'm as skilled at magic. Unless this is weather magic? Just what have you in mind?"

Clubfoot answered in the Guild tongue.

They talked for some time. Whatever they were discussing, it was complicated, judging from Mirandee's frequent questions and the way Clubfoot waved his arms. Orolandes could see that Mirandee didn't like it. He edged closer to those inseparable colleagues, Wavyhill and the Warlock, and asked, "What's going on?"

"Necromancy," said the skull. "Very technical. Can you climb that rock with a pack?"

"Yes. But why is Mirandee—"

"We didn't discuss it with her before. She didn't know what was involved."

"Then—"

"No!" Mirandee snapped. "If it has to be done, I'll do it. Otherwise I wouldn't let you do it either. Orolandes!" She turned her back on Clubfoot, whose face was a study in mixed emotions: sorrow and relief. Mirandee was biting her lower lip.

Orolandes went up alone, barefoot, using as fingerholds and toeholds those crevices and irregularities whose pattern just hinted at serpent-scales worn smooth. There were potholes in the great smooth expanse of the World-Worm's head: real potholes this time, worn by rain pooling to dissolve rock. Orolandes chopped with the sword point—the blade was uncannily hard—until he had joined adjacent potholes into a knob that would hold the line.

Mirandee toiled up the line. There was nothing Orolandes could do from up here except hurt for her, fear for her. The slope wouldn't kill her if she slipped, but it would remove skin and the flesh beneath, and she might break a leg at the end . . .

But she arrived intact, panting. She said no word to Orolandes. She spilled the pack he had carried up. She selected a chain of tiny silver links and arranged it in a circle. She drew symbols with a piece of red chalk. She looked up.

"Give me your sword," she said.

Orolandes didn't move. "What's it all about?"

"I don't think you want to know."

"Tell me, love."

She sagged. "Necromancy. Magical power derived from death, from murder. We need enough power to waken a half-dead god. We're going to get it by murdering the World-Worm."

"Oh. More death. Isn't there any other way?"

"I tried to think of one. Don't you believe me?"

"Yes, of course. Of course I believe you."

"Curse it, Orolandes, the World-Worm is dead *now*. The land has shifted and broken its back in places: it's not even the shape of a snake any more. The wind has worn it away, scales and skin and flesh. If we revived it completely, right now, it would die almost immediately. It's *dead*, but it doesn't know it yet, and we can take advantage of that. Give me your sword."

He did.

"Stand well back," she said, and turned to her work.

The song she sang was unpleasant, grating. Orolandes felt numbness in his toes and fingers and a black depression creeping into his soul. He watched as the dusty stone within the ring of silver turned dusty pink.

Mirandee raised the sword, holding the hilt tightly in both hands. She brought it down hard. Still singing, she pounded on the hilt with a rock until the blade was entirely sheathed.

The mountain shuddered. Orolandes flattened, gripping rock, ready for the next quake. Far back along the mountain chain to the south, he saw motion and churning dust.

The mountain shuddered and spilled Clubfoot's little pile of stones. The Warlock cursed in his mind, but he started chanting immediately. *Let my enemy's heart be mine, let my enemy's strength be mine*—Wavyhill sang the counterpoint next to the Warlock's ear, while Clubfoot worked at moving rocks.

It was hard work, and Clubfoot was in haste. Without the ladder of stones, they could not aim their spells into the cavern. Sweat ran down his cheeks and his neck, and he hurled his cloak from him and kept working. Poor Clubfoot, he couldn't even curse. The Warlock sang on and watched the rock pile grow.

High enough. Clubfoot mumbled over a dry branch until it blazed, hurled it through the hole and went up the rocks after it. The Warlock followed more slowly, accepting Clubfoot's assistance. He could feel the power in him now. The World-Worm's life had fed him.

The last god seemed to move in the firelight; but it was illusion. Its marble arms gripped the World-Worm's tooth as tightly as ever.

Wake and see the world . . . They sang the spell he and Clubfoot had sung for Wavyhill, the song for reviving the dead. Wavyhill's voice quavered and shifted. Wavyhill was frightened, and rightly. This could cost him his own not-quite-life. The Warlock could feel the *mana* leaving him.

In the middle of the chant his voice left him. He managed to finish the phrase, then signalled Clubfoot with a very ancient gesture, a finger across his throat. Clubfoot moved in smoothly. Wavyhill sang on, in an echoless voice that did not pause for breath.

The tree limb had almost burned out. The statue's eyes picked up the firelight like cat's-eye emeralds. The Warlock made his exaggerated passes, and worried. *Let your heart beat, let your blood flow . . .* Would a spell worked to revive men revive a god?

The song ended.

The marble statue did not move.

At last Clubfoot sighed and turned from the black opening. He stumbled down the ladder of stones. The Warlock followed. He was exhausted. The soreness in his throat felt permanent.

"I feel rotten," said Orolandes. Shoals of shifting corpses floated past his memory. He sat slumped with his chin on his knees. He could not think of a reason ever to move again. "We killed the World-Worm. How could anything be worth that?"

"It's the spell," Mirandee said. "I feel rotten too. Live with it."

"I'm glad I'm not a magician."

"No, you don't have what it takes."

"What does it take?"

Her black hair was a curtain around her, rendering her anonymous. "It takes another kind of courage. You know what I can do, given the power. Cause solid rock to flow like soft clay in invisible hands. Walk on clouds. Read minds, or take them over, or build illusions more real than reality. Kill with a gesture: one moment a hale and dangerous man, the next a mass of meat already decomposing. I can wake the dead to ask them questions. All those things, and other things I know how to do: they make a hash of what a mundane would call common sense. What scares the wits out of the mundanes is knowing how *fragile* our reality is. Not many can take that." She shifted a little, but the tent of hair still hid her. "Swordsman, I think we made a mistake, getting so involved with each other."

He nodded. In retrospect it seemed almost ridiculous, how dependent he had been on this woman. "It's no basis for a lifelong love affair, is it? I'm glad you said it first."

When she said nothing, he added, "You read my mind by accident. You must know a spell to break you loose."

"I do."

The sun was warm and bright, and here they sat on the biggest corpse in the world. He had felt so good this morning. Where had it gone?

The witch-woman said, "You're around thirty, aren't you? A child, no more. I'm over seventy. The boy and the old lady, the witch and the swordsman. They don't go," she said sadly. "That's not to say we should give up sex. That was good."

"You pulled me out of a bad period. I guess you know I'm grateful."

"You're just not in love any more. Nor am I."

"Right."

Mirandee seemed to drift off into a private reverie of her own.

Orolandes was feeling better. The awful death-wish depression was leaving him. It was good to end a love affair this easily, with no hatred, no recriminations, no guilt . . .

He saw her stiffen.

She stood abruptly. "Let's get down."

"Not so fast," he said as she wound the line round her waist and backed toward the drop. "You're in too much of a hurry. Curse it, slow down, you'll get killed that way!"

Mirandee ignored him. She went down backward, properly, but too dangerously damn fast. "Slow down!" he ordered her.

"No time!"

Huh? Well, it was her neck. He watched her descend.

"I think I've chanted my last spell," the Warlock whispered. His throat felt dry as dust.

"This isn't the end," said Clubfoot. "Only the first attack. We'll talk it over with Mirandee. Figure out what went wrong. Try again."

"Sure."

"I chanted youth spells for you once. I can do it again," said Clubfoot, "once we land the Moon." He paused. "That sounds insane."

"Maybe it is."

They sat slumped against the corpse of the World-Worm. It felt like sandstone now, crumbly soft rock that the winds would wear away. The magicians were exhausted, even Wavyhill, who had not spoken in minutes.

"No maybe about it," Clubfoot said suddenly. "It's crazy. How long have there been men in the world? A couple of thousand years at least, right? Maybe more. Maybe a lot more. But the *mana* was still rich in the world when some unknown god made men. And they used it."

"Of course they did," said the Warlock. "Why not?"

"The names of the great magicians come down to us. Alhazred, Vulcan the Shaper, Hera—Look, what I'm getting at is this. There were a couple of thousand years of *mana* so rich that none of us, no magician of these last days, has the skill to use it. His spells would kill him. Do you believe that nobody in those last two thousand years ever tried to land the Moon? *Nobody?*"

"Why should they?"

"Because it's pretty! And not all those old masters were completely sane, Warlock. And some of the sane ones served mad emperors, like Vulcan served Trillion Mu."

"All right. They tried. Certainly they failed. Maybe they weren't desperate enough."

"Maybe. Another thing. If we don't know what keeps the Moon up, we sure as Fate don't know why. One of the gods put it up, maybe; or many gods; or even a being of unknown power and unknown nature, something that doesn't live on a world at all. If we don't know why the Moon was put there, how can we dare call it down? We don't even dare drain it of *mana*, because we don't know what ancient spells that might ruin."

"You make sense," the Warlock said with some reluctance. "I've even been wondering if it matters to anyone but us."

"Well, of course it matters . . ." Clubfoot trailed off.

"Are you sure? Animals die. Classes of animals die. Civilizations die. New things come to take their places. Take Prissthil. The sky-stone is gone, but is

Prissthil hurting? It's a thriving village, a trade center. The guard: his grandfather was a magician, but he's not hurting. The Nordiks had captive magicians, and what did they want from them? Magic swords, and nothing else! Even the Frost Giants are happy enough with their god dormant. The strong ones adapt."

"I wonder what Mirandee's in such a hurry about? She's coming down awfully fast."

The Warlock didn't hear. He said, "Maybe Piranther was right. We use Roze-Kattee directly, get what good we can out of the last god. Wavyhill, what do you think?"

"I want to die," said Wavyhill.

"What?"

"It's not worth it. Another ten years of life, another hundred, and so what? People die. Even World-Worms die, and gods, and magicians."

"Wavyhill, what's got into you?"

"Nothing. Nothing's got into me. What could get into a dead man? I don't feel good, I don't feel bad. I guess I like it that way. Turn me off, Warlock. Use the spell we used to break through the World-Worm's cheek. It won't even hurt."

"Are you sure?"

"I'm sure," Wavyhill said without regret.

Mirandee found them that way, apathetic and dreamy-eyed, when she reached them out of breath and still trying to run. "Where is it?" she demanded.

The Warlock looked up. "What? Oh, the god. It sleeps on."

"Troll dung it does! Can't you *feel* it?"

"Feel what?"

"Why it's soaking up all the love and all the madness it can reach! *Feeding* on it!"

The Warlock stood up fast. Of course, he'd been stupid, they'd all three slipped into sanity without noticing! Sweet reason and solid judgement and philosophical resignation, these were not common among sorcerers. As he scrambled up the piled stones behind Clubfoot, he wondered what had tipped off Mirandee, who *was* stable and sensible. Then he remembered the Greek swordsman.

Clubfoot put his head in the hole. His voice was muffled. "Curse, we forgot to bring a torch! Mirandee, would you—"

The sandstone wall next to them fell outward. A splinter of rock nicked the Warlock's cheek; another struck Wavyhill, *tok!* Slabs of rock fell and smashed to sand, and behind them the last god stepped forth.

God of love and madness, was it? Roze-Kattee seemed a god of madness alone. It was shaggy with coarse hair, hair that covered its face and chest, baring only the eyes. Its eyes blazed yellow-white, brighter than the daylight. Orolandes had called it small, but it wasn't; it was bigger than the Warlock . . . and it was growing before their eyes.

Its pointed ears twitched as it looked around at its world. Already its head was above the magicians, and it did not see them. Alien thoughts formed in the Warlock's mind, crushingly powerful.

ALONE? HOW CAN I BE ALONE? I CALL YOU ALL TO ANSWER, YOU WHO RULE THE WORLD . . .

The last god was male and female both. Its male organs were mounted below and behind the vagina, in such a way that it could probably mate with itself. And this was embarrassingly clear, because the magicians were now looking up between the tremendous hairy pillars of its legs. It was still growing!

How? Where did it find the power? Roze-Kattee's range must be growing with its size, with its power. The Warlock had never anticipated this: that as the last god, Roze-Kattee was beyond competition. Every madman and every lover must now serve it as a worshipper.

Wavyhill snarled in the Warlock's ear. "Get hold of yourselves! Clubfoot, quick, what's your true name? Warlock, wake him up!"

Mirandee and Clubfoot were still gaping. The Warlock shook Clubfoot's shoulder and shouted, "Your true name!"

"Kaharoldil."

Wavyhill sang in the Guild tongue. *My name is Kaharoldil, I am your father and mother* . . . The Warlock joined, making Wavyhill's gestures for him. After a moment Clubfoot joined them. It was the old loyalty spell they were using, a spell the Warlock had once rejected as unethical. It decreased the intelligence of its victims. But now he only wondered if it would work.

They had come ill-equipped, and moved too fast. Too much had been forgotten about the gods. Perhaps nobody had ever known enough.

Roze-Kattee was a hairy two-legged mountain now. Its head must be halfway up the World-Worm's head. And still it grew. The Warlock imagined chill sanity engulfing the Frost Giants and their Nordik masters, sweeping over the Greek islands, crossing Asian and African mountains; wars ending as weaker armies surrendered to stronger, or as farmers-turned-soldiers dropped their spears and returned in haste to harvest their crops; husbands returning to wives, and wives to husbands, for remembered fondness and remembered promises, old habits and the neighbors' approval. Already Roze-Kattee had changed the world.

Orolandes lay on his back on the crumbly rock, looking up at the sky.

He had tried a drug once. Something an American was carrying. The red man had burned leaves in a fire, and Orolandes and some of his troop had sniffed the smoke. He had felt like this, then. Abstracted. Able to view himself, his friends, his environs, from a godlike distance and with godlike clarity.

It had not seemed worthwhile to follow Mirandee down the mountain. Whatever she and the others were planning, it could hardly be worthy of his attention.

Even the guilt was gone. That was nice.

There was a muffled booming somewhere far away. He ignored it.

Then a section of rock the size of a parade ground, not far from where he was lying, settled and hesitated and dropped away. Thunder sounded below him.

The corpse of the World-Worm was decomposing.

Orolandes moved by reflex. He swept gear into his pack (leaving gear on the battlefield could get you killed next time), donned the pack and went backward down the rope. He tried to keep his weight on the rock, not on the line. The knob of rock could crumble. His life was at stake, and Orolandes truly did not have the gift for abstraction.

I CALL YOU TO ANSWER, YOU WHO RULE THE WORLD . . .

Orolandes stiffened. Those were *not* his thoughts. He looked around.

He was then halfway down the slope, several hundred feet up. He saw a beast-thing with glowing yellow eyes, eyes level with his own. The great eyes locked with his, considered him, then turned away.

Orolandes continued to descend.

Certainly it would have been easy to let go. His muscles ached from the strain of climbing . . . but the hurt didn't seem to matter either. It was easier to follow his training.

I am Kaharoldil, your teacher and your wet-nurse and your ancestors' ghosts. I tell you things for your own good. Wavyhill and Mirandee and Clubfoot sang, and the Warlock's fingers made patterns in the air.

Roze-Kattee heard.

The tall ears twitched, the head swiveled, the blazing yellow eyes found them clustered on the ground. Roze-Kattee dropped to knees and hands, the better to observe them.

Wavyhill said, "Ah, never mind."

Right. What did it matter? Clubfoot had stopped singing too. Roze-Kattee covered the sky; its yellow eyes were twin suns. The Warlock sat down, infinitely weary, and leaned back against crumbling rock to watch the last god grow.

A thought formed, and tickled. Roze-Kattee was amused.

YOU WOULD USE A LOVE-SPELL ON ME?

Why, yes, a loyalty spell was a form of love spell. They'd been silly.

SILLY AND PRESUMPTUOUS. BUT YOU HAVE WAKED ME FROM MY DEATH SLEEP. HOW MAY I REWARD YOU?

The Warlock thought about it. Truly, he didn't know. What must be would be.

YOU WISHED TO BRING DOWN THE MOON? Again the thought tickled. PERHAPS I WILL.

"Wait," said Clubfoot, but he did not go on.

Now the Warlock imagined a fat sphere, blue and bluish-brown and clotted white. He sensed a watery film of life covering that sphere . . . and he sensed how thin it was. Remove the life from the world, and what would have changed?

This resignation, this fatalism, this dispassionate overview of reality went far beyond mere sanity, thought the Warlock. Roze-Kattee had practiced his power long before men ever put names to it. Now he imagined a smaller sphere, its rough surface the color of Wavyhill's skull. It cruised past the larger sphere in a curved path. Now it stopped moving, then began to drift toward the larger sphere. Now the spheres bumped, and deformed, and merged in fire. A sticky cloud of flame began to cool and condense.

IS THIS WHAT YOU WANTED?

"No," Mirandee whispered.

"No!" Wavyhill shouted. "No, you maniac! We didn't know!"

BUT IT IS WHAT I WANT. I CAN LIVE THROUGH THE TIME OF FIRE. I NEED THE . . . STATE OF THINGS THAT LETS GOD LIVE, THAT WARPS DEAD REALITY TO LIVING REALITY. WITH THE DEAD MOON'S AID I WILL PEOPLE THE CHANGED EARTH WITH MY CHILDREN. BECAUSE YOU HAVE SERVED ME, I WILL CREATE EACH OF YOU OVER AGAIN.

The last god had grown so huge that Orolandes couldn't even find it at first. He stepped back from the rope and looked around him. There were the magicians, a good distance away, doing nothing obvious about the menace. There, what he'd taken for a mountain became a pillar of coarse pale hair . . . leading up into a hairy torso . . . Orolandes froze, trying to understand.

Then pictures invaded his mind and sent him reeling dizzily against the rock wall.

Nobody had ever told him that the world was round. After the daydream-pictures stopped flitting through his mind, he remembered that. He remembered that everyone was about to die. But the pictures he had understood so well, grew muddled now, and faded . . .

Never mind. What to do next? Orolandes thought of fleeing; but he wasn't frightened.

HOW CAN I STOP THE MOON IN ITS COURSE? YOU WHO WORK IN A LAND THAT IS ALMOST DEAD, YOU MUST HAVE CONSIDERED THIS. The question came with crushing urgency, and Orolandes thought frantically. How would a Greek soldier go about stopping the Moon? Then his head cleared . . .

Well. The last god was proving very dangerous. Perhaps it would be best to kill the thing, Orolandes thought. The magicians seemed in no position to do so, and killing wasn't really their field.

He pulled the silver chain from the back pack. He found the red chalk too, looked at it . . . but he had paid no attention to Mirandee's symbols. Nor to the arm-waving. Best stick with the chain and the sword.

And still he wasn't frightened. It was strange to be thinking this way, as if Orolandes had no more importance than any other man or woman. He had lost even love of self. This was no drug dream. It was like battlefield exhaustion, when he had fought and killed and run and fought until even his wounds no longer hurt and dying meant nothing but a chance to lie down. Thrice he had known that terrible death of self. He had not stopped fighting then.

YES, GOOD. I CAN DO THAT, he thought; and he imagined himself stretching into the sky, growing very thin and very tall.

But it was Roze-Kattee that stood upright and reached skyward. Roze-Kattee's furry legs grew narrow, and the knees went up and up; but Roze-Kattee's torso receded much faster, up through a stratum of broken clouds and onward.

There was no way to reach a vital spot now. Well . . . Orolandes marched toward the last god's foot.

There was now something spidery about Roze-Kattee. The eyes were tiny dots of light, stars faint by daylight and right overhead. The fingers of both hands seemed thin as spiderweb strands: a web enclosing a pale crescent moon. The feet had spread and flattened as if under enormous pressure, and Orolandes had no trouble stepping up onto the foot itself, though it must cover several acres.

At no time did he picture himself as a mosquito attacking a behemoth with cold-blooded murder in mind. Orolandes' sense of humor was stone dead.

He jogged toward the slender ankle. His skin felt puffy. He guessed that the sensation came from Roze-Kattee, and ignored it. He never guessed its origin: most of Roze-Kattee was in vacuum.

The last god's ankle was like an ancient redwood, slender only in proportion. Orolandes looped the silver chain and held it against the furry skin. He thrust through the loop. The blade grated against bone. He withdrew the blade, moved the loop and thrust again. The point scraped bone, found a joint and sank to the hilt. He grasped the hilt in both hands and worked the blade back and forth. Roze-Kattee was slow to respond. Without impatience he withdrew the blade and stabbed again.

HURT! Orolandes yelled and grabbed his ankle. It felt like a snake had struck him. He found no wound . . . but he would not be unwounded long, because Roze-Kattee's spidery hands were descending in slow motion.

Something else had changed. Suddenly it mattered very much whether a Greek swordsman survived. Orolandes ran limping across the last god's foot, swearing through clenched teeth.

The Warlock said, "What?" exactly as if someone had spoken. He shook his head. Now what had startled him? And how had he hurt his foot? He bent to look, but the scream stopped him.

"Orolandes!" Mirandee's scream.

It was a puzzling sight. Roze-Kattee was spread across the view like a child's stick-figure drawing defacing a landscape painting. The scrawled line-figure stooped as if to tie a bootlace. And Mirandee was running toward where a flea seemed to be scuttling across the thing's foot . . .

Then it jumped into perspective, and the Warlock saw Orolandes running for a gap in the World-Worm's cheek. He snapped, "Wavyhill!"

"Here. Somewhere we have lost control."

"He had us controlled till Orolandes distracted him."

"Suggestions?"

"Kill it."

Wavyhill didn't like the taste of that. "How?"

"The Warlock's Wheel."

"You built another one? Why?"

"I was trying for a prescient dream. Success or failure for the Guild meeting. I took the right drugs, and I slept in the right frame of mind, and I had a nice, peaceful, dreamless sleep. Understand? Where I was trying to look . . . no *mana*. So maybe I'd be using a Warlock's Wheel."

Now the swordsman was somewhere inside the World-Worm's mouth. Roze-Kattee reached with spidery fingers into the hole a much tinier Roze-Kattee had broken through the sandstone.

Clubfoot was on the ground, his arms over his face, his body clenched like a fist.

"That's suicide for us both. There's got to be a better way. Warlock, there's *mana* in god-murder. If we can kill it and take its power—"

"How?"

"Mirandee's vampire spell!"

"She'd be cremated, or turned into something shapeless. Could you hold that much power? Could I? Poor Clubfoot's already had more than he can take."

"I hate it. All our work, lost! That's the world's last large source of *mana*, and you talk of burning it out to save a swordsman!"

"To save the world," the Warlock said gently.

"Even Roze-Kattee can't bring down the Moon by *pushing* on it!"

Pain stabbed at the Warlock's hand. Roze-Kattee howled in their brains . . . and was suddenly quiet. It turned to look at them, to study them.

The cavern was black. Orolandes stayed on his hands and knees. Stalagmites he could feel his way around, but a drooping stalactite would take his head off. His foot hurt like fury. He turned left, toward the cavern's main entrance.

Marble pillars tipped with claws blasted their way through the wall and began feeling their way around, knocking World-Worm teeth in all directions.

Now there was light. Orolandes waited.

The hand paused as if bewildered.

Orolandes sprang. He slashed at a knuckle, howled, set himself and slashed again. He ducked under the wounded finger and slashed at another. Nobody who loved Orolandes would have recognized him now, with saliva dripping from his jaws and his face contorted in murder-lust.

The hand reacted at last. It spasmed. Then it cupped and swept through the cavern gathering spires of rock. It gathered Orolandes. He stabbed again, into a joint. Then closing fingers squeezed the breath from him. His eyes blurred . . .

Wavyhill was shouting, "But what about *us*?" when the god's blazing yellow eyes found them. "Never mind," he said. "I think I see."

Those eyes: they could make you not care; they could make you lose interest. But they guaranteed a dispassionate overview and a selfless judgment.

"I don't care if it can bring down the Moon or not. It's got to die," said the Warlock. "The world belongs to the gods or it belongs to men."

"I said I understand. Go ahead."

The Warlock's legs wouldn't hold him. He started to crawl. Orolandes' backpack was yards away, and his knees and hands hurt. Roze-Kattee's vast spidery hand emerged from the cavern.

"Come *on*."

"This is my top speed. Hell, at least I did it to myself."

"What?"

"This is where it ends, the killing of Glirendree. Maybe I made the wrong choice. It was a long time ago . . ."

The young magician had had to leave his home . . . again. Somehow his spells lost power. It happened to everyone. Irritated, but curious too, the Warlock had devised an experiment.

He had made a simple copper disk and set two spells on it. One was simple and powerful: it held the metal together, gave it near-infinite tensile strength. The other spun it. He put no upper limit on that spell.

And when the Wheel had destroyed itself, he knew.

He had kept the secret for more than a century. But the demon-sword Glirendree had come to challenge him . . .

"I didn't have anything else that would kill it." The Warlock spilled the pack and picked a copper disk out of the litter. "I couldn't let Glirendree run loose, could I? Then the secret spread like a brushfire. The battle made too good a story."

"You and your damn Wheel."

"The magic goes away and never comes back. All the magicians panicked. You made a whole discipline out of murder and resurrection. Piranther and his band scrambled for a place of safety. Rynildissen City barred magicians—"

"Do it. Before we're stopped."

The Warlock spoke a word in the old Guild language and let go fast. The Wheel hovered in the air, spinning.

Roze-Kattee reached for them.

The Warlock heard a humming, rising in pitch. Sudden weakness dropped him on his side, limp. The disk glowed dull red. Roze-Kattee's fingers disappeared into the glow, stretching and thinning like smoke in a draft. The Warlock felt no pain from the god, only the god's amazement changing to horror.

Roze-Kattee set its feet and pulled back. Now the disk was yellow-hot. Bursitis, arthritis, kidney stones, all the agony of a body that had lived too long flared and faded, and the Warlock's strength and his senses faded together. His eyes blurred. The disk was a blue-white sun, and Roze-Kattee was pulled into it. The god's panic was thick enough to touch . . . and then that faded too.

Mirandee came picking her way delicately through fallen rock. Her face was above Orolandes when he opened his eyes. "It's all over," she said.

Orolandes sighed. "I've been thinking of giving up magic."

What should have been a joke only made her nod soberly. In daylight spilling through the smashed cavern wall, her hair glowed white. On her shadow-darkened face his caress found roughness and wrinkles.

The daylight was dwindling as they left the cavern. Orolandes saw no trace of Roze-Kattee. He saw a scar of burned and melted rock, and smelled vaporized copper.

It was possible to imagine that the mountain range to the south had the shape of a serpent, or that the earthquake-shattered cavern had some of the symmetry of a snake's mouth. But really, the landscape was quite ordinary. Where magicians had made their last stand, they found the red man curled up and apparently asleep beside what seemed a human skeleton with two skulls.

Mirandee stooped with difficulty. She put a large-knuckled hand on Clubfoot's shoulder and said, "Kaharoldil, speak to me."

"I couldn't handle it," Clubfoot said without moving.

"You can't go mad. Roze-Kattee saw to that. Come on, sit up. We need you."

Clubfoot rolled over and opened his eyes. He touched the two skulls beside him, almost caressingly.

"Nice, wasn't it?" he said, perhaps to the skulls. "Knowing how to grant wishes instead of working for them. Must have been bad when the gods were alive, though. They might grant your prayer, they might grant your enemy's, but they'd certainly grant their own. A god's wishes wouldn't have anything to do with what human beings wanted." Clubfoot looked up at last. "Mirandee, love, we should have remembered what the gods were like. Whimsical. Wilful. They wiped out humanity at least once, and made us over again. These last thousand years were a golden age. We got our prayers granted, but not often, and not too far granted, and it took some skill to do it."

"It's over," Mirandee said.

"Are you both all right?"

Mirandee nodded. Orolandes said, "Nothing broken, I think. I'll have some interesting bruises. I'd have been crushed if the Warlock hadn't distracted the god's attention."

"What do we do next? We're stranded on a mountain with no magic."

"We'll spend the night in the cave," Orolandes said. "Get out of here in the morning. We'll be hungry. You probably summoned all the game in this area. So I'll put my spear back together, and we'll put the pack on you, Clubfoot; it'll be empty anyway. You won't want your tools now. What about the skulls?"

"Might as well leave them. I wish—"

"What?"

"Nothing."

The Magic
May Return

ψ

Table of Contents

2μ

ψ

NOT LONG BEFORE THE END
by Larry Niven

4

A SWORDSMAN BATTLED a sorcerer once upon a time.

In that age such battles were frequent. A natural antipathy exists between swordsmen and sorcerers, as between cats and small birds, or between rats and men. Usually the swordsman lost, and humanity's average intelligence rose some trifling fraction. Sometimes the swordsman won, and again the species was improved; for a sorcerer who cannot kill one miserable swordsman is a poor excuse for a sorcerer.

But this battle differed from the others. On one side, the sword itself was enchanted. On the other, the sorcerer knew a great and terrible truth.

We will call him the Warlock, as his name is both forgotten and impossible to pronounce. His parents had known what they were about. He who knows your name has power over you, but he must speak your name to use it.

The Warlock had found his terrible truth in middle age.

By that time he had traveled widely. It was not from choice. It was simply that he was a powerful magician, and he used his power, and he needed friends.

He knew spells to make people love a magician. The Warlock had tried these, but he did not like the side effects. So he commonly used his great power to help those around him, that they might love him without coercion.

He found that when he had been ten to fifteen years in a place, using his magic as whim dictated, his powers would weaken. If he moved away, they returned. Twice he had had to move, and twice he had settled in a new land, learned new customs, made new friends. It happened a third time, and he prepared to move again. But something set him to wondering.

Why should a man's powers be so unfairly drained out of him?

It happened to nations too. Throughout history, those lands which had been richest in magic had been overrun by barbarians carrying swords and clubs. It was a sad truth, and one that did not bear thinking about, but the Warlock's curiosity was strong.

So he wondered, and he stayed to perform certain experiments.

His last experiment involved a simple kinetic sorcery set to spin a metal disc in midair. And when that magic was done, he knew a truth he could never forget.

So he departed. In succeeding decades he moved again and again. Time changed his personality, if not his body, and his magic became more dependable, if less showy. He had discovered a great and terrible truth, and if he kept it secret, it was through compassion. His truth spelled the end of civilization, yet it was of no earthly use to anyone.

So he thought. But some five decades later (the date was on the order of 12,000 B.C.) it occurred to him that all truths find a use somewhere, sometime. And so he built another disc and recited spells over it, so that (like a telephone number already dialed but for one digit) the disc would be ready if ever he needed it.

The name of the sword was Glirendree. It was several hundred years old, and quite famous.

As for the swordsman, his name is no secret. It was Belhap Sattlestone Wirldess ag Miracloat roo Cononson. His friends, who tended to be temporary, called him Hap. He was a barbarian, of course. A civilized man would have had more sense than to touch Glirendree, and better morals than to stab a sleeping woman. Which was how Hap acquired his sword. Or vice versa.

The Warlock recognized it long before he saw it. He was at work in the cavern he had carved beneath a hill, when an alarm went off. The hair rose up, tingling, along the back of his neck. "Visitors," he said.

"I don't hear anything," said Sharla, but there was an uneasiness to her tone. Sharla was a girl of the village who had come to live with the Warlock. That day she had persuaded the Warlock to teach her some of his simpler spells.

"Don't you feel the hair rising on the back of your neck? I set the alarm to do that. Let me just check . . ." He used a sensor like a silver hula hoop set on edge. "There's trouble coming. Sharla, we've got to get you out of here."

"But . . ." Sharla waved protestingly at the table where they had been working.

"Oh, that. We can quit in the middle. That spell isn't dangerous." It was a charm against lovespells, rather messy to work, but safe and tame and effective. The Warlock pointed at the spear of light glaring through the hoopsensor. "That's dangerous. An enormously powerful focus of *mana* power is moving up the west side of the hill. You go down the east side."

"Can I help? You've taught me *some* magic."

The magician laughed a little nervously. "Against that? That's Glirendree. Look at the size of the image, the color, the shape. No. You get out of here, and right now. The hill's clear on the eastern slope."

"Come with me."

"I can't. Not with Glirendree loose. Not when it's already got hold of some idiot. There are obligations."

They came out of the cavern together, into the mansion they shared. Sharla, still protesting, donned a robe and started down the hill. The Warlock hastily selected an armload of paraphernalia and went outside.

The intruder was halfway up the hill: a large but apparently human being carrying something long and glittering. He was still a quarter of an hour downslope. The Warlock set up the silver hula hoop and looked through it.

The sword was a flame of *mana* discharge, an eyehurting needle of white light. Glirendree, right enough. He knew of other, equally powerful *mana* foci, but none were portable, and none would show as a sword to the unaided eye.

He should have told Sharla to inform the Brotherhood. She had that much magic. Too late now.

There was no colored borderline to the spear of light.

No green fringe effect meant no protective spells. The swordsman had not tried to guard himself against what he carried. Certainly the intruder was no magician, and he had not the intelligence to get the help of a magician. Did he know *nothing* about Glirendree?

Not that that would help the Warlock. He who carried Glirendree was invulnerable to any power save Glirendree itself. Or so it was said.

"Let's test that," said the Warlock to himself. He dipped into his armload of equipment and came up with something wooden, shaped like an ocarina. He blew the dust off it, raised it in his fist and pointed it down the mountain. But he hesitated.

The loyalty spell was simple and safe, but it did have side effects. It lowered its victim's intelligence.

"Self-defense," the Warlock reminded himself, and blew into the ocarina.

The swordsman did not break stride. Glirendree didn't even glow; it had absorbed the spell that easily.

In minutes the swordsman would be here. The Warlock hurriedly set up a simple prognostics spell. At least he could learn who would win the coming battle.

No picture formed before him. The scenery did not even waver.

"Well, now," said the Warlock. "*Well,* now!" And he reached into his clutter of sorcerous tools and found a metal disc. Another instant's rummaging produced a double-edged knife, profusely inscribed in no known language, and very sharp.

At the top of the Warlock's hill was a spring, and the stream from that spring ran past the Warlock's house. The swordsman stood leaning on his sword, facing the Warlock across that stream. He breathed deeply, for it had been a hard climb.

He was powerfully muscled and profusely scarred. To the Warlock it seemed strange that so young a man should have found time to acquire so many scars. But none of his wounds had impaired motor functions. The Warlock had watched him coming up the hill. The swordsman was in top physical shape.

His eyes were deep blue and brilliant, and half an inch too close together for the Warlock's taste.

"I am Hap," he called across the stream. "Where is she?"

"You mean Sharla, of course. But why is that your concern?"

"I have come to free her from her shameful bondage, old man. Too long have you—"

"Hey, hey, hey. Sharla's my *wife.*"

"Too long have you used her for your vile and lecherous purposes. Too—"

"She stays of her own free will, you nit!"

"You expect me to believe that? As lovely a woman as Sharla, could she love an old and feeble warlock?"

"Do I look feeble?"

The Warlock did not look like an old man. He seemed Hap's age, some twenty years old, and his frame and his musculature were the equal of Hap's. He had not bothered to dress as he left the cavern. In place of Hap's scars, his back bore a tattoo in red and green and gold, an elaborately curlicued pentagramic design, almost hypnotic in its extradimensional involutions.

"Everyone in the village knows your age," said Hap. "You're two hundred years old, if not more."

"Hap," said the Warlock. "Belhap something-or-other roo Cononson. Now I remember. Sharla told me you tried to bother her last time she went to the village. I should have done something about it then."

"Old man, you lie. Sharla is under a spell. Everybody knows the power of a warlock's loyalty spell."

"I don't use them. I don't like the side effects. Who wants to be surrounded by friendly morons?" The Warlock pointed to Glirendree. "Do you know what you carry?"

Hap nodded ominously.

"Then you ought to know better. Maybe it's not too late. See if you can transfer it to your left hand."

"I tried that. I can't let go of it." Hap cut at the air, restlessly, with his sixty pounds of sword. "I have to sleep with the damned thing clutched in my hand."

"Well, it's too late then."

"It's worth it," Hap said grimly. "For now I can kill you. Too long has an innocent woman been subjected to your lecherous—"

"I know, I know." The Warlock changed languages suddenly, speaking high and fast. He spoke thus for almost a minute, then switched back to Rynaldese. "Do you feel any pain?"

"Not a twinge," said Hap. He had not moved. He stood with his remarkable sword at the ready, glowering at the magician across the stream.

"No sudden urge to travel? Attacks of remorse? Change of body temperature?" But Hap was grinning now, not at all nicely. "I thought not. Well, it had to be tried."

There was an instant of blinding light.

When it reached the vicinity of the hill, the meteorite had dwindled to the size of a baseball. It should have finished its journey at the back of Hap's head. Instead, it exploded a millisecond too soon. When the light had died, Hap stood within a ring of craterlets.

The swordsman's unsymmetrical jaw dropped, and then he closed his mouth and started forward. The sword hummed faintly.

The Warlock turned his back.

Hap curled his lip at the Warlock's cowardice. Then he jumped three feet backward from a standing start. A shadow had pulled itself from the Warlock's back.

In a lunar cave with the sun glaring into its mouth, a man's shadow on the wall might have looked that sharp and black. The shadow dropped to the ground and stood up, a humanoid outline that was less a shape than a window view of the ultimate blackness beyond the death of the universe. Then it leapt.

Glirendree seemed to move of its own accord. It hacked the demon once lengthwise and once across, while the demon seemed to batter against an invisible shield, trying to reach Hap even as it died.

"Clever," Hap panted. "A pentagram on your back, a demon trapped inside."

"That's clever," said the Warlock, "but it didn't work. Carrying Glirendree works, but it's not clever. I ask you again, do you know what you carry?"

"The most powerful sword ever forged." Hap raised the weapon high. His right arm was more heavily muscled than his left, and inches longer, as if Glirendree had been at work on it. "A sword to make me the equal of any warlock or sorceress, and without the help of demons, either. I had to kill a woman who loved me to get it, but I paid that price gladly. When I have sent you to your just reward, Sharla will come to me—"

"She'll spit in your eye. Now will you listen to me? Glirendree *is* a demon. If you had an ounce of sense, you'd cut your arm off at the elbow."

Hap looked startled. "You mean there's a demon imprisoned in the metal?"

"Get it through your head. *There is no metal.* It's a demon, a bound demon, and it's a parasite. It'll age you to death in a year unless you cut it loose. A warlock of the northlands imprisoned it in its present form, then gave it to one of his bastards, Jeery of Something-or-other. Jeery conquered half this continent before he died on the battlefield, of senile decay. It was given into the charge of the Rainbow Witch a year before I was born, because there never was a woman who had less use for people, especially men."

"That happens to have been untrue."

"Probably Glirendree's doing. Started her glands up again, did it? She should have guarded against that."

"A year," said Hap. "One year."

But the sword stirred restlessly in his hand. "It will be a glorious year," said Hap, and he came forward.

The Warlock picked up a copper disc. "Four," he said, and the disc spun in midair.

By the time Hap had sloshed through the stream, the disc was a blur of motion. The Warlock moved to keep it between himself and Hap, and Hap dared not touch it, for it would have sheared through anything at all. He crossed around it, but again the Warlock had darted to the other side. In the pause he snatched up something else: a silvery knife, profusely inscribed.

"Whatever that is," said Hap, "it can't hurt me. No magic can affect me while I carry Glirendree."

"True enough," said the Warlock. "The disc will lose its force in a minute anyway. In the meantime, I know a secret that I would like to tell, one I could never tell to a friend."

Hap raised Glirendree above his head and, two-handed, swung it down on the disc. The sword stopped jarringly at the disc's rim.

"It's protecting you," said the Warlock. "If Glirendree hit the rim now, the recoil would knock you clear down to the village. Can't you hear the hum?"

Hap heard the whine as the disc cut the air. The tone was going up and up the scale.

"You're stalling," he said.

"That's true. So? Can it hurt you?"

"No. You were saying you knew a secret." Hap braced himself, sword raised, on one side of the disc, which now glowed red at the edge.

"I've wanted to tell someone for such a long time. A hundred and fifty years. Even Sharla doesn't know." The Warlock still stood ready to run if the swordsman should come after him. "I'd learned a little magic in those days, not much compared to what I know now, but big, showy stuff. Castles floating in the air. Dragons with golden scales. Armies turned to stone, or wiped out by lightning, instead of simple death spells. Stuff like that takes a lot of power, you know?"

"I've heard of such things."

"I did it all the time, for myself, for friends, for whoever happened to be king, or whomever I happened to be in love with. And I found that after I'd been settled for a while, the power would leave me. I'd have to move elsewhere to get it back."

The copper disc glowed bright orange with the heat of its spin. It should have fragmented, or melted, long ago.

"Then there are the dead places, the places where a warlock dares not go. Places where magic doesn't work. They tend to be rural areas, farmlands and sheep ranges, but you can find the old cities, the castles built to float which now lie tilted on their sides, the unnaturally aged bones of dragons, like huge lizards from another age.

"So I started wondering."

Hap stepped back a bit from the heat of the disc. It glowed pure white now, and it was like a sun brought to earth. Through the glare Hap had lost sight of the Warlock.

"So I built a disc like this one and set it spinning. Just a simple kinetic sorcery, but with a constant acceleration and no limit point. You know what *mana* is?"

"What's happening to your voice?"

"*Mana* is the name we give to the power behind magic." The Warlock's voice had gone weak and high.

A horrible suspicion came to Hap. The Warlock had slipped down the hill, leaving his voice behind! Hap trotted around the disc, shading his eyes from its heat.

An old man sat on the other side of the disc. His arthritic fingers, half-crippled with swollen joints, played with a rune-inscribed knife. "What I found out—oh, there you are. Well, it's too late now."

Hap raised his sword, and his sword changed.

It was a massive red demon, horned and hooved, and its teeth were in Hap's right hand. It paused, deliberately, for the few seconds it took Hap to realize what had happened and to try to jerk away. Then it bit down, and the swordsman's hand was off at the wrist.

The demon reached out, slowly enough, but Hap in his surprise was unable to move. He felt the taloned fingers close his windpipe.

He felt the strength leak out of the taloned hand, and he saw surprise and dismay spread across the demon's face.

The disc exploded. All at once and nothing first, it disintegrated into a flat cloud of metallic particles and was gone, flashing away as so much meteorite dust. The light was as lightning striking at one's feet. The sound was its thunder. The smell was vaporized copper.

The demon faded, as a chameleon fades against its background. Fading, the demon slumped to the ground in slow motion, and faded further, and was gone. When Hap reached out with his foot, he touched only dirt.

Behind Hap was a trench of burnt earth.

The spring had stopped. The rocky bottom of the stream was drying in the sun.

The Warlock's cavern had collapsed. The furnishings of the Warlock's mansion had gone crashing down into that vast pit, but the mansion itself was gone without trace.

Hap clutched his messily severed wrist, and he said, "But what happened?"

"*Mana*," the Warlock mumbled. He spat out a complete set of blackened teeth. "*Mana*. What I discovered was that the power behind magic is a natural resource, like the fertility of the soil. When you use it up, it's gone."

"But—"

"Can you see why I kept it a secret? One day all the wide world's *mana* will be used up. No more *mana*, no more magic. Do you know that Atlantis is tectonically unstable? Succeeding sorcerer-kings renew the spells each generation to keep the whole continent from sliding into the sea. What happens when the spells don't work any more? They couldn't possibly evacuate the whole continent in time. Kinder not to let them know."

"But . . . that disc."

The Warlock grinned with his empty mouth and ran his hands through snowy hair. All the hair came off in his fingers, leaving his scalp bare and mottled. "Senility is like being drunk. The disc? I told you. A kinetic sorcery with no upper limit. The disc keeps accelerating until all the *mana* in the locality has been used up."

Hap moved a step forward. Shock had drained half his strength. His foot came down jarringly, as if all the spring were out of his muscles.

"You tried to kill me."

The Warlock nodded. "I figured if the disc didn't explode and kill you while you were trying to go around it, Glirendree would strangle you when the constraint wore off. What are you complaining about? It cost you a hand, but you're free of Glirendree."

Hap took another step, and another. His hand was beginning to hurt, and the pain gave him strength. "Old man," he said thickly. "Two hundred years old. I can break your neck with the hand you left me. And I will."

The Warlock raised the inscribed knife.

"That won't work. No more magic." Hap slapped the Warlock's hand away and took the Warlock by his bony throat.

The Warlock's hand brushed easily aside, and came back, and up. Hap wrapped his arms around his belly and backed away with his eyes and mouth wide open. He sat down hard.

"A knife always works," said the Warlock.

"Oh," said Hap.

"I worked the metal myself, with ordinary blacksmith's tools, so the knife wouldn't crumble when the magic was gone. The runes aren't magic. They only say—"

"Oh," said Hap. "Oh." He toppled sideways.

The Warlock lowered himself onto his back. He held the knife up and read the markings, in a language only the Brotherhood remembered.

AND THIS, TOO, SHALL PASS AWAY. It was a very old platitude, even then.

He dropped his arm back and lay looking at the sky.

* * *

Presently the blue was blotted by a shadow.

"I told you to get out of here," he whispered.

"You should have known better. What's *happened* to you?"

"No more youth spells. I knew I'd have to do it when the prognostics spell showed blank." He drew a ragged breath. "It was worth it. I killed Glirendree."

"Playing hero, at your age! What can I do? How can I help?"

"Get me down the hill before my heart stops. I never told you my true age—"

"I knew. The whole village knows." She pulled him to sitting position, pulled one of his arms around her neck. It felt dead. She shuddered, but she wrapped her own arm around his waist and gathered herself for the effort. "You're so thin! Come on, love. We're going to stand up." She took most of his weight onto her, and they stood up.

"Go slow. I can hear my heart trying to take off."

"How far do we have to go?"

"Just to the foot of the hill, I think. Then the spells will work again, and we can rest." He stumbled. "I'm going blind," he said.

"It's a smooth path, and all downhill."

"That's why I picked this place. I knew I'd have to use the disc someday. You can't throw away knowledge. Always the time comes when you use it, because you have to, because it's there."

"You've changed so. So—so ugly. And you smell."

The pulse fluttered in his neck, like a hummingbird's wings. "Maybe you won't want me, after seeing me like this."

"You can change back, can't you?"

"Sure. I can change to anything you like. What color eyes do you want?"

"I'll be like this myself someday," she said. Her voice held cool horror. And it was fading; he was going deaf.

"I'll teach you the proper spells, when you're ready. They're dangerous. Blackly dangerous."

She was silent for a time. Then: "What color were *his* eyes? You know, Belhap Sattlestone whatever."

"Forget it," said the Warlock, with a touch of pique.

And suddenly his sight was back.

But not forever, thought the Warlock as they stumbled through the sudden daylight. When the *mana* runs out, I'll go like a blown candle flame, and civilization will follow. No more magic, no more magic-based industries. Then the whole world will be barbarian until men learn a new way to coerce nature, and the swordsmen, the damned stupid swordsmen, will win after all.

Ψ

EARTHSHADE
by Fred Saberhagen

♃

WHEN ZALAZAR SAW the lenticular cloud decapitate the mountain, he knew that the old magic in the world was not yet dead. The conviction struck him all in an instant, and with overwhelming force, even as the cloud itself had struck the rock. Dazed by the psychic impact, he turned round shakily on the steep hillside to gaze at the countenance of the youth who was standing beside him. For a long moment then, even as the shockwave of the crash came through the earth beneath their feet and then blasted the air about their ears, Zalazar seemed truly stunned. His old eyes and mind were vacant alike, as if he might never before have seen this young man's face.

"Grandfather." The voice of the youth was hushed, and filled with awe. His gaze went past Zalazar's shoulder, and on up the mountain. "What was that?"

"You saw," said Zalazar shortly. With a hobbling motion on the incline, he turned his attention back to the miracle. "How it came down from the sky. You heard and felt it when it hit. You know as much about it as I do."

Zalazar himself had not particularly noticed one small round cloud, among other clouds of various shape disposed around what was in general an ordinary summer sky. Not until a comparatively rapid relative movement, of something small, unnaturally round, and very white against the high deep blue had happened to catch the corner of his eye. He had looked up directly at the cloud then, and the moment he did that he felt the magic. That distant disk-shape, trailing small patches of ivory fur, had come down in an angled, silent glide that somehow gave the impression of heaviness, of being on the verge of a complete loss of buoyancy and control. The cloud slid, or fell, with a deceptive speed, a speed that became fully apparent to Zalazar only when the long path of its descent at last intersected age-old rock.

"Grandfather, I can feel the magic."

"I'm sure you can. Not that you've ever had the chance to feel anything like it before. But it's something everyone is able to recognize at once." The old man took a step higher on the slope, staring at the mountain fiercely. "You were born to live with magic. We all were, the whole human race. We're never more than half alive unless we have it." He paused for a moment, savoring his own sensations. "Well, I've felt many a great spell in my time. There's no harm in this one, not for us, at least. In fact I think it may possibly bring us some great good."

With that Zalazar paused again, experiencing something new, or maybe something long-forgotten. Was it only that the perceived aura of great spells near at hand brought back memories of his youth? It was more than that, probably. Old wellsprings of divination, caked over by the years, were proving to be still capable of stir and bubble. "All right. Whatever that cloud is, it took the whole top of the mountain with it over into the next valley. I think we should climb up there and take a look." All above was silent now, and apparently tranquil. Except that a large, vague plume of gray dust had become visible above the truncated mountain, where it drifted fitfully in an uncertain wind.

The youth was eager, and they began at once. With his hand upon a strong young arm for support when needed, Zalazar felt confident that his old limbs and heart would serve him through the climb.

They stopped at the foot of an old rock slide to rest, and to drink from a high spring there that the old man knew about. The midsummer grass grew lush around the water source, and with a sudden concern for the mundane Zalazar pointed this out to the boy as a good place to bring the flocks. Then, after they had rested in the shade of a rock for a little longer, the real climb began. It went more easily for Zalazar than he had expected, because he had help at the harder places. They spoke rarely. He was saving his breath, and anyway he did not want to talk or even think much about what they were going to discover. This reluctance was born not of fear, but of an almost childish and still growing anticipation. Whatever else, there was going to be magic in his life again, a vast new store of magic, ebullient and overflowing. And feeding the magic, of course, a small ocean at least of *mana*. Maybe with a supply like that, there would be enough left over to let an old man use some for himself . . . unless it were all used up, maintaining that altered cloud, before they got to it . . .

Zalazar walked and climbed a little faster. *Mana* from somewhere was around him already in the air. Tantalizingly faint, like the first warm wind from the south before the snow has melted, but there indubitably, like spring.

It was obvious to the old man that his companion, even encumbered as he was by bow and quiver on his back and the small lyre at his belt, could have clambered on ahead to get a quick look at the wonders. But the youth stayed patiently at the old man's side. The bright young eyes, though, were for the most part fixed on ahead. Maybe, Zalazar thought, looking at the other speculatively, maybe he's a little more frightened than he wants to admit.

Maybe I am too, he added to himself. But I am certainly going on up there, nevertheless.

At about midday they reached what was now the mountaintop. It was a bright new tableland, about half a kilometer across, and as flat now as a certain parade ground that the old man could remember. The sight also made Zalazar think imaginatively of the stump of some giant's neck or limb; it was rimmed with soil and growth resembling scurfy skin, it was boned and veined with white rocks and red toward the middle, and it bubbled here and there with pure new springs, the blood of Earth.

From a little distance the raw new surface looked preternaturally smooth. But when you were really near, close enough to bend down and touch the faint new warmth of it, you could see that the surface left by the mighty plane was not *that* smooth; no more level, perhaps, than it might have been made by a small army of men with hand tools, provided they had been well supervised and induced to try.

The foot trail had brought them up the west side of what was left of the mountain. The strange cloud in its long, killing glide had come down also from the west, and had carried the whole mass of the mountaintop off with it to the east. Not far, though. For now, from his newly gained advantage upon the western rim of the new tabletop, Zalazar could see the cloud again.

It was no more than a kilometer or so away. Looking like some giant, snow white, not-quite-rigid dish. It was tilted almost on edge, and it was half sunken into the valley on the mountain's far side, so that the place where Zalazar stood was just about on a horizontal level with the enormous dish's center.

"Come," he said to his young companion, and immediately led the way forward across the smoothed-off rock. The cloud ahead of them was stirring continually, like a sail in a faint breeze, and Zalazar realized that the bulk of it must be still partially airborne. Probably the lower curve of its circular rim was resting or dragging on the floor of the valley below, like the basket of a balloon ready to take off. In his youth, Zalazar had seen balloons, as well as magic and parade grounds. In his youth he had seen much.

As he walked, the raw *mana* rose all around him from the newly opened earth. It was a maddeningly subtle emanation, like ancient perfume, like warm air from an oven used yesterday to bake the finest bread. Zalazar inhaled it like a starving man, with mind and memory as well as lungs. It wasn't enough, he told himself, to really do anything with. But it was quite enough to make him remember what the world had once been like, and what his own role in the world had been.

At another time, under different conditions, such a fragrance of *mana* might have been enough to make the old man weep. But not now, with the wonder of the cloud visible just ahead. It seemed to be waiting for him. Zalazar felt no inclination to dawdle, sniffing the air nostalgically.

There was movement on the planed ground just before his feet. Looking down without breaking stride, Zalazar beheld small creatures that had once been living, then petrified into the mountain's fabric by the slow failure of the world's *mana*, now stirring with gropings back toward life. Under his sandaled foot he felt the purl of a new spring, almost alive. The sensation was gone in an instant, but it jarred him into noticing how quick his own strides had suddenly become, as if he too were already on the way to rejuvenation.

When they reached the eastern edge of the tabletop, Zalazar found he could look almost straight down to where a newly created slope of talus began far below. From the fringes of this great mass of rubble that had been a mountaintop, giant trees, freshly slain or crippled by the landslide, jutted out here and there at deathly angles. The dust of the enormous crash was still persisting faintly in the breeze, and Zalazar thought he could still hear the last withdrawing echoes of its roar . . .

"Grandfather, look!"

Zalazar raised his head quickly, to see the tilted lens-shape of the gigantic cloud bestirring itself with new apparent purpose. Half rolling on its circular rim, which dragged new scars into the valley's grassy skin below, and half lurching sideways, it was slowly, ponderously making its way back toward the mountain and the two who watched it.

The cloud also appeared to be shrinking slightly. Mass in the form of vapor was fuming and boiling away from the vast gentle convexities of its sides. There were also sidewise gouts of rain or spray, that woke in Zalazar the memory of ocean waterspouts. Thunder grumbled. Or was it only the cloud's weight, scraping at the ground? The extremity of the round, mountain-chopping rim looked hard and deadly as a scimitar. Then from the rim inwards the appearance of the enchanted cloudstuff altered gradually, until at the hub of the great wheel a dullard might have thought it only natural.

Another wheelturn of a few degrees. Another thunderous lurch. And suddenly the cloud was a hundred meters closer than before. Someone or something was maneuvering it.

"Grandfather?"

Zalazar spoke in answer to the anxious tone. "It won't do us a bit of good to try to run away." His own voice was cheerful, not fatalistic. The good feeling that he had about the cloud had grown stronger, if anything, the nearer he got to it. Maybe his prescient sense, long dormant, had been awakened into something like acuity by the faint accession of *mana* from the newly opened earth. He could tell that the *mana* in the cloud itself was vastly stronger. "We don't have to be afraid, lad. They don't mean us any harm."

"They?"

"There's—someone—inside that cloud. If you can still call it a cloud, as much as it's been changed."

"*Inside* it? Who could that be?"

Zalazar gestured his ignorance. He felt sure of the fact of the cloud's being inhabited, without being able to say how he knew, or even beginning to understand how such a thing could be. Wizards had been known to ride *on* clouds, of course, with a minimum of alteration in the material. But to alter one to this extent . . .

The cloud meanwhile continued to work its way closer. Turn, slide, ponderous hop, gigantic bump and scrape. It was now only about a hundred meters beyond the edge of the cliff. And now it appeared that something new was going to happen.

The tilted, slowly oscillating wall that was the cloudside closest to the cliff had developed a rolling boil quite near its center. Zalazar judged that this hub of white disturbance was only slightly bigger than a man. After a few moments of development, during which time the whole cloud-mass slid majestically still closer to the cliff, the hub blew out in a hard but silent puff of vapor. Where it had been was now an opening, an arched doorway into the pale interior of the cloud.

A figure in human shape, that of a woman nobly dressed, appeared an instant later in this doorway. Zalazar, in the first moment that he looked directly at her, was struck with awe. In that moment all the day's earlier marvels shrank down, for him, to dimensions hardly greater than the ordinary; they had been but fitting prologue. This was the great true wonder.

He went down at once upon one knee, averting his gaze from the personage before him. And without raising his eyes he put out a hand, and tugged fiercely at his grandson's sleeve until the boy had knelt down too.

Then the woman who was standing in the doorway called to them. Her voice was very clear, and it seemed to the old man that he had been waiting all his years to hear that call. Still the words in themselves were certainly prosaic enough. "You men!" she cried. "I ask your help."

Probably *ask* was not the most accurate word she could have chosen. Zalazar heard himself babbling some reply immediately, some extravagant promise whose exact wording he could not recall a moment later. Not that it mattered, probably. Commitment had been demanded and given.

His pledge once made, he found that he could raise his eyes again. Still the huge cloud was easing closer to the cliff, in little bumps and starts. Its lower flange was continually bending and flowing, making slow thunder against the talus far below, a roaring rearrangement of the fallen rock.

"I am Je," the dazzlingly beautiful woman called them in an imperious voice. Her robes were rich blue, brown, and an ermine that made the cloud itself look gray. "It is written that you two are the men I need to find. Who are you?"

The terrible beauty of her face was no more than a score of meters distant now. Again Zalazar had to look away from its full glory. "I am Zalazar, mighty Je," he answered, in a breaking voice. "I am only a poor man. And this is my innocent grandson—Bormanus." For a moment he had had to search to find the name. "Take pity on us!"

"I mean to take pity on the world, instead, and use you as may be necessary for the world's good," the goddess answered. "But what worthier fate can mortals hope for? Look at me, both of you."

Zalazar raised his eyes again. The woman's countenance was once more bearable. Even as he looked, she turned her head as if to speak or otherwise communicate with someone else behind her in the cloud. Zalazar could see in there part of a corridor, and also a portion of some kind of room, all limned in brightness. The white interior walls and overhead were all shifting slightly and continually in their outlines, in a way that suggested unaltered cloudstuff. But the changes were never more than slight, the largescale shapes remaining as stable as those of a wooden house. And the lady stood always upright upon a perfectly level deck, despite the vast oscillations of the cloud, and its turning as it shifted ever closer to the cliff.

Her piercing gaze returned to Zalazar. "You are an old man, mortal, at first glance not good for much. But I see that there is hidden value in you. You may stand up."

He got slowly to his feet. "My lady Je, it is true that once my hands knew power. But the long death of the world has crippled me."

The goddess' anger flared at him like a flame. "Speak not to me of death! I am no mere mortal subject to Thanatos." Her figure, as terrible as that of any warrior, as female as any succubus of love, was now no more than five meters from Zalazar's half-closed eyes. Her voice rang as clearly and commandingly as before. Yet, mixed with its power was a tone of doomed helplessness, and this tone frightened Zalazar on a deeper level even than did her implied threat.

"Lady," he murmured, "I can but try. Whatever help you need, I will attempt to give it."

"Certainly you will. And willingly. If in the old times your hands knew power, as you say, then you will try hard and risk much to bring the old times back again. You will be glad to hazard what little of good your life may have left in it now. Is it not so?"

Zalazar could only sign agreement, wordlessly.

"And the lad with you, your grandson. Is he your apprentice too? Have you given him any training?"

"In tending flocks, no more. In magic?" The old man gestured helplessness with gnarled hands. "In magic, great lady Je? How could I have? Everywhere that we have lived, the world is dead. Or so close to utter deadness that—"

"I have said that you must not speak to me of death! I will not warn you again. Now, it is written that . . . both of you must come aboard. Yes, both, there will be use for both." And, as if the goddess were piloting and powering the cloud with her will alone, the whole mass of it now tilted gently, bringing her spotless doorway within easy stepping distance of the lip of rock.

Now Zalazar and Bormanus with him were surrounded by whiteness, sealed into it as if by mounds of glowing cotton. White cushioned firmness served their feet as floor or deck, as level always for them as for their divine guide who walked ahead. Whiteness opened itself ahead of her, and sealed itself again when Bormanus had passed, walking close on Zalazar's heels.

The grinding of tormented rock and earth below could no longer be heard as the lady Je, her robes of ermine and ultramarine and brown swirling with her long strides, led them through the cloud. Almost there was no sound at all. Maybe a little wind, Zalazar decided, very faint and sounding far away. He had the feeling that the cloud, its power and purpose somehow regained, had risen quickly from the scarred valley and was once more swiftly airborne.

Je came to a sudden halt in the soft pearly silence, and stretched forth her arms. Around her an open space, a room, swiftly began to define itself. In moments there had grown an intricately formed chamber, as high as a large temple, in which she stood like a statue with her two puny mortal figures in attendance.

Then Zalazar saw that there was one other in the room with them. He muttered something, and heard Bormanus at his side give a quick intake of breath.

The bier or altar at the room's far end supported a figure that might almost have been a gray statue of a tormented man, done on a heroic scale. The figure was youthful, powerful, naked. With limbs contorted it lay twisted on one side. The head was turned in a god's agony so that the short beard jutted vertically.

But it was not a statue. And Zalazar could tell, within a moment of first seeing it, that the sleep that held it was not quite—or not yet—the sleep of death. He had been forbidden to mention death to Je again, and he would not do so.

With a double gesture she beckoned both mortals to cross the room with her to stand beside the figure. While Zalazar was wondering what he ought to say or do, his own right hand moved out, without his willing it, as if to touch the statue-man. Je, he saw, observed this, but she said nothing; and with a great effort of his will Zalazar forced his own arm back to his side. Meanwhile Bormanus at his side was standing still, staring, as if unable to move or speak at all.

Je spoke now as if angry and disappointed. "So, what buried value have you, old man? If you can be of no help in freeing my ally, then why has it been ordained for you to be here?"

"Lady, how should I know?" Zalazar burst out. "I am sorry to disappoint you. I knew something, once, of magic. But . . ." As for even understanding the forces that could bind a god like this, let alone trying to undo them . . . Zalazar could only gesture helplessly. At last he found words. "Great lady Je, I do not even know who this is."

"Call him Phaethon."

"Ah, great gods," Zalazar muttered, shocked and near despair.

"Yes, mortal, indeed we are. As well you knew when you first saw us."

"Yes, I knew . . . indeed." In fact he had thought that all the gods were long dead, or departed from the world of humankind. "Any why is he—like this?"

"He has fallen in battle, mortal. I and he and others have laid siege to Cloudholm, and it has been a long and bitter fight. We seek to free his father, Helios, who lies trapped in the same kind of enchantment there. Through Helios' entrapment, the world of old is dying. Have you heard of Cloudholm, old mortal? Among men it is not often named."

"Ah. I have heard something. Long ago . . ."

"It stifles the *mana*-rain that Helios cast ever on the Earth. With a fleet of cloudships like this one, we hurled ourselves upon its battlements—and were defeated. Most of the old gods lie now in tormented slumber, far above. A few have switched sides willingly. And all our ships save this one were destroyed."

"How could they dare?" The words burst from Bormanus, the first he had uttered since boarding the cloud-vessel. Then he stuttered, as Je's eyes burned at him: "I mean, who would dare try to destroy such ships? And who would have the power to do it?"

The goddess looked at the boy a moment longer, then reached out and took him by the hand. "Lend me your mortal fingers here. Let us see if they will serve to drain enchantment off." Bormanus appeared to be trying to draw back, but his hand, like a baby's, was brought out forcibly to touch the statue-figure's arm. And Zalazar's hand went out on its own once more; this time he could not keep it back, or perhaps he did not dare to try. His fingers spread on rounded arm-muscle, thicker by far than his own thigh. The touch of the figure made him think more of frozen snake than flesh of god. And now, Zalazar felt faint with sudden terror. Something, some great power, was urging the freezing near-death to desert its present captive and be content with Zalazar and Bormanus instead. But that mighty urging was mightily opposed, and came to nothing. At last, far above Zalazar's head, as if between proud kings disputing across some infant's cradle, a truce was reached. For the moment. He was able to withdraw his hand unharmed, and watched as Bormanus did the same.

The goddess Je sighed. It was a world-weary sound, close to defeat yet still infinitely stubborn. "And yet I am sure that there is *something* in you, old man . . . or possibly in your young companion here. Something that in the end will be of very great importance. Something that must be found . . . though I see, now, that you yourselves can hardly be expected to be aware of what it is."

He clasped his hands. "Oh great lady Je, we are only poor humans . . . mortals . . ."

"Never mind. In time I will discover the key. What is written anywhere, I can eventually read."

Zalazar was aware now of a strong motion underneath his feet. Even to weak human senses it was evident that the whole cloud was now in purposeful and very rapid flight.

"Where are we going?" Bormanus muttered, as if he were asking the air itself. He was a very handsome youth, with dark and curly hair.

"We return to the attack, young mortal. If most of our fleet has been destroyed, well, so too are the defenses of Cloudholm nearly worn away. One more assault can bring it into my hands, and set its prisoners free."

Zalazar had been about to ask some question, but now a distracting realization made him forget what it was. He had suddenly become aware that there was some guardian presence, sprite or demon he thought, melded with the cloud, driving and controlling it on Je's commands. It drew for energy on some vast internal store of *mana*, a treasure trove that Zalazar could only dimly sense.

Now, in obedience to Je's unspoken orders, the light inside the room or temple where they stood was taking on a reddish tinge. And now the cloud-carvings were disappearing from what Zalazar took to be the forward wall. As Je faced in that direction, pictures began to appear there magically. These were of a cloudscape first, then of an earthly plain seen from a height greater than any mountain's. Both were passing at fantastic speed.

Je nodded as if satisfied. "Come," she said, "and we will try your usefulness in a new way." With a quick gesture she opened the whiteness to one side, and overhead. A stair took form even as she began to climb it. "We will see if your value lies in reconnoitering the enemy."

Clinging to Bormanus' shoulder for support, Zalazar found that the stairs were not as hard to negotiate as he had feared, even when they shifted form from one step to the next. Then there was a sudden gaping purple openness above their heads. "Fear not," said Je. "My protection is upon you both, to let you breathe and live."

Zalazar and Bormanus mounted higher. Wind shrieked thinly now, not in their faces but round them at some little distance, as if warded by some invisible shield. Then abruptly the climbing stair had no more steps. Zalazar thought that they stood on an open deck of cloud, under a bright sun in a dark sky, in some strange realm of neither day nor night. The prow of the cloudship that he rode upon was just before him; he stood as if on the bridge of some proud ocean vessel, looking out over deck and rounded bow, and a wild vastness of the elements beyond.

Not that the ship was borne by anything as small and simple as an earthly sea. The whole globe of Earth was already so far below that Zalazar could now begin to see its roundness, and still the cloudship climbed. All natural clouds were far below, clinging near the great curve of Earth, though rising here and there in strong relief. At first Zalazar thought that the star-pierced blackness through which they flew was empty of everything but passing light. But presently—with, as he sensed, Je's unspoken aid—he began to be able to perceive structure in the thinness of space about him.

"What do you see now, my sage old man? And you, my clever youth?" Je's voice pleaded even as it mocked and commanded. Her fear and puzzlement frightened Zalazar again. For the first time now he knew true regret that he had followed his first impulse and climbed a chopped-off mountain. Where now was the good result that prescience had seemed to promise?

"I see only the night ahead of us," responded Bormanus. His voice sounded remote, as if he were half asleep.

"I . . . see," said Zalazar, and paused with that. Much was coming clear to him, but it was going to be hard to describe. The cloud structures far below, so heavy with their contained water and their own mundane laws, blended almost imperceptibly into the base of something much vaster, finer, and more subtle. Something that filled the space around the Earth, from the level of those low clouds up to the vastly greater altitude at which Zalazar now stood. And higher still . . . his eyes, as if ensnared now by those faery lines and arches, followed them upward and outward and ever higher still. The lines girdled the whole round Earth, and rose . . .

And rose . . .

Zalazar clutched out for support. Obligingly, a stanchion of cloudstuff grew up and hardened into place to meet his grasp. He did not even look at it. His eyes were fixed up and ahead, looking at Cloudholm.

Imagine the greatest castle of legend. And then go beyond that, and beyond, till imagination knows itself inadequate. Two aspects dominate: first, an almost invisible delicacy, with the appearance of a fragility to match. Secondly, almost omnipotent power—or, again, its seeming. Size was certainly a component of that power. Zalazar had never tried to, or been able to, imagine anything as high as this. So high that it grew near only slowly, though the cloudship was racing toward it at a speed that Zalazar would have described as almost as fast as thought.

Then Zalazar saw how, beyond Cloudholm, a thin crescent of Moon rose wonderfully higher still; and again, beyond that, burned the blaze of Sun, a jewel in black. These sights threw him into a sudden terror of the depths of space. No longer did he marvel so greatly that Je and her allied powers could have been defeated.

"Great lady," he asked humbly, "what realm, whose dominion is this?"

"What I need from you, mortal, are answers, not questions of a kind that I can pose myself." Je's broad white hand swung out gently to touch him on the eyes. Her touch felt surprisingly warm. Her voice commanded: "Say what you see."

The touch at once allowed him to see more clearly. But he stuttered, groping for words. What he was suddenly able to perceive was that the Sun lived at the core of a magnificent, perpetual explosion, the expanding waves of which were as faint as Cloudholm itself, but none the less glorious for that. These waves moved in some medium far finer than the air, more tenuous than even the thinning air that had almost ceased to whistle with the cloudship's passage. And the waves of the continual slow sun-explosion bore with them a myriad of almost infinitesimal particles, particles that were heavy with *mana*, though they were almost too small to be called solid.

And there were the lines, as of pure force, in space. In obedience to some elegant system of laws they bore the gossamer outer robes of the Sun itself, to wrap the Earth with delicate energy . . . and the *mana* that flowed outward from the Sun, great Zeus but there was such a flood of it!

The Earth was bathed in warmth and energy—but not in *mana*, Zalazar suddenly perceived. That flow had been cut off by Cloudholm and its spreading wings. (Yes, Zalazar could see the pinions of enchantment now, raptor-wings extending curved on two sides from the castle itself, as if to embrace the whole Earth — or smother it.) Through them the common sunlight flowed on unimpeded, to make the surface of the world flash blue and ermine white. But all the inner energies of magic were cut off . . .

Zalazar realized with a start that he was, or just had been, entranced and muttering, that someone with a mighty grip had just shaken his arm, that a voice of divine power was urging him to speak up, to make sense in what he reported of his vision.

"Tell clearly what you see, old man. The wings, you say, spread out from Cloudholm to enfold the Earth. That much I knew already. Now say what their weakness is. How are they to be torn aside?"

"I . . . I . . . the wings are very strong. They draw sustaining power from the very flow of *mana* that they deny the Earth. Some of the particles that hail on them go through — but those are without *mana*. Many of the particles and waves remain, are trapped by the great wings and drained of *mana* and of other energies. Then eventually they are let go."

"Old fool, what use are you? You tell me nothing I do not already know. Say, where is the weakness of the wings? How can our Earth be fed?"

"Just at the poles . . . there is a weakness, sometimes, a drooping of the wings, and there a little more *mana* than elsewhere can reach the Earth."

Suddenly faint, Zalazar felt himself begin to topple. He was grabbed, and upheld, and shaken again. "Tell more, mortal. What power has created Cloudholm?"

"What do I know? How can I see? What can I say?"

He was shaken more violently than before, until in his desperate fear of Je he cried: "Great Apollo himself could not learn more!"

He was released abruptly, and there was a precipitous silence, as if even Je had been shocked by Zalazar's free use of that name, the presence of whose owner only his mother Leto and his father Zeus could readily endure. Then Zalazar's eyes were brushed again by Je's warm hand, and he came fully to himself.

Cloudholm was bearing down on them. "And Helios is trapped up there?" Zalazar wondered aloud. "But why, and how?"

"Why?" The bitterness and soft rage in Je's voice were worthy of a goddess. "Why, I myself helped first to bind him. Was I made to do that, after opposing him and bringing on a bitter quarrel? I do not know. Are even we deities the playthings of some overriding fate? What was Helios' sin, for such a punishment? And what was mine?"

Again Zalazar had to avert his gaze, for Je's beauty glowed even more terribly than before. And at the same time he had to strive to master himself, hold firm his will against the hubris that rose up in him and urged him to reach for the role of god himself. Such an opportunity existed, would exist, foreknowledge told him, and it was somewhere near at hand. If he only . . .

His internal struggle was interrupted by the realization that the cloudship no longer moved. Looking carefully, Zalazar could see that it had come to rest upon an almost insubstantial plain.

Straight ahead of him now, the bases of the walls of Cloudholm rose. And there was a towering gate.

Je was addressing him almost calmly again. "If your latent power, old mortal, is neither of healing nor of seeing, then perhaps it lies in the realm of war. That is the way we now must pass. Kneel down."

Zalazar knelt. The right hand of the goddess closed on his and drew him to his feet again. He arose on lithely muscular legs, and saw that the old clothing in which he had walked the high pasturelands had been transformed. He was clad now in silver cloth, a fabric worked with a fine brocade. His garments hung on him as solidly as chain mail yet felt as soft and light as silk. They were at once the clothing and the armor of a god. In Zalazar's right hand, grown young and muscular, a short sword had appeared. The weapon was of some metal vastly different from that of his garments, and yet he could feel that its power was at least their equal. On his left arm now hung a shield of dazzling brightness, but seemingly of no more than a bracelet's weight.

The front of the cloudship divided and opened a way for the man who had been the old herdsman Zalazar. The thin cloudstuff of the magic plain swirled and rippled round his boots of silver-gray. His feet were firmly planted, and though he could plainly see the sunlit Earth below, he knew no fear that he might fall.

He glanced behind him once, and saw the cloudship altering, disintegrating, and knew that the nameless demon who had sustained it had come out now at Je's command, to serve her in some other way.

Then Zalazar faced ahead. He could see, now, how much damage the great walls of Cloudholm had sustained, and what had caused the damage. Other cloudships, their insubstantial wreckage mixed with that of the walls they had assailed, lay scattered across the plain and piled at the feet of those enduring, fragile-looking towers. Nor were the wrecked ships empty. With vision somehow granted him by Je, Zalazar could see that each of them held at least one sleep-bound figure of the stature of a god or demi-god. They were male or female, old-looking or young, of divers attributes. All were caught and held, like Phaethon, by some powerful magic that imposed a quiet if not always a peaceful slumber.

Now, where was Je herself? Zalazar realized suddenly that he could see neither the goddess nor her attendant demon. He called her name aloud.

Do not seek me, her voice replied, whispering just at his ear. *Make your way across the plain, and force the castle gates. With my help you can do it, and I shall be with you when my help is needed.*

Zalazar shrugged his shoulders. With part of his mind he knew that his present feelings of power and confidence were unnatural, given him by the goddess for her own purposes. But at the same time he could not deny those feelings—nor did he really want to. Feeling enormously capable, driven by an urge to prove what this divine weapon in his new right hand could do, he shrugged his shoulders again, loosening tight new muscles for action. Beside him, Bormanus, who had not been changed, was looking about in all directions alertly. With one hand the lad gripped tightly the small lyre at his belt, but he gave no other sign of fear. Then suddenly he raised his other hand and pointed.

Coming from the gates of Cloudholm, which now stood open, already halfway across the wide plain between, a challenger was treading thin white cloud in great white boots.

Zalazar, watching, raised his sword a little. Still the goddess was letting him know no fear. He who approached was a red-bearded man, wearing what looked like a winged Nordik helm, and other equipment to match. He was of no remarkable height for a hero, but as he drew near Zalazar saw that his arms and shoulders under a tight battle-harness were of enormous thickness. He balanced a monstrous war-hammer like a feather in one hand.

I should know who this is, Zalazar thought. But then the thought was gone, as quickly as it had come. Je manages her tools too well, he thought again, and then that idea too was swept from his mind.

The one approaching came to a halt, no more than three quick strides away. "Return to Earth, old Zalazar," he called out, jovially enough. "My bones already ache with a full age of combat. I yearn to let little brother Hypnos whisper in my ear, so I can lie down and rest. I don't know why Je bothered to bring you here; the proper time for humans to visit Cloudholm is long gone, and again, is not yet come."

"Save your riddles," Zalazar advised him fearlessly. This, he thought, in a moment of great glory and pride, this is what it is like to be a god. And in his heart he thanked Je for this moment, and cared not what might happen in the next.

"Oho," Red-beard remarked good-humoredly. "Well then, it seems we must." And the sword and hammer leapt together of themselves, with a blare as of all war-trumpets in the world, and a clash as of all arms. It lasted endlessly, and at the same time it seemed to take no time at all. Zalazar thought that he saw Red-beard fall, but when he bent with some intention of dealing a finishing stroke, the figure of his opponent had vanished. Save for Bormanus, who had prudently stepped back from the clash, he was apparently alone.

Well fought! Je's voice, from invisible lips, whispered beside his ear. There was new excitement in the words, an undertone of savage triumph.

Zalazar, triumphant too—and at the same time knowing an undercurrent of dissatisfaction, for these deeds were not his of his own right—moved on toward the open gate. He had gone a dozen strides when something—he thought not Je—urged him to look back. When he did, he could now see Red-beard, hammer still in hand, stretched out upon the cloud. There was no sign of blood or injury. At Red-beard's ear a winged head was hovering, whispering a compulsion from divine lips. And on the face of the fallen warrior there was peace.

Why do you pause? Je demanded in her hidden voice. She required no answer, but Zalazar must go on. All Je's attention, and Zalazar's too, was bent now upon the open castle gate. It slammed shut of itself when he was still a hundred strides away. Now he could see that what he had taken for carved dragon heads on either side of the portal were alive, turning fanged jaws toward him.

Zalazar glanced at the lad who was walking so trustingly at his side, and for the first time since landing on the cloud-plain he knew anxiety. "Lady Je," he prayed in a whisper, "I crave your protection for my grandson as well as for myself."

I give what protection I can, to those I need. And I foresee now that I will need him, later on . . .

The dragons guarding the gate stretched out their necks when Zalazar came near; fangs like bunched knives drove at him. The shield raised upon his left arm took the blows. The sword flashed left, lashed right.

Zalazar stepped back, gasping; he looked to see that Bormanus, who had kept clear, was safe. Then Zalazar willed the swordblade at the great cruciform timbers of the gate itself. They splintered, shuddered, and swung back.

Je's triumph was a shrill scream, almost soundless, inarticulate.

Zalazar knew that he must still go forward, now into Cloudholm itself. He balanced the shield upon his left arm, hefted the sword again in his right hand. He drew a deep breath, of ample-seeming air, and entered the palace proper.

He came to door after door, each taller and more magnificent than the last, and each swung open of itself to let him in. Around him on every hand there towered shapes that should have been terrible, though he could see them only indistinctly. Something told him which way he must go. And he pressed on, through one royal hall and chamber after another . . .

. . . until he had entered that which he knew must be the greatest hall of all. At the far end of it, very distant from where he stood, Zalazar saw the Throne of the World. It was guarded by a wall of flame, and it was standing vacant.

As Zalazar's feet brought him closer to the fire, he saw that it was centered on a plinth of cloud, that supported another man-like figure, like that of tortured Phaethon but larger still.

It is Helios, said Je's disembodied whisper. *Pull him from the flames, restore him to his throne, and* mana *will rain upon the Earth again.*

The flame felt very hot. When Zalazar probed it with his sword, it pushed the swordblade back. "But what power is this that imprisons him? Je?"

Do not ask questions, mortal. Act.

Zalazar stalked right and left, seeking a way around the flames or through them. The figure inside them did not seem to be burned or tormented by the terrible heat, but only bound. But Zalazar as he approached the tongues of fire had to raise first one hand, and then his shield, to try to protect himself from radiance and glare. The only way to reach the bound god seemed to be to leap directly into the flames, or through them.

Zalazar tried. Unbearable pain seared at him, and the tongues of flame seized him like hands and threw him back. The instant he was clear of the flames, their burning stopped; he was unharmed.

Je shrieked words of compulsion in his ear. Zalazar wrapped himself in his silvery cloak, raised his shield, brandished his sword, and tried again. And was thrown back. And yet again, but all to no avail. And still Je made him try. She stood near now in her full imaged presence.

And yet again the tongues of fire gripped Zalazar, and hurled him flying, sprawling. When Zalazar saw that the metal of his shield was running now in molten drops, he cried aloud his agony: "Spare me, great Je! What will you have from me? Only so much can you make of me, so much and no more."

"I will make whatever I wish of you, mortal. We are so near, so very near to victory!" Her gaze turned to Bormanus, and she went on: "There is a way in which we can augment our power, as I foresaw. Murder will feed great magic."

Zalazar came crawling along the floor, toward the goddess's feet. He made his hand let go the sword. Only now he realized that no scabbard for it had ever been given him. "Goddess, do not demand of me that I kill my own flesh and blood. It will not bring you victory. I was never a great wizard, even in my youth. No Alhazred, no Vulcan the Shaper. Though even before I met you I had convinced myself of that. A warrior? Conqueror? No, I am not Trillion Mu either, though I have killed; and yours and your demon's power could sustain me in combat for a time even against Thor Red-beard himself. But I cannot do more. Even murder will not give me power enough. And if it could, I will not—"

In fishwife rage, Je lost her self-control. "What are you, thing of clay, to argue with me?" She grabbed Bormanus and forced him forward, bent down so that his neck was exposed for a swordstroke. "Earth is mine to deal with as I will, and you are no more than a clod of earth. Kill him!"

"Destroy me if you will, goddess. If you can. I will not kill him."

Je's eyes glowed, orange fire from a volcano. "I see that I have maddened you with my assistance, until you think you are a demigod at least. You are not worth destruction. If I only withdraw my sustaining power, you will both fall back to Earth and be no more than bird-dung when you land. Where will you turn for help if I abandon you?"

Zalazar, on his feet again, turned, physically, looking for help. The half-melted shield now felt impossibly heavy, weighing his left arm down. The brocade of his god-garments hung on him now like lead. The last time the flames had thrown him, some of their pain had remained in his bones. At a thought from Je, the cloud-floor of the palace would open beneath his feet. He would have a long fall in which to think things over.

The Throne of the World was empty, waiting. No help there. But still he was not going to murder.

Je's voice surprised him in its altered tone. It was less threatening now. "Zalazar, I see that I must tell you the truth. It need not be Helios that you place on the Throne when you have gained the power. It could be me."

"You?"

"The truth is that it could even be yourself."

"I?" Zalazar turned slowly. Looked at the Throne again, and thought, and shook his head. "I am only a poor man, I tell you, goddess. Alone and almost lost. If it is true that I can choose the Ruler of the World, well, it must be some cruel joke, such as you say that even gods are subject to. But if the choice is truly mine to make, I will not give it to you. As for taking it myself, I, I should not. I have no fitness, or powers, or wealth, or even family."

Silence fell in Cloudholm. It was an abrupt change; a stillness that was something more than silence had descended. Zalazar waited, eyes downcast, holding his breath, trying to understand.

Then he began to understand, for the last three words that he himself had spoken seemed to be echoing and re-echoing in the air. All his life he had been a poor nomad with no family at all.

Even the flames of Helios' prison seemed to have cooled somewhat, though Zalazar did not immediately raise his head to look at them. When it seemed to him that the silence might have gone on for half an hour, he did at last look up.

He who had walked with Zalazar as his companion had at last taken the lyre from his belt, and the others were allowed to recognize him now.

Je had recoiled, cringing, herself for once down on one knee, with averted gaze. But Zalazar, for now, could look.

White teeth, inhumanly beautiful and even, smiled at him. "Old man, you have decided well. One comes to claim the Throne in time, and Thanatos will be overcome, and your many-times-great-grandsons will have to choose again; but that is not your problem now. I send you back to Earth. Retain the youth that Je has given you—it is fitting, for a new age of the world has been ordained, though not by me. And memories, if you can, retain them too. Magic must sleep."

Bright, half-melted shield and silver garments fell softly to the floor of cloud, beside the sword. Zalazar was gone.

The bright eyes under the dark curls swept around. The god belted his lyre and unslung his bow. There was a great recessional howling as Je's demon-servant fled, and fell, and fled and fell again.

Je raised her eyes, in a last moment of defiance. The winged head of Hypnos, already hovering beside her ear, silently awaited a command.

"Sleep now, sister Je. As our father Zeus and our brothers and sisters sleep. I join you presently," Apollo said.

ψ

MANASPILL
by Dean Ing

♃

"KEEP YOUR HEAD down, Oroles," Thyssa muttered, her face hidden by a fall of chestnut hair. Cross-legged on the moored raft, his lap full of fish-net, little Oroles had forgot his mending in favor of the nearby commotion.

Though the lake was a day's ride end-to-end, it was narrow and shallow. Fisher folk of Lyris traversed it with poled rafts and exchanged rude jokes over the canoe, hewn from an enormous beech, which brought the Moessian dignitary to Lyrian shores. The boy did not answer his sister until the great dugout bumped into place at the nearby wharf, made fast by many hands. "Poo," said Oroles, "foreigners are more fun than mending old Panon's nets. Anyhow, King Bardel doesn't mind me looking."

Thyssa knew that this was so; Lyrians had always regarded their kings with more warmth than awe. Nor would Boerab, the staunch old war minister who stood at the king's left, mind a boy's curiosity. The canoe was very fast, but skittish enough to pitch dignity overboard when dignitaries tried to stand. And what lad could fail to take joy in the sight? Not Oroles!

Yet Thyssa knew also that Minister Dirrach, the shaman standing alert at the young king's right elbow, would interpret a commoner's grin as dumb insolence. "The shaman minds," she hissed. "Do you want to lose favor at the castle?"

Grumbling, six-year-old Oroles did as he was told. Thus the boy missed the glance of feral hunger that Dirrach flicked toward the nubile Thyssa before attending to his perquisites as minister to King Bardel of Lyris.

Dirrach seemed barely to sway nearer as he spoke behind young Bardel's ear: "The outlander must not hear you chuckling at his clumsiness, Sire," he suggested in a well-oiled baritone.

Bardel, without moving: "But when I can't laugh, it seems funnier."

"Averae of Moess is devious," the shaman replied easily, while others rushed to help the outlander. "If you think him clumsy, you may falsely think yourself secure."

Bardel gave a grunt of irritation, a sound more mature than his speaking voice. "Dirrach, don't you trust anybody?"

"I have seen duplicity in that one before," Dirrach murmured, and swayed back to prevent further interchange. Truly enough, he had known Averae before, and had been uneasy when he recognized the Moessian. Dirrach breathed more easily now that he had slandered the man in advance. Who knew what crimes the outlander might recall? Then Averae stood on the wharf, and Bardel stepped forward.

Thyssa had not noted the shaman's glance because her attention was on the king. In the two years since his accession to the Lyrian throne, Bardel had grown into his royal role—indeed, into his father's broad leather breastplate—without entirely losing the panache of spirited youth. Tanned by summer hunts, forearms scarred by combat training with the veteran Boerab, the young Lyrian king fluttered girlish hearts like a warm breeze among beech leaves. And while Bardel watched the Moessian's unsteady advance with calm peregrine eyes, Thyssa saw a twinkle in them. Flanked by Boerab and Dirrach, arms and enchantment, Bardel of Lyris was a beloved figure. It did not matter to most Lyrians that his two ministers loathed each other, and that Bardel was just not awfully bright.

Thyssa, fingers flying among the tattered nets, seemed not to hear the royal amenities. Yet she heard a query from Averae: " . . . Shandorian minister?" And heard Boerab's rumbled, " . . . Escorted from the Northern heights . . . tomorrow." Then Thyssa knew why the castle staff and the fat merchants in Tihan had been atwitter for the past day or so. It could mean nothing less than protracted feasting in Bardel's castle!

To an Achaean of the distant past, or even to Phoenicians who plied the Adriatic coast to the far Southwest, this prospect would have inspired little awe. No Lyrian commoner could afford woven garments for everyday use; only the king and Boerab carried iron blades at their sides, each weapon purchased from Ostran ironmongers with packtrains of excellent Lyrian wine.

Nor would the royal castle in Tihan have excited much admiration from those legendary outlanders. Some hundreds of families lived in Tihan, thatched walls and roofs protected by stout oak palisades surrounding town and castle on the lake's one peninsula. Bardel's castle was the only two-story structure capacious enough to house king, staff, and a small garrison mostly employed for day-labor.

The pomp that accompanied Bardel's retinue back to nearby Tihan would have brought smiles to Phoenician lips but as Thyssa viewed the procession, her eyes were bright with pride. "Remind me to brush your leather apron, Oroles," she smiled; "if you are chosen to serve during feast-time, there may be red meat for our stew." Unsaid was her corollary: *and since I must play both father and mother to you, perhaps I too will make an impression on someone.*

Old Panon was less than ecstatic over the job on his nets. "Your repairs are adequate, Thyssa," he admitted, then held an offending tangle between thumb and forefinger; "but Oroles must learn that a knot needn't be the size and shape of a clenched fist. Teach him as I taught you, girl; nothing magic about it."

"Nothing?" Oroles frowned at this heresy. "But Shaman Dirrach enchants the nets every year."

"Pah," said the old man. "Dirrach! The man couldn't—ah, there are those who say the man couldn't enchant a bee with honey. Some say it's all folderol to keep us in line. *Some say,*" he qualified it.

"Please, Panon," said Thyssa, voice cloudy with concern. "Big-eared little pitchers," she ruffled the ragged hair of Oroles, "spill on everyone. Besides, if it's folderol how do you explain my father's slingstone?"

"Well—" The old man smiled, "maybe some small magics. It doesn't take much enchantment to fool a fish, or a rabbit. And Urkut *was* an uncanny marksman with a sling."

At this, Oroles beamed. The boy had no memory of the mother who had died bearing him, and chiefly second-hand knowledge of his emigrant father, Urkut. But the lad had spent many an evening scrunched next to the fireplace, hugging his knees and wheedling stories from Thyssa as she stirred chestnuts from the coals. To the girl, a father who had seen the Atlantic and Crete had traveled all the world. One raised across the mountains beyond Lyris was an emigrant. And one whose slingstone was so unerring that the missile was kept separate in Urkut's waistpouch, was definitely magical. Indeed, the day before his death Urkut had bested Dirrach by twice proving the incredible efficacy of his sling. It had come about during an aurochs hunt in which Bardel, still an impressionable youth, and Boerab, an admirer of Urkut, had been spectators.

As Thyssa heard it from the laconic Boerab, her father's tracking skill had prompted young Bardel to proclaim him "almost magical." Dirrach, affronted, had caused a grass fire to appear behind them; though Boerab left little doubt that he suspected nothing more miraculous in the shaman's ploy than a wisp of firewick from Dirrach's pack. Challenged to match the grass fire, Urkut had demurred until goaded by Bardel's amusement.

Slowly (as Thyssa would embroider it, matching her account with remembered pantomime while gooseflesh crawled on Orole's body), the hunter Urkut had withdrawn a rough stone pellet from his wallet. Carefully, standing in wooden stirrups while his pony danced in uncertainty, Urkut had placed pellet in slingpouch. Deliberately, staring into Dirrach's face as he whirled the sling, Urkut had made an odd gesture with his free hand. And then the stone had soared off, not in a flat arrowcourse but in a high trajectory to thud far off behind a shrub.

Dirrach's booming laughter had stopped abruptly when, dismounting at the shrub, Urkut groped and then held his arms aloft. In one hand he'd held his slingstone. In the other had been a rabbit.

Outraged by Dirrach's claims of charlatanry, Urkut had done it again; this time eyes closed, suggesting that Boerab retrieve stone and quarry.

And this time Boerab had found a magnificent cock pheasant quivering beside the slingstone, and Urkut had sagaciously denied any miraculous powers while putting his slingstone away. It was merely a trick, he'd averred; the magic of hand and eye (this with a meaningful gaze toward Dirrach). And young Bardel had bidden Urkut sup at the castle that night. And Urkut had complied.

And Urkut had died in his cottage during the night, in agony, clutching his belly as Thyssa wept over him. To this day, even Dirrach would admit that the emigrant Urkut had been in some small way a shaman. *Especially* Dirrach; for he could also point out that *mana* was lethal to those who could not control it properly.

Now, with a sigh for memories of a time when she was not an orphan, Thyssa said to the aged Panon: "Father always said the *mana* was in the slingstone, not in him. And it must have been true, for the pellet vanished like smoke after his death."

"Or so the shaman says," Panon growled. "He who took charge of Urkut's body and waistpouch as well. I heard, Thyssa. And I watch Dirrach—almost as carefully as *he* watches *you.*" The fisherman chose two specimens from his catch; one suitable for a stew, the other large enough to fillet. "Here: an Oroles'-worth, and a Thyssa-worth."

The girl thanked him with a hug, gathered the fish in her leather shift, leapt from raft to shore with a flash of lithe limbs. "May you one day catch a Panonworth," she called gaily, and took the hand of Oroles.

"He watches you, girl," old Panon's voice followed her toward the palisades of Tihan. "Take care." She waved and continued. Dirrach watched everybody, she told herself. What special interest could the shaman possibly have in an orphaned peasant girl?

There were some who could have answered Thyssa's riddle. One such was the gaunt emissary Averae, whose dignity had been in such peril as he stood up in his Moessian canoe. Not until evening, after an aurochs haunch had been devoured and a third flagon of Lyrian wine was in his vitals, did Averae unburden himself to Boerab. "You could've knocked me into the lake when I spied your friend, the shaman," Averae muttered.

"Or a falling leaf could've," Boerab replied with a wink. "You're a landlubber like me. But be cautious in naming my friends," he added with a sideways look across the table where Dirrach was tongue-lashing a servant.

"You've no liking for him either?"

"I respect his shrewdness. We serve the same king," Boerab said with a lift of the heavy shoulders. "You know Dirrach, then?"

"When your king was only a pup—I mean no disrespect for him, Boerab, but this marvelous wine conjures truth as it will—his father sent Dirrach to us in Moess to discuss fishing rights near our shore."

"I was building an outpost and only heard rumors."

"Here are facts. Dirrach had full immunity, royal pardons, the usual," Averae went on softly, pausing to drain his flagon. "And he abused them terribly among our servant girls."

"You mean the kind of abuse he's giving now?" An ashen-faced winebearer was backing away from Dirrach.

A weighed pause: "I mean the kind that leaves bite scars, and causes young women to despise all men."

Boerab, a heavy womanizer in his time, saw no harm in a tussle with a willing wench. But bite scars? The old warrior recalled the disappearance of several girls from farms near Tihan over the past years, and hoped he could thrust a new suspicion from his mind. "Well, that explains why we never arranged that fishing treaty," he said, trying to smile. "Perhaps this time Lyris and Moess can do better."

"Trade from Obuda to the Phoenician coast is more important than punishment for a deviate," Averae agreed. "Do you suppose we'll find Shandor's folk amenable?"

"Likely; they have little to lose and much to gain."

"Even as you and I," Averae purred the implication.

"Even as your king and mine," Boerab corrected. "Just so we'll understand one another, Averae: I'm happy as I am. Wouldn't know what to do with presents from Moess or Shandor, even without strings attached. If Lyris and the lad—ah, King Bardel—prosper, I'm content."

"Fair enough," Averae laughed. "I'm beginning to be glad your *mana* was strong during our border clash."

Boerab, startled, spilled his brimming flagon. "My *what?* Save that for commoners, Averae."

"If you insist. But it's common knowledge in Moess that our shaman spent the better part of his *mana* trying to sap your strength in that last battle. Practically ruined the poor fellow."

Boerab studied the lees in his wine. "If anybody put a wardspell on me, he's kept it secret." The barrel chest shook with mirth. "Fact is, I had high-ground advantage and grew too tired to move. If you want to believe, then believe in a safespot. For myself, I believe in my shield."

Boerab could hardly be blamed for denying the old legends. The entire region was rich in relics of forgotten battles where mighty shamans had pitted spell against spell, *mana* against *mana,* irresistible ax versus immovable shield. The mound that Boerab had chosen for his stand was a natural choice for a combat veteran; other warriors had chosen that spot before him. On that spot, magical murder had been accomplished. On that spot no magic would work again, ever. Boerab had indeed defended a safespot upon which all but the most stupendous *mana* was wasted.

All Boerab's life had been spent in regions nearly exhausted of *mana.* Of course there had been little things like Urkut's tricks, but—Boerab did not commit the usual mistake of allowing magic to explain the commonplace. Instead he erred in using the commonplace to explain magic. Thus far, Boerab was immeasurably far ahead.

"I'd drink to your shield, then," Averae mumbled, "if that confounded winebearer were in sight."

Boerab's eyes roamed through the smog of the lignite fire as he roared for more wine. By now the king and Dirrach were too far in their flagons to notice the poor service. Boerab promised himself that for the main feast, he'd insist on a winebearer too young to crave the stuff he toted. *Ah; Urkut's boy*, he thought. *Too innocent to cause aggravation.*

As to the innocence of Oroles, the grizzled warrior was right. As to the consequences of innocence he could scarcely have gone farther wrong.

Thyssa, late to rise, was coaxing a glow from hardwood embers when she heard a rap on her door. "Welcome," she called, drawing her shift about her as the runner, Dasio, entered.

"In the royal service," said Dasio formally. The youth was lightly built but tall, extraordinary in musculature of calf and thigh; and Thyssa noted the heaving breast of her childhood friend with frank concern.

"Are you ill, Dasio? You cannot be winded by a mere sprint across Tihan."

"Nor am I. I'm lathered from a two-hour run. Spent the night with the Shandorians; they'll be here soon—with a surprise, I'll warrant," Dasio said cryptically, taking his eyes from Thyssa with reluctance. Seeing Oroles curled in a tangle of furs: "Ah, there's the cub I'm to fetch; and then I can rest!"

Choosing a motherly view, Thyssa set a stoneware pot near the coals. "Tell them Oroles was breaking his fast," she said. "You don't have to tell them you shared his gruel. Meanwhile, Dasio, take your ease." She shook her small brother with rough affection. "Rise, little man-of-the-house," she smiled. "You're wanted—" and glanced at Dasio as she ended, "—at the castle?"

The runner nodded, stirred the gruel as it began to heat, tasted and grimaced. "Wugh; it could use salt."

"Could it indeed," Thyssa retorted. "Then you might have brought some. Our palates aren't so jaded with rich palace food as some I might name."

A flush crept up the neck of the diffident youth. Silently he chided himself; though Thyssa and Oroles still lived in Urkut's cottage, they did so with few amenities. Without even the slenderest dowry, Dasio knew, the girl was overlooked by the sons of most Tihaners.

Presently, Oroles found his sandals and apron, then joined Dasio over the gruel. "What have I done now," he yawned.

It was as Thyssa hoped. After one dutiful mouthful that courtesy required, Dasio set her at ease. "The palace cook will brief you, runt. Big doings tonight; bigger than last night. If you can keep your feet untangled, maybe you can ask for a slab of salt—to jade your palates," he added with a sidelong grin at Thyssa.

Moments later, the girl ushered them outside. "Watch over him, Dasio," she pleaded. "And thanks for his employ."

"Thank old Boerab for that," said the youth. "But I'll try to keep the cub out of the wine he'll pour tonight." Then, while Oroles tried to match his stride, Dasio trotted slowly up the dirt road toward high ground and the castle.

The Shandorians arrived in midafternoon, and all Tihan buzzed with the surprise Dasio had promised. Everybody knew Shandor had funny ideas about women, but conservative Tihaners grumbled to see that the emissary from Shandor was a handsome female wearing crimson garments of the almost mythical fabric, silk; and her eyes were insolent with assurance. Thyssa, contracting a day's labor for a parcel of a merchant's grain, knew it first as rumor.

Dirrach learned of it while powdering a lump of lightest-tinted lignite coal in his private chamber. It was the shaman's good fortune that such stuff was available, since when powdered it was unlikely to be as visible when sprinkled from shadow into fire as was charcoal or the sulphur which he used for other effects. It was the region's good fortune that Dirrach's "magics" had never yet tapped genuine *mana*.

Dirrach heard his door creak open; turned to hide his work even as he opened his mouth to blast the intruder. Only one man in all Lyris had the right to burst in thus. "Who dares to—oh. Ah, welcome, Bardel," he ended lamely; for it was that one man.

"Can you believe, Dirrach?" The king's face was awash with something between delight and consternation as he toed the door shut. "Boerab and I just did the welcomes — and where were you anyhow — oh, here I guess; and the Shandorian has a girl for a servant. Which is fine I suppose, because she's a woman. The emissary, I mean. Is a *woman!*"

Dirrach drew a long breath, moving away from his work to draw Bardel's attention. Too long had he suffered the prattle, the presumption, the caprice of this royal oaf. Perhaps tonight, all that could be remedied. "Shandor puts undue value on its females, as I have told you." He hadn't, but Bardel's shortsword outspanned his memory.

"The Shandorian's a bit long in the tooth for me," Bardel went on, "but firm-fleshed and — uh — manly, sort of. But where do we seat a woman at a state feast? You take care of it, Dirrach; Boerab's rounded up the kitchen staff. I'm off to the practice range; that crazy Gethae — the Shandorian — would pit her skill with a bow against mine. A woman, Dirrach," he laughed, shaking his head as he ducked out the door. His parting question was his favorite phrase: "Can you *believe?*"

Dirrach sighed and returned to his work. No believer in the arts he surrogated, the shaman warmed to his own beliefs. He could believe in careful preparation in the feast hall, and in mistrust for outlanders who could be blamed for any tragedy. Most of all, Dirrach could believe in poison. The stuff had served him well in the past.

Dirrach's seating arrangements were clever, the hanging oil lamps placed so that he would be partly in shadow near the fireplace. The special flagstone rested atop the bladder where Dirrach's foot could reach it, and specially decorated flagons bore symbols that clearly implied who would sit where. The shaman's duties included tasting every course and flagon before it reached the royal lips, though poison was little used in Lyris. Dirrach congratulated himself on placing the woman across from him, for Dirrach's place was at the king's side, and anything the woman said to Bardel could be noted by the shaman as well. A second advantage was that women were widely known to have scant capacity for wine; Gethae would sit at the place most likely to permit unmasking of a shaman's little tricks; and if Gethae denounced him it could be chalked up to bleary vision of an inebriate who could also be accused of hostile aims. Especially on the morrow.

Yet Gethae showed herself to good advantage as she swept into the castle with her new acquaintances. "I claim a rematch," she said, laying a com-
panionable hand on Boerab's shoulder gorget. "Bardel's eye is a trifle too
good today." Her laugh was throaty, her carriage erect and, Dirrach admitted, almost kingly. Already she spoke Bardel's name with ease.

Bardel started to enter the hall, stumbled as he considered letting the
stately Gethae precede him but reconsidered in the same instant that such
courtesy was reserved for the mothers of kings. "I was lucky, Gethae — ooop,
damn flagstones anyhow; ahh, smells good in here; oh, *there* you are,
Dirrach," Bardel rattled on with a wave. Actually the hall stank of smoke and
sweat — but then, so did the king.

Boerab introduced Dirrach to the Shandorian whom he treated as an
equal. "Sorry you were busy here, Dirrach," the old soldier lied manfully.
"This sturdy wench pulls a stronger bow than I thought possible."

"Put it down to enthusiasm," said Gethae, exchanging handclasps with
Dirrach. Her glance was both calculating and warm.

"Huh; put it down to good pectorals," Boerab rejoined, then raised his
eyes to heaven: "Ulp; ghaaaa . . ."

"I accept that as a compliment," said Gethae, smiling.

Dirrach saw that such compliments were justified; the Shandorian's
physical impact could not be denied, and a man like Boerab might find his
judgment colored with lust. But Dirrach's tastes were narrow and, "I fear we
have prepared but rough entertainment for a lady," said the shaman in cool
formality.

"I can accept that too," she said, still smiling as she peered at the fast
table. "Ho, Averae: I see we're to be kept apart."

Averae of Moess found his own place with a good-natured gibe to the
effect that a small plot with Shandor would have been a pleasure. Plainly,
the shaman saw, this woman enjoyed the company of men without considering herself one. Had he only imagined an invitation in her smile of
greeting?

Dirrach found that it had not been mere imagination. All through the
courses of chestnut bread, beef and fowl, beer and honeycake, the shaman
shifted his feet to avoid the questing instep of the long-legged Gethae. At
one point Dirrach felt his false-bottomed flagstone sink as he hastily moved

his foot, saw reflection in Gethae's frank dark eyes of a sudden flare in the fireplace. But Gethae was stoking a fire of another sort and noticed nothing but Dirrach himself. The shaman took it philosophically; he could not help it if Gethae had an appetite for men in their middle years. But he would not whet that appetite either, and pointedly guided Bardel into dialogue with the woman.

Eventually the beer was replaced by a tow-headed lad bearing the most famed product of Lyris: the heady wine of the north lakeshore. Gethae sipped, smacked, grinned; sipped again. Very soon she pronounced her flagon empty and beamed at the boy who filled it. "The lad," she said to one and all, "has unlocked Lyris's wealth!"

All took this as a toast and Gethae winked at the boy, who winked back. "I predict you'll go far,—ah, what's your name, lad?"

"Oroles, ma'am," said the boy, growing restive as others turned toward the interchange. "I've already gone as far as the end of the lake."

"You'll go farther," Gethae chuckled.

"Here's to travel," said the king. "Keep traveling around the table, Orolandes."

Dutiful laughter faded as the boy replied; servants did not correct kings. "Oroles, please sir—but you're almost right."

Boerab, in quick jocularity: "In honor of the great Orolandes, no doubt."

"Aw, you knew that, Boerab," said the boy in gentle accusation, and again filled Gethae's flagon, his tongue between his teeth as he poured. The boy's innocent directness, his ignorance of protocol, his serious mien struck warm response first from Averae, himself a grandfather. Averae began to chuckle, then to laugh outright as others joined in.

Little Oroles did not fathom this levity and continued in his rounds until, perceiving that his own king was laughing at him, he stopped, hugging the wine pitcher to him. The small features clouded; a single tear ran down his cheek.

Boerab was near enough to draw Oroles to him, to offer his flagon for filling, to mutter in the boy's ear. "No fear, lad; they're laughing for you, not at you."

Gethae could not tell whether Boerab was praising or scolding the boy and resolved to generate a diversion. With a by-your-leave to Bardel she stood. "At such a merry moment, a guest might choose to pay tribute."

"Ill-said," from Averae, "because I wish I'd said it first." More merriment, fueled by alcohol.

"I yield," Gethae mimed a fetching swoon, "to Moess—for once."

Bardel understood enough of this byplay to lead the guffaws. Averae bowed to the king, to the woman, then performed quick syncopated handclaps before turning expectantly toward the door.

A blocky Moessian—it was poor form to seat one's bodyguard at a state feast—entered, arms outstretched with obvious effort to hold their burden. At Averae's gesture, the man knelt before the beaming young king.

"May you never need to use it, sire," from Averae.

Bardel took the wicked handax, licked its cold iron head to assure himself of its composition. It was a heavy cast Ostran head, hafted with care, and as Bardel swung it experimentally the applause was general.

Except for Dirrach. The shaman muttered something unintelligible and Bardel's face fell. "This pleased me so," said the king, "that I forgot. Trust Dirrach to remind me: no weapons in the feast hall. No, no, Averae," he said quickly; "you gave no offense. Boy," he offered the ax to Oroles, "have a guard put this in my chamber. I'll sleep with it tonight."

So it shall be mine tomorrow, thought Dirrach.

Oroles, cradling the wine pitcher in one arm, took the ax with his free hand. Its weight caused him nearly to topple, a splash of golden liquid cascading onto the flagstones. Dirrach was not agile enough and, winesplattered to his knees, would have struck the boy who bolted from the hall with wine and weapon.

But: "A boy for a man's job," Boerab tutted. "At least we have wine to waste."

Dirrach quenched his outward anger, resumed his seat and said innocently, "I fear we have given offense to Moess." He knew the suggestion would be remembered on the morrow, despite Averae's denial which was immediate and cordial.

Then it was Gethae's turn. The Shandorian reached into her scarlet silken sleeve, produced a sueded pouch, offered it to Bardel with a small obeisance.

"What else might Shandorians have up their sleeves," murmured Dirrach with false bonhomie.

"A body search might reward you," Gethae replied in open invitation. Dirrach did not need to respond for at that moment Bardel emptied the pouch into his hand. There was total silence.

"Oh damn," Gethae breathed, and chuckled; "I'd hoped to keep them damp." Bardel, perplexed, held several opaque porous stones. One, by far the largest, was the size of a goose egg, set into a horn bezel hung from a finely braided leather loop. The others were unset and all had been smoothed to the texture of eggshell.

Dirrach almost guessed they were gallstones, for which magical properties were sometimes claimed. Instead he kept a wise look, and his silence.

Gethae retrieved the great stone. "Here; a bit of magic from the northern barbarians, if you'll stretch a point." She extended her tongue, licked the stone which actually adhered to the moist flesh until she plucked it away, held it aloft. Even Dirrach gasped.

The properties of hydrophane opal were unknown even in Shandor; Gethae had been jesting about magic. The Shandorians had imported the stones from the north at tremendous expense; knew only that this most porous of opals was dull when dry but became a glittering pool of cloudy luminescence when dampened. As the moisture evaporated, the stone would again become lackluster. Thus the Sandorians did not suspect the enormous concentration of *mana* which was unlocked by moistening a hydrophane.

Had Gethae known the proper spell, she could have carved away the Tihan peninsula or turned it all to metal with the power she held. Even her fervent prayer for strength to pull a Lyrian bow had been enough earlier, before the opals in her pouch had dried. Yet none of this was suspected by Gethae. Her fluid gesture in returning the huge gem to Bardel was half of a stormspell. She, with the others present, interpreted the sudden skin-prickling electricity in the air as the product of awe.

Bardel took the gift in wonderment. "Spit is magic?"

"Or water, wine, perspiration," Gethae chuckled. "I have heard it argued that oil scum on water creates the same illusion of magical beauty. And has the same natural explanation." She shrugged. "Don't ask me to explain it; merely accept it as Shandor's gift."

This called for another toast. "Where the devil is that winebearer?" Bardel asked.

Oroles scurried back from his errand to pour. Even Bardel could see the boy trembling in anticipation of punishment, saw too that the outlanders had taken a liking to the slender child. With wisdom rare in him, Bardel suddenly picked up the smallest of the opals, still opaque and dry. The king ostentatiously dipped the pebble into his wine, held it up before Oroles, who marveled silently at the transformation. "For your services," said Bardel, "and for entertainment." With that he dropped the opal, the size of a babe's thumbnail, into the hand of Oroles.

Bardel acknowledged the applause, hung the great hydrophane amulet around his own sweaty neck, pledged packtrains of Lyrian wine as gifts for Moess and Shandor. "And what say you of outlander magics," he asked of the glum Dirrach. It was as near as Bardel would come to commanding a performance from his shaman. He knew some doubted Dirrach's miracles, but Bardel was credulous as any bumpkin.

Dirrach grasped his talisman of office, a carved wand with compartmented secrets of its own, and waved it in the air. "Iron strikes fire on stone," he intoned; "stone holds inner fire with water. But true *mana* can bring fire to fire itself." It only sounded silly, he told himself, if you thought about it. But the powdered lignite in the wand would keep anybody else from thinking about it.

Dirrach knew where the fireplace was, did not need to look over his shoulder as he manipulated the wand and trod on the false flagstone, feeding pungent oil to the blaze. He felt the heat, saw astonishment in the eyes of his audience, smiled to see Oroles cringe against the wall. He did not realize that the flames behind him had, for a moment only, blazed *black*. The gleaming hydrophanes of Bardel and Oroles were near enough that Dirrach's wandpass had called forth infinitesimal *mana* in obedience to a reversal gesture-spell. It did not matter that Dirrach was wholly incompetent to command *mana*. All that mattered was the *mana* and the many means for its discharge as magic. Knowingly or not. The jewel at Bardel's throat glimmered with unspent lightnings.

Unaware of the extent of his success, and of the enormous forces near him, Dirrach mixed blind luck with his sleight-of-hand and his hidden-lever tricks. The shaman was a bit flummoxed when two white doves fluttered up from the false bottom of his carven chair; he'd only put one bird in there. He was similarly pensive when the coin he "found" in Averae's beard turned out to be, not the local bronze celt Dirrach had palmed beforehand, but a silvery roundish thing which Averae claimed before either of them got a good look at the picture stamped on it. Inspection would have told them little in any case: the Thracian portrait of Alexander was not due to be reproduced for centuries to come.

And when a spatter of rain fell inside, all assumed that it was also raining *outside*; even royal roofs leaked a bit. At last Gethae sighed, "My compliments, Dirrach. But tell me: how did you breed mice to elk? That was subtly done."

Indeed it was; so subtly that only Gethae had noticed the tiny antlered creatures that scampered across hearthstones and into the fire during one of Dirrach's accidental spells. Dirrach did not know if his leg was being pulled, and only smiled.

Bardel called for more wine when the shaman claimed his *mana* was waning. Oroles was pouring when Averae asked what credence might be placed in the tales of ancient shamans.

"Much of it is true," replied Dirrach, taking an obligatory sip from Bardel's flagon, thinking he lied even as he gazed at the truth gleaming darkly on Bardel's breast. "Yet few of us know the secrets today. You'd be surprised what silly frauds I've seen; and as for the nonsense I hear from afar: well—" Aping a lunatic's expression, hands fluttering like his doves, Dirrach began a ludicrous capering that brought on gales of mirth. And while his audience watched the wand he tossed into the air, Dirrach dropped a pinch of death into the king's flagon. There was enough poison there to dispatch a dozen Bardels. Dirrach would feign illness presently, and of course the winebearer would later be tortured for information he did not have.

But there was information which Dirrach lacked, as well. He would never have performed a gestural wardspell, nor given anyone but himself the gift of conversing with other species, had he known just what occult meanings lay in his mummery.

* * *

The next day was one of sweltering heat, and did nothing to sweeten the odor of the fish Thyssa was filleting outside Panon's smokehouse. "Oroles, turn these entrails under the soil in Panon's garden," she called. "Oroles!"

The boy dropped his new treasure into his waistpouch, hopped from his perch on a handcart and scrambled to comply after muttering something, evidently to thin air.

"Don't complain," she said, tasting perspiration on her lips.

"I wasn't," said Oroles. "Did you know the castle midden heap is rich with last night's leavings and, uh, suc—succulent mice?"

"How would you know," she asked, not really listening.

"Oh—something just tells me."

Despite her crossness, Thyssa smiled. "A little bird, no doubt."

Pausing to consider: "That's an idea," the boy said, and trudged off, head averted from his burden.

Hidden from Thyssa by the smokehouse, Oroles could still be heard as he distributed fish guts in the garden. "Don't take it all," he said. "I'm supposed to plant this stuff." Thyssa thought she heard the creak of an old hinge, clucking, snapping. "No I'm not; you're talking people-talk," Oroles went on. More creaking. No, not a hinge. What, then? "There's a ferret under the cart that can do it too. Funny I never noticed it before." Creak, pop. "All right, if you promise not to steal grain."

There was more, but Thyssa first investigated the cart. A dark sinuous shape streaked away nearly underfoot to find refuge in Panon's woodpile; there *had* been a ferret hiding there! Thyssa crept to the edge of the smokehouse, spied Oroles dividing his offal between the dirt and a raven that was half as large as he. Neither seemed to fear the other. If she hadn't known better, Thyssa would have sworn the two were actually exchanging the polite gossip of new acquaintances. But the boy didn't seem to be in danger, and he had few enough playmates. Thyssa tiptoed back to her work, waved the flies away, and chose another fish from the pile.

Presently Oroles returned, searched around the cart, then began to string fillets onto withes. "I wonder if the shaman is sick in the head," he said.

"Not he," Thyssa laughed. "Why would you think that?"

"He keeps squatting at his window, running back to leap into bed when servants appear, going back to the window—you know," Oroles said vaguely.

Dirrach's chamber upstairs in the castle faced the dawn, away from Panon's cottage. Oroles would have had to climb a tree to see such goings-on. "Your little bird told you," said Thyssa.

"Quite a big one," Oroles insisted, as a raven flapped away overhead. Thyssa felt the boy's forehead. Such behavior was not at all usual for Oroles.

Dirrach did not step outside his chamber until he spotted Bardel near the vineyards with the outlanders. The shaman had retired from the feast with complaints of a gripe in his belly, fully expecting to wake to the sweet music of lamentations from servants. Told of Bardel's vineyard tour, Dirrach suspected a ruse; continued to fake his illness; told himself that Boerab must go next. Dirrach *knew* the poison had gone into the flagon, had seen Bardel swill it down.

Maybe the fool had thrown it all up soon after Dirrach took his leave. Yes, that had to be the answer. The only other possibility was some inexplicable miracle. Well, there were other paths to regicide. One path would have to be chosen while the outlanders were still available as suspects.

At the noon meal, the king glowed with health and camaraderie. "Try some more stew, Dirrach; just the thing to settle your innards."

"Aye, and to bank your fires for negotiations," Gethae put in. "Bardel wouldn't hear of serious talk while you were indisposed."

"Bardel was nearly indisposed himself, this morning," Averae grunted. Noting Dirrach's sudden interest, he continued: "Set your entrails right before your king runs out of luck."

Boerab grunted at this understatement; but courtesy forbade outright mention of a king's death. "Made me dizzy to watch him, Dirrach; climbing like a squirrel to fetch grapes that were still unripe."

A king, engaged in such foolishness! Dirrach's face mirrored the thought.

"It wasn't the climb that impressed me, so much as the fall," Gethae said, her hand tracing the tumble of a falling leaf. She went on to describe Bardel's acrobatic ascent, the gleam of the hydrophane on his breast as he sweated to the topmost extent of a vine high in a beechtree.

Bardel, deluded that such childish heroics made the right impression: "I don't think I missed a branch on the way down."

"Brought enough of them down with you," Boerab snorted. "What a thump you made!"

Dirrach picked at his food, wondering how much of the tale was decoration. Taking it at half its face value, Bardel should now be lying in state—and in a basket, at that.

From Gethae: "I've never seen better evidence of a wardspell."

At this, Bardel thanked his shaman for his coronation wardspell, now several years old and, in any case, known by Dirrach to be pure counterfeit. Or was it? Dirrach silently enumerated the scars and bruises sustained by Bardel since the coronation; rejected his wardspell out of hand. Still, something was accountable for a flurry of bizarre events—and all since the previous evening. Was the woman teasing him with covert hints? Dirrach allowed himself to wonder if one of the outlanders was a true shaman, and felt his flesh creep. Forewarned, a wise man would take careful note of further anomalies.

Mindful of royal duties, anxious to show himself equal to them in the very near future, Dirrach suggested a brief attendance to local matters before the open-ended negotiations. While emissaries lounged at one end of the chamber, Bardel settled several complaints from citizens of Tihan and vicinity. The runner, Dasio, rounded up petitioners quickly—all but one, for whom Dasio had promised to plead.

When a squabble between farmers had been concluded, Bardel stood up. "Is that the last, runner?"

"Yes, sire, . . .

"Well then, . . ."

"And no, sire," Dasio said quickly. "I mean, there is one small matter, but of great import to the girl, Thyssa." Dasio saw the king's impatience, felt the cold stare of Dirrach. Yet he had promised, and: "She begs the special attention of the shaman but dared not leave her work to make petition."

Bardel sat back in obvious pique. Dirrach opened his mouth to deny the petition; remembered the visitors. "Quickly then," he said.

"The girl fears for her brother, Oroles. She thinks he is suddenly possessed; and truly, the cub is not himself. Thyssa craves audience with our wise shaman, and is prepared to pay in menial labor."

"Thyssa? Oh, the daughter of Urkut," Bardel said.

Dirrach's eyes gleamed as he recalled the girl. Prepared to do services for him, was she? But time enough for that when Dirrach occupied the throne. "Next week, perhaps," he muttered to Bardel.

"But her brother was the pup I rewarded last eve," Bardel mused. "He seemed only too normal then. What exactly is his trouble?"

Alarms clamored in Dirrach's mind as Dasio blurted, "He thinks he talks with animals, sire. And in truth, it seems that he does!"

The shaman leaned, muttered into the royal ear. "The shaman will make compassionate treatment before this day is done," Bardel said, parroting what echoed in his ear. So saying, he concluded the session.

Following Dasio to the girl's cottage, Dirrach applauded himself for the delay he had caused in negotiations. The outlander runners, in search of boundary clarification, would need three days for round trips to Shandor and Moess. In that time, a crafty shaman might learn more of these evidences of true occult power and perhaps even circumvent the luck of a king.

Dasio had alerted Thyssa to expect the shaman; traded worried glances with her as Dirrach strode into the cottage. Dirrach waited until the girl and Oroles had touched foreheads to his sandal before bidding Dasio leave them.

"The boy knows why I come?" Dirrach kept the edge off his voice, the better to interrogate them. The more he looked on Thyssa, the more honeyed his tones became.

Thyssa had told the boy, who rather enjoyed his sudden celebrity. "He's never acted this way before," she said, wringing her hands, "and I thought perhaps some fever—"

Dirrach made a few stately passes in the air. A faint chittering reached them from outside. The opal of Oroles nestled in the boy's waistpouch unseen and, somewhere in the distance, a dog howled in terror. Kneeling, Dirrach took the boy's arms, then his hands, in his own. No trembling, no fever, no perspiration; only honest dirt. "His fever is in his bones, and will subside," Dirrach lied, then pointed to a cricket at the hearth. "What does the insect say, boy?"

"Bugs don't say much, 'cause they don't know much," was the prompt reply. "I tried earlier; they just say the same things: warm, cold, hungry, scared—you know. Bugs ain't smart."

"How about mice?"

"A little smarter. What does 'horny' mean?"

Dirrach would have shared a knowing smile with Thyssa, but saw her acute discomfort. To Oroles he said, "It seems that your ability comes and goes."

"It went today while I was working under Panon's raft. You have to strip and swim under. You know those baitfish he keeps alive in a basket? Not a word," Oroles said in wonderment.

Dirrach persisted. The boy showed none of the fear or caution of a small boy perpetrating a large fraud; but to ensure Dirrach of the sister's pliant services, Oroles must seem to be mending. The shaman hinted broadly that cubs who lied about *mana* could expect occult retribution, adding, "Besides, no one would believe you."

Oroles said stolidly, "You would. A raven told me he watched you running to and fro from your bed to your window this morning."

"The raven lied," Dirrach said quickly, feeling icy centipedes on his spine.

"And the ferret is angry because Dasio is standing between him and a rat nest, right outside."

Dirrach flung open the door. In the dusk he saw Dasio patiently waiting nearby, his feet less than a pace away from a well-gnawed hole in the foundation wattling. No sign of a ferret—but then, there wouldn't be. Dirrach contained a mounting excitement, sent the girl away with Dasio, and began testing the boy further. Though lacking clear concepts of experimental controls, the shaman knew that he must verify the events, then isolate the conditions in which they occurred.

An hour later, Dirrach stood at lakeside with a shivering and very wet Oroles, smiling at the boy. He no longer doubted the gift of Oroles; had traced its *mana* first to clothing, then to waistpouch, finally to proximity of Oroles with the tiny stone in the pouch. Such knowledge, of course, must not be shared.

Teeth chattering, Oroles tugged his leather breechclout on and fingered his waistpouch. "Can I have my gleamstone back?"

"A pretty bauble," said Dirrach, eyeing its moonlit glitter; "but quite use-less."

"Then why can't I have it back?"

Dirrach hesitated. The boy would complain if his treasure were taken, and no breath of its importance could be tolerated. If the boy should drown now? But too many people would wonder at Dirrach's peculiar ministra-tions. Ah: there were other, larger stones; one of which just might explain much of young Bardel's escapes from death. Imperiously: "Take the gleam-stone, cub; I can get all of them I want."

"The raven told you, I bet," Oroles teased.

Dirrach led the boy back to the cottage, subtly leading the conversation where he willed. Before taking his leave, he learned that Oroles's winged crony had admired the gleamstone, had claimed to know where a great many of them could be found near a warm spring in the northern moun-tains. It was not difficult to frighten the lad into silence, and to enlist him in the effort to locate a spring whose warm waters might have curative power. Dirrach returned to the castle in good spirits that night, resolved to keep his curtains drawn in the future.

After a dull morning spent on details of safe-passage agreements, the out-landers were amenable to an afternoon's leisure. They groaned inwardly at Bardel's proposal, but the deer hunt was quickly arranged. Dirrach would have preferred to wait in Tihan, the sooner to hear what his small conspira-tor might learn of the thermal spring; but the shaman had been absent from state affairs too much already; who knew what friendships Bardel might nur-ture with outlanders in the interim? Dirrach's fingers itched for a *mana*-rich hydrophane; the sooner he could experiment with them, the better for him. The worse for others.

A series of small things suggested to Dirrach that the great stone at Bardel's throat was constantly active. When Boerab stood in his stirrups by the king's side and waved their beaters toward a ridge, both men found themselves unhorsed comically. They cursed the groom whose saddle knots had slipped, but it was Dirrach's surmise—a lucky guess—that knot-loosening spells were easy ones, even by accident. Far better, Dirrach thought, if he could surreptitiously try spells while within arm's reach of

Bardel—but the king was much too alert and active during a hunt, and at the negotiation table such incantatory acts would be even more obvious. And always the shaman kept one eye on the winged motes that swept the sky, and thought of ravens.

The hunt was not a total loss for Dirrach, who cozened a wager from his king early in the afternoon. "One of the Shandorian gems, is it?" Bardel laughed. "Fair enough! If I can't capture my quarry intact, a stone is yours."

"But if he does, Dirrach, you have an iron axhead to hone," Boerab grinned. "Bit of honest labor would do you no harm," and the warrior rode off with his king.

The deer they surprised in the small ravine amounted almost to a herd. His foolhardiness growing by the minute, Bardel was in his glory. His shaggy mountain pony fell on the slope but, with preternatural agility, Bardel leapt free to bound downward as deer fled in all directions. Gethae fumbled for an arrow, but with a savage cry of battle Bardel fell on the neck of the single stag from above, caught it by backsweeping antler tines, wrenched it crashing to earth beneath him in a flurry of brush and bellowing.

Scrambling to avoid the razor hooves, whooping for the joy of it, Bardel strove to choke the stag into submission, and king and quarry tumbled into the dry creekbed. Something arced away, butterfly-bright in the sun, and Bardel's next whoop was of pained surprise. The stag found firm footing. Bardel, now impeded by a limp, was not so lucky. With a snort of terror the stag flew up the ravine and Boerab, bow drawn, feathers brushing his cheek, relaxed and saluted the animal with a smile. It had been too easy a shot.

While Boerab shared his smile with Gethae (for she had witnessed his act of mercy), others were hurrying to Bardel. It was Averae who found the great opal amulet adorning a shrub, its braided thong severed in the melee, and Dirrach who noted silently that possession was nine parts of the *mana*.

Bereft of his protection, Bardel had immediately sustained a gash below the knee. Bardel accepted the bleeding more easily than Boerab's rough jests about it; jokingly questioned the shaman's old wardspell; retied the gem at his throat; and resumed the hunt. But the king was sobered and his leg a bit stiff, and on their return to Tihan Bardel made good his wager. Boerab saw to the battle wound while Dirrach, pocketing an opal the size of a sparrow egg, retired to "rest" until evening.

Trembling with glee, Dirrach set the opal on a tabletop to catch the late sun in his chamber. He discovered the knot-loosening spell after sundown, and wasted time gloating while a warm breeze dried the last of the moisture from the hydrophane. Dirrach became glum as the spell seemed less effective with each repetition. The knock at his door startled him.

"Dasio the runner, sire," said a youth's voice. "I bring the girl Thyssa and her brother, Oroles. They said it was your wish," he finished tentatively. Unheard by the shaman, Dasio murmured to the girl: "If you should scream, many would hear. I've heard ill rumors of our shaman with—"

The door swept open to reveal a smoothly cordial Dirrach. With more expertise in sorcery, the shaman could have the girl at his whim; it was the brat who might hold the key to that darker desire for power. Affecting to ignore Thyssa: "I hope your mind is clearer tonight, boy, come in—but come alone."

Thyssa, stammering: "Our bargain, sire, I uh—might sweep and mend as payment while you examine the boy."

"Another time. The cub does not need distraction," Dirrach snapped, closing the heavy door. He bade Oroles sit, let the boy nibble raisins, listened to his prattle with patience he had learned from dealing with Bardel. He approached his topic in good time.

Oroles trusted in the shaman's power, but not in his smile. It became genuine, however, when Oroles admitted that the raven had pinpointed the thermal spring. "He brought proof," said Oroles. "It's at the head of a creek a few minutes west of Vesz. Is there a place called Vesz? Do ravens like raisins? This one wants better than fish guts. Do you have a pet, shaman?"

It was worse than talking with Bardel, thought Dirrach. "The village of Vesz is near our northeastern boundary, but several creeks feed the place."

"Not this one. It disappears into the ground again. The raven likes it because humans seem afraid to drink there. On cool mornings it smokes; is that why?" Oroles narrowed his eyes. "I think that's dumb. How could water burn?"

Dirrach rejoiced; he had seen warm water emit clouds of vapor. Three ridges west of Vesz, the boy went on, now straying from the subject, now returning to it. Dirrach realized that such a spot should be easy to locate on a chilly dawn.

Gradually, the shaman shaped his face into a scowl until the boy fell silent. "It's well-known that ravens lie," Dirrach said with scorn. "I am angry to find you taken in by such foolishness." He paused, gathered his bogus anger for effect. "There is no such spring or creek. Do not anger me further by ever mentioning it again. To anyone! Pah! You ought to be ashamed," he added.

Oroles shrank from the shaman's wrath as he withdrew a nutshell from his waistpouch. "Maybe there's no smoking water, but there's this," he insisted, employing the shell like a saltshaker.

"And where does the lying raven say he stole this?" Dirrach licked his lips as he spied, in the damp sprinkle of loam, a few tiny nodules of opalescence.

"Scraped from an embankment, fifty wingbeats south of the spring," said Oroles. "Sure is slippery dirt; my pouchstring keeps loosening."

Dirrach feigned disinterest, stressed the awful punishments that would surely await Oroles if he repeated such drivel to others. Dirrach could hear a murmur of male and female voices in the hall. "Your sister fears for your empty head, boy," Dirrach repeated as he opened the door. "Do not worry her again with your gift of speaking with animals." He ushered Oroles through, careful to show ostentatious concern for the boy, caressed the small shoulder as he presented Oroles to his sister.

And then Dirrach realized that the voices had been those of Boerab and the formidable Gethae, who strolled together toward the old warrior's chamber, tippling from a pitcher of wine. Both had paused to look at Dirrach in frank appraisal.

The shaman dismissed the youngsters, nodded to his peers, said nothing lest it sound like an explanation. Gethae only glanced at the spindly form of Oroles as he retreated, then back to Dirrach. One corner of her mouth twitched down. Her nod to Dirrach was sage, scornful, insinuating as she turned away.

Dirrach thought, *That's disgusting; he's only a little cub!* But Gethae would have agreed. Dirrach returned to his chamber and his experiments, Bardel and his guest to theirs.

* * *

The Shandorian runner was gone for two days, the Moessian for three; ample time for Dirrach to reassure himself that the fresh windfall of *mana* was genuine and resided, not in outlander sorcery, but in hydrophane opals. By tireless trial, error, and indifferent luck the shaman had enlarged his magical repertoire by one more spell. It would summon a single modest thunderbolt, though it was apt to strike where it chose, rather than where Dirrach chose. In that time he fought small fires, quailed at fog-wreathed specters, and ducked as various objects flew past him in his chamber. But as yet he had not been able to bring any of these phenomena under his control.

It was no trick to arrange a surface-mining expedition "on the king's business" — Bardel rarely bothered to ask of such things — and to stress secrecy in his instructions to the miners. Ostensibly the men sought a special grit which might be useful in pottery glaze. Dirrach was adamant that the stuff must be kept dry, for he had learned two more facts. The first was that the things were potent only when damp. The second was that only so much *mana* lay dormant in an opal. Once drained by conversion of its potential into magic, the stone might still achieve a dim luster; but it would no longer summon the most flatulent thunderclap or untie the loosest thong. The specimen won from Bardel was still, after many experiments, mildly potent; but the pinpoint motes in the loam sample were already drained of *mana*.

Dirrach saw his miners off from the trailhead above Tihan, giving them the exhausted grit as a sample. He regretted his need to stay in Tihan, but the outlanders required watching. The ten packass loads, he judged, would easily overmatch the *mana* of Bardel's great amulet.

"If you succeed, send a messenger ahead on your return," was Dirrach's last instruction before the packtrain lurched away toward a destination a day's hike to the north.

Dirrach turned back toward Tihan, imagining the paltry castle below him as he would have it a month hence, when he'd learned the spells. Stone battlements to beggar the ancient Achaeans; gold-tipped roofs; vast packass trains trundling to and fro; fearsome heraldic beasts of living stone, like those of legend, guarding his vast hoard of opals. And of course, a stockade full of wenches wrested as tribute from Moess, Shandor, Obuda, — it occurred to Dirrach that he was still thinking small. He must, obviously, conjure his great castle directly atop the thermal spring. It would stand on vapor, and soar into the clouds!

All the world would tremble under the omnipotent gaze of the great King Dirrach. Why not the great God Dirrach? Nothing would be impossible, if only he avoided some lethal experiment. A real wardspell was necessary, but so far he had not duplicated his accidental success with Bardel. A hot coal could still blister the shaman's finger; a pinprick could still pain him. Hurrying to the castle, Dirrach pondered ways to steal the great stone from Bardel's breast. He considered seeking out the cub, Oroles, to employ the raven as a spy—yet that would soon be unnecessary, he decided.

For Oroles, the raven was not the only spy. In Panon's smokehouse, the fisherman took a load of wood from the boy, chose a billet. "Don't ask *me* why all Tihan is edgy," he grunted. "Ask your friend, the ferret. Better still, don't. You'll have me believing in your gift, pipsqueak."

"I can't ask Thyssa," Oroles complained, "'cause the shaman said not to. But everybody's so jumpy . . ."

Panon coughed, waved the lad out with him, brought a brace of cured fillets for good measure. "Huh; and why not? Green clouds form over the castle, fires smoulder on cobblestones near it, thunder rolls from nowhere,—some say the outlanders bring wizardry."

"What do you say, Panon?"

"I say, take these fillets home before the flies steal them from you," smiled the old man. "And steer clear of anything that smacks of sorcery." He did not specify Dirrach, but even Oroles could make that connection.

Panon's smile lingered as he watched the boy depart. If the old tales could be believed, neither Oroles nor Thyssa had much to fear from most magical events. Both had hearts so pure as to comprise a mild wardspell— even though Panon had often seen Thyssa embroidering her tales of the redoubtable Urkut; intoning foreign words of his, copying outlander gestures as her father had done to entertain her once. The girl had a marvelous memory for such things, but little interest in the occult. Besides, Panon mused, if such incantations worked, why was Thyssa not wealthy? Panon shrugged, winced, rubbed his shoulder. If his rheumatism was any guide, all Lyris would soon be enriched by summer rains.

Try as he might for the next two days, Dirrach could not entice Bardel into another wager, nor further physical risks. At length Averae exclaimed in the parley room, "I do believe Dirrach craves your amulet, sire, more than he wants a parley. Why not just give it to him and be done with it?" Dirrach maintained his composure while writhing inside.

"Because it's mine," laughed Bardel. "I even sleep with it."

Boerab exchanged a smile with Gethae and murmured, "To each his own."

"To each somebody else's," she rejoined, then cocked an eyebrow at the shaman; "however small."

Because Bardel joined in the general laughter, Dirrach imagined that he was being mocked by all present. The anxiety, frustration, and juggled plans of Dirrach kindled an anger that boiled to the surface; Dirrach leaped to his feet. The moist opal in his waistpouch validated his dignity as Dirrach unleashed his easiest spell with all the gestural strength he could summon, cloaked in verbiage. "Let those who think themselves superior be loosened from conceit," he stormed.

The next instant, all but the invulnerable Bardel were grasping at the clothing as every knot within five paces was loosened.

Oil lamps fell from lashings to bounce from floor and table. Boerab and the outlanders fought to hold their clothing—and Dirrach himself was depantsed.

Without a word, eyes flashing with contempt, Gethae gathered her clothing and strode out, living proof that she could combine nudity with pride. Averae sputtered and fumed, his gaunt rib cage heaving with pent rage as he struggled to regain his finery.

As for Boerab, the staunch warrior faced Dirrach over the head of their openmouthed king, leather corselet and gorget at Boerab's feet. "*Mana* or mummery, Dirrach," he roared, "that was a stupid mistake! You've affronted guests; friends!"

Dirrach retied his trousers, fumbled with waistpouch, a furious blush on his features. "The first offense was theirs," he said huskily. "High time you learned a little respect."

"I'll show respect for lumps on your head," Boerab replied, taking a step forward. "Stop me if you can."

"Hold, Boerab," cried the king, finally on his feet. "What will our guests think?"

"They'll think we need to strangle that piss-witted child molester," said Boerab. But Dirrach had already fled into the hall.

"Who is king here, you or I?" Dimly, Bardel recognized the need for a regal bearing; for a measured response to this sudden turn. "For all you know, Dirrach could turn you into a toad, Boerab."

Averae, who had watched the confrontation in silence, now spoke. "Well spoken, sire. It strikes me that you may have need for more than one shaman. A balance of powers, as it were."

"But we don't have—" Bardel began, and stopped.

"You have only Dirrach," Averae said for him and added gently, "We know that, Bardel; but mutual loathing and mistrust are brittle bases for a treaty. With Dirrach, I fear—I fear I'm giving counsel where none is asked," he finished quickly.

"No, go ahead and say it," Boerab urged. "Everybody knows our fine shaman is a sodomizer of children."

"Everybody but me," said Bardel, aghast.

"And who was to tell you?" Boerab spread his big hands, then launched into a description of what he and Gethae had witnessed outside Dirrach's chamber. As usual, the tale grew in the telling.

Averae was not surprised. "Dirrach is unwelcome in Moess because he preyed sexually on the young," he said without embellishment.

In the hallway, Dirrach ground his teeth as he listened, enraged at the irony of it. The king was still ignorant of his real transgressions, but seemed ready to punish him for imagined ones!

"Have Dirrach confined in his chamber," said the king sadly, "until I can decide what must be done. If you *can* confine him," he added with sudden awareness.

"Cold iron is rumored to block any spell," Averae said mildly.

"And I have an idea where we can locate another who's adept, or could become so, at Dirrach's specialty. I don't think I really thought it possible until now—the mumbo-jumbo, I mean," Boerab said.

Dirrach heard heavy footfalls, thought of the cast-iron ax, and ducked into a shadowed alcove as Boerab huffed past. The shaman could not return to his chamber now—but perhaps he would not need to.

At dusk, Dirrach emerged from hiding. By turning his tunic inside out and jamming sandals into his belt, the shaman passed unrecognized in the dusty byways of Tihan. Twice he melded with shadows as men clattered by, clumsy with bronze weapons they seldom used. Dirrach felt certain he could command their fear, or at any rate their trousers, in a confrontation. Yet the uproar would locate him. Thunderbolts might not help. Dirrach made his way unseen to a hayrick near the palisades, climbed atop it, and sniffed a breeze chill with humidity as he burrowed into the hay for the night. He willed the rains to hurry; they kept most folk indoors.

Summoned in early morning, Thyssa ran with her friend Dasio before a damp wind as Dirrach, in his perch at palisade height, scanned northern hills for sight of a messenger of his own. While the girl made a fetching obeisance to Bardel, wondering what her sin might be, Dirrach spotted his man astride a packass. Shouldering a stolen mattock, blinking dust from his eyes, Dirrach trudged out from the untended palisade gate into the teeth of the wind to intercept his man.

In the castle, Thyssa was tongue-tied with astonishment. "I, sire? Bubbut, *I*?" Her pretty mouth was dry as she stared up at her king. "But shamans are men, and I know nothing of necromancy or—I, sire?"

"Oh, stand up, Thyssa, he's not angry—are you, Bardel?" Boerab dug a gentle elbow into Bardel's ribs. No, not angry, Boerab judged; but perhaps a bit bewitched. How like the dunderhead to notice beauty only when it lay beneath his nose!

"I'm told you might be of great service to Lyris," Bardel began, "if you can but recall your father's ancient spells. Dirrach has crimes to answer for. The question is, could you replace him?"

Slowly, Thyssa was persuaded that this was no trick to convict her of forbidden arts, and no royal jest. She admitted the possibility that Urkut, in his tale-spinning, might have casually divulged knowledge of occult powers which he had learned in distant lands. Urkut's failure to make full use of such knowledge might be ascribed to disinterest, fear of its misuse, or even to a blocking spell. Added Boerab, who did most of the coaxing: "Now it's time to find out, Thyssa. How well do you recall Urkut's tales, and what secrets might they hold?"

Thyssa nodded, then closed her eyes in long reverie. It seemed an age before a smile of reminiscence tugged at her lips. Hesitant at first, Thyssa knelt before cold ashes in the fireplace. A few gestures mimed placement

of invisible kindling, whirling a nonexistent firestick, other actions not so
transparently pantomimic—and then the barest wisp of smoke sought the
flue. With practice, she coaxed a flame upward, but turned in fear toward
Bardel, who bent near, his huge sweat-stained amulet swinging like a pendulum.

Too dull-witted to consider the dangers, Bardel grinned at her and
winked: "Now try it on the flagstones."

Flagstones burned, too. The problem was in quenching them. Thyssa
finally thought to reverse her gestures and after some failures, sighed as the
flame winked out. Thyssa was, of course, wholly innocent of the oral short-
hand equivalents which sorcerers of old had used. Thyssa wondered aloud
why Urkut had never put such spells to work around the cottage, then
recalled another of her father's anecdotes. She got it right on the third try.
Boerab made her erase the spell, laughing nervously as an oak table levitated toward the roof. Again, the reversal worked when she did everything in
order; the heavy table wafted down.

Urkut's spell over food was not to be deduced as a preservation spell just
yet. Thyssa tried it on their noon meal of bread, beer and fruit, but nothing
obvious happened and the experiment was soon consumed. Thyssa had no
inkling, yet, that their lunch could have been stored for a century without
losing its freshness.

His belly full, Bardel urged the girl to devise some spell of a more war-
like nature. "The sort of thing that gave warlocks their name," he said. "We
may need it; don't forget, Dirrach is at large."

Boerab shuddered. "And if it goes awry? Thyssa toys with thunder as it is."

"The nearest my father got to a curse, so far as I know, was when he'd
speak of shamans and their powers," she reflected. "Then he'd say a prayer
for deliverance—and do something like this." She began a two-handed ritual; paused with a frown, reversed it; began anew with a nod of satisfaction.

The trapspell, far older than any of them could know, was very special.
Lacking *mana* to energize it, Urkut had never known—until too late—
whether it worked. Fundamentally it was a shrinkspell, positively polarized
against evil and those who employed it by magical means. Only those present—the king, the girl, the warrior, and a mouse near the hearth—could be

the beneficiaries, and then only in proximity to a source of *mana*. As with the preservation spell, nothing spectacular happened; but the room grew oppressively warm.

"I guess I forgot something," Thyssa sighed.

Boerab, rising: "You're the best judge of that. But perhaps you'd best stop for now. Think back, and make haste slowly; as for me, I'll just make haste. There's bad weather brewing and we'll never find Dirrach in a storm."

"I hope it cools things off," Bardel nodded; "even my amulet is hot."

Thyssa took her leave, welcoming warm rain on her face as she hurried homeward. It did not seem like the kind of weather that would cool Tihan much.

Dirrach's messenger bore the best possible news, and estimated that the grit-laden packass train was no more than a half-hour behind. The man had no way of knowing Dirrach's outlaw status and dutifully returned, on the shaman's orders, to direct the packtrain toward a new destination. Jubilant, Dirrach took shelter from intermittent wind-driven showers under a stand of beeches. From his promontory, he could see groups of Tihaners searching lofts and hayricks. It would be necessary to commandeer an outlying farmhouse and to detain the miners until he had puzzled out ways to make himself invincible.

And how long might that take? Perhaps he should retreat further into the hills with his *mana*-rich ore. Later he could return with gargoyles, griffons, even armies of homunculi . . .

As the little group of miners struggled from their protected declivity into the open, heading for their new rendezvous, Dirrach allowed himself a wolfish grin. Then his features altered into something less predatory as he watched the packtrain's advance.

The skins over the packs gleamed wetly, and the lead miner fought a cloud of biting flies—or something—so dense that Dirrach could see it from afar. Then pack lashings parted—untied themselves, Dirrach surmised—and both skins began to flap in the wind. The lead packass took fright, bucked, stampeded the animals behind it, and in the space of three heartbeats the procession erupted into utter mind-numbing chaos.

FLASH BLAMMmm . . .

A great light turned the world blue-white for an instant, thunder following so close that it seemed simultaneous. Now the miners waved, sought to slow the maddened animals, and fled through clouds of grit as the pack contents whirled downwind, spilled into the air by the leaping beasts.

One miner disappeared in a twinkling. A packass, then another, flew kicking and hawing in the general direction of Tihan—but at treetop level, a sight so unnerving that miners scattered in terror. Paralyzed with impotent rage, Dirrach knew that a trickle of water into one of the packs had triggered a series of events; a series that had scarcely begun.

As the storm waxed, Dirrach hurried toward one pack animal in an attempt to save some of its load without getting downwind of it. Dirrach had seen a man vanish in the stuff, but could not know the man had reappeared safely under his bed in Tihan. The packass saw Dirrach, rolled its eyes, grew fangs the length of shortswords, roared a carnivore's challenge. Dirrach scrabbled into a tree with a bleat of stark horror. From his perch, he could see clouds of fine grit blowing over palisades into Tihan in a monumental *mana*spill.

Old Panon blinked as a grit-laden gust of wind whirled past him at the dock; steadied himself above his nets with outflung arms. He could never recall later what he muttered, but the next moment he stood amid a welter of fish, all flopping determinedly from the lake into his pile of net. Panon sat down hard.

On merchant's row, the bronzeworker followed a reluctant customer outside in heated exchange over prices. A blast of wind peppered them both and suddenly, his heel striking something metallic, the customer sprawled backward onto a pathway no longer muddy. It was literally paved for several paces with a tightly interlocked mass of spearheads, plowpoints, adzes, trays; and all of gleaming iron.

The tanner was wishing aloud for better materials when he ducked out of the foul weather to his shop. He found his way blocked by piles of fragrant hides.

The produce merchant spied a farmer outside, rushed out to complain of watered milk, and braved a gritty breeze. The men traded shouted curses before discovering that they stood ankle-deep in a cowflop carpet. It spread down the path as they fled, and more of it was raining down.

An aging militiaman paused in his search for Dirrach to surprise his young wife, and found that he had also surprised one of the castle staff. The younger man cleared a windowsill, but could not evade the maledictions that floated after him. He hopped on through the gathering storm, his transformation only partial, for the moment a man-sized phallus with prominent ears. He elicited little envy or pity, since most of Tihan's folk had problems of their own.

Bardel was informed by a wide-eyed Dasio who could still run, though for the time being he could *not* make his feet touch the ground, that the end of the world had arrived. The king howled for Boerab, aghast as more citizens crowded into the castle toward the only authority they knew.

One extortionate shopkeeper, perched on the shoulder of his haggard wife, had become a tiny gnome. The castle cook could still be recognized from his vast girth, but from the neck up he seemed an enormous rat. Bardel saw what the citizens were tracking into the castle, wrinkled his nose, and stood fast. "BOERABBBB!"

The old soldier stumped in, double-time, sword at ready, but soon realized he was not facing insurrection. "It pains me to say this," he shouted over the hubbub, "but Thyssa may have made some small miscalculation—"

"All this, the doings of one girl?" Bardel's wave took in the assembled throng.

It was Dirrach's erstwhile messenger, breathless from running, who set them right. "No, my lords," he croaked. "The shaman! I saw it begin with my own eyes." Convinced as always of Dirrach's powers, the man attached no value to the windborne grit. Thus he did not describe it, and a great truth passed unnoticed.

"Shaman . . . Dirrach . . . the molester," several voices agreed, as Boerab and his king exchanged grim nods.

Bardel motioned the eyewitness forward, hardly noticing that the knee-high shopkeeper was already beginning to grow to his original size. "Tell us what you know of Dirrach," said the king, "and someone fetch the girl, Thyssa."

★ ★ ★

Sodden and mud-splattered, Dirrach made his way unchallenged in waning light to the unoccupied cottage of Thyssa. He moved with special care, avoiding accidental gestures, forewarned by personal experience that the hydrophane fallout was heavier in some places than in others. He no longer entertained the least doubt that Bardel enjoyed magical protection so long as he wore the amulet.

Face-to-face intrigue was no longer possible, and Dirrach judged that raw power was his best option. It should not be difficult to wrest the small stone from Oroles. Far greater risk would lie in finding the means to steal the king's great opal. Perhaps an invisibility spell; Dirrach had seen the passage of some unseen citizen as footprints appeared in one of Tihan's muddy paths. The shaman had seen Bardel lose his amulet once through accident, knew that it could be lost again through stealth.

Dirrach plotted furiously, filing vengeful ideas as he ravaged the small cottage in search of the waistpouch of little Oroles. He knew it likely that the boy had it with him, but trashing the place was therapeutic for Dirrach.

If the locus of power lay in hydrophanes, then none but Dirrach himself could be allowed to have them during the coming power struggle. Once Bardel was dead—and stiff-necked Boerab as well, by whatever means possible—the shaman could easily fill the power vacuum he had created. Time enough then to organize a better mining foray!

Dirrach paused at the sound of approaching footfalls, strained to pull himself up by naked rafters, and stood near the eaves in black shadow. One of the voices was a youthful male; Dirrach held his one-piece bronze dagger ready.

"I'll be safe here," said Thyssa, just outside.

"So you say," replied Dasio, "but I'd feel better if you let me stay. Why d'you think the outlanders packed up and left so fast, Thyssa? As the Shandorian woman said, 'only fools fight *mana*.' Who knows what curse Dirrach will call down on Lyris next?"

Stepping into view below Dirrach, the girl shook her head. "I can't believe he intended all this, Dasio." There was something new in Thyssa's tone as she closed the door; something of calm, and of maturity.

Dirrach heard footsteps diminish outside, grinned to himself. He had no way of knowing why this peasant girl's self-confidence had grown so, and did not care. One of the rafters creaked as the shaman swung down.

Thyssa whirled to find Dirrach standing between her and the door. "Where is the cub? No, don't scream," the shaman ordered, the dagger his authority.

"Cleaning a huge pile of fish with a friend," she said. "Perhaps Panon should thank you for them, Dirrach. And don't worry, I won't scream. It may be that you and I have some things in common."

At that moment, Oroles burst into the cottage. Dirrach grasped the lad, enraged both by the surprise and the girl's treatment of him as an equal. Oroles squalled once before Dirrach's hand covered his mouth. Sheathing his dagger quickly, Dirrach wrenched the lad's waistpouch away and cuffed Oroles unconscious. Then Thyssa did cry out.

The shaman was not certain he could silence her quickly and made a snap decision. "The cub is hostage to your silence," he snarled, slinging the boy over one shoulder.

Thyssa's hands came up, churning a silent litany in the air. "I don't think so," she said, and Dirrach found himself rising helplessly into the eaves again. He dropped the boy, who fell on bedding, then locked one arm over a rafter as Thyssa reached into a corner. She brought out a wickedly tined fish spear.

Thyssa, advancing, clearly reluctant with the spear: "Even a rabbit will protect her young."

Dirrach saw that the tines of bone were bound to the spearshaft with a sinew, invoked his simplest spell with one hand, and barked a laugh as the sharp tines fell from their binding. But something else happened, too; something that startled Thyssa more than the loss of her weapon. She stepped back, hugged the boy to her, gazed up at Dirrach in fresh awe.

Dirrach felt distinctly odd, as if the rafter had swollen in his embrace. "Get me down," he hissed in hollow braggadocio, "or I turn you both to stone!"

Thyssa reversed the levitation spell, naive in her fear of his power—though that fear was fast being replaced by suspicion. The shaman released the rafter as he felt the return of his weight—or some of it, at least. He sprawled on the packed earth, then leaped to his feet and stared up at the girl.

Up? He glanced at himself. His clothing, his dagger, all were to the proper scale for Dirrach; but he and his equipment were all a third their former size. Thyssa's trapspell, dormant until now, had energized in response to his evil intent with magic.

The shaman's fall had been a long one for such a small fellow and, in his fury, Dirrach summoned a thunderbolt. The flash and the sonic roll were dependable.

And so was the trapspell. Thyssa covered her ears for a moment, blinking down at a twice-diminished Dirrach. His dagger was now no larger than a grassblade and fear stayed his steps. Obviously the girl had done this; what if she stepped on him while he was only a hand's length tall?

Little Oroles stirred, and Thyssa kissed the boy's brow. She was shaken but: "I was wrong, shaman," she said evenly. "We have nothing in common."

Her eyes held no more fear, but Dirrach thought he saw pity there. This was too much to bear; and anyway, he already had the boy's *mana*stone. Dirrach snarled his frustration, squeezed through a crack in the heavy wall thatch, hurled himself out into the night.

Had the trapspell depended on windblown particles of opalescent grit, Dirrach might have grown tall within the hour. But Thyssa's spell had drawn on the *mana* of Bardel's amulet, and the shaman had a long skulk to the castle.

His mind, and other things, raced with him before the keening of a fitful wind. He listened for telltale human sounds, found that he could easily hide now, kept his small bronze fang in his fist. Dirrach recalled the vines that climbed past the royal chamber and knew that stealth was a simple matter for one of his size. Now and then he paused to listen. It seemed that even the leaves teased him as they scurried by.

At last he reached the castle wall, planning headlong. Once he had cut his way through the upper-story thatch, he could hide in the king's own bedchamber and wait for the king to sleep. And Bardel slept like the dead. A predator of Dirrach's size and cunning could easily sever the amulet cord, steal the protecting *mana*stone, then slice through a king's royal gullet. After that, he promised himself; after that, old Boerab. It was a shame that Averae had already fled, but a grisly vengeance could be brewed later for that one; for the girl; for all of them.

He sheathed his tiny dagger, tested a rope of ivy, and began to climb. Then he froze, heart thumping as he perceived the eyes that watched him with clinical interest; eyes that, he realized with shock, had been on him for some time . . .

Three days after the storm, a healing sun had gently baked away the last vestige of moisture in the dust of Tihan. Citizens tested their old oaths again and found that it was once more possible to enjoy an arm-waving argument without absurd risks.

After a week, Bardel called off the search for his elusive shaman, half-convinced that Thyssa had imagined Dirrach's shrinkage and half-amused at the idea of danger from such an attenuated knave. But he did allow Boerab to post dogs around the castle, just in case.

Boerab's ardor to collar the shaman went beyond duty, for Gethae of Shandor had been spicy tonic for a veteran campaigner, and blame for her leave-taking could be laid squarely upon Dirrach. The garrison joke was that Boerab had exchanged one lust for another.

Thyssa refused to leave her cottage. "I'm comfortable there, sire," she explained, "and Oroles would soon be spoiled by palace life. Besides, my, ah, friends might be too shy to visit me here." She turned toward Boerab. "Intercede for me, old friend!"

Boerab slapped an oak-hard thigh and laughed. "Fend for yourself, girl! Just threaten to levitate your king. Or turn him to stone; you're capable of it by now, aren't you?"

"No," Thyssa admitted sheepishly. "And I don't seem to be inspired unless I'm in my king's presence. But I'll spend some time practicing here daily, if that is your wish."

Bardel kicked at a flagstone. "Why not, uh, spend some time with me just for amusement? I have eyes, Thyssa. Your friends aren't *all* bashful; only Dasio. And all your other friends are new ones. What does that tell you?"

"Just as you are, Bardel," Thyssa replied, "and what does *that* tell me?"

"Damnation! What does my runner have that I don't?"

After a moment: "Long familiarity—and shyness," she said softly. She exchanged a glance with Boerab and did not add, *and wit.*

Bardel pulled at his chin, sighed. "I've offered you everything I can,

Thyssa. My larder and my staff are at your orders. What more can we do to seal your allegiance?"

She smiled. "But Lyris has always had that. One day I'll move to the castle, after Oroles has grown and—" she paused. "Oh, yes; there is something you can do. You might have those dogs taken away."

Boerab: "They won't harm you."

"It's not for my sake. Oroles has a friend who lives around the castle. The dogs disturb it greatly."

Bardel's smile was inquisitive: "*Around* the castle?"

"A ferret, sire," she said, blushing. "Oroles no longer claims to talk with animals, except for one. Don't ask me how, but he's convinced me that he really can do it. You have no idea how much he learns that way."

The men exchanged chuckles. "Let's wait for news of Dirrach," Boerab said, "and then I'll remove—"

"Oh, that's another thing," said Thyssa. "Oroles tells me the ferret spied a tiny manlet the other night, and it described Dirrach perfectly. It watched our shaman do the strangest things.

"Oroles told the ferret that it was lucky Dirrach hadn't seen it; that the shaman was a bad man."

"Quite right," said Boerab. "I'll double the dogs."

"I'm not finished," Thyssa went on. "The ferret replied that, on the contrary, it found Dirrach a lot of fun. In its own words: delicious."

A very, very long silence. Boerab, hoarsely: "I'll remove the dogs."

Bardel: "I wonder if you could make ferrets become very large, Thyssa. You know: guard duty, in Lyris's defense."

Thyssa: "I wonder if you would want them thus. They are not tame."

"Um; good point," said the king. "Seems a shame, though. If you can talk with them, looks like you could tame them."

"Only that one," Thyssa shrugged, and bade them farewell in time to meet Dasio for a stroll.

The secret of the hydrophanes was intact. Not even the ferret knew that one of Dirrach's opals remained, permanently damp, in a corner of the animal's belly.

Tihan's folk were to learn caution again during rainy weather, though with each hapless employment the *mana* was further leached from the glittering motes in Tihan's soil and roof thatches. Meanwhile, Lyrians began to gain repute for a certain politeness, and greater distance from their king. It occurred to no one that politeness, like other inventions, is a child of necessity.

As a consequence of the *mana*spill, even the doughty Boerab agreed that *mana* was a hazardous reality which few cared to explore. If a king's presence was fecund with *mana*, then perhaps royalty bore divine rights. Europe's long experiment had begun.

ψ

"... BUT FEAR ITSELF."
by Steven Barnes

♃

THE DOOR OPENED slowly, a slender wedge of light falling, widening on the porch. A withered hand fumbled at the latch, finally holding the screen door open so that a small, sinewy shadow could enter.

"There you are, T'Cori," Judith said, bending stiffly to scoop the tortoiseshell kitten into her arms. "Momma was afraid you weren't coming back tonight. That might have been very bad." She scratched its ear, listening to the bubbling sounds it made. T'Cori backed her head against Judith affectionately. "No, Momma needs you tonight."

Judith peered out into the street, her dark sunken eyes unblinking as they searched for movement. She shook her head slowly and closed the door, mouth drawn into a taut line.

She set T'Cori down by a saucer of milk in the kitchen, then walked slowly back into the living room, lowering herself into her sewing chair, a vast, flowery thing that nearly swallowed her whole. One thin hand pressed against her chest and she closed her eyes, listening to the labored workings of an ancient and worn machine. "No," she whispered sternly. "No. Not yet.

Not tonight." For an instant, there was shooting pain along her arm and she inhaled deeply, sucking air in slow, desperate gulps, opening her eyes again as the pain receded. "Tomorrow," she said, the color coming back to her face. "Tomorrow. Tonight is mine."

There was a knock on the door, three raps, then two. A smile wound its way onto her face and she pushed herself out of the chair, paused to adjust a black-rimmed portrait of a dark smiling man which sat upright on the mantel.

"He's come, Josh," she said to the picture. "He's a good boy." Tears burned at her eyes; she fought them and won.

Again, the knock on the door. Judith walked to the front door and opened it again, swinging the screen door wide for the gangling young man who stood in the dim glow of the porch light.

"Good evening, Aunt Judith," he said, stepping into the room. He pecked her on the cheek and she returned it, scowling.

"You growing a beard, boy?" She closed the door and waved him to an overstuffed chair across from her sewing chair. A single white candle burned on the table.

He nodded and handed her a small brown bag. "Tryin' to. Here. Just some milk and eggs, but the freezer looked a little empty last time I was over."

Judith clucked happily as she took the bag into the kitchen. "Bless you, Ronald."

The young man crossed one denimed leg over the other and stretched back in his chair until he heard grinding sounds in his neck. T'Cori popped into his lap and he wiggled a finger behind her ear as he looked around the room he knew so well. In nearly every spare inch of space, there were plants. Potted ferns, sweet potatoes floating in water, long-stemmed roses cut weeks ago and in some miraculous way still a symphony of bright reds and yellows. Creepers wound about thin doweling set high in the wall, and a miniature citrus tree bore grafted branches of oranges, limes and lemons, surviving with only window light and love for nourishment. There was more, much more, but he refused to waste time cataloguing, instead breathing deeply of the sweet, sharp perfumes that filled the air.

Judith shuffled in from the kitchen, a plate of oatmeal raisin cookies balanced in one hand, a glass of milk in the other. Ronald filled his grin with sweetness and wet, and sighed contentedly.

"Uncle Josh would be proud of you," she said, her gaze unwavering as she studied him. She lowered herself back in her chair. "A college man now. Where do the years go? It seems like last week when you came up to the front door and asked if we had any bottles you could haul."

"Mmmfh," he said, then paused to swallow. "I can still remember his answer, too: 'Don't ever ask folks to give you nothing, boy. You ain't gonna make no money like *that*. You got to give 'um a piece of yourself.' And he took that old corncob monster out of his mouth, dragged me into the back-yard, and taught me how to hoe." He laughed, high with old memories. "You people were always mighty good to me. I couldn't love you more if you had actually been kin." He seemed embarrassed, and attacked another lumpy brown pastry ferociously.

"He . . . We loved you, too." He tried to tell himself that he was imag-ining things, but there was something . . . unnerving about the way her eyes were set. Something unfamiliarly restrained about her voice. "You learned fast. You knew how to work, boy, and how to listen. Even when Josh was just . . . tellin' stories."

The tension left him. "My God . . ." a sudden disapproving stare, ". . . uh, my gosh, how could I help but listen? All that about Pirander and Ibandi and the magic that used to be in the ground. You wait. In between botany classes I'm going to find an excuse to do a paper on African folk myths, and blow *everybody* away."

Judith looked at him for a long, painful moment, then spoke. "Perhaps you will. Perhaps not."

He paused in mid-mouthful. "Why not? They were great stories."

The last cookie was eaten, and she waited until he had drained his glass. She sat, watching him silently until he began to shift in his seat. "There was one last story, Ronald. One that Josh always wanted to tell you."

Broad muscular shoulders hunched in confusion. "Why didn't he? I'm a little old for stories now."

"No." Her voice crackled in the room, more force in it than he had ever heard, and he found himself recoiling.

"Aunt Judith? Are you . . ." He started from his chair.

She waved him back, angry with herself, now. "I'm sorry, boy. It's just—there is one last story, and you must hear it." The room's shadows deepened the wrinkles in her face until it seemed like a piece of dark, dried fruit.

"Well . . ." He slumped back into his seat until its softness engulfed his body. "Sure." He found his smile again. "This is your time, Judith. All you said was that you wanted to see me before I left for college. I came running. Lay it on me."

She stood slowly, gathering her thoughts. "Josh told you about the magic, the *mana*, and how greedy, foolish men used it up with their spells and ceremonies. Pirander brought the news of the vanishing power to his homeland, and to his twin brother, Ibandi."

"Right. I remember now. Pirander took his followers to Australia. They became the Abos, right?"

"Correct." She smiled. "But we never did tell you what became of Pirander's brother, Ibandi. He was also a mighty wizard, one more farsighted than his brother. If *mana* was going to run out, then it was of no use to move to more and more remote lands. Eventually it would be gone from everywhere, forever. Ignoring that fact was merely abandoning future generations."

She pulled an ancient world globe from a darkened corner of the room, and spun it until she reached Africa, then traced a finger down until she reached Johannesburg, then just a hair southwest. "This is where they lived, Ibandi and his followers, and where they stayed. The one change was that they began using the remaining magic to amass knowledge, knowledge that would be used in a final, desperate attempt to find a source of *mana* that would never dry up, that might serve them for generations yet undreamed of."

A wrinkle of curiosity touched Ronald's face. "And did they succeed . . . ?"

You will lead. That was what the dream had said to him, as clearly as a clean wind whipping through the grass. *You will lead.* Nagai fought to keep his excitement from bubbling past the wall of control. He squatted on his string-tight haunches, hands resting easily on his thighs.

He watched the Dinga priest speak to Pulolu, the elder Father of the

Ibandi. Every ten days the priest came, his sagging belly painted with runes, and his head festooned with gaudily dyed feathers. Nagai didn't like the man, although, or perhaps because, he always smiled, and sometimes laughed with a booming voice. The Mothers and Fathers had always told him that the Dinga were their friends, that in exchange for a little food, the Dinga protected them from enemies. That the Ibandi owed the Dinga much.

Nagai waved a fly away from his offering, watched the priest posture. Why would they need the protection of the Dinga? Was not all the Body in accord? Something about it made him feel sour in the stomach. The girl ahead of him in the line stood, bearing her armload of tubers. The Dinga priest smiled, the sharp tips of his teeth brushing fleshy lips.

Nagai stood, felt a droplet of perspiration trickle down his back, and calmed himself. He forced a neutral expression to his face and strode forward. The boy halted, bare toes gripping dirt and tiny pebbles as he extended his bowl of fruit. "A gift to our friends," he said automatically.

The priest patted his head with a great moist hand, and Nagai chewed at his lower lip. The fat man picked up one of the yellow ovals and buried his teeth in it, his eyes widening in pleasure as the juice welled up over and dribbled down a stubbled cheek.

Another pat on the head. Nagai smelled the sourness of the other's body. *Fear. This man is afraid.* But that was absurd. If they were of the Body there would be nothing . . .

"You Ibandi," the fat priest said, laughing, eyes tiny and wet. "How do you call up such magic from this soil? Do the plants listen to you?"

Nagai smiled.

The priest chuckled again, and passed the basket to the Dinga warrior who stood behind him. The man stacked the basket into the cart waiting, now almost filled with the week's offerings.

The Ibandi lad ran from the gate as soon as his burden was lifted, and made for the nearest stand of fruit trees. Reaching them, he stopped and looked back at the front gate and slow-moving line of contributors to the Dinga cart. Most were older than his sixteen years: Nagai had only been allowed to make offering for the past four months.

It was part of the process of becoming a Father. Or, for that matter, a

Mother. Slowly, he was being eased out of his childhood, taking on a few more responsibilities, gradually learning what it was to be a Coordinator.

But what was he feeling from the Dinga? He didn't understand, not at all. The cart was finally filled, and began to move out of the gate, pulled by four men. Always the same men. Always staring straight ahead, silent, unblinking.

Once, the first month of Nagai's contributions, he had come close to one of the four men, standing in front of him and watching as a fly crawled across the doughy face, across an open eye without a blink. Ashan, his father, had taken Nagai by the hand and led him away quickly, refusing to answer questions.

Still the Coordinators, both Mothers and Fathers, refused to talk about it. "You will learn," was the most response that ever came, before the inevitable smile and "why don't you go play now?"

The boy watched as the gate closed behind the Dinga priest and his cart, and the Coordinators walked back into the central village with drawn, worried faces.

A child ran up to one of them, and there was an automatic warm smile and hug; the ugly moment had passed. Nagai stretched, breathing deeply to cleanse lungs and mind. Immediately he felt the gentle knowledge tickling at him like a feather, and the joy came bubbling up out of his worry like fresh cold water. "I come, sister."

Nagai ran from the grove into the central village compound, taking a moment to spin from the path of three running children. One of them, a dark, sweet-faced child who giggled "Nagai!" turned on her heel and stopped. "You're going to be a Father today." She grinned challengingly.

He shook his head at her. "Everybody knows more than me."

"That's why you're going to be a Father. You don't know enough to be a kid anymore." He swatted at her playfully and she took off, chasing after her friends, now disappearing around a hut.

He tried to find a speck of irritation to hurl after her, and came up empty. She was right. He couldn't feel the *mana* as once he could. As any child in the village could. But he knew things now. He knew more of the world outside the high fence. He knew of the Dinga, and their fear. And soon, he would be a Father, a Coordinator. And he would guide the children, as he had been guided from earliest memory, *coordinating* their feelings into the fields and streams. Keeping the Ibandi centered in the Body. And as a part of the Body, they were fed by the forests, the streams, the fruit of the earth.

These were the earliest truths he could remember. *Life is your birthright. As an organ of the Body, you need fear nothing but fear itself.* Fear was corruption and death. Fear was cramping muscles and a clouded mind. Fear was anger, and hatred, and all things evil.

And the Dinga priest had smelled of it.

The old woman at the front flap of the birthing hut nodded toothlessly as she stepped aside. "It is time."

Daytime vanished as the flap swung down. Within, the only light was the glow of a tiny brazier.

The birthing hut was large enough for twenty at a time, and it was filled. Except for Nagai, no male Ibandi older than five years was in the room. Seven children sat in a ring surrounded by twelve ancient Ibandi women who sat, legs folded and eyes closed, humming softly. The children giggled as if they were being tickled, the liquid sounds of their pleasure weaving into a melody that complemented the humming of the older women.

In the center of the circle of moaning women was Nagai's mother, Wamala. Her legs were crossed, her hands rested easily on her knees. Her moist plump face was peaceful. The dim light in her womb grew brighter.

She chanted softly:

"Ibandi, lord of the Ibandi, bring forth thy new daughter bloodlessly, in peace and purity. Ibandi, lord of the Ibandi, grant her thy strength. Ibandi, lord of the Ibandi—"

The women in the hut chanted and sang, perspiration running in their age-furrowed faces. Musk-sweet incense hazed the air blue.

Wamala's body shuddered, each tremor rippling outward from the glow beneath her navel. Her eyes focused on her son, and her chin bobbed in acknowledgement. The light in her belly grew brighter still, and extended past her skin to shimmer in her lap. The chanting of the elders grew more intense, and the light began to congeal.

At first, just the suggestion of an infant's form shifted within the light, then huge dark eyes formed, pinpoints of sparkle within the greater glow. Gradually shadow filled in detail, and arms, legs and trunk emerged. The haze faded and the infant, air still shimmering about it, blinked slowly with translucent lids.

Mylé, the senior midwife of the Ibandi, stood heavily. Twisted with years, she moved as if her joints were filled with sand. "Ibandi be praised, a girl child." She stalked across the hut like a black crab, only her face animated. "Come." She took Nagai's hand in a brittle grip. "You're a man now, boy."

Silent, he let her lead him to the center of the circle. Nagai dropped to one knee before his mother.

"Nagai."

He touched her outstretched hand to his cheek. "Mother." The tiny glowing thing in her lap gurgled. Its aura expanded until it filled the hut, washing a jeweled spectrum over the skins and woven mats that covered the walls.

Nagai drooped his shoulders, and searched within himself for the fluttering tingle that would focus his sister's *mana*.

From a loose cloud, the cascade of light condensed into tendrils, snaking and darting in the air all about her. She bubbled with delight.

"She is pure magic," he murmured.

"As are all children," Wamala said. "As were you, once." She was tired, and the strain of the ritual rasped in her voice. But her eyes were alive as they scanned the taut planes and gentle contours of his body. "You have seen the bloodless birth now. You have not been allowed to witness it in eleven years."

His sister tried to wrap him in her light, but it fuzzed to mist under her control. "I had almost forgotten. Almost."

"Now is your time for learning," Wamala breathed, her eyes fighting to close. "You are ready for Fatherhood now. Go—your sister will comfort me. Go. There is much to be learned and done."

He touched his lips to her forehead, and then even more gently to the head of his sister. "When she is named, I would like to be present."

"Perhaps. We will see what the Mothers say. Go now. Go to the Fathers." Her voice weakened, and he knew that it was time for him to leave.

One of the midwives lifted Wamala slightly, sliding a layer of moisture-absorbent matting beneath her.

"Leave now," Mylé whispered. "She must release the birth water, and it is not for you to see."

He stood and bowed. "Mother," he said, treasuring the word, knowing that it would never again have the same meaning between them. "Good-bye." Her eyes closed, glazing, and he backed out of the hut and left.

Some of the children waited outside the birthing hut. Many were nude, small black bodies glistening with the afternoon heat. Others wore clothing as their bodies began to ripen with age: those with younger brothers and sisters would soon be eligible as Coordinators. Those without . . . he saw among them the familiar face of Bolu, his hair woven like a child's, incongruous above the corded body. But everyone of the tribe knew that Bolu's mother would never have another child. Bolu would remain hers, caring for her until the day she died. Only then would he ever be permitted beyond the Gate. Only then might he seek Fatherhood.

Nagai sang to them wordlessly, touching their hands as he walked back to the front gate. He touched their minds and felt them laugh, feeding him *mana*. It seemed as if each of them were giving him a single thread, a single silver strand that he wove into a cocoon about himself. And there, in his womb of energy, he could feel things he had forgotten, and truly knew himself as part of the Body. But now he just played with it joyfully, knowing that today was the true beginning of his life.

At the front gate he didn't have to explain or ask, it was opened for him, that he might go and find his father, Ashan. He was not turned away at the Gate, or told to find a Father to guide and protect him. He was of age, and now had a sister. He might well be a Coordinator, a Father, by the end of the day.

He ran past the outer fields where grains and tubers were coaxed from the earth, hopping over irrigation ditches and seedlings as he sped. What would it be like? The world of the Coordinator's mind. The Mothers used the children for bloodless birth, for healing, for growing food. The Fathers used them for hunting, fishing and luring.

He heard the rush of the stream, and knew that Ashan would be somewhere near. Nagai brushed the reeds aside and started to yell.

Something fierce and wet clinched his ankle. Nagai hopped back, shaking his foot violently, stifling a yelp of surprise. He kicked free and scrambled back three paces before stopping to see what it was.

The arm had thick, grayish skin, its elbow clumsily articulated. Higher up towards the shoulders it was spotted with tufts of hair that ran up into the scalp, where they joined a ragged shock of dark brown mane.

Its eyes flared greenly up at the boy, and short sharp teeth clacked feebly together.

Even as Nagai watched, the fire died, and the thing's body relaxed with finality. Nagai jumped as a broad hand clapped on his shoulder.

"You did not feel me, and you did not feel the Ghoul. You are indeed a Man now."

Nagai's eyes darted from the alien corpse to his father. Ashan's face was unlined, except for three rows of parallel scars that ran vertically on each cheek. His hair was dusted with gray, but the extreme erectness of his carriage made Time an abstraction.

"A Ghoul?" The puzzlement in his voice was genuine.

"It should never have come so near to the village." His father's expression was difficult to read, something stirring behind the placid brown mask that confused Nagai terribly. "It is an enemy of our—friends—the Dinga."

"But father . . ." Nagai found his attention returning time and again to the body of the Ghoul. Its muscles were growing flaccid. "Why didn't the Dinga keep it away? Why have I never seen one before?" The Ghoul was half-covered in water. Already, scavengers were investigating the possibilities.

"The Ghouls are a were-people, and came to our land in search of— sustenance."

"Why didn't our friends keep it away if it is dangerous?"

"The Ghouls are powerful."

"More powerful than our friends?"

His father seemed to wince at the word. "Very nearly. The Dinga won the war, but it has drained them. They have used much *mana*." Ashan nudged the sodden Ghoul with the tip of his sandal. The corpse twitched, then was still.

"Why did they come here?"

"*Mana*," Ashan said.

"But . . . why *here*? *Mana* is everywhere."

His father sighed, and sat the boy down on the grass. "There are many things that you do not yet understand. One is that not all people use the life-force as we do. Some use it to move objects, or change metals, or create life. This takes great concentrations of *mana*, nowadays only to be found in rare areas, like ours. We, the Ibandi, use it only to harmonize ourselves with Nature, to teach us of the Body. Only in the bloodless birth do we violate natural order, that we might bring our children into the world knowing nothing of pain or fear. There is *mana* in children, great power, but they begin to lose it as they learn fear. They are cut off from the flow of Nature."

"And the Ghouls? The Dinga?"

Ashan shook his head proudly. "No. This is our secret. They work their crude magics, draining power from the earth, or—" he looked sharply at his son who sat, fascinated, "—from the bodies of men. And their eyes are blind to the gentle *mana* that flows to us from stars and sun and moon. Too subtle for such as the Dinga to understand or use. A pattern connecting all living things into the Body."

He stretched out his hand and pointed to the lush greens and browns of the plain they lived on, to the mountains far to the north. "Once, a piece of star struck this plain, and spread its power throughout. It is for this that the Ghouls fought the Dinga."

Nagai couldn't take his eyes from the Ghoul. Dead, without a mark on its body. Already it was losing color. Starved for *mana*?

Ashan sounded thoughtful. "Perhaps I should wait for the Fathers to tell you these things, but you need to understand as much as you can, if you are to . . ."

Nagai had heard that silence before. It was an impassable void that told him that his father had already said too much.

Ashan stood, pulling his son to his feet. They walked to a spot near the nets, where another Father Coordinated four small, laughing children. The air about them shimmered as with heat.

The *feel* of their *mana* was in the air. He knew that he could guide them, Coordinate them. He felt the hunger growing, the empty feeling in his stomach. He wanted to reach out, to join with them and call fish to the nets, to repel insects and diseases from the crops . . .

"Soon, you will be a man. Already, I know you feel the waning of the strength you knew as a child." Ashan's eyes were sharp and alive as he drew near. "You will continue to lose *mana* and gain knowledge—if you become a Father this day."

"I am ready."

"Are you?" His father extended his hand. "Flow with me."

Father and son extended palms until they were within a hair of contact. Fingers upright, the hands danced together, only the barest layer of air separating them. Ashan fluttered his fingers, and Nagai responded fluidly, again, the fractional distance maintained. Small, then larger circles and patterns. Never separating more than a hair's breadth, never touching. Finally, the lean, corded arm of the older man dropped to his side. Ashan nodded approval. "You have learned."

"I am ready."

"The first challenge is ready for you—has been ready for days." He clasped his son's shoulder. "Once, centuries ago—" His face grew strained, and again Nagai felt the oddness. "Before the Dinga came, my father's father many times removed was the king of our people."

"But we have no kings . . ." Nagai sputtered, remembering the dream. "We need no kings. Our friends . . ."

"Yes," Ashan said bitterly. "Our friends, the Dinga." He leaned close, until Nagai could scent the sharpness of his breath. "But perhaps one day we will need kings again. And perhaps we will not need friends. You must be prepared."

Although unanswered questions swam in his head like nervous fish, Nagai nodded his confidence. "I am ready."

"Then go. The first test awaits."

The sick feeling returned to the pit of Nagai's stomach. If there had been food there, he would have found a waste ditch to empty it into. But his stomach had been empty for two days, since Wamala had first entered her birthing cycle.

He squatted, clearing his mind, minding his breathing, feeling his

weight sink into the ground. The more he relaxed the more it tingled. Not
the same as he had as a child, though; then, it had seemed that the world
was a crisscrossing spiderweb of energy that flowed from all directions, gossamer threads that could be woven by the skill of a Coordinator.

Once, his father had shown him a piece of rock, glassy gray and pitted
deeply on the surface. There was so much *mana* in it that it burned him to
be near it. He had vomited immediately, while Ashan beamed with pride.

But now, consciousness of the strands was a dim, elusive thing, found
only in the deepest states of relaxed wakefulness. He yearned to be a
Coordinator.

Olo grinned at him from the other side of the Amphitheater. There was
a diagonal chunk of tooth missing low on the left side and Nagai laughed
back at him. He remembered the game of tag that had ended with his own
arm skinned from wrist to elbow, and Olo's mouth bloodied against a rock.
Olo had won.

Younger and leaner than Nagai, Olo was not yet so knowledgeable, but
his vision was clearer. . . .

There were no children in the Amphitheater, only the gathered Mothers
and Fathers, sitting quietly on the ground in concentric rings. Wamala sat
across the ring from Ashan, with the Mothers. She was pale, and sat wrapped
in blankets, but would not be dissuaded: she had come to see her son.

There was one other within the ring: Weena. Her hair had been braided finely, in tight rows and swirls, proclaiming her preparedness for
Motherhood.

Nagai tried not to think of her, to think only of the contest to come. Was
it truly only three months since the three of them had run, playing as children play, through the streets and groves? Only three months since the
Fathers had prepared her for Motherhood. She had ceased playing with the
children after that night, and had begun her wait for the first eligible Father.

Today. It would be either Nagai or Olo.

Through half-lowered lids Nagai measured the sweet curves of her
naked body, and the strength of her eyes. Even at this distance he felt her,
and knew that he had to have her.

Olo stood, Nagai unfolding from his crouch in the same moment.

Slowly, as if a drum were beating in a distant corner of the village, their feet began to move in unison, tamping down the hard-packed dirt of the Amphitheater.

They approached each other, and Nagai felt Olo's *mana* and knew his opponent, younger, to be the more powerful. But this was not a contest of strength, and Nagai was unconcerned.

The two of them were close now, and both turned sideways, their shoulders almost grazing before each slipped to a side and slid by the other without touching.

A sound began, deep in their throats. It echoed their breathing, deep and organic to the movement. Not singing, not speaking, but something that blended with the rhythms of feet and swaying bodies until it became impossible to say which throat made what sound.

Nagai swirled and capered, the contortions of his waist expanding his lungs again. For an instant he grew dizzy, then he found the balance between himself and Olo, and the two of them moved in the Body as sound filled the Amphitheater.

At last there was a disturbance above them, a fluttering of wings, and both dancers paused, their torsos halting in mid-twist. On each, the light oil of exertion reflected the afternoon's waning light, highlighting the tautly muscled planes and valleys of their bodies.

Nagai stood with his arms splayed out to the sides, directly behind him the frozen figure of Olo. Nagai could feel his rival's heat, smell his sweat. His stomach burned, and he slowed his breathing to a crawl, relaxing, relaxing . . .

The fluttering grew closer, but still neither looked up. Once there was a quick flash of a tiny white figure, then nothing but fluttering.

Olo trembled a bit, then relaxed. Nagai felt it, and visualized as he did when a child: Spiderwebs. Silken strands of life. One to the other. Living things, sacred things. All interlocked by the strands. Every living thing . . .

Sound, very close, of settling wings, then the weight of a small body on his shoulder. Nagai turned his head, smiling to the tiny white bird that sat there, cocking its head as if mystified with its own actions.

A sigh of release, echoed by the Coordinators, and Olo stepped away from Nagai. As he left the Amphitheater, he was biting his lower lip savagely. There would be blood.

Nagai stood alone, facing Weena. She rose to her feet in a floating spiral and glided to him, searching his face and body with her eyes.

She was perhaps two inches shorter than he, and stood very straight, her body covered only with a tiny woven breech cloth. When she became a Mother, she would cover her breasts as well, but not until then.

Their eyes met, and he felt himself being drawn to her, as if he could lose himself in the depths of swirling brown. He stayed very still.

She took his hand. "Come." Again, the Coordinators sighed.

The second trial was conducted in a small unadorned hut behind the groves, near the fence. Weena walked ahead of him. He felt lightheaded, and tried to center his thoughts. What would this be . . . ?

She brushed aside the bead curtain and beckoned him inside. Brushing past her nearly burned his skin. They sat across from each other in the darkening room and savored the tension. The moisture and heat, the sweet sight and smell of her made him feel giddy.

"I lost my Childhood three moons ago," Weena said simply. "But I must have a mate to become a Mother."

"As must I to become a Father." Again Nagai thought of Olo's bitten lip. "Olo will wait until the next moon, and again contest. I hope he attains . . ." Nagai smiled mischievously. "But I am glad that he will not attain with you."

Only the barest flicker of her expression showed joy. "Olo will win Fatherhood one day. Today, we must deal with what is. I am a woman, and with you, could be Mother. If you pass your third trial, I can make you Father. Will you open yourself to me? Will you let me know you, that I might choose?"

Perspiration had blossomed on her cheeks, tiny beads slighter than dewdrops. Her expression was still, only the rise and fall of her shoulders, the gentle swell of full young breasts, spoke of life.

He had to trust. This was not the Weena he had played games and skinned knees with. The nights she had spent with the Fathers had changed her. His body knew the difference, and it tightened his stomach to dwell on it.

"Yes," he said finally. A trickle of sweat worked its way out of his armpit to slide down his side.

She reached out and touched his thigh just above the knee. Her fingertips warmed him.

Touch me, she said without speaking. Not in words, not in images but with the sudden creation of a *void.* He stretched out to touch, conscious of her hand sliding gradually up his thigh, the heat increasing until it became almost, but not quite, unpleasant.

Their eyes met across a space of a few inches, and they breathed each other's breath and formed the Body as they sat, crosslegged. She felt the tenseness of his body, the locked muscles and emotional scars that made him retreat from her.

She spoke softly as she touched him. "We are born in perfection. As we learn fear we lose vision, we lose suppleness, we lose contact with the Body. This is a consequence of understanding, of growing older. Fear is the destroyer. Only Love can give us back our perfection, for a few precious moments we are pure beings again, in the Oneness of the Body. If I join with you I will take your fear and pain, and let you see what once you saw as an infant. For that instant, you will have both knowledge and understanding, and you will become a Coordinator, reborn and renewed."

Nagai felt the tension leaving his body with the gentleness of her touch, and he could *see,* could feel the *mana* about him as he hadn't felt it for more years than he cared to remember. He felt it warm and cleanse him, clinging without pressure and guiding without judgment. The heat within him flared, the light clouding his vision.

She drew back. "No. Not until the third trial." Her voice was heavy and slurred, with a heaviness that balanced the lightness he felt in his own body. He wanted to beg her to continue, but sensed that it would be wrong.

For long moments she seemed burdened, then she straightened her back and exhaled sharply. Her smile relieved him.

"Yes," she said softly. "We need each other. You and I can understand each other." She sighed deeply. "Here is the next piece of knowledge that you need, Nagai. All things, especially living things, are like the mushroom. Mushrooms live in clumps, but are apparently separate entities. Only looking to their roots can one see that such a clump, with a dozen flowerings, is actually one creature.

"So are we all. All things that exist are forms of the same thing, only Pain and Fear prevent us from seeing the roots, or the invisible seeds that spread life. We perceive things as being different—in sizes, colors, locations and times. These are but the flowerings. The roots are in the Body.

"We understand this as children, as infants, as small clumps of life in the womb. Pain and Fear prevent the energy of life from flowing freely through us, and we lose what once we understood, replacing Understanding with its shadow, Knowledge.

"Nagai, we are the only ones who know that children brought into the world without violence, in an atmosphere rich in love and *mana* are open, and free, and can feel the connective energies. They are protected from the world, that they might stay within the Body totally, for in becoming a Coordinator you gain perspective, and lose the natural acceptance of things.

"Love gives it back to us. When we lie together, you and I, I will take you into my body and you will take me into yours. I will show you things that you have long forgotten, and give you peace."

"And I will see . . ." He left the question hanging. Nagai felt his limbs tremble with anticipation.

"What I see. You need me, and I need you. Together, we will make a child. You, and I, and our child will make up one small Oneness of the Body."

She stood, bending to trace her finger along his jawline. "Do not try to understand. You cannot. It must be shown." Her tone dropped, and she lowered her eyes shyly. "We belong to each other now, Nagai. For Always." They touched, and Nagai wanted only to stay with her, to learn the secrets hidden behind the warm brown eyes.

Torchlight flickered and popped in the Amphitheater. Only the Fathers were there. Their faces were heavily lined with stains, and together, in perfect harmony, they swayed to and fro in the gloom.

Nagai stood before them, silent, as the Eldest stepped slowly to the center of the Amphitheater. Age had eaten Pulolu's face into a ruined hollow. He walked in a rhythm of threes; foot, foot and the probing tip of a gnarled cane.

"Young Nagai, you seek Fatherhood. A woman has chosen you, so your final test lies with us—" his voice was a hissing sound. "The Fathers."

"I am ready."

"So you believe. If you would win the scars of Fatherhood, you must show that you can Coordinate the *mana*.

Nagai repeated the ritual words that his father had prepared him to say. "I have shown this, with the first test."

"You must show that you are ready to be absorbed into the Body."

Nagai stood tall, tasting the power and the victory that would soon be his. "I have shown this also, by the second test."

The old man shook his head. "It may be better for you to refuse your Fatherhood, young one."

Nagai's hands clenched in shock. This was not part of the ceremony! He searched the faces of the men ringing the fire, and learned nothing. Even Ashan's face seemed a stranger's.

"N-no," he stammered. "I am ready."

Pulolu clucked, deep in his throat. "We pray you are."

"Give me my task," he said firmly, reassured to hear his voice ringing clear and strong.

"Your task is to bring the children of the village — every one of them — here to the Amphitheater. Here, you will join with them, Coordinate them — and slay the Dinga."

The sound of the last words rang in Nagai's ears, burning like drops of flaming oil. His tongue seemed clumsily thick. "But — but why? They are our friends — they protect us — "

"From themselves, Nagai. You were spared the truth, as are all the children. Today you learn."

There was a murmur of agreement from the assembled Fathers.

"Three hundred years ago the Dinga came to our land, seeking the power in the earth. They are a wicked people, who had renewed their own powers by ritual murder when the *mana* grew short. Only the cleverness of our forefathers spared us a bloody fate, for they were more powerful than we. But they could not grow food as we grow it, or fish or hunt as we. So we have supplied them with food, half of our crops and catches, in exchange for peace to live our lives."

Nagai tried to find words that expressed the empty confusion in his gut. "But we — we can continue, can we not? Surely we need not spill blood."

Thoughts tumbled from mind to mouth in a torrent. "And—and if they are more powerful than we, how can I destroy them?"

"The were-people," Pulolu said with certainty. "They changed everything here. They warred with the Dinga for months."

The young man's mouth hung open numbly. "I never knew."

"We have paid a heavy price to insulate you from such knowledge, such pain. Your task now is to repay what we have given you. The Dinga defeated the were-people, but now their strongest wizards lie in exhaustion. The *mana* in the ground is gone. Tomorrow, or the day after, they will hunger, and they will look to the closest source of life-energy at hand—the Ibandi. This time, fruits and fishes will not dissuade them. This time," and his voice was a cold and unyielding wind. "We must strike first."

Nagai was silent. Reds and blacks crowded the edges of his sight, and he smelled his own fear.

Fear the destroyer, his mind echoed, and he shut it down desperately. "Time. I need time to think."

"No!" Pulolu shrieked now, corded throat stretching as he lifted his face to Nagai. "It must be done now! Now! Tonight! Or we lose everything!"

"But—"

"No arguments. Accept or decline, that is all."

Nagai felt his legs buckling, and smelled a now-familiar aroma from the men of the circle, something that he had never smelled from them before. Sour. Heavy.

They can fear. Coordinators can fear. The ground seemed to drop from beneath his feet. Knowledge did not protect from Fear. Vision continued to deteriorate . . .

In that moment he understood—*he was the most powerful member of the Ibandi*. For that day, that moment, no other Ibandi had as much Vision and Knowledge simultaneously.

Only he could do it. Only he could save the Ibandi. Their eyes stretched out to him in hunger. *You will lead.*

There could be only one answer, but his voice still cracked.

"I accept."

The children of the Ibandi were eighty in number, and they sat, child by dark child, in concentric rings, dotting the Amphitheater.

Even to the very young ones, they sat in total silence, bodies still and waiting. No sleepiness, no wandering of attention, although the sun had disappeared beneath the horizon five hours earlier. Even Nagai's sister was among them, cradled in the arms of Olo. Bolu the man-child was there, quiet, waitful, an infant's eyes peering out of his stubbled face.

Nagai crouched in the center of the rings, balanced on the balls of his feet.

The children fed him *mana*. He felt the lines appear, invisibly thin things that connected one infant to another, to child, to adolescent. The lines radiating from the youngest children were hottest, purest. Nagai gathered them with his mind. Forgotten totally was the great mass of the Coordinators who stood back from the circle. Watching. Hoping.

He spun and tightened with his mind until the strands became visible light, ropy luminescent bands that crisscrossed about them until it became a net, then a solid cocoon of light that surrounded the children in a glowing hemisphere.

One with the Body, he imaged with every deepening breath. Until the flesh seemed to melt from his bones, and a cool cleansing wind whistled in his mind. And he soared, seeing . . .

The torches and lights of the Dinga flickered, casting wraiths of darkness on the walls of their adobe homes. The fat cattle mulling in the pens sniffed the air, and even the guards pacing the edge of the city hunched their shoulders and peered into the darkness.

There is a void here . . .

Men and women of the Dinga turned in their beds. A few awoke and strained with tired ears for sounds that never came.

There is sickness here . . .

The Dinga priest awoke, staring blindly into the darkness. His tongue slid dryly over the points of his teeth, and he roused himself to a sitting position. There was nothing to be heard in his small, bare room, and no light to see. He knelt up from the thin mat he slept on, and groped out for his robe.

Come, creatures of the earth, creatures of the air. There is death, and wickedness, and disease here. It is a corruption of the Body.

The temples of the Dinga were silent and still, except for one, where a single robed priest genuflected, then prostrated himself before a swollen-bellied idol. A brazier nearby cast a dull glow, scenting of burnt herbs and blood.

And from the forests they came. From the ground. From the skies.

There is corruption here. On the morrow it rises to slay.

A single scream split the night, and a naked figure dashed from a hut and rolled in the street, clawing at face and body. Tiny biting things, stinging things, scrabbled on his skin, and the man writhed in the gutter, groans of pain and fear babbling in his throat.

He was not alone. From every corner of the city there came cries, screams as all of the vermin that dwelled in chimney and larder and sewer, all of the flying things that should have slept in bunches within paper nests, and the terrible red ants that bit so fiercely and relentlessly, poured into the homes and onto the bodies of the Dinga people.

In the temple, the priest staggered, slamming into curtains and tables, screaming as he staggered toward the altar. He clawed at his eyes, but the crushed bodies of dozens of their kin did nothing to dissuade the winged demons that plucked and darted.

He stumbled into the brazier, knocking it to the ground and falling atop it. His body jerked spastically.

At last he twitched more gently, as the screams and sobs of the Dinga died away into the night, and finally there was silence.

The sounds of screaming were lifted in the wind, carried to the Ibandi. They stood, the Coordinators, Mothers and Fathers, outside the dome of light Nagai had spun on the Amphitheater grounds. When the whispering screams faded away, no man or woman there could mistake the message in the silence.

The stars glared pinpoint-bright and cold. The light from the cocoon cast twisted, dim shadows.

Only the sound of tense breathing, and the distant cough of a wild dog filled the still air of the village.

Then the hemisphere began to waver, and it appeared that tiny balls of light were peeling back from the surface. The hole looked like a wound ripped in living flesh.

Nagai stood there, staring at them, through them. There was no anger in his voice, or even accusation. The words were almost toneless, but for a massive fatigue lingering beneath the surface that threatened to bow him.

"You didn't tell me. You never told me—" His eyes would not focus, even when he looked directly at Pulolu. His throat quivered. "They hurt so much—the Body believed me and destroyed the diseased flesh, but their *pain*, their *fear!*"

A hint of pleading crept in now, and his body sagged before he caught himself. "How could you? Why didn't you tell me how much it would *hurt?*"

Wamala took an uncertain step toward him, but she stopped short as if she had run into a glass wall.

"Nagai—you don't need to fear me—"

He looked at her curiously, trying to remember something lost in a jumble of pain.

"Mother? Why . . . ?"

She whined, trying to speak. Fingernails splintered against the air, and she dug at the ground with her feet. "Give me my baby," she sobbed finally. "Give me your sister."

Slowly, painfully slowly, he shook his head. "No. All of you must live with the knowledge of what you did, as must I. The children must never know." He clutched himself, trembling with the effort to remain erect. "Oh, mother, it burns—" He caught himself again, and his eyes focused at last. "I'm taking them. I'm taking them where you won't find them, and when they're safe, I will die."

"But the children!" Pulolu hobbled forward, mouth working numbly. "You have not the knowledge. If you take them, they will never learn enough—"

"That may be true," Nagai hissed, "but they will still be more than you." At last he took a backwards step, his chest heaving with effort. "None of you—none of you interrupt me, or try to stop me, or you will die."

He retreated into the ruptured hemisphere. It healed behind him sluggishly.

Pulolu turned to the others, searing them with his gaze. "We cannot allow this thing," he said weakly. "The children cannot . . . cannot survive without us."

"What can we do?" The question arose spontaneously from a dozen throats.

The Eldest looked to the stars, the bright, cold clusters of light that dominated the night sky. "It is Nagai who has proven weak. For the good of the Ibandi, he must die."

"No!" Wamala screamed. Ashan stood beside her, gripping her shoulders as she twisted.

"You cannot kill my son," Ashan said. "His is the Power now. None match him in strength."

Pulolu peered up at Ashan, stared until Nagai's father turned away from the ancient, pitted face. "Are you of the Body?" Pulolu edged closer, until Ashan gave ground. "Do you speak for the Body, which lives forever, or for Ashan, a bit of flesh which will one day putrefy?"

"I speak . . ." A great sigh went out of him, like water out of a ruptured skin. "For the Body, of course . . ." Ashan felt Wamala's body tense in his arms. "But—but who could do this thing? He refused to even let his mother touch him."

"Yes . . . but he had already broken ties with her. There is another, who had just begun to live her bond. Yes, another . . ."

He scanned the group until he found Weena. Small, bright-eyed Weena, shrinking back from him into an unyielding wall of human flesh.

"No . . ."

There was silence again, save for the shuffling footsteps of old Pulolu. He reached out a clawed hand to touch her face. "Would you have your people die? Would you doom the children?"

"I wouldn't . . . but I couldn't hurt Nagai." She fumbled for words. "We are joined—"

"He is no loner Nagai!" Pulolu screamed, his voice rising to a painfully high pitch. "He has allowed his weakness to eat away at him. He was an inadequate vessel for his power."

Weena tried to run, but strong arms held her fast.

"Would you let the Ibandi die? Would you kill the children, and us, and yourself, that one imperfect organ of the Body might live? Would you thus damn yourself?"

There were tears in her eyes, but they only welled hugely, did not spill, until she shook her head slowly, miserably. Until she heard Pulolu's grunt of satisfaction.

Weena had been washed and anointed. Her skirtlet was dyed in flower patterns, and her cheeks were painted in wedding glyphs. She stood holding a basket of fruits and yellow vegetables, just outside the shimmering barrier. Her small, exquisitely lovely face was expressionless, and there was no trace of emotion in the voice that softly called.

"I am here, Nagai. I am yours. I will enter your world, or I will die. The choice is yours." She waited long anxious heartbeats, then took a short step forward, then another, until her balance committed her to the final step, and she crossed the barrier. At first there was searing heat, and light so bright it turned closed eyelids into sheets of flame. Then she was through.

It was cold within, and very dark. Each exhalation fogged and hung in the air like pale butterflies. She waited for her eyes to adjust.

At last she could see a few small, still figures—the children of the Ibandi. They lay splayed about as if in exhaustion, limbs and torsos overlapping in a giant sprawl. They made no movement or sound.

In the middle of them, cross-legged and staring at her emptily, sat Nagai.

He seemed not to be breathing at all, merely sitting, waiting, his face the face of a dead man. His mouth hung slack.

Weena stepped over the unmoving form of an infant, one part of her mind trying to ignore the way it was curled up on one side like a tiny corpse. The other part tried to identify it. Whose child was that? Whose puffy-cheeked baby? It lay in dreamless sleep. Protected from Knowledge, from Pain and Fear by the ashen figure of Nagai.

His eyes were red and wide. She stepped over a final child and held her basket of fruit out to him. Her body was racked with chills.

Slowly, as if the impulses crawled along his nerves like spiders climbing webs, he pulled his mouth closed.

His voice was a faint rattle. "Why . . ." he said, then yawned torpidly. "Why have you come?"

"I came—"

One hand worked its way up out of his lap, a single finger raised. Her words jammed in her throat like chunks of splintered bone.

"No lies," he hissed.

The urge to turn and run was a physical thing, tugging at her like snare lines. She felt the cold penetrating her body, numbing the marrow.

"It is not safe for you, here," Nagai said, each word heaved out with a sigh.

"I came . . . because I am yours. You are mine. We are pledged."

For all the change in his visage, she might have been squawking or squealing instead of speaking words.

Then . . . something crept into his eyes that she had never seen in him, or any other being. A longing or need beyond the need for food or shelter or even breath. A deathly fatigued desperation. "I wish . . ." Then he dropped his head to the ground. "No, you must leave."

She knelt before him, setting her bowl down, and brought her face very close to his. "We belong to each other."

"No . . ." he said, trying to find the strength to turn away.

The muscles in her arms trembled as she came closer, lifting his chin to gaze at him.

She felt his need. Smelled it, sweet and sour in her mind. It rang in her ears like the rushing blood of a burst heart. Like a torrent rushing to fill the void she came to him, and all thoughts were swept away.

Still he fought, for an instant more he fought to control himself, then something shattered. Tears spilled from his eyes and he reached for her hungrily, felt her warmth melting the ice that filled his belly, felt himself drifting, soaring . . .

Weena awoke first. She twisted away from Nagai's sleeping body and clutched a hand to her stomach, sobbing in the darkness.

Nagai's peaceful expression made the pain recede for a moment, then she remembered why she was there. Weena reached into the basket, under the cool firm shapes, and pulled the knife. She curled her fingers around it carefully. An iron blade, wound with fiber at the hilt, five inches of edge and point nestled in her fist.

Gasping now, she got one hand braced on Nagai's shoulder and levered him over onto his back. Voices screamed in her ears, fingers of dead hands crawled up the lining of her stomach.

Fear like this never dies, unless . . .

For the last time, she bent over and kissed him on the throat, on the warm hollow so recently discovered. He slept on, peacefully.

Then she raised her hand, screaming her pain and sorrow, and drove the knife with all her strength up under the ribs and into her heart.

Nagai awakened slowly, listening for the voices, feeling for the cold, or the crawling fingers, but there was nothing. Without turning, he knew what he would see.

Weena lay curled on her side, her face calm now. Her hands still grasped the knife buried under her ribs. He brushed her cheek, walking its roundness to the long curve of her neck.

The children were waking. They rubbed their eyes with tiny fists, and yawned. Olo touched Weena, uncomprehending but unafraid. He stood, and picked up one of the babies.

Nagai gathered up their *mana* and exhaled a thin, even stream. The dome about them began to glitter, then glow. It burst into sparks and dissolved.

The Mothers and Fathers stood outside the shielded area, clustered, silent, staring.

No movement, no challenge. Nagai felt nothing for them. The strands, the slender strands that had bound him to the Ibandi were broken, lost forever.

Without a word, the children formed into a ragged line, the largest carrying the smallest. All heads were directed toward Nagai, at the head of the line.

Mothers sang to their infants, Fathers threatened and promised, but all eyes remained on Nagai. No parent could cross the thin, shimmering barrier that surrounded the line.

Pulolu spiderwalked to the front of the line, his mouth working silently. "You dare not!" he screamed at Nagai. "What you do is sacrilege!"

Nagai's gaze was focused on the horizon and beyond. Without glancing down at the Eldest he said: "Sacrilege? And what of the task you set me to?"

The old man flinched back. "It was for you! It was for the children."

"You lie," Nagai whispered. "It was for your fear."

"They will be separated from the Body."

"Your fear has already done that. There is no route to the Body through you."

"Many will die . . ."

"We all die. To go is to die. To stay with you, in this place, is worse."

Without another word, they walked from the village of the Ibandi, toward the mountains to the north. None tried to stop them. Nagai passed his mother and father on the way out. Wamala swallowed and looked away from him, but his father nodded shallowly, almost imperceptibly, and Nagai found the trace of a smile to give them.

"Nagai!" Pulolu screamed, waving his stick. "May you rot in the sun! Ibandi damn you for what you do here! May your belly crawl with worms—"

The line moved on, out of the gate and the village, out of sight of the Ibandi forever.

Judith stopped talking and swallowed hard. Ronald was sunk back in his chair and gazed at her over the top of the candle that now burned low in its holder.

Finally, he cleared his throat. "And what happened then?" he asked uneasily. "What happened to the children?"

"They suffered. Some died of exposure, some starved. Some merely sickened." She retreated back from the candle flame until her face was lost in shadow, and her voice sounded like a thing from the dead, distant past. "Nagai and the other children coped as well as they could. Some of them were adopted by other tribes. Some fell prey to slavers. . . ." The words drained away. Her eyes were reflecting pools within the shadow, and he could see that her hands were knotted and tensed until they seemed to fuse with the chair arms.

Ronald felt something cool brush the back of his neck, and warmed it with his hand. He smiled warily. "Well . . . that's really something." A broader laugh, now. He tried vainly to pierce the darkness that shrouded the reflecting pools. "It's sure a lot different from the other stories. . . ." He half-rose from the chair, glancing at the door, to his wristwatch, to her unblinking eyes. "I guess I oughta be going now—"

"No. It is not a story. It is true." Her voice was a whisper that carried clearer than a shout, and there was a terrible acid, churning in his stomach.

"It is true. The story has passed from husband to wife, from mistress to man, for more years than I can guess." Now she leaned out of the shadow, and the light made her face seem all grooved shadow and burning eyes. "And the knowledge—what is left of it, has passed, too—"

Ronald felt the breath rasping in his throat and stood, horrified.

"It's true, Ronald, it's true." Her voice was begging now, the words tumbling out like children's blocks. "And there is only one obligation—to pass it on. I received it from Josh. I told him that I couldn't do it, couldn't pass the gift to a man I wasn't married to. He never pressured me. He knew. . . ."

She stood facing him, her body shaking. "But my time is coming, I can feel it now. And I know that it would be wrong to die without passing on what is left of the gift. The Vision."

He raised his hands to his ears to block out her sound, drowning, terrified of the old woman who stood before him, craving something he could never give. "No! This is a lie." Suddenly there was understanding in his face, and he lowered his hands. "God, Judith. Oh, Lord, I should have known. Living here alone . . . I know how attached you were to Uncle Josh." He spoke quietly, pityingly. "I can find someone for you to talk to—"

She shook her head sadly, and reached into a side pocket, pulling out a seed, a single, small, yellow seed. "I knew you could not believe. Neither did I, at first. I must show you what I can."

T'Cori sat on the table, licking her paw, and didn't flinch as Judith took her in a withered hand. The kitten curled there, purring.

Judith milked her cheeks several times, then spat into her right palm, onto the seed. Then she closed her eyes and relaxed, humming almost imperceptibly.

T'Cori's purr deepened, and it looked up at him, eyes half-lidded. Its head grew heavy and it snuggled down into her left palm with a sighing growl.

For a few seconds there was nothing. No sound, no movement. So still was Judith's body that Ronald wondered . . .

Then the seed, in the small pool of clear fluid, began to split. A slender tendril of stalk worked its way out as he watched, and a gossamer network of root pushed free from the opposite side. In the space of two minutes it reached a length of five inches, absorbing the liquid in her palm until it lay there, dry and impossible, a tiny plant barely five minutes old.

The room whirled around him. She opened her eyes. There was no madness there, no lust, no danger. It seemed that they were windows to another time, a time when miracles were commonplace, and where Ronald had never walked except in dreams.

"You . . ." he licked his lips with the dry tip of his tongue. "You can teach me this?"

She shook her head. "No. I *must* teach you. Please, Ronald. There is no one else to give it to."

He leaned on the top of his chair, feeling his youth and strength, seeing the life stretching before him like an open road. And suddenly he saw her, truly saw her, not as an aging, weathered body, but as a spirit cloaked in human flesh, a spirit joined to a heritage stretching back to prehistory. A spirit begging him to help keep the heritage alive.

"What . . . what must I do?" he said at last, his voice unrecognizable.

She nodded, and gently deposited T'Cori on the table, and with the same hand cupped the candle flame. A whiff of breath and it wavered sharply, then died.

She faced him across the gulf of darkness and years, and held her hand out to him. Ronald looked at it uncertainly, then watched his own reach out to take it. Her hand was firm, and dry. And warm.

STRENGTH

by Poul Anderson and Mildred Downey Broxon

♃

NIGHT STILL HELD the western horizon when Shalindra found the dead sea-unicorn. It stretched sleek amid kelp, timbers, and storm-drowned birds.

* * *

The sorceress knelt in the wet sand. Zaerrui had mentioned that once, in his travels a hundred years ago, he had seen a cup carved from such a horn. A king drank from it to ward off poison.

One of the beast's great brown eyes stared skyward at the wheeling gulls. Soon they would land and feast. Shalindra stroked the flank—cold in death, but not fish-slimy. What must it be like when alive?

Behind the ragged peaks of the Heewhirlas the sky glowed pale. This early, Shalindra walked the beach alone, but soon the townspeople, too, would be out searching for gale-brought treasure.

Doubtless any of them would offer her the horn but doubtless, also, he would exact a price: most likely a healing spell. Those were failing everywhere. She must hoard her magic, in hope of making her son Llangru strong, or at least controlling the tremor in his hands so he could learn to write.

She sighed and looked down at the huge dead beast. The spiral horn measured a good cubit longer than Shalindra stood tall. She pulled. It held fast.

She needed a saw sharp enough to cut bone. There was probably one back at the library, but to find it would take time. Meanwhile someone else might claim her prize. Best not to squander power on a warding spell; best, instead, to hurry.

In her haste, stumbling over the littered beach, she almost fell across the man.

He lay tangled amid seaweed, his hair sand-grimed, his clothing drenched. For a moment she thought him drowned. Then his chest moved.

Shalindra stepped back a pace. Whence could he have come, if not from the sea? The fingers that dug into the wet sand were unwebbed, and the last merfolk had vanished years ago. No visitors came to Tyreen since the glacier had sealed Icehold Pass. This was no merman, but neither was he of her country. His rough dun tunic was of foreign cut, and he was stockier than folk from hereabouts.

He took another shallow breath. *Too slow.* Shalindra nerved herself to touch his hand. Icy, and his lips were blue. She shook his shoulder; his head lolled. After an eternity he breathed again.

She could see no hurt, yet he would not wake. In wintertime she'd seen folk stumbling with cold, wits slowed enough that they eventually lay down to sleep forever. She shook him again. No response.

Panicked, she looked about. This was taking valuable time. In earlier days she could have warmed him with spells, wakened him, set his blood moving, but she no longer carried charms now that magic was fading. She could abandon him—*no*. Evil would spring from such a deed. She sighed.

She needed strong muscles. Not far off was Gilm's cottage. The carpenter and his grown son could help carry the stranger home. She ran and beat on the door.

Gilm swung it open. He grumbled about the stiffness in his back and hands, but he and his son came. They lifted the man as if he were a kitten.

Shalindra went ahead to make things ready. She must light a fire, gather blankets, brew tea, anything to restore warmth.

Up the ramp to the College, where merfolk formerly squelched from the water, bearing fish and sunken treasures; she spared scarcely a glance for the dragons that flanked the gate. Once they had gleamed with iridescent scales: now legs, tail, and trunk were dull gray. They had almost turned to stone. One bent its head as she passed.

The library was the only building that had not slumped to rubble. Here Shalindra and Llangru made their home, amid moldering books no one else could read.

She pushed open the door—its rusting hinges creaked—and stopped, surprised. Already fire blazed, a kettle steamed, and the long copper tub gleamed on the hearth. Llangru was holding blankets near the heat. He looked up when he saw her. His hands twitched, and the blankets tumbled.

His eyes sought the outlander. Strange eyes, they were, gray-blue bordered with paleness. They were often dreamy, but at this moment seemed intent. "I watched you find him, Mother," the boy said. "I knew you'd want warmth. Is he badly hurt?"

Shalindra frowned, puzzled, but voiced no question as Gilm and his son shuffled through the door. "Where you want him, lady?" Gilm growled.

"Over there, near the fire."

They set the man down and backed away, casting fearful glances at the shadows. "It's a cruel cold day for m' hands," Gilm hinted.

"Thank you for your help," said Shalindra. The two left as quickly as they could. She bent over the victim; he still breathed shallowly. "Help me strip him," she ordered Llangru, then bit her lip as the boy fumbled at fastenings. *Keep silence, it's not his fault he was born that way.* "Better yet, fetch more blankets."

It was difficult for a frail woman to remove his clothing—he lay a dead weight—but at last she heaped the sodden garments on the floor. Where sun had not seared him, his skin gleamed white. She had not seen an unclad man since Zaerrui died—and that was ten years gone, while she was pregnant with Llangru.

This man was of ordinary height, shorter by far than Zaerrui, but he would weigh as much or more: powerful muscles bulged arms, shoulders, and thighs. His chest was broad. He must be used to heavy work. Square-jawed and blunt-nosed, his features were somewhat rugged. In the manner of the Southerners, he wore his brown hair short, and was accustomed to shave his beard, though several days' worth of stubble showed.

"Help me lift him," Shalindra told Llangru. Mother and son strained, and finally eased the stranger into the steaming tub. "More hot water."

First came shivering, then awareness returned. The man opened gray eyes. She answered his unspoken question: "You are in the town of Tyreen, in the old College library where I make my home. I found you on the beach, half-dead. Who are you, and whence from?"

The cracked lips parted. She leaned forward to catch the words: "I am Brandek. I was on a ship, trying to—teach men—" He swallowed. Yes, his accent was Southern. In the years before the pass closed, folk from Aeth had often visited the College to confer with Zaerrui.

"Never mind talking," Shalindra said. She helped him from the tub, wrapped him in warm blankets, and fed him hot tea. "You can tell us all about it later."

He slipped into slumber. Shalindra thought she might leave Llangru on watch, and go back to the beach, but suddenly Gilm knocked on the door.

The old carpenter grinned, held out the sea-unicorn horn, and said, "See what I found on the strand, lady. It's yours in trade for a bit of magic."

"Thank you," Shalindra said. "What do you wish?"

He spread knotted fingers. "It's m' hands and back, they pain me sore. Make the hurt go away, an' I'll give ye this pretty thing."

Shalindra held the horn. White, slender, spiral, it was heavy with *mana*. Any fool could see that. "Very well," she said, "sit down."

The healing spell would not last, and Gilm would complain he had been cheated, if she did not add something special. For a few moments she admired the flawless beauty of the horn, before picking up a rasp. She felt almost physical anguish as she scraped. There, that much should suffice. She measured out the usual herbs and powdered pearl, and mixed the medicine with wine. Zaerrui's wine. She whispered the activating spell and handed Gilm the goblet. "Here, drink. This will help for a time." She watched him gulp; she'd brewed it bitter.

After the carpenter left she picked up what remained of the horn, a great length, but flawed, now. She set it in the corner, against a stack of musty books. It no longer held power to help Llangru. Perhaps nothing did.

She looked down at Brandek. *The fault, stranger, is yours. There you lie. Were you worth it?*

The moon had swung through two full cycles when Brandek returned to Shalindra's home. First, as propriety required, he had moved elsewhere after he could walk again. The household of Kiernon the blacksmith had been glad to take him in for the sake of hearing about the world beyond Tyreen and its hinterland; no outlander had crossed these ever-narrowing horizons for years. The place was soon beswarmed by people just as eager for news. His vigor regained, Brandek set about earning his keep. When he learned how lacking in huntsman's skills they were hereabouts, though big game was frequently seen, he offered to lead forth a party of young men and teach them something. First, he discovered, it was necessary to prepare weapons for the chase, mainly spears, knives, and slings. With metal become scarce and precious, he chipped stone into points and edges, an art he had seen practiced in wild parts of the South but must largely re-invent himself. Thereafter he must drill his would-be followers in the use of these things. At last they were ready.

Their band was gone so long that kinfolk worried, for it made countless mistakes—but it learned from them, and came home triumphant.

Next day Brandek laid across his shoulder a haunch of venison that he had smoked in the field. Stepping out of Kiernon's door, he turned

toward the abandoned College of Wizards where Shalindra dwelt alone
with her son.

It was a bleakly bright summer morning. Wind harried white clouds
through the sky so that their shadows and its whistling swept through grass-
grown, ruin-lined streets. Gray-green with glacial flour, the Madwoman
River poured noisily into a bay where whitecaps danced on water the hue of
steel. On the southern bank, rubble heaps and snags of towers marked the
totally abandoned half of Tyreen. There had been no sense in anyone living
across the stream after the bridge collapsed and only rafts were available.
Beyond lay the country where Brandek had been hunting. Often he had
spied fallen buildings in those reaches, for that had once been a land of great
plantations. Now it was tundra and taiga, bearing naught but grass, moss,
dwarf birch and willow, gnarled shrubs. They called it the Barren in Tyreen,
and no one in living memory had gone far into it—for what could a man
find there to keep himself alive?

Brandek struck out northerly through the town. The village, rather, he
thought: just a few hundred souls remained. After weather spells failed and
the glaciers marched south, while pests and murrains that were no longer
checked by magic ravaged the farms, famine had taken off most of the population. Disease, cold, storm, fighting for scraps accounted for others.
Eventually a certain balance had been struck, but everyone who could think
knew how precarious it was.

Kiernon's house was better than most. Being clever with his hands, the
smith had shored up a crumbling structure, even made an addition of timbers salvaged from tenantless places, roughly dovetailed together and
chinked with mud. He had ample time for that, since no new iron ever
came in and implements were wearing out, rusting away, or getting lost.
(Still, the demand for repairs, paid for in kind, was sufficient to keep his family reasonably well off.) Striding along, Brandek passed dwellings that were
little more than caves grubbed out of wreckage, or lean-tos against remnant
walls. The bright colors of bricks, the occasional grace of a colonnade, the
vividness of a phoenix in a mosaic of which half was gone, somehow made
the scene doubly forlorn.

What people he met were less miserable than their surroundings . . .
thus far. They were of his own race, though usually lighter-complexioned,

sometimes blond, and might have been taller than him had not under-nourishment stunted growth. However, they were wiry, and his young hunters had not lacked endurance. Their clothes, such as he necessarily wore, would have seemed archaic in Aeth—tunic and trousers for men, long gowns for women, hooded cloaks for both sexes—but were, after all, generally old, when wool and linen were in short supply; if dyes had faded, the patching and darning were carefully done.

Brandek did not encounter many persons. Most were out tending their meager fields and sparse flocks, gathering firewood, fishing along the river and bay shores. Those who stayed behind were children, housewives, the aged, the sick, the rare artisan like Kiernon. They hailed him in friendly wise. The meat he had gotten made him a hero.

"Hoy, my son told me how you tied a rack of antlers off a reindeer skull to your head, and threw a skin over your back, and went on all fours to within spearcast of the herd," said Hente the weaver. "And that hooked stick of yours for throwing the spear, he claims it doubles the range and force. Won't you show the rest of us?"

"Of course," Brandek replied, a bit curtly. He was impatient to be on his way. "You've a whale of a lot to learn here."

"A what? A whale of a lot? Hee, hee! That's a clever 'un. A Southern turn of speech, eh?" Hente cocked his head and regarded the burly man closely. "You're settling down for good, then, are you?"

Brandek shrugged. "I've no choice. Therefore I'd better do what I can to make this place fit to live in."

"Hoy, you're a gruff 'un, aren't you?" Hastily, Hente smiled. "Um, you'll be wanting a wife, and my daughter Risaya—well, I think you might like meeting her."

"No doubt. Later." Brandek nodded and went on. Hente stared after him. The weaver had little else to do, these days, and hunger was often a guest at his board.

Crossing Searoad, Brandek reached the College. Well-nigh all its proud buildings had fallen; he could look across weedy grounds and the ruins and hovels beyond, to city walls in nearly as bad repair. He cursed under his breath, not for the first time. Like any prosperous, populous community, Tyreen had made lavish use of magic. Indeed, because of this institution in its midst, it had been still more prodigal of *mana* than most were. When enchantments began to fail, so did the delicate, fantastic works, or the massive ones, which they had upheld against gravity and weather. Knowledge was lacking of how to rebuild in mundane fashion. The rot had gnawed less far inward in his homeland, but he had seen it there too—yes, in Aeth itself, which had been the capital of an empire that reckoned Tyreen a rich provincial town.

One hall of the College survived, in part. Ivy crawled over amber-hued masonry, would pry it asunder in due course, meanwhile hid friezes and inscriptions. Windows gaped glassless or were crudely boarded up. A fountain before the entrance held rainwater in its basin but did not spring any more, and its statue of a dancing maiden was lichenous and blurred. Nevertheless, here was a shelter of a sort for many books, and for Shalindra and her boy.

Llangru sat on the stairs, rocking to and fro. His gaze was vacant and he did not seem to notice the newcomer. He was towheaded, handsome of face, but small and thin for his nine or ten years of age, unkempt despite everything his mother could do.

Brandek found her in the library, reading. A sunbeam like a flickery swordblade came in an ogive window and fell on time-browned pages; in that light, those shadows, the volumes shelved behind seemed to stir, and the sound of the wind was as if they sighed. Wrapped in a cloak against the chill, her slight form was hidden from him. He saw only a finely shaped face, large brown eyes, waist-length cataract of russet hair.

"Oh—" She peered nearsightedly before recognition came. Well, he thought, she'd scarcely seen him since he left her. "Brandek of Aeth! What do you wish?"

"To give you this," he said. The nearby table being piled high with tomes, he laid the meat down on the carpetless, stone-flagged floor. "I reckoned you could use it."

"Why—" She rose, stooped over and handled it, straightened and looked at him in wonder. "I know not how to thank you."

"No thanks needed, lady," he growled. "You saved my life, didn't you?" He paused, forcing himself, before he could add: "I hope I gave no offense. If I did, well, I was newly hauled from the sea and half out of my head from grief at lost shipmates and, and everything."

"Oh, no, you never did," she murmured.

"Then why—I mean, everybody else wanted to hear what I could tell of the South. You never came to listen. Why not?"

She winced. Her gaze dropped. "I . . . don't like crowds." He could barely hear her. "Llangru would have wanted to come along, and . . . too many of them have been cruel to him . . . because he is different. . . . I kept hoping you would visit us."

"I should have, but it seemed I was always busy, finding my way around, getting things set up for that hunt, and then off on it—Shalindra, I came as soon as I could, honestly." Brandek smote fist into palm. The noise cracked loud through the dusty stillness. "But you—they—they're so *ignorant*! They don't see what's under their noses. And chaos take it, this is a survival matter. I'll have to live here too, you know. And I admit I'm not a very patient man."

She smiled and touched his arm. "Well, you came. Now I can hear your story at leisure, as I'd wanted to. Sit down." She pointed to an elaborately carved chair opposite hers. "I'll brew us a pot of tea—No." She laughed, and the clarity of that sound challenged the gloom around them. "I've some wine left that my husband made. Noble stuff; I swear that whatever magic he used has not gone out of *it*. A guest from Imperial Aeth, who's brought such a magnificent gift, yes, surely this is worth a small bottle."

In addition, she fetched bread and cheese—not much, for she had little—and she and Brandek settled down to a lively conversation. They had heard something about each other from third parties, but this was their first chance to become really acquainted.

Brandek was shorter-spoken. "I was a younger son of a baron at home. It's barons and petty kings there; the Empire is just a memory. The climate is milder than here, but not notably, and worse every year. I saw things falling apart, the same as they've already done for you, and wondered what to do about it. Hunting—hunting was always a pleasure of mine, and I learned a lot from the wild tribes that've drifted into the Homptoleps Forest, these past hundred years. But I also thought we might try reviving coastwise shipping, get in contact with lost provinces, start trade again and—Well, I had a ship built and headed north, exploring. Without magic, she proved unseaworthy, for the wrights had small skill. She foundered in the storm, outside Tyreen Bay. I clung to a plank, and that's all I remember till I woke up in your care. Everybody else must have drowned." He grimaced. "No way for me to return, hey? North and east, the mountain passes are choked by the glaciers. South, the Barren is too wide; it's rich in wildlife close by, but I found that farther on it's still almost empty and a man would starve before he got across. So here I am."

Shalindra told her story at greater length, though there was actually less of it. Her husband, Zaerrui, had been the dean of the College, a wizard as learned and accomplished as the dwindling of *mana* in the world allowed. She was his tenth wife, for he was centuries old and had never been able, in this gaunt age, to cast a longevity spell on anyone else. Yet he and Shalindra were happy, and she was carrying their firstborn when suddenly the enchantment that kept him young guttered out and—She did not care to talk about that. Since, she had lived by the scant magic, ever less, that she commanded, and by trading off possessions for food, and by what work she could get as a scribe or clerk or the like; she was nearly the last literate person in Tyreen.

Mostly, talking with Brandek, she sounded him out about the South, as her fellow townsfolk had done. Did she press him too closely, or did he simply feel too deep a wound? He could not say. He only knew that at last he exclaimed: "The demons take that! Cities, books, riches, peace, leisure, yes, farms, metals—they're done! They're going the way the magic has gone, and you'll go too if you don't learn how to live in the world we've got."

She stiffened in her chair. "What do you mean?"

"You people! Fumbling around on your niggard acres, with your starveling livestock, when more and more big game is moving south ahead of the glaciers, elk, reindeer, boar, horse, aurochs, wisent, mammoth. . . . You're trying to patch up junkheaps like, like this building, when you could find out how to make shelters that're warm and weather-tight." His fist struck his knee. "I tried to give the old world new life, by my ship. The sea taught me better. Now I've got to teach all of you!"

Shocked, she whispered, "Do you mean we should give up our whole civilization—all the old ways—and become savages? No!" Pride straightened her back and squared her shoulders. "Quit if you wish, Brandek. I had expected more from a man of Aeth, but do as you will. I, though, I am a sorceress in my own right, the wife of the dean of the College—yes, *still* his wife—and mother of his son. No, I'll not betray that heritage. Nor will Llangru after me."

They glared at each other before changing the subject. He left as soon as decently possible, and their parting was cool.

Autumn was drawing to a close, and Shalindra dreaded the coming season. Rain-raw wind whined through the windows, and the College fountain brimmed with sodden leaves. Snowdrifts soon would smother Tyreen. Each year the frost fell earlier.

As always, when cold crept down the stone halls, Llangru sickened. Formerly Shalindra's medicines could soothe the rattle in his chest and cool his fever, but of late they availed little. Each winter's illness left him more weakened. Even in summer he coughed. If only, Shalindra thought, they could stay warm and dry . . .

Today he lay flushed, eyes bright, staring at something his mother could not see. He held out his arms, spread his fingers, and chanted, "Soaring, over glittery waves. Fish like silver needles. Winds cradle me. Tyreen lies tiny, far down. The boys romp in the street. I could stoop on them, but why bother? It's cool and blue here, the sun warms my wings, the fish below me dance for joy—"

Shalindra sponged his forehead. He often babbled thus, claiming to be a hawk, a fox, once a great shambling bear—Llangru, who had never walked the Barren or the forest. He had merely seen wild animals in books. Llangru spent his life cowering in the library, hidden from the jeers and taunts of normal children. The townsfolk knew him to be sincere in his claims, so they thought him mad. *Had Zaerrui lived, could he have helped his son?*

The boy needed fruit, fresh vegetables, milk—for perhaps the twentieth time that day, Shalindra opened her larder. The shelves gleamed bare. One hook, amid an empty dozen, held a shoulder of smoked elk: a gift from Brandek. Its gamy taste was strange to one used to fat beef cattle. Yet it was the sole meat Shalindra had, and she was grateful for whatever Brandek did to preserve it. Long ago, spoilage was no problem; a simple spell kept meat and produce fresh. But over time, magic had faded. She remembered going to her larder one morning to fix Zaerrui a festive breakfast; she had opened the door and gagged at corruption.

Now her problem was finding anything to eat. Brandek brought food, sometimes a silent leaving on the doorstep, but charity made a bitter meal.

Tyreen ate better, though; Brandek was teaching his hunting band new ways. Kiernon's son Destog, for instance, scorned to work in metal. He'd fashioned a spear and hunted for a living. The spearpoint was flint. Brandek's work, likewise. Knives made by Destog's father lay broken and rusted.

Again Shalindra examined the shelves. She might have overlooked something. The smoked meat, part of a cheese, a crust of bread—that was all. Most of her possessions she had bartered away. Last to go were the carved chair, her ivory boxes, the circlet that once bound her hair. Naught remained but the books. She would not part with those. Had she wished to, they were valueless. Tyreen no longer wanted even a writing of births, deaths, and marriages.

Shalindra raised her hands to her face. Her last gold bracelet slid down a thin arm. *No, I'll not trade that. Not Zaerrui's wedding gift.* It would buy food for a short time, but soon that, too, would be eaten. *So what's to do? I'm scarcely a sorceress any longer.*

Old Abba, for instance, was among her failures: Shalindra had helped her for years, until abruptly the potions no longer worked. The laundress had sickened and died in weeks. Her family thought Shalindra had willfully held back magic. *But there is no magic left. At least not in me.*

An idea struck her. She laughed, a choking sound, quickly stifled. She did not wish to rouse Llangru. Since Abba's death, Tyreen lacked a laundress. Well, Shalindra did know how to make soap, and washing was an honorable task, not like being someone's kept woman, or worse. The townsfolk might not need a scribe, but they did need clean clothes.

She dragged out the big copper tub and inspected it. Dents and spots worn thin were plentiful, but it should hold together for a while. She checked on Llangru a final time and set forth seeking work.

Shalindra knelt by the tub, scrubbing. Llangru, a book propped on his lap, read aloud. On demand he could fetch more hot water, but he was too clumsy for any real labor.

The shirt she washed was patched. How long since anyone had had strong new linen, cotton, wool? Hente the weaver sat idle. His sons had joined Brandek's band, and fed their parents.

Llangru read on: "To ensure fair weather for a festival, take clippings from the mane of a white unicorn, the oily tears of a merchild, and, in an amethyst flask, gather dragon's breath. On the night of the dark moon mix these together—"

Shalindra lifted the shirt. How long since unicorns pranced or merfolk swam, how long since the College's guardian dragons had last moved?

Gently, she wrung out soapy water. The shirt came apart in her hands. Rough hands, work-reddened; no longer the fingers Zaerrui had kissed.

Cloth garments were vanishing. Brandek and his hunters wore animal hides, harsh on the skin and clumsily sewn. She looked at the blue fabric of her gown. It hung soft against her body, draped in pleasing folds, but the hem was threadbare and the sleeves were patched.

She wiped a soapy arm across her eyes, lest Llangru see her tears.

Day at midwinter was brief and pale in this land, when clouds did not make twilight of it or snowstorms strike men with white blindness. Brandek could seldom go to sleep at nightfall or sit quietly in the house he had occupied. It was too cold and dark. He had been using odd moments to carve fat-burning lamps out of soapstone, but as yet he had only three. Hence he became a frequenter of the last tavern in Tyreen. The magical light-globes there were extinct too, but you needed no more than hearth-glow to drink by. Besides, he usually enjoyed the company; and if nothing else, it was well to be friendly, for some people resented his rapid rise to dominance.

One night was frozenly clear. A full moon cast long shadows from the east and made the snow sheen and glisten. Beneath it he saw the peaks of the Heewhirlas thrust whiter still above the horizon. Elsewhere, stars thronged heaven and the Silver Torrent cataracted in the same silence that made the scrunch of his boots on the snow seem loud. His breath went ghostly before him.

The cold slid fingers past his garments. Fur and leather were better than cloth, but none of the men who tried had yet perfected the art of preparing these materials, nor had any woman—in this case, Hente's daughter Risaya, anxious to impress the great hunter—grown skillful at making clothes from them. Well, that would come with experience, Brandek knew. He hefted the flint-headed spear he carried, and his free hand dropped to the obsidian knife at his hip. Several men, himself included, were already good at shaping stone.

So much to learn, discover, master—A sigh sent Brandek's breath flying. He often thought that the existence of *mana* had finally proven more a curse than a blessing. When it was exhausted through use, mankind knew very little else. Without it, the race would have developed techniques which depended only on the enduring aspects of the world. For instance, there must be a better way to light a dwelling than by a wick afloat in a bowl of grease; but no one was likely to hit upon any when countless different inventions were more urgently needed.

He saw the Green Merman ahead and lengthened his stride. The tavern was formerly the house of someone who could not pay magicians to help in the construction. Hence it abided, though much decayed in the timbers, amidst hillocks which had been more pretentious neighbors. Light seeped dim around the edges of warped door and shutters. Smoke billowed from a hole in the roof, where tiles had been removed when spells no longer kept weather balmy.

Wolves began to howl. They sounded like a large pack, and right outside the North Gate. Belike they were in quest of livestock; it was becoming impossible to keep herds or flocks safe from predators. More than once Brandek had raged at the owners, that they wasted time trying when the coastal plain and the mountains held abundant wild game.

Their sons usually agreed with him, and that had broken several families, and that had earned him added reproaches by Shalindra. Brandek flung the tavern door wide and stamped in. "Red wine, a mug of it!" he roared.

The air made his eyes and lungs sting. Just four men clustered at the single table, amidst unrestful thick shadows. Money was meaningless, and few could spare goods to swap for the diminishing store of drink. Brandek had ample credit from the pelts he brought out of the wilderness, and endeared himself to chosen fellow patrons by treating them.

Tonight they spoke no welcome but sat tense. Even muffled by walls, it was as if the sudden wolf-howls had pierced them. Terbritt the landlord must swallow before he could say, huskily, "I'm sorry. No more wine."

"What?" Brandek was astounded. "I've seen—"

"Yes, sir, two barrels were left. After that, no more wine, ever. And Jayath, the chirurgeon, you know, he and a lot of others came to tell me it should be kept for those who're in pain or need his knife. The Lord Mayor's taken charge of it."

Brandek uttered an oath, then curbed his temper. For the most part, city government had become a solemn farce. He, the outlander, had already gained more real power, merely by showing people how to survive and browbeating them into doing so. He had still less faith in the chirurgeon; fate deliver him from ever falling into those untrained hands!

However, many did trust Jayath, and the belief doubtless strengthened them. Therefore turning the wine over to him was a move toward solidarity, in this divided and demoralized community.

"All right," Brandek said. "Beer will do. It'd better."

Nobody chuckled. He settled down on a bench next to Gilm the carpenter, who mumbled, "Soon no more beer, either. Drink it while it's there." He had obviously been setting an example. With abrupt violence, he banged his goblet on the table. "I got credit. Gave Terbritt the two halves of a saw after it broke today. Next to last saw in my kit. Terbritt says he'll have Kiernon turn it into knives. No way to make a new saw, o' course. Who needs cabinets or cedar chests any longer, anyway? Houses? Why, the wood we can pull out o' the ruins is generally rotten, and the Northern forests are under the glacier, and no ships bring timber from the South." He hiccoughed. "My son began in my trade too, you remember. He'll not end in it. No call for carpenters. What'll he *do?*"

Brandek clapped the man's shoulder. "Let him learn hunting, or stone-chipping, or any of a host of crafts that really are needed. I'll be glad to teach him what I can."

"Teach him to be a . . . a savage!"

The wolf chorus, which had quieted, broke forth again. Wisnar, who farmed, traced a sign across his broad breast. His beard fell that far down; not many razors remained. (Brandek had acquired one and used it regularly, as a way of maintaining he was no enemy of civilization.) "What's that you do?" asked Lari, who had been a merchant and now lived by trading away what remained in his warehouses. Fear shrilled through his voice.

"I make the mark of my family," Wisnar told them, "hoping my fore-bears will guard me against yonder demons; for the gods died long ago."

The landlord stiffened where he stood tapping the beer. "Hold on," he exclaimed. "I'll not have another Alsken in this house."

Wisnar bridled, dread half lost in indignation. "I'm no such thing. You ought to know me better than that, all of you."

"An Alsken?" asked Brandek. "What do you mean?"

Anxious to smooth matters over, Terbritt said fast: "Alsken was a man of this town, a few years ago, who claimed he had found a stone so full of *mana* that he was now as mighty a sorcerer as . . . as Zaerrui was of old. Many believed him, and in their need showered him with gifts and did his every bidding. But then it was found he had nothing more, really, than sleight of hand and other such tricks. A mob tore him apart, and the building he was in as well. I'm sorry, Wisnar. I spoke too fast. You're no charlatan like that, I'm sure. I was only anxious lest the Green Merman suffer."

The farmer shook his head. "No, I'm no fraud, I make no claims for myself. I told you what I did—beseech, just beseech my forefathers to help me. It may well be that they're bones in their graves, as dead as magic itself. But—" He grimaced as if in pain. "But what harm in calling on them, when we who live are helpless against those demons out there?"

"Those?" Brandek protested. "They're only wolves."

"Only!" Wisnar yelled. "If you knew their cunning, if you knew the harm they've wrought me—If they aren't demons themselves, then they're possessed. And what shall stand between us and them?"

"But I'd not call on ghosts for help," Lari quavered. "Who knows what ghosts might want?"

A shudder ran around the table. Terbritt's hand slopped the beer he set down before Brandek. The wolves howled louder. From afar, a mammoth trumpeted. A groan arose, and two men covered their eyes.

Aged Fyrlei alone sat as still as the Southerner. Once he had been the town's interpreter for the last of the merfolk who came trading; he had been accustomed to the unhuman. Yet it could be seen that he thrust his quiet-ness upon himself, and what he said was: "The magic is gone. But muster your courage, lads, the courage to hope that Our Father of the Tusks will be merciful to us."

"Would he take an offering, do you think?" Lari asked.

Brandek's fist crashed on the board. "Let him offer to us!" he answered, deep in his throat. "A walking hoard of meat, bone, hide, ivory—You dread him simply because his kind has very lately come down from the North. What other cause is there? Stop quaking at every change that happens along, and use your common sense." He made a spitting noise. "If you have any."

"Too much has changed, too soon," Terbritt said, and slumped down onto the bench.

"Aye," Fyrlei murmured, "everything now is unknown. We're like sailors on a rudderless boat adrift in a fog. Nothing is left us but courage, and it must stand naked."

"Then don't weaken it by whimpering," Brandek snapped at them all.

His words did not lash them into a healthy anger as he wished. They sat huddled in their terror. Wisnar did retort, with dull resentment, "You're no help yourself, fellow. You throw you weight around like a legate of the Empire. But the Empire's dust on the wind, and what you really do is turn our children against us."

"I try to show them how Tyreen can best survive," Brandek said in a milder tone. He would not openly admit what he realized, that he was often too overbearing. Such was his nature, and the terrible plight of these people did not make him patient with fecklessness.

"Yes, like that boy in your hunting party who met his death last month," Wisnar answered.

"He saw something strange at the riverside, where we were," Brandek explained for the dozenth time. "He panicked, bolted off, went through thin ice, and drowned before we could reach him. The strange thing turned out to be no more than another beast new to these parts—a rhinoceros, we'd call it in Aeth, though this was woolly—a calf, at that, surely strayed from its mother." He did not remind them that a third of his band had refused to help kill the animal, and later nobody at home would touch the valuable carcass. They supposed a nameless evil force must be in it, and knew not how to cope.

He had requested aid of Shalindra. She could pretend to cast a spell and annul the curse. Appalled, she refused to debase the art which had been her husband's and her own. Let it lie honorably in its grave. Besides, who could tell what misfortune might indeed come of a thing which had already claimed one life? He had snarled and stamped off. Inwardly, almost reluctantly, he mourned that this had further widened the rift between them.

Fyrlei nodded his white head. "Aye, Brandek, you mean well and you do well," he said. "You show us ways of coping with the material world, ways we'd never have thought of by ourselves. However, you are no visionary. You spoke of common sense. How can that exist when *nothing* makes sense any more?"

The question pierced. The old man had wisdom of a sort. If the heart went altogether out of them, whatever skills they gained, the folk of Tyreen would not have long to live.

Brandek's hand closed on his crude wooden goblet, as though to splinter it. The wolves and the mammoth chanted through the night around him.

A warm spring breeze scurried into the courtyard, bearing a whiff of Brandek's latest project. He had discovered some new way to cure hides. In Shalindra's opinion, the stench was even more offensive than in the old method of scraping and drying.

Hente, the weaver, grieved at the advent of leather garments, but since weather-spells had failed, the flax crops were blighted. Wolves, driven south before the ice, harried the sheep and made wool unobtainable. Folk simply had no way to produce cloth. Hente's youngest son tanned skins for a living.

Shalindra poured hot water into the fountain and started a wash. Little enough work was left for her; each week more clothes fell to tatters.

The pleasant morning had tempted Llangru out of the compound. She let him go; she could not shelter him forever. Already he stood nearly as tall as his mother. In a few years he would shoot up into manhood.

What life will there be for him, then? Her son lacked the brute strength to face this world.

Soft-shod feet shuffled across cobbles. She turned and gasped. Llangru's face was a sheet of gore. His tunic flapped over skinned knees, and his knuckles were raw. Tears had traced dirty paths down his cheeks. Behind him loomed Brandek, dressed for the hunt.

Shalindra sprang forward. "What have you done to him?" she shrilled, though she knew the question was stupid. Brandek did not harm children.

"It's only a bloody nose," the Southerner said. "They always look dramatic. It's mostly stopped running. Wash your face, young man. You've scared your mother."

Llangru nodded gravely and stepped over to the fountain. It was full of laundry, so he cupped water in his palms. Last winter Shalindra's copper tub had holed through. No one knew how to patch it. The fountain, which was granite, endured. The dancing maiden's outstretched hand held a bowl of fat-and-ash soap.

Shalindra watched the worst of the blood rinse away. Brandek was right, the injuries were minor. She was ashamed of her outburst. "Come inside," she said, "and you both can tell me what happened."

Brandek sat on the floor, his back against a pile of books. Most of Shalindra's furniture was gone, broken or traded. He gulped herb tea from a fragile ceramic cup. Around its rim writhed red-and-golden dragons. Llangru and Shalindra drank from wooden mugs.

"I was walking out Searoad, by the market, when I heard shouting. There was Llangru in a knot of older boys—six of them, but he was putting up a good fight. I think Mintu led them, as usual. He's the one with the loud mouth. I should take that bully out hunting aurochs—if he brings a good supply of dry breeks!"

Llangru, who sat between his mother and Brandek, nodded. "It was Mintu. He didn't like what I said."

"I've told you not to get into arguments with those boys," Shalindra began, but Llangru cut her off.

"Mintu was telling lies. He said he'd gone hunting alone and killed an elk. It was too big to drag home, and a pack of wolves ate it. He killed most of them, too. He said he was every bit as good a hunter as Brandek, and knew how to chip sharper spearpoints. I couldn't let him go on bragging like that, so I told them I'd seen what really happened."

Shalindra frowned. Her son often had wild fancies.

He continued: "Mintu never killed any elk. He's scared to be out alone, and he made so much noise in the woods that even the weasels were laughing. He found an elk that had been dead since last fall. They don't even *have* antlers in the spring." He looked up at Brandek. "You know that; you told me."

The man nodded.

"It was by the river, upstream, mostly just bones. He'd borrowed his father's saw. He finally cut one antler loose, but he was too lazy to take the other, so he left it and came back with a made-up story. I saw it all."

"Llangru," Shalindra said, "how far upstream was this, did you say?"

"Most of a morning's walk, for Mintu. I flew."

"You flew." Shalindra's tone was flat.

"Of course. I was an eagle. I like that. You can see everything, and swoop down on rabbits, but I feel sorry for them, they squeal so. You can soar with the sun warm on your wings and the world tiny down below. The roof on the library is gray-green, and tiles are missing on the west wing, where the ceiling leaks. You can hardly *see* the dragon statues—" His eyes were brilliant.

Shalindra slapped him. Llangru's head rocked back; his nose dripped fresh crimson. Aghast, Shalindra looked at her blood-smeared palm. "I, I shouldn't have struck you, dear," she stammered. "But you shouldn't tell stories."

"That's what Mintu said, before they beat me." Llangru set down his mug and shuffled from the room.

Silence settled, broken only by fire-hiss and the boom of a wind turning raw. Brandek frowned but held his peace, while Shalindra stared into the depths of her mug. The wood was warped and cracking. He had told her hot liquids caused that, and added with a laugh that the tavern had no such problem. Well, he swilled enough of its beer—

Finally Brandek spoke. "The business was more serious than Llangru told you. Those boys were afraid. They were ready to tear him apart for being different. If I hadn't come along they might have killed him. I don't know what I think of his story, but they half believed it, Mintu most of all."

"Llangru has always been a strange one," Shalindra admitted. If she gazed straight ahead, into the fire, she could almost imagine that Zaerrui sat in his accustomed chair. But if she looked he would not be. And the chair was gone too, traded off last autumn. She gulped. "Maybe it's my fault. Llangru's father died before he was born." She bit her lip.

"Tell me," Brandek urged.

Shalindra was about to refuse, but words spilled forth: "It was a fine fall day eleven years ago. We were expecting a guest from Olanna, beyond the mountains. Zaerrui and the scholar wished to confer on why magic was fading, and whether anything might bring it back.

"We flew to meet the party at Icehold Pass. It was an easy journey, Zaerrui on his great black griffin, I on my winged unicorn.

"The air was crisp as apples. We raced, and arrived before our guests. As we landed, we could see them far off down the road. The scholar did not care to fly, so his group moved more slowly. While we waited, I told Zaerrui what I'd learned by divination that morning: I was carrying his son.

"He whooped for joy: *We'll name him Llangru!* He spun me a veil of sunbeams, and wove a crown of golden leaves. A simple magic, that. Only a small, simple magic." She swallowed. She dared not weep.

"Then it happened. Zaerrui clutched his chest. His hair bleached white, and his face wrinkled. He gasped one word: *Run.* I did not want to leave him; he hurled a lightning bolt, and my mount screamed and took flight. His own griffin stood like black stone. I looked back once to see the mountains slump and the glacier grind green ice across the pass; then my unicorn fluttered earthward like an autumn leaf, and died.

"When I reached Tyreen, my feet were bleeding, and I was half-starved. The town had fallen to rubble. Folk crouched amid wreckage. Snow howled early that year. When spring came, the pass did not open.

"I took shelter in the College library, and here I bore Llangru, Zaerrui's last son."

Silence, again. A gust through an empty window fluttered some sheets of paper that lay on the table, weighted down by a useless scrying stone. Shalindra had been practicing calligraphy, lest her work stiffen her fingers till she also lost that equally useless art.

"And was Llangru always—the way he is?" Brandek's question was soft.

"Yes," she said. "He talked at the normal age—nothing wrong with his mind—but he had trouble learning to feed himself and walk. I don't know the reason, or what went awry. It may be that the magic that wards babes has faded too."

"All magic is going, Shalindra, you know that. There was just so much in the world, and men used it up. We can only keep on, and in different ways. It won't be easy." Brandek leaned forward, almost touching her. "I have an idea I want to try this summer. Boats."

"You nearly died when your ship sank," the woman said, a trifle shocked. "Haven't you seen enough of the sea?"

"I dared too much. This time I'm minded to build small craft, not sailed but paddled, to venture no farther than the mouth of Tyreen Bay. We could do offshore fishing, and gather eggs on Geirfowl Island. Maybe, as our skill grows, we can advance to larger vessels and longer trips, begin re-opening coastwise trade routes—" He went on.

Shalindra merely half-listened, until he mentioned hides. She remembered the stench.

"I'm finding new ways of treating leather. We can already make it supple, for clothing, but now we can make it strong and waterproof as well. I can cover a wooden frame, lashed together, with skins smeared in grease. Given careful stitching, that should produce a reliable hull."

It was if Shalindra heard the drip, drip, drip from the west wing in every downpour. "Hides can keep water out?"

"Yes," said Brandek, "if first you cure them in—"

Excitement flared through her. "But that means I can save the books! The damp is killing them! Look at that stack, I've been trying to dry them by the fire. The rain comes in through holes in the roof that nobody can repair. A watertight shelter—"

Brandek reached back and took a volume. The cover was black with mildew. He opened it; moisture had freckled the pages. "Longevity spells," he grunted, and shook his head. "Those haven't worked for years—generations, most places. What's the use?" He set the book on the floor.

Shalindra rose. Staggering under the weight, she returned it to the stack. "If you misfile an item in a library this size—" she gestured at shelves stretching endless down the gloom of halls beyond this chamber—"you have lost it."

Brandek shrugged. "And what if you have? I'm educated, like you, and you've taught your boy, but how many others in Tyreen care a belch about writing? You've told me how you couldn't find recent employment as a scribe. People are cold, hungry, and afraid. Better they learn to hunt, make tools, build shelters, not read crumbling books of worthless wizard-lore."

"Worthless wizard-lore!" The words stung Shalindra like a slap. "Barbarian! Would you make all men illiterate? Have them trust naught but half-remembered tales?"

Brandek flushed, gnawed his lip, and finally replied: "Haven't we squabbled about this often enough? Books were good to have once. Today . . . they might serve to start fires." He shook his head. "No, I can't spare you any hides for their shelter. We'll need all we can get, and then some, to make those coracles." His curbed anger broke loose and he almost shouted, "Or would you rather keep reading until everybody starves to death in this ice-trap that's got us?"

"Well I know," Shalindra said, word by word, "that the ice has us trapped. My Zaerrui's bones lie beneath it. Would that they were yours instead."

She turned her back. Brandek sprang up. She heard something crunch, and turned again. In his haste he had kicked his cup across the floor and it shattered, the fragile ancient cup for guests. She saw a dragon's eye gleam gold on one fragment, as if to cast a look of despair upon the world.

She held her tone steady. "So you've smashed that too, as you'd smash everything else that was ours. You'll never rest, will you, till you've ground the last spark of civilization under your heel and we're all filthy, stinking savages, hunkered in caves with blood on our hands. Tell me, Brandek, shall we still cook our meat then, or do you want us to forget about fire also?"

"You seemed well pleased to eat the meat I left here, while you huddled among your precious books," he growled, and snatched a volume from the nearest shelf. "A *Dictionary of the Mer-Tongue.* How fine! What a shame the merfolk are gone!" He chose another at random. "*Raising the Dead.* Yes, I can see how you'd like that, Shalindra. You're more at home with the dead than the living, no?" He dropped both tomes. The spines broke. Loose pages swirled across the room. "Meanwhile you take in laundry from the village. That's the best your sorcery can do for you, and you refuse to learn anything new." He drew an uneven breath. "Teeth of doom, woman, it's magic that is dead. Give it a decent burial and come alive again yourself!"

Shalindra knelt, gathering scattered paper. Her hands shook. Brandek was right, in his way: her powers were gone. How many more years could she do heavy labor? Tears blurred her vision, and she turned away.

There, in the corner, gleamed something white and slender. She remembered, suddenly, what it was. She surged to her feet and strode across the room.

The sea-unicorn's horn was long, heavier than it looked. She laid hold of the spiral-curved lance. "Get out," she said. "Get out. Take this with you. It was the price of your life. I made a poor bargain. This, at least, once held *mana.*" She proffered it, point first. *He thinks I'll stab him.* She stifled a laugh.

His eyes narrowed; he touched the hilt of his knife, then let his hands fall, and backed away. He fumbled at the latch; the door creaked open. He gathered his spear, throwing-stick, and ax. In his furs, he looked like a savage. He began to say something. Shalindra threw the horn after him. It shattered on the cobbles beyond. "Take it, you barbarian," she screamed, "and begone!"

Llangru pushed past her. "Brandek, don't leave," the boy pleaded. Shalindra leaned against the wall, put an arm across her eyes, and wept.

She heard Llangru stumble after Brandek, calling. The man soon outdistanced him. Llangru called once more, gave up, and started back. Afar, a mammoth trumpeted, harbinger of the oncoming ice.

Cren, son of Wisnar, and Destog, son of Kiernon, waited as agreed outside the Great Gate. It was no longer much more than a hill of tumbled blocks, from which a sculptured head, noseless, stared blindly eastward. The youths were about the same age, probably twenty winters. Though Cren was blond and Destog dark, somehow they looked alike as they stood there. Perhaps it was their outfits, garb of fur-trimmed leather, spear in hand, throwing stick and knife tucked into belt, two extra spears and a sleeping bag and packet of dried meat secured by thongs across the back. Or perhaps it was their build. Undernourished in childhood, they shared a leanness which long tours on the hunt, after Brandek came, were turning rangy. In their eyes, too, was a feral quality Tyreen had never known before.

"What kept you sir?" Cren asked.

"A spot of trouble. Never mind about that," Brandek snapped. Inwardly he recognized that it had been well to rescue Llangru, but wrong to dawdle with Shalindra when his followers expected him. Why had he done it? Did some remnant of witchcraft still cling to her? "Let's be off. The morning's already old."

"Where are we bound this time?" Destog inquired eagerly.

Brandek's plan had been to go after horse. A herd had been spied yesterday, north of here. A large party would alarm the beasts too early, but a few men, sound of wind and limb, could get sufficiently close that, when the creatures did bolt, they could run one down, driving it between them as wolves do. Lately he had been experimenting with a noose on a long cord, to cast around the neck of an animal, but this was a skill which would take a while to develop.

Now he looked east, away from the town, across miles whose emptiness was scarcely broken by a few tumbledown, abandoned farm buildings, until the snowpeaks of the Heewhirlas caught his glance. "Yonder," he said, with a gesture. Bear had become plentiful in the uplands. Newly roused from winter sleep, such a brute would be gaunt and savage, but nonetheless a prize. And he *needed* a fight.

The others were astonished. "Spring is a dangerous season in the mountains," Cren blurted. "Avalanches—"

Brandek fashioned a sneer. "Stay behind if you're afraid."

"I'm not!" Yet Cren added hesitantly, "It's just that you're always telling us yourself, sir, the chase is risky enough without taking chances we don't have to."

"But you mean we've got to discover how to get along in any kind of conditions, don't you, sir?" Destog's earnest question sealed the matter. Brandek felt he could hardly change his mind after it, though beneath the seething, a part of him regretted his impulse. Leading people starved for certitudes, he must always pretend to a kind of *mana* of his own.

He nodded and set forth at a steady lope. His disciples came behind. They could maintain the pace, with brief pauses, till evening, when it would have brought them well into the chaotic lands below the heights.

They could not spare breath for talk, however, and Brandek found himself locked up with his thoughts.

All his spears were tied to his shoulders. He gripped the ax he bore until knuckles stood white. It was another experiment of his, a flint blade set through a haft. After numerous failures, he dared hope that the lashings of shrunken rawhide would keep stone wedded to wood; but only heavy use would show if he had really found his way to making a trustworthy tool.

Wedded—He might as well go ahead and marry Hente's daughter Risaya. She wasn't bad-looking, and she had acquired the necessary new skills faster than most. Of course, Kiernon's youngest had a fullness about her suggesting she'd be a lively bedmate, as well as bearing him strong children. . . . They were chaste and monogamous in Tyreen, but he was the most desirable husband material they knew; and he must have offspring— daughters to bind him in family alliances, sons to aid him and in the end, if he lived to be old, care for him; and his loins often burned.

Curse Shalindra, anyhow! Too long had he buzzed about that slim body, that deep mind—no, that skinny, nearsighted, daydreaming jackdaw. Most of her childbearing years were behind her, too; she was doubtless good for three or four yet, but could expect to lose at least one in infancy. . . . Why should he care? She and her books and her useless brat—He was being unfair. Llangru couldn't help his own helplessness and bore it with a certain gallantry. But why had she and Brandek gone on, month after month, when nearly every meeting ended in a fight?

Well, whatever he owed her, he had paid back a hundredfold; and today she herself had screamed that there never was any debt, and had flung the token of it at his feet.

Must she take so hard the breaking of a cup? How like her. Oh, yes, Brandek thought, it had been a pretty object and he was sorry. He even wished he could offer her a replacement, however crude; but his attempts to make vessels of fired clay, during the winter, had come to naught. That was evidently an art whose development would take more time than anyone could spare, these days, from creating the means of stark survival.

His bootsoles whispered on stone. At the Great Gate, Searoad became Aiphive Way and ran across the coastal plain, over Icehold Pass, to the rich province beyond . . . formerly. Without magical maintenance, rains washed out the shallow bed, thin paving blocks slid apart and roots of grass cracked them to bits, the thoroughfare was already a mere trace and in a century or two would be erased. For that matter, the pass had been choked on the day when Shalindra was widowed.

Brandek glanced about him. To right and left he glimpsed stumps. Orchards had been cut down for firewood after frost killed them. Everywhere else, the grass of springtime billowed, pale green, beneath a wind that came sliding chill off the ocean. The air was full of water and earthy odors. Clouds scudded white; their shadows scythed across the land. Birds clamored aloft in huge flocks. Brandek wondered if he could find a means to cast a dart that high. Ahead, the range shouldered above the horizon, blue-gray where it was not whitened. He made out that tower-like peak men called the Bridegroom. A scowl seized his brow. He turned off the dying road, toward a different height, around which ice crystals flurried and glittered, the one they called Ripsnarl.

At eventide, the party made camp below that mountain. Although they were well into the chaotic land by then, they heard wolves howl after sunset, and later a deep-throated roar.

Once the Heewhirlas had lifted sheer from the coastal plain. Legend said that a god had fashioned them thus, to create a dramatic pattern. But gods died and magic faded, and at last no force remained to uphold those forms. When they slumped, great chunks of them came crashing down to make a jumble below the remaining steeps. This wreckage provided some grazing for chamois, and ample dens for bear and cave lion. These sought most of their food in the outer parts, strewn across miles. There boulders the size of houses, or whole walls of them, gave weather-shelter to plant life that in turn nourished animals.

A night in such a coppice had not calmed Brandek. He had slept ill in his bag, quarreling with Shalindra in his very dreams. At dawn, he was brusque with his companions.

"We'll spend the day separately, in search of spoor," he told them. "We'll meet here before dark, exchange information, and lay our plans. Don't forget for a moment how easy it is to lose your way hereabouts. Keep taking bearings on peaks and sun, but don't trust them much; rain or fog or whatever can blot them out of your sight. So memorize landmarks as you go, and make marks where you can. If you do get lost, don't panic. Settle down, wait till you see the sky again, and work your way toward the west. You'll come out in the open eventually, and be able to locate this camp." He paused. "If not, we're better off without you."

They reddened at his unwonted condescension. Usually he had been genial and sympathetic, in his bluff fashion. "Yes, sir," Cren said, while Destog's features showed hurt. The young men took up their loose spears and went in different directions.

Brandek lingered for a bit. Oaths muttered from him. Half were aimed at himself. He was being a fool, he knew. What sense in taking out on those lads his fury at Shalindra? And what did it matter in the first place what she said or did? She and her weird boy—yes, that was why the children persecuted Llangru. A strangeness possessed him, and in a world from which the comforting, controlling, explaining *mana* had departed, strangeness was a terror, therefore an object of hatred. Those two were ghosts and did not know it. Then let her stop haunting him!

He spat and struck off on his own.

Scrub birch, nestled on the side of a granite windrow, fell behind. He wound and climbed among masses between whose somberness the shadows and the cold lay heavy. Mists drifted in streamers under a sky that was wan and splashed with cirrus clouds. The colors of lichen, clumps of grass, patches of moss fairly shouted, so rare were they. Now and then somewhere, a raven croaked. Mechanically, Brandek recorded his location in his mind; but otherwise he wandered almost at random, scamping his search for signs of big game.

If only Shalindra—he thought. If only Shalindra— She was no weakling. He had to concede her that much. Look how she struggled to maintain herself. And she was bright, she could learn what she needed to learn. Doubtless she would never be the best cook or denkeeper that a huntsman might have; but she could, for instance, turn her gift for things like calligraphy toward the making of decorated garments for which neighbors would trade what they themselves brought forth, including help with everyday tasks. . . . Brandek's ax clove air. Forget her!

Seeking to do that, he harked back to Aeth, his city that he would never see again. He called forth palaces, parks, porticos, kinfolk, friends, populace—and found surprisingly little homesickness in his heart. The city was a crumbling shell; most of what few people remained grubbed the earth beyond its walls and had no hope; the few who kept a little wealth were as obsessed with the past as *she* was, if not more. It was his impatience with their sort, as much as anything else, which had driven him to make his expedition and thus at last to Tyreen. Here the future lay, here most were winning to a readiness to grapple with the world as it was, and he liked them for that. Why must she hold out, and why must he care?

A sunbeam struck between clouds to dazzle him. Suddenly he noticed that he had been scrambling for hours and was hungry. Yet that was not what halted him. It was something that, in the brightness, leaped forth at his attention.

Huntsman's habit made him look around before he examined the sight more closely. He was halfway up a long slope on the lower flank of Ripsnarl. Grass and wildflowers grew in patches between scattered boulders. Well below him was a mossy hollow in among such rocks, intensely green against their gray. Ahead, the stone wilderness reared sharply toward a bank of talus beneath darkling palisades; above those, wind-whirled crystals of dry snow, wherein rainbow fragments danced, hid the spike of the mountain. He heard the air yowling up there.

What stood immediately before him was a mass twice the size of any other in view, the bulk of a large house. The side that loomed over him as he confronted it was nearly flat. Had some natural force cloven the stone, long ago, or some magic? Certainly magic had been at work here, for a symbol had been chiseled into this face. Its boundary was a circle, a fathom across. Otherwise it was so eroded that he could only see it was of labyrinthine complexity.

Did it, though, bear kinship to signs he had encountered on cliffs in the South? Brandek bent close in wonderment. His forefinger tried to trace faint lines and curves. A shiver went through him as he identified a *vai*, that letter of the hieratic alphabet which was never used in writing. The memory of how potent it had been in gramarie was still too sharp.

The raven flapped overhead. Somehow, abruptly, that winged blackness reminded Brandek of Llangru and the boy's claims about faring forth in animal guise. It didn't seem like childish fabulation. Llangru was too desperately serious about it. He didn't even act like a child trying to deny that his father was dead, trying in a way to *be* that father and wield forces which themselves were forever vanished.

But if he wasn't daydreaming or play-acting, what then? Brandek's lips tightened. He had seen more than one person driven by despair to seek refuge in delusion. And those had been able-bodied adults. Llangru, frail and unripe soul in a body that from birth had been encumbered—Was Llangru simply insane?

Poor Shalindra. . . . Impulse outraced thought. Brandek retraced the sign while he spoke its name, "*Vai*," which means "I guard."

Earth rumbled and grated. Through his bootsoles and into his bones, he felt shock waves hit. The great stone shuddered. Lesser boulders toppled or rolled. In a tidal roar, the scree poured downward.

Brandek spun on his heel and bounded ahead of the slide. If those shards caught him, they would cut him into flitches. It flashed across his mind—a wisp of power to hold mountains in place had remained in yonder emblem. He drained it off when he uttered the formula. Ripsnarl slumped further.

A hammerblow cast him into night.

As he returned to day, he was not aware of pain. Instead, he was dazedly surprised by the silence. So vast was it, after the noise before, that he lay in it as if in ocean depths, as if he had become a merman. The wind around the peak sounded fugitively faint. His heartbeat was no louder.

He tried to raise himself. Then the agony smote. Darkness blew ragged across his vision. He heard his voice scream.

After a while he grew capable of careful small movements, and thus of learning what had happened to him. His right shin lay across a track plowed by the round rock which had overtaken him and come to rest several yards off. Though his mind was still clumsy and anguish dragged at every thought, he decided that it had knocked him down and passed over his leg. Soil had cushioned him somewhat, little blood seemed to have been lost, but he saw the slight bend under his knee. That, as well as what he felt, told him the shinbone was broken.

His right arm wouldn't obey him, either. Every attempt at motion sent lightnings through him. The upper bone was likewise fractured. He guessed he had fallen with arms flung out and landed on that one in just the wrong way, the force of the boulder behind him.

The rest of his body throbbed within his garments. He must have bruises from head to foot and be missing a good bit of skin, but there didn't seem to be anything worse the matter. Not that that would make much difference. He had barely escaped the talus. Pieces lay around him, and the main mass now began mere feet away. Higher aloft, half buried, the runic stone looked strangely forlorn.

Brandek almost wished the slide had caught him. He'd be free of this torture—No!

He began to curse. He cursed the mountain up the west side and down the east, roots and crown and the stupid god who erected it, for minutes, with the riches of oath and obscenity that a sailor commanded. It cleared his head and brought back a measure of strength. When he was done, he was ready to fight.

To remain here was sure death; Cren and Destog would never find him in time. The odds were overwhelming that they never would at all, nor any search party they might fetch. But at least if he had water he would live longer and thus have a tiny chance. Moss in the hollow that he had noticed betokened moisture. A frightful distance to go, in his present state: but the only way for him.

He rolled to his left side, overbalanced, and fell prone on grit and flinders. Pain seethed; icy sweat spurted forth, runneled inside his clothes and reeked in his nostrils. He mastered himself. The spears and pack of rations on his back had toppled him. With his usable hand and his teeth, he loosened their thongs. The ax he must leave behind, but he would not be without food and some means of doing battle.

With one arm and one leg, dragging his gear, he crawled.

Often in the hours that followed, the pain wore him down. He must lie half conscious, shivering, until at last he could hitch himself onward. The sun descended; the horizon flamed above far Tyreen; stars blinked forth overhead; his breath smoked in deepening cold, and he saw frost form on the stones over which he crept.

When he reached his goal, it was past midnight and he knew he could travel no more. The moss was soft and dank under his belly. A rivulet trickled through it. He sucked up water for a very long time before his body stopped feeling withered and merely hurt. By now he was almost used to hurting. It should not keep him from the rest that was his next necessity. Of course, he thought in a distant part of his mind, water like this must draw animals. Maybe big flesh-eaters were among them. Somehow he got to the largest of the boulders which loomed murkily around, that he might have his back against it. He arranged his weapons ready to his left hand, and toppled into unawareness.

That night Llangru cried Brandek's name in his sleep, but when Shalindra went to comfort him he turned toward the wall. He was silent and listless all the following day. By sunset he lay feverish, making small-animal sounds. Shalindra poured him a decoction of willowbark—that potion, at least, still worked—but he gagged on the bitterness.

"Brandek . . . broken . . . freezing . . ." Again and again, the same words. Shalindra struggled with her pride, conquered it, and sent for Brandek, merely to learn that he'd gone hunting the day before yesterday. *Right after we quarreled.* When he returned—let it be soon!—she would ask him to see Llangru. He would come for the boy's sake, no matter how angry he was with her. He was gruff but kind. His gifts had fed them through the winter and he had never sought anything in return, despite her being a woman and alone.

Her cheeks burned. Why even think of that? Brandek could have any of a dozen girls, young, sturdy helpmeets and childbearers. Doubtless he had made his choice, and would soon wed. No matter for her concern. They could not talk together without flying at each other.

After he came back she would strive to be pleasant for Llangru's sake. Against a sudden dread: of course he would come back. The sea itself had not slain him. He was a veteran hunter.

That evening Destog brought word to his father, Kiernon the smith. He and Cren had drawn lots, and the latter stayed behind to search, though they held scant hope. They'd seen no smoke, and, in yonder trackless country full of half-mythic beasts. . . .

Shalindra was on her way home from the Lord Mayor's palace. She'd sought wine for Llangru, and had been told that Tyreen's precious and dwindling store was not to be wasted on a useless witling. Beyond the door of the Green Merman she heard voices mutter, and Brandek's name was mentioned. She entered and saw Destog; were they back from the hunt already?

". . . get a large party to search for him," Destog was saying. "Surprising he'd come to grief, but, well I had the notion his mind was mostly elsewhere."

"What will we *do?*" That was Kiernon's basso. He spread work-roughened hands.

Shalindra had to know. She drew her cloak about her and stepped full into the ill-lit room. Soapstone lamps, newly made, guttered on shelves and the table. Brandek's design. Their smoke, combined with man-sweat and stale beer, stung her eyes. The men hushed their talk. Many more than usual were present; they must have gathered to discuss appalling news. Benches scraped as some of the older ones rose. The youngsters eyed her with indifference.

"I overheard—" she said into the abrupt silence, "someone is missing? Brandek?"

"Aye, lady," Gilm slurred. He was far-gone in drink. "Destog, here, brought word. Away in the chaos country, they were, and him beyond finding in that jumble, I'm thinking."

Shalindra turned pale. Her knees buckled and she slid to the floor.

Gilm lurched forward, slopping his beer. "Catch her, quick! Eh, there, what ails ye, lady?" He rose and shook his head. "She's fainted. We'd best get her home. Funny thing, her takin' on like that, she and Brandek was never friends."

Again it was night and the stars mercilessly brilliant. Among them the Silver Torrent glimmered along a frozen course, and sometimes a meteor darted. Though the moon had not yet risen, light was enough to show hoarfrost pale on rocks and moss, and the rivulet agleam. Its tiny tinkle was the only sound Brandek could hear, save for the breath that rattled through his lungs. By dawn the water would be ice.

He drew his good knee under his chin and hugged his good arm around it, trying to hold a trifle of warmth. If he just had his sleeping bag, he could crawl into that. But it was back in camp. Cold had soon wakened him last night. During the day he had gotten some rest. Now came the long watch until morning. It might be as well this way—lions, wolves, and their ilk did most of their work after sunset—but it deepened the weariness in him, hour by hour.

He had no means of kindling fire, and the fire in his body smoldered low. Pain was lessened a little. Partly that was because he had splinted the broken leg, lashing it to a spearshaft grounded in his boot, and kept the broken arm inside his coat with the hand under his belt. However, he recognized that whatever slight relief he felt was also due to the numbness of fatigue.

How long had he to live? Water was here in plenty, and food sufficient; you didn't leave rations unguarded for animals to find, but packed them along. He had scant appetite, must indeed force himself to fuel his flesh against chill. Yes, he thought, starvation would not move in on him as fast as exposure and exhaustion.

He downright wished that a beast of prey would arrive first. He meant to go out fighting, no matter how feebly, and to thrust a spear down the gullet of a bear was better than to sit trying to defy these nights, like Shalindra defying the future.

Better? Easier? She had never borne a weapon, but she had overcome more than he could imagine, by enduring it. How far away, how dreamlike she seemed.

—He started out of a drowse. What? The sound repeated. *Hoo-oo* . . . an owl. His bad side protested as he turned his head in search.

The owl had landed on a tall rock not far off. It was one of the great white ones that were moving south ahead of the glaciers. Starlight filled its eyes and made it doubly spectral. *Hoo-oo*, it said again. In a dull fashion, he wondered why. The tone was softer than he had ever heard before from its kind, almost caressing.

Bitterness surged in him. "Oh, yes," he said aloud, "you're welcome to pick my bones, but not till I'm done with them." He fumbled about, closed fingers on a stone, and threw it left-handed. He missed, of course. Yet it should have frightened the owl off. It didn't. The bird simply cocked its head and continued to stare at the man.

A shudder which was not from cold passed through him. He had found to his woe that a ghost of magic lingered in this desolation. It was gone, but was there more?

The owl spread wings. For a moment it held quiet thus, like a talisman of snow. Then it lifted. In three silent circles, it swung over Brandek's head before departing westward.

* * *

Gilm and Kiernon bore Shanlindra to the library and sent Risaya, Hente's daughter, to care for her and her ailing son. The tall young woman sat by the fire and stitched skins, her movements deft.

Garments for Brandek? Shalindra wondered, and began shaking anew, despite her warm wrap. Finally she spoke. "How—how is Llangru?"

"Much the same," Risaya said. "He was sleeping when— Oh, here he comes!"

Wraithlike, the boy padded into the main room. His nightshirt hung loose, and his face seemed all huge blue eyes, with the strange gray ring around the iris. He held out his palms to the hearth. "Brandek has no fire," he said. "He shivers at night."

Risaya dropped her sewing. "What did you say, boy? How can you know anything about Brandek?" Her tone was shrill. She gulped and gathered back her work.

"Surely you dreamed it," Shalindra said. "You've been feverish." But Llangru had fallen ill before word of Brandek came. He had not left the library. How could he know?

Llangru shook his head. "You always say I dream things, Mother, or scold me for making them up. But I was there. I just got back. I *know*."

"We've all heard your wild stories," Risaya jeered. "No one believes them. You should be ashamed. What would Brandek say?"

"Brandek never laughs at me. I saw, and I *know*." With an attempt at dignity, the boy stumbled from the room.

He scurried down dark streets to the Green Merman. Inside, men still huddled and talked. "We've got to go out tomorrow and search," Destog argued. "We can't quit until we're sure."

"Ah, he's dead already," Hente mumbled, "as will we all be soon. Probably lose half our party in the jumbled lands. It's not worth it, just to bring home a corpse."

Llangru shivered. Most of these persons thought him half-witted, and their children taunted him, but he had a duty. He stepped forward into the lamplight. The greasy beer-soaked table reached to his breast.

Laughter greeted him. "A bit young for taverns, aren't you, boy?" Terbritt japed. And from Gilm: "Is your mother all right? Do she and Risaya know you're out?"

Llangru took a deep breath. Now, more than ever, he must not stammer. "I-it's Bran-Bran-Brandek. He-he's alive. I know where he is."

Mirth barked around the table. "I, I, I do so. *I saw him.*" He gulped. "He's on the west face of Ripsnarl, near the bottom. There was an avalanche. You couldn't find him 'mongst all those rocks, but I found him from above, and on my way back I noticed how to get there on foot. I can guide you."

Laughter tried to start afresh, but sputtered into silence. They stared. A couple of them drew signs in the air. After many heartbeats, Destog rose from his bench and whispered, "How did you do that?"

"I went. I flew." Llangru struggled against tears. "He's hurt, Brandek is, his leg and his arm both. He's freezing, and I saw lions not far off, hunting, only there wasn't any game nearby, so they'll be hungry and look farther tomorrow—" The tears burst forth, but on a tide of rage. Llangru clenched his fists and stamped. "And you sit here!" he screamed. "He taught you how to hunt, and make weapons, and keep food, and, and everything . . . and the first time *he* needs help, you just sit here!"

Kiernon the smith chewed his lip and stared at the table. Hente muttered, "The boy's crazy," and Lari whispered, "Magic is gone."

Then Fyrlei said, most quietly, "It has seemed thus. But now I wonder if a little remains after all."

Llangru swayed back and forth. "Ay-ah, ay-ah," he chanted, "it's cold and dark, the man lies by the water, hurt, he cannot run, and lions prowl. I found him, he did not know me and threw a stone at me, but I came back to take you to him. Ahh—Hoo-oo, hoo-oo." His fingers crooked like talons. In the flickery gloom, his eyes seemed to glow golden.

Destog took a step forward and reached out a hand. The boy shrank back. "NO!" he coughed, in a voice not altogether human.

Most of the company sat stiff, or leaned away as far as they could without rising and perhaps drawing that eerie gaze. Fyrlei kept moveless, save for the lips within his white beard that said, "Here is either madness indeed, or something new and powerful. If it is simply madness, what do you risk by heeding?"

A flame leaped in Destog. "Yes!" the youth shouted. "Llangru, the *men* of Tyreen will follow us."

Kiernon rose massive to his feet and said, "Count me among them when we're ready, son. That won't be till dawn, I suppose, and most won't be in shape to travel as fast as you. But we ought to reach Brandek by tomorrow's eventide, if this—" his tone stumbled—"this child really is a seer." He forced a smile. "Meantime, suppose I try persuading his mother to let him go along."

The sun went down once more. A single crimson streak marked the place, beneath the purity of a westering planet. In that direction the sky was green; eastward it darkened to violet and the earliest stars trod forth. There Ripsnarl peak stood windless under its snows. This would be another clear upland night, cold, cold.

Brandek woke when the lion roared nearby. He was barely half aware of that noise or what it meant. His skull seemed hollowed out, he could no longer sense a heartbeat, and pain was like the rocks everywhere around, eternal but apart from him.

Yet when the beast surmounted a ridge of debris and poised on top, he felt a certain comfort. Here came his last battle, and then peace. She was a lioness, her tawny flanks vague in the dusk but eyes luminous in the forward-thrusting head. He did see her tail switch, and heard the rumble from her throat.

Brandek reached for a spear. Sitting, he braced its butt against the boulder on which he leaned. If he was lucky, he might catch her charge on the sharp-flaked point. Doubtless that would not kill her, but she'd know she'd been in a fight.

A second and a third lioness appeared on either side of the first. A new roar echoed among the stones; their male waited behind them. Brandek sighed. "Very well," he said. "This'll be quick, anyhow."

Something stirred at the edge of vision. He glanced aloft and saw an arctic owl. Was it the same as last night's? It acted as strangely, wheeling about and winging off at an unnatural speed.

The first lioness finished studying him and flowed down the rubble-heap. Her comrades followed. When they reached the moss, they moved to right and left. Brandek grinned. "Don't worry," he croaked. "I'm not about to make a break for it."

The lead lioness gathered herself for the final dash.

"*Yaaah!*" cried from above. Brandek saw a hand ax—his own design—fly through the air, end over end. It struck her in the ribs. That was a heavy piece of flint, with keen edges. He heard the thunk. Blood ran forth, black in this dimness. She growled and crouched back. Her companions went stiff.

Brandek twisted his head around and saw men spring from between the boulders, into the hollow. They brandished spears, axes, knives, torches, they threw stones, they formed a wall in front of him. More by voice than sight, he recognized Cren, Destog, Kiernon, Wisnar—He fell into an abyss.

—When he came to himself, he was lying among them. They squatted, stood, danced, babbled their joy or bellowed their triumph. Few more stars were in sight; he had not been unconscious for long. The lions must be gone. Of course they would be, he thought. Animals are too sensible for bravado. They're off after easier game, to nourish themselves and their young.

Brandek's head was on Destog's lap. The youth stroked his hair with anxious gentleness. "Are you well, sir?" he breathed.

If Brandek had had the strength, his laughter would have made the mountain ring. He did achieve a chuckle. "I haven't caught the sniffles," he replied in a whisper. Wonder smote. "How did you find me . . . and this many of you?"

Awe possessed the dimly seen face above him. "Llangru."

As if that had been a signal, the boy came into sight. Men stepped aside to make a way for him. "He guided us." Kiernon's words were an under-groundish mumble. "We took turns carrying him on our shoulders, till . . . near the end, suddenly he swooned. When he woke after a while, he said we must hurry, because you were in great danger. So we did—"

The son of Shalindra knelt down at Brandek's side, smiled shyly into his eyes, and murmured, "I'm glad. You were always good to us."

Rain turned the world dull silver. It brawled over the roofs of Tyreen and gurgled between walls. The Madwoman River ran swollen, and from afar one heard the sea shout. The air was raw. Yet as she passed a hillock which had been a house, Shalindra saw that a tree which grew from it had broken into full blossom.

The door of Brandek's dwelling was never barred, for he had nothing to fear from his tribe. Besides, she came in daily to care for his needs. Nobody disputed the right of Llangru's mother to do that.

Entering, discarding her leather cloak, she must grope through weak lamplight till her pupils widened and she saw him, wrapped in furs, sitting up in bed. Restless, awkward, his left hand used a piece of charcoal to sketch plans for a weir upon a scrap of hide. "How are you?" she asked.

"Pretty well," he said. "I hobbled around some more on a pair of sticks this morning, and it didn't hurt. I can do a few things with my arm, also. Let me show you." He raised it in its splints. "Oh, yes, I'll soon be as good as new, and more annoying." His gaze sought hers. "Thanks to you," he added, not for the first time.

She winced at the memory. When he, brought back home, refused the attentions of Jayath the chirurgeon, she had gone to her books. There she found anatomical drawings. Holding those before her, she directed the sinewy hands of Kiernon as the smith properly set the broken bones. Brandek had declined wine, saying it ought to be saved for worse cases. He had not screamed. He had not even fainted. But he had lain mute and white throughout the following day.

Afterward, though—She busied herself setting forth wooden bowls and filling them with the fish she had cooked in leaves and clay and brought here in a skin. It was lucky, she thought, that in the murk he could not see how she flushed. "Everybody will rejoice to hear that," she said. "They need you."

Brandek stirred uneasily. "I hope they don't think they can't get along without me. Someday—tomorrow or fifty years hence, no matter which— they must. They've got to learn the tricks of staying alive in the world as it's become." He plucked at the wisent robe across his lap. "So much to do," he grumbled, "and I must lie in this stinking hovel. Caves, or shelters under overhanging cliffs, or tents, or . . . or nearly anything . . . would be more comfortable, and we'd get fewer people falling sick. Yes, I think Llangru would fare better too. But first we have to find our way to the *how* of such things. This very year I begin, after I'm truly on my feet again."

He sank back against a rolled-up bearskin. His left hand reached toward her. His voice dropped. "Of course," he said low, "that means the end of your books and other treasures. We can't save them if we move out. We can only take along in our heads what knowledge they give us that we can use, like how to treat fractures. I'm sorry, Shalindra."

He seldom spoke at such length, or so mildly.

She gave him his food and sat down on a bedside stool, a bowl on her knees. "It can't be helped," she sighed. "I've come to see that." As you have come to regret it, my dear, her mind added. Which is worth many books to me.

She took a chunk of fish. Utensils of metal and porcelain would presently belong to the past, like tableware. Maybe a craftsman could produce substitutes of wood, bone, or horn, but probably none would have the time. They would be too busy inventing tools more urgently needed by hunters on the fringe of the glacier. She might as well practice how to eat in mannerly wise with her fingers.

"It's the future, you know," he said. "Like it or not, it is. And you . . . you're not just borne along helpless, Shalindra. You can have a great deal to say about how it goes, in your own right and through Llangru." He paused. "After all, in spite of his power, he's still a boy. He still has much to learn from you and—and any stepfather he might get."

Her pulse, her blood cried out. She barely kept from spilling her dish.

Brandek stared at the shadows beyond his bed. "Where is he today?" he asked. "He usually comes here with you."

"He may arrive later," she replied in chosen words. "He told me he meant to—Well, do you remember Mintu, that brat who took the lead in persecuting him because he was odd? Mintu had become his most abject follower, after what happened. Llangru told me he thinks he . . . he will need helpers . . . and he had ideas about what Mintu can do. They were going to experiment with a drum and—I don't know what."

"You know more than I do," Brandek said. "I'm so ignorant about magic that I nearly got myself killed under the Heewhirlas. I'm sure of nothing except that it's not altogether gone from the world, and some of it remains in him. You, your studies—" He turned his head to her. "Can you tell me more?"

She had expected this, once he regained strength and, with it, his liveliness of mind. Again he reached out, and this time she gave him her hand. His closed around it, hard, warm, comforting. "I've ransacked the library and my own thoughts, of course," she said, while she brought her face near his because she was talking softly. "I've discovered little. This is such a new phenomenon. However—the principle is basic, that anything different, peculiar, has a certain amount of *mana* by virtue of that same differentness. And Llangru was always a strange one, wasn't he?" Of a sudden she heard herself add, "I don't imagine any other children I bear will be like him—" and stopped in total confusion and saw Brandek's mouth curve happily upward.

The smile died. His glance went past her. She twisted about and saw Llangru.

Today the slight form moved with catlike grace. She wondered: in what shape would his soul next travel forth?—and shivered. How dank the house was. Yes, open-air life would be hard, but would in truth be healthier.

Llangru had not shed his rain-wet cape. From the cave of its hood, his gaze sought Brandek. Those eyes gleamed like a lynx's. He raised a hand in salute and declared with a gravity beyond his years, "Chieftain, Mintu's drumming sent me out of my body and I met the Reindeer Spirit. He told me a big herd of them is moving this way, and we can have plenty of meat. But he also told me this will not be—they will go elsewhere—unless we give him and them their due respect."

Breath hissed between Shalindra's teeth. Her grip on Brandek tightened.

He took the news calmly, almost matter-of-factly. "Aye," he said, nodding, "I thought it'd come to something like this."

"What do you mean?" Shalindra gasped. Llangru sat down on the floor at her feet, cross-legged, facing the brightest of the lamps.

"Why, we're no longer masters of the world," Brandek told her. "We're back *in* the world, as much as animals or trees or stones or anything. What was killing our souls was that we didn't realize this, we had no idea of where we belonged or what we should believe or how we should behave. . . . I found, myself, skill's not enough."

Understanding rushed through Shalindra. "No," she whispered, "it isn't. But we'll always have a few among us who are wise about the hidden things." She bent her mind toward her son, though her hand stayed with Brandek's. "What should we do, then, to please the reindeer?" she asked.

"I do not yet know," Llangru answered, "but I will find out."

The first of the shamans fixed his eyes upon the lamp flame.

More Magic

TABLE OF CONTENTS

ψ

THE LION IN HIS ATTIC
A TALE OF THE WARLOCK'S ERA
by Larry Niven

♃

BEFORE THE QUAKE it had been called Castle Minterl, but almost nobody outside Minterl remembered that. Small events drown in large ones. Atlantis itself, an entire continent, had drowned in the tectonic event that sank this small peninsula.

For seventy years the seat of government had been at Beesh, and that place was called Castle Minterl. Outsiders called this drowned place Nihilil's Castle, for its last lord, if they remembered at all. Three and a fraction stories of what had been the South Tower still stood above the waves. They bore a third name now: Lion's Attic.

The sea was choppy today. Durily squinted against bright sunlight glinting off waves. Nothing of Nihilil's Castle showed beneath the froth.

The lovely golden-haired woman ceased peering over the side of the boat. She lifted her eyes to watch the South Tower come toward them. She murmured into Karskon's ear, "And that's all that's left."

Thone was out of earshot, busy lowering the sails; but he might glance back. The boy was not likely to have seen a lovelier woman in his life, and as far as Thone was concerned, his passengers were seeing this place for the first time. Karskon turned to look at Durily and was relieved. She looked interested, eager, even charmed.

But she *sounded* shaken. "It's all gone! Tapestries and banquet hall and bedrooms and the big ballroom . . . the gardens . . . all down there with the fishes, and not even mer-people to enjoy them . . . that little knob of rock must have been Crown Hill . . . Oh, Karskon, I wish you could have seen it." She shuddered, though her face still wore the mask of eager interest. "Maybe the riding-birds survived. Nihilil kept them on the roof."

"You couldn't have been more than . . . ten? How can you remember so much?"

A shrug. "After the Torovan invasion, after we had to get out . . . Mother talked incessantly about palace life. I think she got lost in the past. I don't blame her much, considering what the present was like. What she told me and what I saw myself, it's all a little mixed up after so long. I saw the traveling eye, though."

"How'd that happen?"

"Mother was there when a messenger passed it to the king. She snatched it out of his hand, playfully, you know, and admired it and showed it to me. Maybe she thought he'd give it to her. He got very angry, and he was trying not to show it, and that was even more frightening. We left the palace the next day. Twelve days before the quake."

Karskon asked, "What about the other—?" But warning pressure from her hand cut him off.

Thone had finished rolling up the sail. As the boat thumped against the stone wall he sprang upward, onto what had been a balcony, and moored the bowline fast. A girl in her teens came from within the tower to fasten the stern line for him. She was big as Thone was big: not yet fat, but hefty, rounded of feature. Thone's sister, Karskon thought, a year or two older.

Durily, seeing no easier way out of the boat, reached hands up to them. They heaved as she jumped. Karskon passed their luggage up and joined them, leaving the cargo for others to move.

Thone made introductions. "Sir Karskon, Lady Durily, this is Estrayle, my sister. Estrayle, they'll be our guests for a month. I'll have to tell Father. We bring red meat in trade."

The girl said, "Oh, very good! Father will love that. How was the trip?"

"Well enough. Sometimes the spells for wind just don't do anything. Then there's no telling where you wind up." To Karskon and Durily he said, "We live on this floor. These outside stairs take you right up past us. You'll be staying on the floor above. The top floor is the restaurant."

Durily asked, "And the roof?"

"It's flat. Very convenient. We raise rabbits and poultry there." Thone didn't see the look that passed across Durily's face. "Shall I show you to your rooms? And then I'll have to speak to Father."

* * *

Nihilil's Castle dated from the last days of real magic. The South Tower was a wide cylindrical structure twelve stories tall, with several rooms on each floor. In this age nobody would have tried to build anything so ambitious.

When Lion petitioned for the right to occupy these ruins, he had already done so. Perhaps the idea amused Minterl's new rulers. A restaurant in Nihilil's Castle! Reached only by boats! At any rate, nobody else wanted the probably haunted tower.

The restaurant was on the top floor. The floor below would serve as an inn, but as custom decreed that the main meal was served at noon, it was rare for guests to stay over. Lion and his wife and eight children lived on the third floor down.

Though "Lion's Attic" was gaining some reputation on the mainland, the majority of Lion's guests were fishermen. They often paid their score in fish or in smuggled wines. So it was that Thone found Lion and Merle hauling in lines through the big kitchen window.

Even Lion looked small next to Merle. Merle was two and a half yards tall, and rounded everywhere, with no corners and no indentations: His chin curved in one graceful sweep down to his wishbone; his torso expanded around him like a tethered balloon. There was just enough solidity, enough muscle in the fat, so that none of it sagged at all.

And that was considerable muscle. The flat-topped fish they were wrestling through the window was as big as a normal man, but Merle and Lion handled it easily. They settled the corpse on its side on the center table, and Merle asked, "Don't you wish you had an oven that size?"

"I do," said Lion. "What is it?"

"Dwarf island-fish. See the frilly spines all over the top of the thing? Meant to be trees. Moor at an island, go ashore. When you're all settled the island dives under you, then snaps the crew up one by one while you're trying to swim. But they're magical, these fish, and with the magic dying away—"

"I'm wondering how to cook the beast."

That really wasn't Merle's department, but he was willing to advise. "Low heat in an oven, for a long time, maybe an eighth of an arc," meaning an eighth of the sun's path from horizon to horizon.

Lion nodded. "Low heat, covered. I'll filet it first. I can fiddle up a sauce, but I'll have to see how fatty the meat is. . . . All right, Merle. Six meals in trade. Anyone else could have a dozen, but you . . ."

Merle nodded placidly. He never argued price. "I'll start now." He went through into the restaurant section, scraping the door on both sides, and Lion turned to greet his son.

"We have guests," said Thone, "and we have red meat, and we have a bigger boat. I thought it proper to bargain for you."

"Guests, good. Red meat, good. What have you committed me to?"

"Let me tell you the way of it." Thone was not used to making business judgments in his father's name. He looked down at his hands and said, "Most of the gold you gave me, I had spent. I had spices and dried meat and vegetables and pickle and the rest. Then a boat pulled in with sides of ox for sale. I was wondering what I could sell, to buy some of that beef, when these two found me at the dock."

"Was it you they were looking for?"

"I think so. The lady Durily is of the old Minterl nobility, judging by her accent. Karskon speaks Minterl but he may be of the new nobility, the invaders from Torov. Odd to find them together . . ."

"You didn't trust them. Why did you deal with them?"

Thone smiled. "Their offer. The fame of Lion's Attic has spread throughout Minterl, so they say. They want a place to honeymoon; they had married that same day. For two weeks' stay they offered . . . well, enough to buy four sides of ox and enough left over to trade *Strandhugger* in on a larger boat, large enough for the beef and two extra passengers."

"Where are they now? And where's the beef?"

"I told . . . Eep. It's still aboard."

The Lion roared. "*Arilta!*"

"I meant to tell Estrayle to do something about that, but it—"

"Never mind, you've done well."

Arilta came hurrying from the restaurant area. Lion's wife resembled her husband to some extent: big-boned, heavy, placid of disposition, carrying her weight well. "What is it?"

"Set the boys to unloading the new boat. Four sides of beef. Get those into the meat box fast; they can take their time with the other goods."

She left, calling loudly for the boys. Lion said, "The guests?"

"I gave them the two leeward rooms as a suite."

"Good. Why don't you tell them dinner is being served? And then you can have your own meal."

The dining hall was a roar of voices, but when Lion's guests appeared the noise dropped markedly. Both were wearing court dress of a style that had not yet reached the provinces. The man was imposing in black and silver, with a figured silver patch over his right eye. The lady was eerily beautiful, dressed in flowing sea green and a centimeter taller than her escort. They were conversation-stoppers, and they knew it.

And then a man came hurrying to greet them, clapping his hands in delight. "Lady Durily, Lord Karskon? I am Lion. Are your quarters comfortable? Most of the middle floor is empty; we can offer a variety of choices—"

"Quite comfortable, thank you," Karskon said. Lion had taken him by surprise. Rumor said that he was what his name implied, a were-lion. He was large, and his short reddish-blond hair might be the color of a lion's mane; but Lion was balding on top, and smooth-shaven, and well-fed, with a round and happy face. He looked far from ferocious. . . .

"*Lion! Bring 'em here!*"

Lion looked around, disconcerted. "I have an empty table in the corner, but if you would prefer Merle's company . . ."

The man who had called was tremendous. The huge platter before him bore an entire swordfish filet. Durily stared in what might have been awe or admiration. "Merle, by all means! And can you be persuaded to join us, Lion?"

"I would be delighted." Lion escorted them to the huge man's table and seated them. "The swordfish is good—"

"The swordfish is *wonderful!*" Merle boomed. He'd made amazing progress with the half-swordfish while they were approaching. "It's baked with apricots and slivered nuts and . . . something else, I can't tell. Lion?"

"The nuts are soaked in a liqueur called *brosa*, from Rynildissen, and dried in the oven."

"I'll try it," Karskon said, and Durily nodded. Lion disappeared into the kitchen.

The noise level was rising toward its previous pitch. Durily raised her voice just high enough. "Most of you seem to be fishers. It must have been hard for you after the mer-people went away."

"It was, Lady. They had to learn to catch their own fish instead of trading. All the techniques had to be invented from scratch. They tell me they tried magic at first. To breathe water, you know. Some of them drowned. Then came fishing spears, and special boats, and nets . . ."

"You said *they?*"

"I'm a whale," said Merle. "I came later."

"Oh. There aren't many were-folk around these days. Anywhere."

"We aren't all gone," Merle said, while Karskon smiled at how easily they had broached the subject. "The mer-people went away, all right, but it wasn't just because they're magical creatures. Their life-*styles* included a lot of magic. Whales don't practice much magic."

"Even so," Karskon wondered, "what are you doing on land? Aren't you afraid you might, ah, change? Magic isn't dependable anymore . . ."

"But Lion is. Lion would get me out in time. Anyway, I spend most of my time aboard *Shrimp*. See; if the change comes over me there, it's no problem. A whale's weight would swamp my little boat and leave me floating."

"I still don't see—"

"Sharks."

"Ah."

"Damn brainless toothy wandering weapons! The more you kill, the more the blood draws more till . . ." Merle shifted restlessly. "Anyway, there are no sharks ashore. And there are books, and people to talk to. Out on the sea there's only the singing. Now, I like the singing; who wouldn't? But it's only family gossip, and weather patterns, and shoreline changes, and where are the fish."

"That sounds useful."

"Sure it is. Fisherfolk learn the whale songs to find out where the fish are. But for any kind of intelligent conversation you have to come ashore. Ah, here's Lion."

Lion set three plates in place, bearing generous slabs of swordfish and vegetables cooked in elaborate fashions. "What's under discussion?"

"Were-creatures," Karskon said. "They're having a terrible time of it almost everywhere."

Lion sat down. "Even in Rynildissen? The wolf people sector?"

"Well," Durily said uncomfortably, "they're changing. You know, there are people who can change into animals, but that's because there are were-folk among their ancestors. Most were-folk are animals who learned how to take human form. The human shape has magic in it, you know." Lion nodded, and she continued. "In places where the magic's gone, it's terrible. The animals lose their minds. Even human folk with some animal ancestry, they can't make the change, but their minds aren't quite human either. Wolf ancestry makes for good soldiers, but it's hard for them to stop. A touch of hyena or raccoon makes for thieves. A man with a touch of lion makes a good general, but—"

Merle shifted restlessly, as if the subject were painful to him. His platter was quite clean now. "Oh, to hell with the problems of were-folk. Tell me how you lost your eye."

Karskon jumped, but he answered. "Happened in the baths when I was thirteen. We were having a fight with wet towels and one of my half-brothers flicked my eye out with the corner of a towel. Dull story."

"You should make up a better one. Want some help?" Karskon shook his head, smiling despite himself. "Where are you from?"

"Inland. It's been years since I tasted fresh fish. You were right, it's wonderful." He paused, but the silence forced him to continue. "I'm half Torovan, half Minterl. Duke Chamil of Konth made me his librarian, and I teach his legitimate children. Lady Durily descends from the old Minterl nobility. She's one of Duchess Chamil's ladies-in-waiting. That's how we met."

"I never understood shoreside politics," Merle said. "There was a war, wasn't there, long ago?"

Karskon answered for fear that Durily would. "Torov invaded after the quake. It was an obvious power vacuum. I gather the armies never got this far south. What was left of the dukes surrendered first. You'll find a good many of the old Minterls hereabouts. The Torovans have to go in packs."

Merle was looking disgusted. "Whales don't play at war."

"It's not a game," Karskon said.

Lion added, "Or at least the stakes are too high for ordinary people."

* * *

There was murky darkness, black with a hint of green. Blocky shapes. Motion flicked past, drifted back more slowly. Too dark to see, but Karskon sensed something looking back at him. A fish? A ghost?

Karskon opened his good eye.

Durily was at the window, looking out to sea. Leftward, waves washed the spike of island that had been Crown Hill. "There was grass almost to the top," Durily said, "but the peak was always a bare knob. We picnicked there once, the whole family . . ."

"What else do you remember? Anything we can use?"

"Two flights of stairs," Durily said. "You've seen the one that winds up the outside of the tower, like a snake. Snake-headed, it used to be, but the quake must have knocked off the head."

"Animated?"

"No, just a big carving . . . um. It could have been animated once. The magic was going out of everything. The mer-people were all gone; the mainlanders were trying to learn to catch their own fish, and we had trouble getting food. Nihilil was thinking of moving the whole court to Beesh. Am I rambling too much, darling?"

"No telling what we can use. Keep it up."

"The inside stairs lead down from the kitchen, through the laundry room on this floor and through Thone's room on the lower floor."

"Thone." Karskon's hand strayed to his belt buckle, which was silver and massive—which was in fact the hilt of a concealed dagger. "He's not as big as Lion, but I'd hate to have him angry with me. They're all too big. We'd best not be caught . . . unless we, or *you*, can find a legitimate reason for being in Thone's room?"

Durily scowled. "He's just not interested. He sees me, he knows I'm a woman, but he doesn't seem to care . . . or else he's very stupid about suggestions. That's possible."

"If he's part of a were-lion family—"

"He wouldn't mate with human beings?" Durily laughed, and it sounded like silver coins falling. No, he thought, she wouldn't have had trouble seducing a young man . . . or *anything* male. *I gave her no trouble. Even now, knowing the truth. . . .*

"Our host isn't a were-lion," she said. "Lions eat red meat. We've brought red meat to his table, but he was eating fish. Lions don't lust for a varied diet, and they aren't particular about what they eat. Our host has exquisite taste. If I'd known how fine a cook he is, I'd have come for that alone."

"He shows some other signs. The whole family's big, but he's a lot bigger. Why does he shave his face and clip his hair short? Is it to hide a mane?"

"Does it matter if they're lions? We don't want to be caught," Durily said. "Anyone of them is big enough to be a threat. Stop fondling that canape sticker, dear. On this trip we use stealth and magic."

Oddly reluctant, Karskon said, "Speaking of magic . . ."

"Yes. It's time."

"You're quite right. They're hiding something," Lion said absently. He was carving the meat from a quarter of ox and cutting it into chunks, briskly, apparently risking his fingers at every stroke. "What of it? Don't we all have something to hide? They are my guests. They appreciate my food."

"Well," said his wife, "don't we all have something worth gossiping about? And for a honeymooning couple—"

At which point Estrayle burst into a peal of laughter.

Arilta asked, "Now what brought that on?" But Estrayle only shook her head and bent over the pale yellow roots she was cutting. Arilta turned back to her husband. "They don't seem loving enough somehow. And she so beautiful, too."

"It makes a pattern," Lion said. "The woman is beautiful, as you noticed. She is the Duchess's lady-in-waiting. The man serves the Duke. Could Lady Durily be the Duke's mistress? Might the Duke have married her to one of his men? It would provide for her if she's pregnant. It might keep the Duchess happy. It happens."

Arilta said, "Ah." She began dumping double handfuls of meat into a pot. Estrayle added the chopped root.

"On the other hand," Lion said, "she is of the old Minterl aristocracy. Karskon may be too—half anyway. Perhaps they're not welcome near Beesh because of some failed plot. The people around here are of the old Minterl blood. They'd protect them, if it came to that."

"Well," his wife said with some irritation, "which is it?"

Lion teased her with a third choice. "They spend money freely. Where does it come from? They could be involved in a theft we will presently hear about."

Estrayle looked up from cutting onions, tears dripping past a mischievous smile. "Listen for word of a large cat's-eye emerald."

"Estrayle, you will explain that!" said her mother.

Estrayle hesitated, but her father's hands had stopped moving and he was looking up. "It was after supper," she said. "I was turning down the beds. Karskon found me. We talked a bit, and then he, well, made advances. Poor little man, he weighs less than I do. I slapped him hard enough to knock that lovely patch right off his face. Then I informed him that if he's interested in marriage he should be talking to my father, and in any case there are problems he should be aware of . . ." Her eyes were dancing. "I must say he took it well. He asked about my dowry! I hinted at undersea treasures. When I said we'd have to live here, he said at least he'd never have to worry about the cooking, but his religion permitted him only one wife, and I said what a pity—"

"The jewel," Lion reminded her.

"Oh, it's beautiful! Deep green, with a blazing vertical line, just like a cat's eye. He wears it in the socket of his right eye."

Arilta considered. "If he thinks that's a safe place to hide it, he should get another patch. Someone might steal that silver thing."

"Whatever their secret, it's unlikely to disturb us," Lion said. "And this is their old seat of royalty. Even the ghost . . . Which reminds me. Jarper?"

He spoke to empty air, and it remained empty. "I haven't seen Jarper since lunch. Has anyone?"

Nobody answered. Lion continued. "He was behind Karskon at lunch. Karskon must have something magical on him. Maybe the jewel? Oh, never mind, Jarper can take care of himself. I was saying he probably won't bother our guests; he's of old Minterl blood himself. If he had blood."

They stuffed wool around the door and windows. They propped a chair under the doorknob. Karskon and Durily had no intention of being disturbed at this point. An innkeeper who found his guests marking patterns on the floor with powdered bone, and heating almost-fresh blood over a small flame, could rightly be expected to show annoyance.

Durily spoke in a language once common to the Sorcerer's Guild, now common to nobody. The words seemed to hurt her throat, and no wonder, Karskon thought. He had doffed his silver eye patch. He tended the flame and the pot of blood, and stayed near Durily, as instructed.

He closed his good eye and saw green-tinged darkness. Something darker drifted past, slowly, something huge and rounded that suddenly vanished with a flick of finny tail. Now a drifting current of luminescence . . . congealing, somehow, to a vaguely human shape. . . .

The night he robbed the jewel merchant's shop, this sight had almost killed him.

The Movement had wealth to buy the emerald, but Durily swore that the Torovan lords must not learn that the jewel existed. She hadn't told him why. It wasn't for the Movement that he had obeyed her. The Movement would destroy the Torovan invaders, would punish his father and his half-brothers for their arrogance, for the way they had treated him . . . for his eye. But he had obeyed *her*. He was her slave in those days, the slave of his lust for the lady Durily, his father's mistress.

He had guessed that it was *glamour* that held him: magic. It hadn't seemed to matter. He had invaded the jeweler's shop expecting to die, and it hadn't mattered.

The merchant had heard some sound and come to investigate. Karskon had already scooped up everything of value he could find, to distract attention from the single missing stone. Waiting for discovery in the dark cellar, he had pushed the jewel into his empty eye socket.

Greenish darkness, drifting motion, a sudden flicker that might be a fish's tail. Karskon was seeing with his missing eye.

The jeweler had found him while he was distracted, but Karskon had killed him after all. Afterward, knowing that much, he had forced Durily to tell the rest. She had lost a good deal of her power over him. He had outgrown his terror of that greenish dark place. He had seen it every night while he waited for sleep, these past two years.

Karskon opened his good eye to find that they had company. The color of fading fog, it took the wavering form of a wiry old man garbed for war, with his helmet tucked under his arm.

"I want to speak to King Nihilil," Durily said. "Fetch him."

"Your pardon, Lady." The voice was less than a whisper, clearer than memory. "I c-can't leave here."

"Who were you?"

The fog-wisp straightened to attention. "Sergeant Jarper Sleen, serving Minterl and the King. I was on duty in the watchtower when the land th-th-thrashed like an island-fish submerging. The wall broke my arm and some ribs. After things got quiet again there were only these three floors left, and no food anywhere. I s-starved to death."

Durily examined him with a critical eye. "You seem nicely solid after seventy-six years."

The ghost smiled. "That's the Lion's doing. He lets me take the smells of his cooking as offerings. But I can't leave where I d-died."

"Was the King home that day?"

"Lady, I have to say he was. The quake came fast. I don't doubt that he drowned in his throne room."

"Drowned," Durily said thoughtfully. "All right." She poured a small flask of seawater into the blood, which was now bubbling. Something must have been added to keep it from clotting. She spoke high and fast in the Sorcerer's Guild tongue.

The ghost of Jarper Sleen sank to its knees. Karskon saw the draperies wavering as if heated air was moving there, and when he realized what that meant, he knelt too.

An unimaginative man would have seen nothing. This ghost was more imagination than substance; in fact the foggy crown had more definition, more reality, than the head beneath. Its voice was very much like a memory surfacing from the past . . . not even Karskon's past, but Durily's.

"You have dared to waken Minterl's king."

Seventy-six years after the loss of Atlantis and the almost incidental drowning of the seat of government of Minterl, the ghost of Minterl's king seemed harmless enough. But Durily's voice quavered. "You knew me. Durily. Lady Tinylla of Beesh was my mother."

"Durily. You've grown," said the ghost. "Well, what do you want of me?"

"The barbarians of Torov have invaded Minterl."

"Have you ever been tired unto death, when the pain in an old wound keeps you awake nonetheless? Well, tell me of these invaders. If you can lure them here, I and my army will pull them under the water."

Karskon thought that Minterl's ancient king couldn't have drowned a bumblebee. Again he kept silent, while Durily said, "They invaded the year after the great quake. They have ruled Minterl for seventy-four years. The palace is drowned but for these top floors." Durily's voice became a whip. "They are used as an inn! Rabbits and chickens are kept where the fighting-birds roosted!"

The ghost-king's voice grew stronger. "Why was I not told?"

This time Karskon spoke. "We can't lure them here, to a drowned island. We must fight them where they rule, in Beesh."

"And who are you?"

"I am Karskon Lor, Your Majesty. My mother was of Beesh. My father, a Torovan calling himself a lord, Chamil of Konth. Lord Chamil raised me to be his librarian. His legitimate sons he—" Karskon fell silent.

"You're a bastard?"

"Yes."

"But you would strike against the Torovan invaders. How?"

Durily seemed minded to let him speak. Karskon lifted the silver eye patch to show the great green gem. "There were two of these, weren't there?"

"Yes."

"Durily tells me they were used for spying."

The King said, "That was the traveling stone. Usually I had it mounted in a ring. If I thought a lord needed watching, I made him a present of it. If he was innocent, I made him another present and took it back."

Karskon heaved a shuddering sigh. He had *almost* believed; always he had *almost* believed.

Durily asked, "Where was the other stone?"

"Did your mother tell you of my secret suite? For times when I wanted company away from the Queen? It was a very badly kept secret. Many ladies could describe that room. Your mother was one."

"Yes."

The ghost smiled. "But it stood empty most of the time, except for the man on watch in the bathing chamber. There is a statue of the one-eyed god in the bathing chamber, and its eye is a cat's-eye emerald."

Durily nodded. "Can you guide us there?"

"I can. Can you breathe under water?"

Durily smiled. "Yes."

"The gems holds *mana*. If it leaves Minterl Castle, the ghosts will fade."

Durily lost her smile. "King Nihilil—"

"I will show you. Duty runs two ways between a king and his subjects. Now?"

"A day or two. We'll have to reach the stairwell, past the innkeeper's family."

The ghost went where ghosts go. Karskon and Durily pulled the wool loose from the windows and opened them wide. A brisk sea wind whipped away the smell of scorched blood. "I wish we could have done this on the roof," she said viciously. "Among Lion's damned chickens. Used their blood."

It happened the second day after their arrival. Karskon was expecting it.

The dining room was jammed before noon. Lion's huge pot of stew dwindled almost to nothing. He set his older children to frying thick steaks with black pepper and cream and essence of wine, his younger children to serving. Providentially, Merle showed up, and Lion set him to moving tables and chairs to the roof. The younger children set the extra tables.

Karskon and Durily found themselves squeezing through a host of seamen to reach the roof. Lion laughed as he apologized. "But after all, it's your own doing! I have red meat! Usually there is nothing but fish and shellfish. What do you prefer? My stew has evaporated—*poof*—but I can offer—"

Durily asked, "Is there still fish?" Lion nodded happily and vanished.

Cages of rabbits and pigeons and large, bewildered-looking *moas* had been clustered in the center of the roof, to give the diners a sea view. A salvo of torpedoes shot from the sea: bottle-nosed mammals with a laughing expression. They acted like they were trying to get someone's attention. Merle, carrying a table and chairs, said, "Mer-people. They must be lost. Where the magic's been used up they lose their half-human shape, and their sense too. If they're still around when I put out, I'll lead them out to sea."

Lion served them himself but didn't join them. Today he was too busy. Under a brilliant blue sky they ate island-fish baked with slivered nuts and some kind of liqueur, and vegetables treated with respect. They ate quickly. Butterflies fluttered in Karskon's belly, but he was jubilant.

The Lion had read meat. Of *course* the Attic was jammed, of *course* the Lion and his family were busy as a fallen hive. The third floor would be entirely deserted.

Water, black and stagnant, covered the sixth step down. Durily stopped before she reached it. "Come closer," she said. "Stay close to me."

Karskon's protective urge responded to her fear and her beauty. But, he reminded himself, it wasn't *his* nearness she needed; it was the gem. . . . He moved down to join Durily and her ally.

She arrayed her equipment on the steps. No blood this time: King Nihilil was already with them, barely, like an intrusive memory at her side.

She began to chant in the Sorcerer's Guild tongue.

The water sank step by step. What had been done seventy-odd years ago could be outdone, partially, temporarily.

Durily's voice grew deep and rusty. Karskon watched as her hair faded from golden to white, as the curves of her body drooped. Wrinkles formed on her face, her neck, her arms.

Glamour is a lesser magic, but it takes *mana*. The magic that was Durily's youth was being used to move seawater now. Karskon had thought he was ready for this. Now he found himself staring, flinching back, until Durily, without interrupting herself, snarled (teeth brown or missing) and gestured him down.

He descended the wet stone stairs. Durily followed, moving stiffly. King Nihilil floated ahead of them like foxfire on the water.

The sea had left the upper floors, but water still sluiced from the landings. Karskon's torch illuminated dripping walls, and once a stranded fish. Within his chest his heart was fighting for its freedom.

On the fifth floor down there were side corridors. Karskon, peering into the darkness, shied violently from a glimpse of motion. It was an eel flopping as it drowned in air.

Eighth floor down.

Behind him, Durily moved as if her joints hurt. Her appearance repelled him. The deep lines in her face weren't smile wrinkles, they were selfishness, sulks, rage. And her voice ran on, and her hands danced in creaky curves.

She can't hurry. She'd fall. Can't leave her behind. Her spells, my jewel: Keep them together, or— But the ghost was drawing ahead of them. *Would he leave us? Here?* Worse, Nihilil was becoming hard to see. Blurring. The whole corridor seemed filled with the restless fog that was the King's ghost. . . .

No. The King's ghost had *multiplied.* A horde of irritated or curious ghosts had joined the procession. Karskon shivered from the cold, and wondered how much the cold was due to ghosts rubbing up against him.

Tenth floor down . . . and the procession had become a crowd. Karskon, trailing, could no longer pick out the King. But the ghosts streamed out of the stairwell, flowed away down a corridor, and Karskon followed. A murmuring was in the air, barely audible, a hundred ghosts whispering gibberish in his ear.

The sea had not retreated from the walls and ceiling there. Water surrounded them, ankle-deep as they walked, rounding up the corridor walls and curving over their heads to form a huge, complex bubble. Carpet disintegrated under his boots.

To his right the wall ended. Karskon looked over a stone railing, down into the water, into a drowned ballroom. There were bones at the bottom, and swamp fires forming on the water's surface. More ghosts.

The ghosts had paused. Now they were like a swirling, continuous, glowing fog. Here and there the motion suggested features . . . and Karskon suddenly realized that he was watching a riot, ghost against ghost. They'd realized why he was here. Drowning the intruders would save the jewel, save their fading lives—

Karskon nerved himself and waded into them. Hands tried to clutch him. A broadsword-shape struck his throat and broke into mist. . . .

He was through them, standing before a heavy, ornately carved door. The King's ghost was waiting. Silently he showed Karskon how to manipulate a complex lock. Presently he mimed turning a brass knob and threw his weight back. Karskon imitated him. The door swung open.

A bedchamber, and a canopied bed like a throne. If this place was a ruse, Nihilil must have acted his part with verve. The sea was here, pushing in against the bubble. Karskon could see a bewildered school of minnows in a corner of the bedchamber. The leader took a wrong turn and the whole school whipped around to follow him, through the water interface and suddenly into the air. They flopped as they fell, splashed into more water, and scattered.

A bead of sweat ran down Durily's cheek.

The King's ghost waited patiently at another door.

Terror was swelling in Karskon's throat. Fighting fear with self-directed rage, he strode soggily to the door and threw it open before the King's warning gesture could register.

He was looking at a loaded crossbow aimed throat-high. The string had rotted and snapped. Karskon remembered to breathe, forced himself to breath. . . .

It was a tiled bathroom, sure enough. There was a considerable array of erotic statuary, some quite good. The Roze-Kattee statue would have been better for less detail, Karskon thought. A skeleton in the pool wore a rotting bath-attendant's kilt; that would be Nihilil's spy. The one-eyed god in a corner . . . yes. The eye not covered by a patch gleamed even in this dim, watery light. Gleamed green, with a bright vertical pupil.

Karskon closed his good eye and found himself looking at himself.

Grinning, eye closed, he moved toward the statue, fumbling in his pouch for the chisel. Odd, to see himself coming toward himself like this. And Durily behind him, the triumph beginning to show through the exhaustion. And behind her—

He drew his sword as he spun. Durily froze in shock as he seemed to leap at her. The bubble of water trembled, the sea began to flow down the walls, before she recovered herself. But by then Karskon was past her and trying to skewer the intruder, who danced back, laughing, through the bedroom and through its ornate door, while Karskon—

Karskon checked himself. The emerald in his eye socket was supplying the *mana* to run the spell that held back the water. It had to stay near Durily. She'd drilled him on this, over and over, until he could recite it in his sleep.

Lion stood in the doorway, comfortably out of reach. He threw his arms wide, careless of the big, broad-bladed kitchen knife in one hand, and said, "But what a place to spend a honeymoon!"

"Tastes differ," Karskon said. "Innkeeper, this is none of your business."

"There is a thing of power down here. I've known that for a long time. You're here for it, aren't you?"

"The spying stone," Karskon said. "You don't even know what it is?"

"Whatever it is, I'm afraid you can't have it," Lion said. "Perhaps you haven't considered the implications—"

"Oh, but I have. We'll sell the traveling stone to the barbarian king in Beesh. From that moment on the Movement will know everything he does."

"Can you think of any reason why I should care?"

Karskon made a sound of disgust. "So you support the Torovans!"

"I support nobody. Am I a lord, or a soldier? No, I feed people. If someone should supplant the Torovans, I will feed the new conquerors. I don't care who is at the top."

"We care."

"Who? You, because you haven't the rank of your half-brothers? The elderly Lady Durily, who wants vengeance on her enemies' grandchildren? Or the ghosts? It was a ghost who told me you were down here."

Beyond Lion, Karskon watched faintly luminous fog swirling in the corridor. The war of ghosts continued. And Durily was tiring. He couldn't stay here, he had to pry out the jewel. "Is it the jewel you want? You couldn't have reached it without Durily's magic. If you distract her now you'll never reach the air, with or without the jewel. We'll all drown." Karskon kept his sword's point at eye level. If Lion was a were-lion. . . .

But he didn't eat red meat.

"The jewel has to stay," Lion said. "Why do you think these walls are still standing?"

Karskon didn't answer.

"The quake that sank Atlantis, the quake that put this entire peninsula underwater. Wouldn't it have shaken down stone walls? But this palace dates from the Sorcerer's Guild period. Magic spells were failing, but not always. The masons built this palace of good, solid stone. Then they had the structure blessed by a competent magician."

"Oh."

"Yes. The walls would have been shaken down without the blessing and some source of *mana* to power it. You see the problem. Remove the talisman, the castle crumbles."

He might be right, Karskon thought. But not until both emeralds were gone, and Karskon too.

Lion was still out of reach. He didn't handle that kitchen knife like a swordsman, and in any case it was too short to be effective. At a dead run Karskon thought he could catch the beefy chef . . . but what of Durily, and the spell that held back the water?

Fool! She had the other jewel!

He charged.

Lion whirled and ran down the hall. The ghost-fog swirled apart as he burst through. He was faster than he looked, but Karskon was faster still. His sword was nearly pricking Lion's buttocks when Lion suddenly leapt over the banister.

Karskon leaned over the dark water. The ghosts crowded around him were his only light source now.

Lion surfaced, thirty feet above the ballroom floor and well out into the water, laughing. "Well, my guest, can you swim? Many mainlanders can't."

Karskon removed his boots. He might wait, let Lion tire himself treading water; but Durily must be tiring even faster and growing panicky as she wondered where he had gone. He couldn't leave Lion at their backs.

He didn't dive; he lowered himself carefully into the water, then swam toward Lion. Lion backstroked, grinning. Karskon followed. He was a fine swimmer.

Lion was swimming backward into a corner of the ballroom. Trapping himself. The water surface rose behind him, curving up the wall. Could Lion swim uphill?

Lion didn't try. He dove. Karskon dove after him, kicking, peering down. There were patches of luminosity, confusing . . . and a dark shape far below . . . darting away at a speed Karskon couldn't hope to match. Appalled, Karskon lunged to the surface, blinked, and saw Lion clamber over the railing. He threw Karskon's boots at his head and dashed back toward the King's "secret" bedroom.

★ ★ ★

The old woman was still waiting, with the King's ghost for her companion. Lion tapped her shoulder. He said, "Boo."

She froze, then tottered creakily around to face him. "Where is Karskon?"

"In the ballroom."

Water was flowing down the walls, knee-high and rising. Lion was smiling as at a secret joke, as he'd smiled while watching her savor her first bite of his incredible swordfish. It meant something different now.

Durily said, "Very well, you killed him. Now, if you want to live, get me that jewel and I will resume the spells. If our plans succeed, I can offer Karskon's place in the new nobility, to you or your son. Otherwise we both drown."

"Karskon could tell you why I refuse. I need the magic in the jewel to maintain my inn. With the jewel Karskon brought me, this structure will remain stable for many years." Lion didn't seem to notice that the King's ghost was clawing at his eyes.

The water was chest-high. "Both jewels, or we don't leave," the old woman said, and immediately resumed her spell, hands waving wildly, voice raspy with effort. She felt Lion's hands on her body and squeaked in outrage, then in terror, as she realized he was tickling her. Then she doubled in helpless laughter.

The water walls were collapsing, flowing down. The odd, magical bubble was collapsing around him. Clawing at the stone banister, Karskon heard his air supply roaring back up the stairwell, out through the broken windows, away. A wave threw him over the banister, and he tried to find his footing, but already it was too deep. Then the air was only a few silver patches on the ceiling, and the seawash was turning him over and over.

A big dark shape brushed past him, fantastically agile in the rolling currents, gone before his sword arm could react. Lion had escaped him. He swam toward one of the smashed ballroom windows, knowing he wouldn't make it, trying anyway. The faint glow ahead might be King Nihilil, guiding him. Then it all seemed to fade and he was breathing water, strangling.

Lion pulled himself over the top step, his flippers already altering to hands. He was gasping, blowing. It was a long trip, even for a sea lion.

The returning sea had surged up the steps and sloshed along the halls and into the rooms where Lion and his family dwelt. Lion shook his head. For a few days they must needs occupy the next level up: the inn, which was now empty.

The change to human form was not so great a change for Lion. He became aware of one last wisp of fog standing beside him.

"Well," it said, "how's the King?"

"Furious," Lion said. "But after all, what can he do? I thank you for the warning."

"I'm glad you could stop them. My curse on their crazy rebellion. We'll all f-fade away in time, I guess, with the magic dwindling and dwindling. But not just yet, if you please!"

"War is bad for everyone," said Lion.

ψ

SHADOW OF WINGS
by Bob Shaw

♃

THERE WAS ONCE a magician named Dardash, who—at the relatively young age of 103—decided he had done with the world.

Accordingly, he selected an islet a short distance off the coast of Koldana and built upon it a small but comfortable house that resembled a wind-carved spire of rock. He equipped the dwelling with life's few necessities and moved into it with all his possessions, the most prized of which were twelve massive scrolls in airtight cylinders of oiled leather bound with silver wire. He surrounded his new home with certain magical defenses, and as a final touch that was intended to complete his isolation, he rendered the entire island invisible.

As has already been stated, Dardash had decided he was finished with the world.

But the world was far from being finished with him. . . .

★ ★ ★

It was a flawless morning in early summer, one on which the universe seemed to have been created anew. The land to the east shimmered like freshly smelted gold, deckled with white fire where the sun's rays grazed slopes of sand; and on all other sides the flat blue immensity of the sea challenged Dardash's knowledge of history with its sheer ringing emptiness. It was as though Crete and Egypt and Sumer had never existed or had vanished as completely as the ancient magic-based civilizations that had preceded them. The very air sang a song of new beginnings.

Dardash walked slowly on the perimeter of his island, remembering a time when such mornings had filled him with near-painful joy. It was a time that was lost to him.

Being a magician, he retained a long-muscled and sinewy physique which—except for its lack of scars—resembled that of a superbly conditioned warrior, but his mind was growing old, corrupted by doubt. When the twelve scrolls had first come into his possession, and he had realized they contained spells written in the *mana*-rich dawn-time of magic, he had known with a fierce certainty that he was destined to become the greatest warlock that had ever lived. But that had been almost two score years ago, and he was no longer so confident. In truth, although he rarely admitted it to himself, he had begun to despair—and all because of a single, maddening, insuperable problem.

He reached the northeastern tip of the islet, moody and abstracted in spite of the vitality all around him, and was turning southward when his attention was caught by a flickering whiteness at the far side of the strip of water separating him from the mainland. The coast of Koldana was rocky in that area, a good feeding ground for gulls, but the object he had noticed was too large to be a bird. It was possibly a man in white garments, although travelers were rare in that region. Dardash stared at the brilliant speck for a moment, trying to bring it into sharp focus, but even his keen eyesight was defeated by the slight blurring effect caused by the islet's invisibility screen.

He shrugged and continued his morning walk, returning his thoughts to more weighty considerations. As a man who had traveled the length and breadth of the known world, he could speak every major language and was familiar with the written forms where they existed. The fact that the spells of the twelve scrolls were couched in the Old Language had at first seemed a minor inconvenience, especially for one who was accustomed to deciphering all manner of strange inscriptions. A few months, possibly even a few years, of study would surely reveal the secrets of the old manuscripts, thus enabling him to fulfill his every dream: to become immortal, to assume all the fantastic powers of the dream-time sorcerers.

But he had not allowed for the effect of the ten-thousand-year hiatus.

The old magic-based civilizations, so powerful in the days when *mana* was plentiful everywhere, had in fact been edifices of great fragility; and when the raw stuff of magic had disappeared from the earth, they, too, had crumbled and faded into nothingness. Few relics remained, and those that Dardash had seen or thought he had seen were totally without relevance to his quest. He lacked the necessary key to the Old Language, and as long as it remained impenetrable to him, he would fail to develop anything like his full potential. The doors of destiny would remain shut against him, even though there were places where *mana* had again begun to accumulate, and that had been the principal reason for his retreat from outside distraction. He had elected to devote all his time, all his mental energies, all his scholarship, to one supremely important task: solving the riddle of the scrolls.

Thus preoccupied, and secure behind his magical defenses, Dardash should have been oblivious to the world beyond, but he had been oddly restless and lacking in concentration for some time. His mind had developed an annoying tendency to pursue the irrelevant and the trivial, and as he neared the southern corner of the island, where his house was located, he again found himself speculating about who or what had appeared on the opposite shore. Yielding to impulse, he glanced to the east and saw that the enigmatic white mote was still visible at the water's edge. He frowned at it for a short period, hesitating, then acknowledged to himself that he would have no mental peace until the inconsequential little mystery was solved.

Shaking his head at his own foolishness, he went into his house and climbed the stone stairs to its upper balcony. He had used the spy-mask only the previous day to observe a ship that had appeared briefly on the western horizon, and it was still lying on the low bench, resembling the severed head of a giant eagle. Dardash fastened the mask over his face and turned toward the mainland. Because the spy-mask operated on magical and not optical principles, there was no focusing or scanning to be done: Dardash immediately saw the mysterious object on the coast as though from a distance of a few paces. And he was unable to withhold an exclamation.

The young woman was possibly the most beautiful he had ever seen. She appeared to be of Amorite stock, with the lush black hair and immaculate tawny skin of her race. Her face was that of the perfect lover that all men recognize from dreams but few aspire to touch in reality—dark-eyed and full-lipped, sensuous and willful, generous yet demanding. She was standing ankle-deep in the waters of a narrow cove, a place where she could presume to remain unobserved; and as Dardash watched she unbuttoned her white linen chiton, cast the garment behind her onto the sand, and began to bathe.

Her movements were graceful and languorous, like those of a dance that was being performed for his sole benefit, and his mouth went dry as he took in every detail of her body, followed the course of every runnel of water from splendid breast to belly and slim-coned thigh.

Dardash had no clear idea of how long her toilet lasted. He remained in a timeless, trancelike state until she had left the water, clothed herself, and was gliding away into the rocky outcrop that formed a natural palisade between sea and land. Only when she was lost to his view did he move again. He removed the eagle-mask from his head, and when he surveyed his little domain with normal vision, it seemed strangely bleak and cheerless.

As he descended the stair to the principal chamber in which he did most of his work, there came to Dardash a belated understanding of his recent lackluster moods, of his irritability and lapses of concentration. The decision to devote his entire life to the riddle of the scrolls had been an intellectual one, but he was a composite being, a synthesis of mind and body, and the physical part of him was in rebellion. He should have brought one or more girls from an inland village when he had set up his offshore retreat a year earlier. Many would have been glad to accompany and serve him in exchange for a little basic tutelage in magic, but he had an uneasy feeling it was too late to come to such an arrangement. The women of the region, even the youngest, tended to be a sun-withered, work-hardened lot, and he had just seen the sort of companion he truly craved.

But who was she? Where had she come from, and what was her destination?

The questions troubled Dardash at intervals for the rest of the day, distracting him from the endless task of trying to relate the phonetic writing of the scrolls to the complex abstractions of his profession. It was rare for trade caravans plying between the capital city of Koldana and the northern lands to take the longer coastal route, so she was unlikely to be the daughter or concubine of a wealthy merchant. But what possibilities remained? Only in fables did princesses or others of high birth go wandering in search of knowledge. Reconciling himself to the fact that speculation was futile, Dardash worked until long after nightfall, but in spite of being weary he found it difficult to sleep. His rest was disturbed by visions of the unknown woman, and each time he awoke with the taste of her lips fading from his, the sense of loss was greater, more insistent.

Part of his mood was occasioned by a belief that important opportunities only come once, that the penalty for failing to take action is eternal regret. Hence it was with a sense of near-disbelief, of having been specially favored by the gods, that on the following morning as he walked the eastern boundary of his island he again saw the flicker of whiteness on the mainland. This time, vision aided by memory, he had no trouble interpreting the lazy pulsations and shape changes of the blurred speck. *She* was there again. Undressing, uncovering that splendid body, preening herself, preparing for the sea's caress.

Dardash paused only long enough to unfasten his sandals. He stepped down into the clear water and swam toward the mainland, propelling himself with powerful and economical strokes that quickly reduced the distance to the shore. As he passed through the perimeter of the invisibility screen that protected his islet, he saw the outline of the woman become diamond-sharp in his vision and he knew that from that moment on she would be able to see him. Apparently, however, she was too preoccupied.

It was not until Dardash felt pebbles beneath his hands and stood up, his nearly naked body only knee-deep in water, that she became aware of his presence. She froze in the act of unbuttoning her chiton, breasts partly exposed, and gave him a level stare that signaled surprise and anger but, he was thrilled to note, no hint of fear.

"I had presumed myself alone," she said coldly, her beautiful face queenly in displeasure. "Suddenly the very sea is crowded."

"There is no crowd," Dardash replied, courting her with his smile. "Only the two of us."

"Soon there will only be you." The woman turned, picked up the net pouch that contained her toiletries, and strode away from him toward the narrow entrance to the cove. Sunlight piercing the fine material of her clothing outlined her body and limbs, striking fire behind Dardash's eyes.

"Wait," he said, deciding that a challenge could be the most effective way of capturing her interest. "Surely you are not afraid?"

The woman gave a barely perceptible toss of her head and continued walking, beginning to move out of sight between outcroppings of rock. Impelled by a growing sense of urgency, Dardash went after her with long strides, convinced that were he to fail this time he would never again have a night's peace. He had almost reached the woman, was breathing the scent of her waist-length black hair, when an inner voice warned him that he was behaving foolishly. He halted, turned to check a deep cleft in the rocks to his left, and groaned as he realized he was much too late.

The braided leather whip whistled like a war arrow as it flailed through the air, catching him just above the elbow, instantaneously binding his arms to his sides.

Dardash reacted by continuing his turn, intending to coil the whip farther around his body and thus snatch it from its user's grasp, but there was a flurry of footsteps and a glint of sunlight on armor, and the weight of a man hit him behind the knees, bringing him down. Other armed men, moving with practiced speed, dropped on top of him, and he felt thongs tighten around his wrists and ankles. Within the space of three heartbeats he was immobile and helpless and sick with anger at having allowed himself to be trapped so easily.

Narrowing his eyes against the glare from the sky, he looked up at his captors. There were four men wearing conical helmets and studded leather cuirasses. They did not look like soldiers, but the similarity of their equipment suggested they were in the employ of a person of wealth. A fifth figure, that of the woman, joined them, causing Dardash to turn his gaze away. He had no wish to see a look of triumph or contempt on her face, and in any case his mind was busy with the question of who had instigated the attack against him. In his earlier years he had made many enemies, but most of them had long since died, and latterly he had devoted so much time to his scrolls that there had scarcely been the chance to incur the wrath of anybody who mattered.

"Tell me the name of your master," he said, making himself sound patient and only mildly interested. He wanted to give the impression that he was unconcerned about his safety, that he was holding tremendous magical powers in reserve, although he was actually quite helpless. Most magic required protracted and painstaking preparation, and the ruffians standing over him could easily end his life at any moment if they so desired.

"You'll find out soon enough," the tallest man said. He had a reddish stubble of a beard, and one of his nostrils had been excised by an old wound that had left a diagonal scar on his face.

"You owe him no loyalty," Dardash said, experimenting with the possibilities of the situation. "By sending you against me he has placed you in terrible danger."

Red-beard laughed comfortably. "I must be a braver man than I thought—I feel absolutely no fear."

You will, Dardash vowed inwardly, *if I get out of this alive*. The sobering realization that this could be the last day of his life caused him to lapse into a brooding silence while the four men brought a wooden litter from its place of concealment behind nearby rocks. They rolled him onto it, none too gently, and carried him up the steep slope to the higher ground of the plain that spanned most of Koldana. The woman, now more normally clad in an all-enveloping burnoose, led the way. Dardash, still trying to guess why he had been taken, derived little comfort from the fact that his captors had not run a sword through him as soon as they had the chance. Their master, if he was an enemy worth considering, would want to dispose of him in person— and quite possibly by some means that would give all concerned plenty of time to appreciate what was happening.

When the party reached level ground, Dardash craned his neck, expecting to see some kind of conveyance that would be used to transport him inland, but instead there was a square tent only a few hundred paces away, positioned just far enough from the shore to be invisible from his islet home. The tent had an awning supported on gilded poles, and near it perhaps a dozen horses and pack animals cropped the sparse vegetation. It was obviously a temporary camp set up by a personage of some importance, one who was not prepared to travel far without the trappings of luxury, and it came to Dardash that he would not be kept in ignorance of his fate much longer. He lay back on the litter and feigned indifference.

The woman ran on ahead of the others, presumably to announce their arrival, and when the group of men reached the tent she was holding the entrance flaps aside for them. They carried Dardash into the lemon-colored shade within, set the litter down, and left without speaking, closing the entrance behind them. Dardash, his eyes rapidly adjusting to the change of lighting, saw that he was alone with a plump, heavily mustached man whose skin was as smooth and well oiled as that of a young concubine. He was dressed in costly silks, and Dardash noted with a quickening of interest—and hope—that astrological symbols were woven into the dark blue of his robe. In Dardash's experience, astrologers were rarely men of violence—except of course toward those who made their predictions go wrong, and he was quite certain he had not done anything along those lines.

"I am Urtarra, astrologer at the court of King Marcurades," the man said. "I am sorry at having brought you here by such devious means, but—"

"Devious!" Dardash snorted his contempt. "It was the simplest and most childish trick ever devised."

"Nevertheless, it worked." Urtarra paused to let the implication of his words sink in. "I do hope that doesn't mean that you are simple and childish, because if you are, you will be unequal to the task I have in mind for you."

"You'll learn how childish I am," Dardash promised, his anger growing apace with his new certainty that he was not about to be slain. "You'll learn a great deal about me as soon as I am free of these bonds."

Urtarra shook his head. "I have already learned all I need to know about you, and I am not stupid enough to release you until you have heard my proposal and agreed to work for me." He eyed Dardash's robust frame. "You look as though you could wreak considerable damage, even without magical aids."

Dardash almost gasped aloud at the extent of the other man's presumption. "I don't know what miserable little desire you harbor, but I can tell you one thing: I will never serve you in any way."

"Ah, but you *will!*" Urtarra looked amused as he rearranged the cushions on which he was seated. "The fact of the matter is that I have certain unusual talents, powers which are related to your own in a way. I am a seer. I have the gift of being able to part the veils of time and divine something of what the future holds in store—and I have seen the two of us making a journey together."

"A seer?" Dardash glanced at the planetary symbols on Urtarra's robes. "I don't regard fiddling with abacus and astrolabe as—"

"Nor do I, but young King Marcurades does not believe in any form of magic, not even my modest variety. He is a philosopher, you must understand—one of that breed of men who put their faith in irrigation schemes rather than weather spells, armor rather than amulets. It would be impossible for me to remain at his court were I to use my powers openly. Instead, I must pretend that my predictions spring from the science of astrology. I have nothing against astrology, of course, except that it lacks . . . um . . . precision."

"Your own visions are similarly lacking," Dardash said with emphasis. "I have no intention of making any journey with you, nor will I serve you in any . . . What sort of chore did you have in mind, anyway? The usual unimaginative trivia? Preparing a love potion? Turning useful lead into useless gold?"

"No, no, no, something much more appropriate to a magician of your standing." Urtarra paused to stare into Dardash's face, and when he spoke again his voice was low and earnest. "I want you to kill King Marcurades."

Dardash's immediate and instinctive response was to begin a new struggle to break free of his bonds. He writhed and quivered on the litter, straining to loosen or snap his restraints, but the thongs were stout and had been expertly tied, and even his unusual strength was of no avail. Finally he lapsed into immobility, sweating, his gaze fixed on the roof of the tent.

"Why exhaust yourself?" Urtarra said reasonably. "Does the life of the king mean so much to you?"

"My concern is for my own life," Dardash replied. He had scant regard for rank—a prince had no more standing in his scheme of things than a pot-mender—but the young King Marcurades was a rare phenomenon in that he was a ruler who was universally admired by his subjects. In the five years since he had ascended to the throne of Koldana, Marcurades had secured the country's boundaries, expanded its trade, abolished taxes, and devoted himself to farsighted schemes for the improvement of agriculture and industry. Under his aegis the populace were experiencing stability and prosperity to an unprecedented degree, and in return they were fiercely loyal, from the most illustrious general right down to the humblest farm worker. Dardash found it difficult to conceive of a project more foolhardy than the proposed assassination of such a king.

"Admittedly, no ordinary man could undertake the task and hope to live," Urtarra said, accurately divining Dardash's thoughts, "but you are no ordinary man."

"Nor do I take heed of flattery. Why do you wish the king dead? Are you in league with his heirs?"

"I am acting only for myself—and the people of Koldana. Let me show you something." Urtarra raised one hand and pointed at a wall of the tent. The material rippled in a way that had nothing to do with the breeze from the sea, then seemed to dissolve into mist. Through swirls of opalescent vapor, Dardash saw the erect and handsome figure of a young king standing in a chariot that was being drawn through the streets of the city. Cheering crowds pressed in on each side, with mothers holding their infants aloft to give them a better view, and maidens coming forward to strew the chariot's path with flowers.

"That is Marcurades now," Urtarra murmured, "but let us look forward and see the course which is to be followed by the river of time."

Conjured images began to appear and fade in rapid succession, compressing time, and by means of them Dardash saw the king grow older, and with the passage of the years changes occurred in his mien. He became tight-lipped and bleak-eyed, and gradually the aspect of the royal processions altered. Great numbers of soldiers marched before and behind the king, and engines of war were in evidence. The crowds who lined the routes still cheered, but few infants or maidens were to be seen, and the onlookers were noticeably shabbier of dress and thinner of face.

The prescience that Dardash was experiencing was more than simply a progression of images. Knowledge, foreknowledge, was being vouchsafed to him in wordless whispers, and he knew that the king was to be corrupted by power and ambition, to become increasingly cruel and insane. He was to raise armies and conquer neighboring countries, thus augmenting his military might. Marcurades was to turn his back on all his enlightened reforms and civil engineering projects. Finally he was to attempt to increase his domain a thousandfold, plunging the entire region into a series of terrible wars and catastrophes resulting in the total annihilation of his people.

As the last dire vision faded, and the wall of the tent became nothing more than a slow-billowing square of cloth, Dardash looked at Urtarra with a new respect. "You *are* a seer," he said. "You have a gift which even I can only envy."

"Gift? Curse is a better word for it." For an instant Urtarra's smooth face looked haunted. "I could well do without such visions and the burden or responsibility they bring."

"What burden? Now that you know what is preordained for Koldana and its people, all you have to do is journey to some safe country and live out your life in peace. That's what I'm going to do."

"But I am not you," Urtarra said. "And the events we saw are not preordained. Time is like a river, and the course of a river can be altered; that's why you must kill the king before it is too late."

Dardash settled back on the litter. "I have no intention of involving myself in anything so troublesome and dangerous. Why should I?"

"But you have just *seen* the miseries that are held in store for multitudes—the wars and plagues and famines."

"What's that to me?" Dardash said casually. "I have my own problems to contend with, and very little time in which to do it. I'll make you an offer: You release me now and I will promise to go my separate way without harming you or any of your company."

"I was told you thought only of yourself," Urtarra said, his eyes mirroring a cynical amusement, "but it was hard to believe a man could be so lacking in compassion."

"Believe it." Dardash proffered his bound wrists. "Let's get this over with no more waste of time."

"There is one thing you have not considered," Urtarra said, his voice oddly enigmatic as he rose to his feet and walked to a richly ornamented chest that sat in one corner of the tent. "I am willing to repay you for your services."

Dardash gave a humorless laugh. "With what? Gold or precious stones? I can conjure them out of dung! The favors of that whore who lingers outside? I can recruit a hundred like her in any city. You have nothing which could possibly interest me, Soothsayer."

"That is most regrettable," Urtarra said mildly as he stooped and took something from the chest. "I hoped you might find something worthy of your attention in this."

He turned and Dardash saw that he was holding a piece of parchment, roughly two handsbreadths in length, which had obviously been cut from a scroll. Dardash gave the parchment a bored glance and was turning his head away again when there came a thrill of recognition: It bore lines of writing in the Old Language, the same enigmatic and impenetrable script of his own twelve scrolls. Apart from the compilations of spells that had defeated his understanding for decades, no other matter written in the Old Language had come his way. Dardash tilted his head for a better view, trying to decide what kind of text the fragment represented, and suddenly—as though he had been stricken by a superior magic—he was unable to speak or breathe. His heartbeat became a tumult of thunder within his chest, and bright-haloed specks danced across his vision as he absorbed the realization that the parchment in Urtarra's hands was written in *two* languages.

Under each line of the Old Language was a corresponding line, a mixture of ideograms and phonetic symbols, which Dardash identified as late-period Accosian, one of the near-defunct languages he had mastered many years earlier.

"This is only a fragment, of course," Urtarra said. "I have the remainder of the scroll hidden in a secure place, but if it's of no interest to you . . ."

"Don't toy with me—I don't like it." Dardash briefly considered the fact that the key that would unlock the secrets of his twelve scrolls would make him virtually immortal, with all the incredible powers of the ancient warlocks, and decided he should modify his attitude toward Urtarra. "I admit to having a certain scholarly interest in old writings, and am prepared to offer a fair price for good examples. The assassination of a king is out of the question, of course, but there are many other—"

"And don't you toy with me," Urtarra cut in. "Marcurades has to die; otherwise the entire scroll will be consigned to the fire."

The threat cast a chill shadow in Dardash's mind.

"On the other hand, the world has seen an abundance of kings," he said slowly. "Is it a matter of any real consequence whether we have one more—or one less?"

It was close to noon by the time Dardash had selected the magical equipment he thought he would need and had brought it ashore by raft. He supervised the loading of the material and some personal effects onto two mules, then turned to Urtarra with a slight frown.

"Just to satisfy my curiosity," he said, "how were you able to find my unobtrusive little island? I believed I had it quite well concealed."

"It was *very* well concealed—from the eyes of men," Urtarra replied, allowing himself to look satisfied. "But birds can see it from on high, and you have many of them nesting there."

"What difference does that make?"

"To me, none; to the hawks I have been releasing, a great deal."

"I see," Dardash said thoughtfully, suddenly aware that Urtarra, for all his eunuchoid softness, would make a highly dangerous adversary. "Have you ever thought of becoming a sorcerer?"

"Never! I'm troubled enough by visions as it is. Were I to introduce new elements, I might forfeit sleep altogether."

"Perhaps you're right." Dardash swung himself up into the saddle of the horse that had been provided for him. "Tell me, do you ever foresee your own death?"

"No seer can do that—not until he is ready." Urtarra gave him an odd smile and made a signal to his four guards and the young woman, all of whom were already on horseback and waiting some distance away. They moved off immediately, taking a southeasterly course for Bhitsala, the capital city of Koldana. The plain was shimmering with heat, and at the horizon there was no clear distinction between land and sky.

Dardash, who much preferred the comparative coolness of the coast, had no relish for the four days' ride that lay ahead. Urging his horse forward alongside Urtarra, he consoled himself with the thought that this journey was probably the last he would have to undertake in such a commonplace and uncomfortable manner. When the knowledge reposing in the twelve scrolls was available to him, he would waft himself effortlessly to his destinations by other means, perhaps sailing on clouds, perhaps by methods as yet undreamed of. Until then he would have to make the best of things as they were.

"The woman," he said pensively, "has she any knowledge of what we're about?"

"None! Nobody else must learn what has passed between us; otherwise your power and mine increased a hundredfold couldn't preserve our lives."

"Don't your men regard this expedition as being a little . . . unusual?"

"They are trained never to ask nor to answer questions. However, I have told them what I will tell Marcurades: that you are a superb mathematician and that I need your help in calculating horoscopes. I have spread word that the stars are hinting at some major event, but are doing it in such an obscure way that even I am baffled. It all helps to prepare the ground."

Dardash's thoughts returned to the female figure ahead. "And where did you obtain the woman?"

"Nirrineen is the daughter of one of my cousins." Urtarra gave a satisfied chuckle. "It was fortunate that she was so well qualified for the task I assigned her. Shall I send her to you tonight?"

"That won't be necessary," Dardash said, concealing his annoyance at what he regarded as an insult. "She will come to me of her own accord."

The group trekked across the arid plain—seemingly at the center of a hazy hemisphere of blinding radiance—until, with the lowering of the sun, the horizons became sharp again, and the world was created anew all around them. In the period of tranquillity that preceded nightfall, they set up camp—the stately square tent for Urtarra's sole usage, humbler conical structures for the others—and fires were lit. Nirrineen began to prepare a meal for Urtarra and Dardash, leaving the four guards to cater to their own needs. Dardash chose to stand close to the young woman while she worked, placing her within the orbit of a personal power that was slow-acting but sure.

"You were excellent when we met this morning," he said. "I quite believed you were a princess."

"And I quite believe you are a flatterer." Nirrineen did not raise her eyes from the dishes she was preparing.

"I never employ flattery."

"It exists most in its denial."

"Very good," Dardash said, chuckling, his desire quickening as he realized that the woman kneeling before him was a complete person and not merely a shell of flesh. "Yesterday, when I watched you bathe, I knew—"

"Yesterday?" Her eyes glimmered briefly in the dusk, like twin moons.

"Yes. Don't forget that I'm as much magician as mathematician. Yesterday, by proxy, I stood very close to you for a long time, and knew then that you and I had been fashioned for each other. Like sword and sheath."

"Sword! Can it be that you now flatter yourself?"

"There's but one way for you to find out," Dardash replied easily.

Much later, as they lay together in the darkness, with Nirrineen contentedly asleep in his arms, he exulted in the discovery that his mind had regained all of its former clarity.

He began to consider ways of killing the king.

The city of Bhitsala was clustered around a semicircular bay that provided good anchorage for trading ships. It was protected by a range of low hills that merged with the shoreline at the bay's southern edge, creating a cliff-edged prominence upon which sat the palace of the Koldanian kings. It was a sprawling, multicentered building, the colonnades of which had been sheathed with beaten gold until Marcurades's accession to the throne. One of the young king's first actions after assuming power had been to strip the columns and distribute the gold among his people. The underlying cores of white marble shone almost as brightly, however, and at the end of the day, when they reflected the aureate light of sunset, the dwellers in the city below told their children that the gods had gilded the palace anew to repay Marcurades for his generosity.

Dardash imagined he could sense the universal adoration of the king as he rode into the city, and for him it was an atmosphere of danger. The task he had undertaken would have to be planned and carried out with the utmost care. He had already decided that it must not appear to be a murder at all, but even a naturally occurring illness could lead to suspicions of poisoning; and a magician, a reputed brewer of strange potions and philtres, was one of the most likely to be accused. It was essential, Dardash told himself, that Marcurades's death should occur in public, before as many witnesses as possible, and that it should appear as either a pure accident or, even better, a malign stroke of fate. The trouble was that divine acts were difficult to simulate.

"I have prepared a room for you in my own quarters at the palace," Urtarra said as they passed through the city's afternoon heat and began the gradual climb to the royal residence. "You will be able to rest there and have a meal."

"That's good," Dardash replied, "but first I'm going to bathe and have Nirrineen massage me with scented oils: I've begun to smell worse than this accursed horse."

"My intention was to send Nirrineen straight back to her father."

"No! I want her to stay with me."

"But many women are available at the palace." Urtarra brought his horse closer and lowered his voice. "It wouldn't be wise at this time to share your bed with one who has a special interest in you."

Dardash realized at once that Urtarra's counsel was good, but the thought of parting with Nirrineen—the she-creature who worked her own kind of voluptuous magic on him through the sweet hours of the night—was oddly painful. "Don't alarm yourself; she will know nothing," he said. "Do you take me for a fool?"

"I was thinking only of your own safety."

"There is only one whose safety is at risk," Dardash said, fixing his gaze on the complex architecture of the palace, which had begun to dominate the skyline ahead.

When they reached the palace gates a short time later, Urtarra conferred briefly with his men and sent them on their way to nearby lodgings. Dardash, Urtarra, and Nirrineen were able to ride through the gates after only a perfunctory examination by the captain of the palace guard—yet another indication of the unusual bond that existed between the king and his subjects. Servants summoned by Urtarra led away their horses and mules. Others came forward to carry Dardash's belongings into the astrologer's suite, which was part of a high wing facing the sea, but he dismissed them and moved the well-trussed bundles in person.

While thus engaged he noticed, in one corner of a small courtyard, a strange vehicle that consisted principally of a large wooden barrel mounted on four wheels. At the base of the barrel was an arrangement of cylinders and copper pipes from which projected a long T-shaped handle, and near the top, coiled like a snake, was a flexible leather tube, the seams of which were sealed with bitumen.

"What is that device?" Dardash said, pointing out the object to Urtarra. "I've never seen its like before."

Urtarra looked amused. "You'll see many of Marcurades's inventions before you are here very long. He calls that particular one a fire engine."

"A fire engine? Is it a siege weapon?"

"Quite the opposite," Urtarra said, his amusement turning to outright laughter. "It's for projecting water onto burning buildings."

"Oh? An unusual sport for a king."

"It's more than a sport, my friend. Marcurades gets so obsessed with his various inventions that he spends half his time in the palace workshops. Sometimes, in his impatience to see the latest one completed, he throws off his robes and labors on it like a common artisan. I've seen him emerge from the smithy so covered with soot and sweat as to be almost unrecognizable."

"Doesn't he know that such activities can be dangerous?"

"Marcurades doesn't care about . . ." Urtarra paused and scanned Dardash's face. "What are you thinking?"

"I'm not sure yet." Dardash almost smiled as his mind came to grips with the information he had just received. "Now, where can I bathe?"

"Watch this," Dardash said to Nirrineen as they stood together in the elaborate garden that formed a wide margin between the royal palace and the edge of the cliffs. It was a fresh morning, and the livening breeze coming in from the sea was ideally suited to Dardash's purpose. In his right hand he had a cross made from two flat strips of hardwood, smoothly jointed at the center. He raised his hand and made to throw the cross off the edge of the cliff.

"Don't throw it away," Nirrineen pleaded. She had no idea why Dardash had constructed the cross in the first place, but she had seen him spend the best part of a day carefully shaping the object, smoothly rounding some edges and sharpening others, and obviously she disliked the idea of his labor going to waste.

"But I've grown weary of the thing," Dardash said, laughing. He brought his hand down sharply, in an action like that of a man cracking a whip, and released the cross. It flew from his fingers at great speed, its arms flailing in the vertical plane, gradually curving downward toward the blue waters of the bay. Nirrineen began to protest, but her voice was stilled as the cross, tilting to one side, defied gravity by sailing upward again until it was higher than the point from which it had been launched. It appeared to come to rest in midair, hovering like a hawk, twinkling brightly in the sky. Nirrineen gave a small scream of mingled wonder and terror as she realized the cross was actually returning. She threw herself into Dardash's arms as the strange artifact fluttered back across the edge of the cliff and fell to earth a few paces away.

"You didn't tell me it was bewitched," she accused, clinging to Dardash and staring down at the cross as though it were a live thing that might suddenly attack her.

"There is no magic here," he said, disengaging himself and picking up the cross, "even though I learned the secret from a very old book. Look at how I have shaped each piece of wood to resemble a gull's wing. I've made you a little wooden bird, Nirrineen—a homing pigeon."

"It still seems like magic to me," she said doubtfully. "I don't think I like it."

"You soon shall. See how reluctant it is to leave you." Dardash threw the cross out to sea again in the same manner and it repeated its astonishing circular flight, this time coming to rest even closer to its starting point. Nirrineen leaped out of its path, but now there was more excitement than apprehension in her eyes, and after the third throw she was able to bring herself to pick the cross up and hand it to Dardash.

He went on throwing it, varying the speed and direction of its flight and making a game for both of them out of avoiding its whirling returns. In a short time a group of palace servants and minor officials, initially attracted by Nirrineen's laughter, had gathered to watch the spectacle. Dardash continued tirelessly, apparently oblivious to the onlookers, but in fact paying careful attention to every detail of his surroundings, and he knew—simply by detecting a change in the general noise level—the exact moment at which his plan had succeeded. He turned and saw the knot of spectators part to make way for the approach of a handsome, slightly built young man whose bearing somehow managed to be both relaxed and imperious.

This is a new kind of arrogance, Dardash thought. *Here is a man who feels that he doesn't even have to try to impress. . . .*

The remainder of the thought was lost as he got his first direct look at the young King Marcurades and felt the ruler's sheer psychic power wash over him. Dardash, as a dedicated magician, understood very well that there was more to his calling than the willingness and ability to memorize spells. On a number of occasions he had encountered men—often in ordinary walks of life—who had a strong potential for magic, but never before had he been confronted by a human being whose charisma was so overwhelming. Dardash suddenly found himself taken aback, humbled and confused, by the realization that he was in the company of a man who, had he been so inclined, could have effortlessly eclipsed him in his chosen profession.

"You must be Urtarra's new assistant," Marcurades said in light and pleasant tones. "I trust that you are enjoying your stay in Bhitsala."

Dardash bowed. "I'm enjoying it very much, sire; it is my privilege to serve Your Highness." To himself he said: *Can it, despite Urtarra's visions, be right to kill such a man?*

"I am sorry we could not meet sooner, but the demands on my time are myriad." Marcurades paused and glanced at Nirrineen. "However, I suspect you are in little need of consolation."

Nirrineen smiled and lowered her gaze in a way that, to Dardash's heightened sensibilities, had nothing to do with modesty. *The bitch,* he thought, appalled at the strength of his emotion. *The bitch is ready to give herself to him, right here and now.*

"I couldn't help observing that you cast more than horoscopes," Marcurades said, nodding at the cross that lay on the grass nearby. "That scrap of wood appears to have magical power, but—as I am no believer in hocus-pocus—I surmise it has qualities of form which are not immediately apparent."

"Indeed, sire." Dardash retrieved the cross and, with murder in his heart, began to explain what he knew of the aerodynamic principles that made the circular flights possible. Now that his attitude toward Marcurades had crystallized, the fact that the king addressed him as an equal and chose to wear unadorned linen garments were further evidence of an incredible arrogance, of an overweening pride. It was not difficult to understand how such attributes could decay into a terrible and dangerous insanity, gradually corrupting the young king until he had become a monster the world could well do without.

"As soon as the cross ceases to spin, it falls to the ground," Dardash said. "That shows that it is the fleet movement of these arms through the air which somehow makes the cross as light as thistledown. I have often thought that if a man could build a large cross, perhaps a score of paces from end to end, with arms shaped just so—and if he could devise some means for making it spin rapidly—why, then he could fly like an eagle, soar above all the lands and peoples of this earth."

Dardash paused and eyed the king, choosing his exact moment. "Of course, such a contrivance is impossible."

Marcurades's face was rapt, glowing. "I disagree, Dardash—I think one could be constructed."

"But the weight of the arms—"

"It would be folly to use solid wood for that purpose," Marcurades cut in, his voice growing more fervent. "No, I see light frameworks covered with wooden veneers, or skins, or—better still—silk. Yes, *silk!*"

Dardash shook his head. "No man, not even the mightiest wrestler, could spin the arms fast enough."

"Like all stargazers, you are lacking in knowledge of what can be done with earthly substances like copper and water . . . and fire," Marcurades replied, beginning to pace in circles. "I can produce the power of ten men, of a *horse*, within a small compass. The main problem is to make that power subservient to my wishes. It has to be channeled, and . . . and . . ." Marcurades raised one finger, traced an invisible line vertically and then, his eyes abstracted disks of white light, began to move his hand in horizontal circles.

"From *this* . . . to *this*," he murmured, communing with himself. "There must be a way."

"I don't understand, sire," Dardash said, disguising the exultation that pounded within him. "What are you—?"

"You'll see, stargazer." Marcurades turned back to the palace. "I think I'm going to surprise you."

"And I think I'm going to surprise *you*," Dardash said under his breath as he watched Marcurades ride away. Well satisfied with his morning's work, Dardash glanced at Nirrineen and felt a flicker of cold displeasure as he saw she was gazing at the figure of the departing king with a peculiar intensity.

The sooner my task here is complete, he thought irritably, *the better I'll like it.*

Urtarra's private apartment was a lavishly appointed room, the walls of which were hung with deep-blue tapestries embroidered with astrological emblems. He had apologized to Dardash for the ostentation of its furnishings and trappings, explaining that as he was not truly an astrologer it was necessary for him to put on a bold and convincing show for the benefit of all other residents at the palace. Now he was squatting comfortably on his bed, looking much as he had the first time Dardash had seen him—plump, oily, deceptively soft.

"I suppose I must congratulate you," he said reflectively. "Going aloft in a flying machine is one of the most dangerous things imaginable, and if you bring about the king's death without the use of magic, your triumph has to be considered all the greater. I won't withhold your reward."

"Don't even think of trying," Dardash advised. "Besides, you have missed the whole point of my discourse: I *will* have to use magic. A great deal of magic."

"But if it is simply a matter of waiting until Marcurades and his machine fall from the sky, I don't see—"

"What you don't see is that the machine will not be capable of leaving the ground," Dardash interrupted, amazed that a man of Urtarra's experience could display such naiveté about the natural world. "Not without my assistance, anyway. Man, like all other animals, belongs to the ground, and there is no contrivance—no ingenious combination of levers and springs and feathers—which can raise him out of his natural element.

"Note that I said *natural* element, because it is the essence of magic that it defies nature. I intend to cast a spell over whatever machine Marcurades builds, and with the power of my magic that machine will bear him upward, higher and higher into the realms of the gods, and then—when I judge the moment aright—the gods will become angry at the invasion of their domain by a mere mortal, and—"

"And you'll cancel your spell!" Urtarra clapped his hands to his temples. "It's perfect!"

Dardash nodded. "All of Bhitsala will see their king up there in the sky, far beyond the reach of ordinary men, and when he falls to his death—Who but the gods could be responsible? Even Marcurades cannot aspire to the status of a deity and hope to go unpunished."

"I bow to you, Dardash," Urtarra said. "You have earned my undying gratitude."

"Keep it," Dardash said coldly. "I'm doing a specified job for a specified fee, and there is no more to it than that."

The days that followed required him to make a number of carefully weighed decisions. On the one hand, he did not want to spend much time in the palace workshops for fear of becoming associated with the flying machine in people's minds and thus attracting some blame for the final disaster; on the other hand, he needed to see what was happening so that he could work the appropriate magic. There was a plentiful supply of *mana* in the vicinity of Bhitsala—he could sense it in his enhanced youthfulness and vigor—but he had no wish to waste it with an ill-conceived spell. If *mana* was again returning to the world at large, perhaps sifting down from the stars, it behooved him to conserve it, especially as he aspired to live as a magician for a very long time, perhaps forever.

He was intrigued to see that Marcurades had divided the work of building his flying machine into two entirely separate parts. One team of carpenters was concerned with fashioning four wings of the lightest possible construction. The frameworks over which the silk was to be stretched were so flimsy that strong cords had been used instead of wood in places where the members they joined always tended to move apart. Nevertheless, Dardash noted, the resulting structures were surprisingly stiff, and his respect for Marcurades's capabilities increased, although he knew that all the work of the artisans was futile.

The king had exercised even more ingenuity in the device that was intended to spin the wings. At its heart was a large, well-reinforced copper container beneath which was a miniature furnace. The latter incorporated a bellows and was fired by coals and pitch. The invisible force that springs from boiling water traveled vertically upward through a rigid pipe, at the top of which was a slip ring. Four lesser pipes, all bent in the same direction, projected horizontally from the ring in the form of a swastika. When the furnace was lit, the steam expelled from the end of the pipes caused the swastika to rotate at a considerable speed, and by decreasing pressure losses and improving lubrication and balance, Marcurades was making it go faster every day.

Dardash watched the work without comment. He knew from his reading and a certain amount of experimentation that all should come to naught when the wings were attached to the pipes of the swastika. For no reason he could explain, the faster that wing-shaped objects traveled, the more difficult they became to urge forward, and the resistance increased much more rapidly than one would have expected. Under normal conditions Marcurades's machine would have been able to produce no more than a feeble and faltering rotation of the wings, far short of the speed needed to create the inexplicable lightness required for flight, but the circumstances were far from normal.

Dardash prepared a simple kinetic sorcery and directed its power into the four newly completed wings, altering their unseen physical nature in such a way that the faster they moved, the *less* effort it took to increase their speed even further. He prudently remained in a distant part of the palace when Marcurades assembled his machine for the first time, but he knew precisely when the first test was carried out. An ornate ring he wore on his left hand began to vibrate slightly, letting him know that a certain amount of *mana* was being used up: The wings of the flying machine were spinning in a satisfactory manner.

Dardash visualized the hissing contraption beginning to stir and shiver, to exhibit the desire to leave the ground, and he strained his ears for evidence of one possible consequence. He knew that the king was reckless when in the grip of an enthusiasm, and if he was foolhardy enough to go aloft in the machine in its present form, he would almost certainly be killed, and Dardash would be able to claim his reward earlier than planned. There came no cries of alarm, however, and he deduced that Marcurades had fore-seen the need to control the machine once it soared up from the still air of the courtyard and into the turbulent breezes that forever danced above the cliffs.

I can wait, he thought, nodding his appreciation of the young king's engineering talent. *What are a few more days when measured against eter-nity?*

The news that the king had constructed a machine with which he intended to fly into the heavens spread through Bhitsala and the surrounding regions of Koldana in a very short time. There was to be no public ceremony con-nected with the first flight—indeed, Marcurades was too engrossed in his new activity even to be aware of his subjects' feverish interest in it—but as the stories spread farther and became more lurid there was a gradual drift of population toward Bhitsala.

The city filled with travelers who had come to see the ruler borne aloft on the back of a mechanical dragon, eagle, or bat, depending on which vari-ation of the rumor they had encountered. Bhitsala's lodging houses and tav-erns experienced a profitable upsurge of trade, and the atmosphere of excite-ment and celebration intensified daily, with runners coming down from the palace at frequent intervals to barter the latest scraps of information. People going about their routine business kept glancing up toward the white-columned royal residence, and such was the pitch of expectancy that every time a flock of seabirds rose from the cliffs, an audible ripple of near-hysteria sped through the streets.

Dardash, while keeping himself closely informed of Marcurades's progress, made a show of being disinterested almost to the point of aloofness. He spent much of his time on the balcony of Urtarra's apartment, ostensibly engaged in astrological work, but in fact keeping watch on the western ram-parts of the palace, behind which the flying machine was receiving finish-ing touches. During this period of idleness and waiting he would have appreciated the company of Nirrineen, but she had taken to associating a great deal with certain of the courtesans who attended the king. Urtarra had expressed the opinion that her absence was all to the good, as it meant she had less chance to become an embarrassment, and Dardash had voiced his agreement. But he waxed more moody and surly and ever more impatient, and as he scanned the foreshortened silhouette of the palace he seemed, occasionally, to betray his true age.

"And not before time" was his sole comment when Urtarra arrived one day, in the trembling purple heat of noon, with the intelligence that Marcurades was on the point of making a trial flight. Dardash had already known that a significant event was about to occur, because the sensor ring on his left hand had been vibrating strongly for some time — evidence that the machine's wings were rotating at speed. He had also seen and heard the growing excitement in the city below. The population of Bhitsala appeared to have migrated like so many birds to rooftops and high window ledges, anyplace from which they could get a good view of the forthcoming miracle.

"This is a wonderful thing you are doing for the people of Koldana," Urtarra said as they stood together on the balcony, with the blue curvatures of the bay stretching away beneath them. His voice was low and earnest, as though he had begun to suffer last-minute doubts and was trying to drive them away.

"Just have my payment ready," Dardash said, giving him a disdainful glance.

"You have no need to worry on that . . ." Urtarra's speech faltered as the air was disturbed by a strange sound, a powerful and sustained fluttering that seemed to resonate inside the chest.

A moment later the king's flying machine lifted itself into view above the palace's western extremity.

The four rotating wings were visible in a blurry white disk edged with gold, and slung beneath them was a gondola-shaped basket in which could be seen the figure of the king. Dardash's keen eyesight picked out weights suspended on ropes beneath the basket, giving the whole assemblance the same kind of stability as a pendulum, and it seemed to him that Marcurades had also added extra fitments at the top of the pipe that carried steam to the wing impellers.

A sigh of mingled wonder and adoration rose up from the watching throngs as the machine continued its miraculous ascent into the clear blue dome of the sky. At a dizzy height above the palace, almost at the limit of Dardash's vision, the king reached upward to operate a lever, the insubstantial disk of the wings tilted slightly, and the machine swooped out over the line of cliffs, out over the waters of the bay.

Ecstatic cheering, great slow-pulsing billows of sound, surged back and forth like tidal currents as Marcurades—godlike in his new power—steered his machine into a series of wide sweeps far above the wave crests.

"Now," Urtarra urged. "The time is *now!*"

"So be it," Dardash said, fingering the scrap of parchment on which the spell for the kinetic sorcery was written. He uttered a single polysyllabic word and tore the parchment in two.

At that instant the sun-gleaming shape of the flying machine was checked in its course, as though it had encountered an invisible obstacle. It wavered, faltered, then began to fall.

The sound that went up from the watching multitude was a vast wordless moan of consternation and shocked disbelief. Dardash listened to it for a moment, his face impassive, and was turning away from the balcony when two things happened to petrify him in mid-stride.

Far out across the water, Marcurades's flying machine, which had been tilting over as it fell, abruptly righted itself and began to hover, neither losing nor gaining height. Simultaneously, a fierce pain lanced through Dardash's left hand. He snatched the sensor ring off his finger and threw it to the floor, where it promptly became white-hot. Outside was a pounding silence as every one of Marcurades's subjects, not daring to breathe, prayed for his safety.

"The king flies," Urtarra said in a hushed voice. "He built better than you knew."

"I don't think so," Dardash said grimly. "Look! The machine's wings are scarcely turning. It should be falling!"

He strode to a chest where he had stored some of his equipment and returned with a silver hoop, which he held out at arm's length. Viewed through the metal circle, the hovering aircraft was a blinding, sunlike source of radiance. Dardash felt the beginnings of a terrible fear.

"What does it mean?" Urtarra said. "I don't—"

"That light is *mana*, the raw power behind magic." Dardash's throat had gone dry, thickening and deadening his voice. "Fantastic amounts of it are being expended to keep Marcurades and his machine aloft. I've never seen such a concentration."

"Does that mean there's another magician at work?"

"I wish that were all it meant," Dardash said. He lowered the silver hoop and stared at the flickering mote that was the flying machine. It had begun to move again, slowly losing height and drifting in toward the shore, and Dardash knew with bleak certainty that aboard it was a new kind of man — one who could use *mana* instinctively, in tremendous quantities, to satisfy his own needs and achieve his ambitions. Marcurades could tap and squander *mana* resources without even being aware of what he was doing, and Dardash now fully understood why the future divined for the king had been so cataclysmic. Such power, without the discipline and self-knowledge of the traditional sorcerers, could only corrupt. The *mana*-assisted achievement of each ambition would inspire others, each grander and more vainglorious than the one before, and the inevitable outcome would be evil and madness.

Dardash, all too conscious of the dangerous nature of the energy behind his profession, suddenly foresaw the rise of a new kind of tyrant — the spawning of monsters so corrupted by success and ambition, believing *themselves* to be the fountainheads of power, that they would eventually seek to dominate the entire world, and even be prepared to see it go up in flames if their desires were thwarted.

"I forbid it," he whispered, his fear giving way to resentment and a deep, implacable hatred. "I, Dardash, say—NO!"

He ran back to the chest, driven by the knowledge that with each passing second Marcurades was a little closer to safety, and took from it a slim black rod. The wand had no power in itself, but it served to direct and concentrate magical energies. There was an unexpected noise in the next room and, glancing through the partially opened door, Dardash saw Nirrineen coming toward him. Her expression was one of childish delight, and her hands were at her throat, caressing a gold necklace.

"Look what the king has given me," she said. "Isn't it the most—?"

"Stay out of here," Dardash shouted, trying to control his panic as he realized there was almost no time left in which to accomplish his purpose.

He wheeled to face the balcony and the bright scene beyond it, pointed the wand, and uttered a spell he had hoped never to use, a personal sacrilege, a destructive formula that used *mana* to combat and neutralize *mana*.

The flying machine disintegrated.

Its four wings flailed and fluttered off in different directions, and from the center of the destruction the body of the machine plunged downward like a mass of lead. There was a sputtering explosion as it struck the water, then it was gone, and Marcurades was lost, and all that remained of the young king and all his ambitions were spreading ripples of water and the four slow-tumbling wings that had borne him to his death. A lone seabird shrieked in the pervading silence.

Dardash had time for one pang of triumph, then his vision dimmed and blurred. He looked at his hands and saw that they had withered into the semblance of claws, blotched and feeble, and he understood at once that his brief battle with Marcurades had been even more destructive than he had anticipated. In that one instant of conflict every trace of *mana* in the entire region had been annihilated, and he, Dardash, no longer had access to the magical power that had preserved his body.

"Murderer!" Nirrineen's voice seemed to reach him from another time, another existence. "You murdered the king!"

Dardash turned to face her. "You overestimate my powers, child," he soothed, motioning for Urtarra to move around behind her and block the exit. "What makes you think that a humble dabbler in simple magic could ever—?"

He broke off as he saw Nirrineen's revulsion at his appearance, evidence that more than a century of hard living had taken a dreadful toll of his face and body. Evidence, too, that a momentous event had just taken place. Evidence of his guilt.

Nirrineen shook her head, and with near-magical abruptness she was gone. Her fleeing footsteps sounded briefly and were lost in the mournful wailing that had begun to pervade the room from outside as the people of Bhitsala absorbed the realization that their king was dead.

"You should have stopped her," Dardash said to Urtarra, too weak and tired to sound more than gently reproachful. "She has gone to fetch the palace guard, and now neither of us will ever . . ."

He stopped speaking as he saw that Urtarra had sunk down on a couch, hands pressed to his temples, eyes dilated with a strange horror, seeing but not seeing.

"So it has finally happened to you, Soothsayer: Now you can foresee your own death." Dardash spoke with intuitive understanding of what was happening in Urtarra's mind. "But do not waste what little time remains to you. Let me know that my sacrifice has not been in vain, that the whore wasn't carrying Marcurades's seed. Give me proof that no other *mana*-monsters will arise to usurp magicians and wreak their blind and ignorant havoc on the world."

Urtarra appeared deaf to his words, but he raised one hand and pointed at the opposite wall of the room. The blue tapestries acquired a tremulous depth they had not previously possessed, came alive with images of times yet to be. The images changed rapidly, showing different places and different eras, but they had some elements in common.

Always there was fire, always there was destruction, always there was death on a scale that Dardash had never conceived.

And against those fearful backgrounds there came a procession of charismatic, *mana*-rich figures. Knowledge, foreknowledge, was again vouchsafed to Dardash in wordless whispers, and unfamiliar names reverberated within his head. . . .

Alexander . . . Julius Caesar . . . Tamburlaine. . . .

The sky grew dark with the shadow of thousands of wings; annihilation rained from great airborne ships, creating a lurid backdrop for the strutting figure of Adolf Hitler. . . .

Dardash covered his eyes with his hands and sank to a kneeling position, and remained that way without moving until the sound of heavy footsteps and the clatter of armor told him the palace guards had arrived. And the stroke of the sword, not long delayed, came like a kindly friend, bringing the only reward for which he retained any craving.

Ψ

TALISMAN

by Larry Niven and Dian Girard

♃

THE STRANGER SWUNG his baggage off his horse's back, patted the animal on the side of the neck, and handed the reins to the stable hand. Old Kasan was rarely interested in people; he barely glanced at the stranger. Slanted eyes, round face with a yellow tinge . . .

Kasan led the animal to an empty stall and gave it food and water. Now, the beast was a puzzler. It suffered his ministrations with an air of strained patience. Its tail ended in the kind of brush usually seen on an ass. Kasan fancied that its look was one of tolerant contempt.

"Ah, horse, you underestimate me," Kasan said. "I won't be tending other people's horses forever." Horses did not often mock Kasan's daydreams. This one's nicker sounded too much like a snicker. "It's true! Someday I'll own my own rental stable. . . ." And Kasan fondled the beast's ears and mane, as if to thank it for listening.

Under its shaggy forelock he felt a hard circular scar.

He told Bayram Ali about it when he went in for lunch. "It's a unicorn. The horn's been chopped off. What kind of man would be riding a disguised unicorn?"

The innkeeper said, "Sometimes I wonder why I put up with your stories, Kasan."

"You can feel the stub yourself!"

"No doubt. At least don't be bothering my guests with such tales." And Bayram Ali set a tankard of ale next to Kasan's midday cheese and bread. Kasan opened his mouth to retort, noticed the ale, and kept silent.

And Bayram Ali took counsel with himself.

Strange beasts like the one munching hay in his stable were often found in the company of strange men. The traveler might be a sorcerer, though they were rare these days. More likely he was a magician on his way to Rynildissen. Bayram had seen the man carry two heavy bags up to his room.

It would be interesting to know what was in them and if it would be worthwhile to lighten them a little.

Bayram Ali never robbed his guests. It was a point of honor. He preferred to leave the work and any possible danger to a professional. He looked around the crowded common room. It was smoky and odorous with the scents of cooking and human bodies. There was much laughter and spilling of wine. Unfortunately, most of the light-fingered brethren present had hasty tempers and were too quick to pull a knife. Bayram would not have violence in his inn.

Across the room his small, pretty wife, Esme, was struggling to carry a huge frothy pitcher of ale. Two men were pushing and shoving each other for the honor of carrying it for her. Just beyond them, leaning back on a rough bench with her shoulders against the wall, Sparthera was laughing and yelling at the two combatants.

Sparthera. Bayram Ali grinned broadly. The slim young thief was just what he had in mind. She was daring without being reckless, and had no morals to speak of. They had made more than one bargain in the past.

He pushed his way across the room, pausing to grab up the pitcher his wife was carrying and slam it down in front of a customer. He knocked the combatants' heads together, sending them into hysterical laughter, and sent Esme back to the kitchen with a hearty slap on her firm round backside.

"Ay, Sparthera!"

The thief laughed up at him. She was finely built and slender, with a tangled mass of tawny hair and high, firm breasts. Her large hazel eyes were set wide over a short, straight nose and full red lips.

"Well, Bayram Ali, have you come over to knock my head against something too?" She hooked her thumbs in the belt of her leather jerkin and stretched out a pair of lean leather-clad legs.

"No, little thief. I wondered if you had noticed a certain stranger among my guests."

"Oh?" She had lost the smile.

Bayram Ali sat down on the bench next to her and lowered his voice. "A smooth-skinned man from the East, with bulging saddlebags. His name is Sung Ko Ja. Old Kasan says he came riding a unicorn, with the beast's horn cut off to disguise it."

"A sorcerer!" Sparthera shook her head firmly. "No. I'd as soon try to rob the statue of Khulm. I don't want anything to do with sorcerers."

"Oh, I hardly think he's a sorcerer," the innkeeper said soothingly. "No more than a magician, if that. A sorcerer wouldn't need to disguise anything. This man is trying to avoid drawing attention to himself. He must have something a thief would want, hmm?"

Sparthera frowned and thought for a moment. No need to ask the terms of the bargain. It would be equal shares, and cheating was expected. "All right. When he comes down to the common room for dinner, or goes out to the privy, let me know. I'll go up and look around his room."

It was several hours before Sung Ko Ja came back down the stairs. The sun was just setting, and Esme and her buxom daughters were beginning to serve the evening meal. Sparthera was sitting at one of the small tables near the kitchen door. Bayram Ali brushed by her with a pot of stew.

"That's the one," he whispered. "With the slanted eyes. His room is the third on the left."

Only Sparthera's eyes moved. Around forty, she thought, and distinctly foreign: round of face, but not fat, with old-ivory skin and dark almond eyes and the manner of a lord. He seemed to be settling in for dinner. Good.

Sparthera moved quickly up the stairs and along the hall, counting doors. The third door didn't move when she pushed on the handle. She tried to throw her weight against it and couldn't; somehow she couldn't find her balance.

A spell?

She went along to the end of the hall where one small window led out onto the first-story roof. Outside, a scant two feet of slippery thatch separated the second-story wall and a drop to the cobblestones in the stableyard.

The sun had set. The afterglow was bright enough to work in . . . perhaps not dark enough to hide her? But behind the inn were only fields, and those who had been seeding the fields were gone to their suppers. There was nobody to watch Sparthera work her way around to the window of the magician's room.

The narrow opening was covered with oiled paper. She slit it neatly with the tip of the knife she always carried, and reached through. Or tried to. Something blocked her.

She pushed harder. She felt nothing, but her hand wouldn't move.

She swung a fist at the paper window. Her hand stopped jarringly, and this time she felt her own muscles suddenly lock. Her own strength had stopped her swing.

She had no way to fight such magic. Sparthera hung from the roof by her hands and dropped the remaining four feet to the ground. She dusted herself off and reentered the inn through the front.

Sung Ko Ja was still eating his meal of roast fowl, bread, and fruit. Bayram Ali was hovering around with one eye on the magician and the other on the stairs. Sparthera caught his eye.

He joined her. "Well?"

"I can't get in. There's a spell on the room."

The innkeeper's face fell; then he shrugged. "Pity."

"I want very much to know what that man has that he thinks is so important." She bit one finger and considered the ivory-skinned man dining peacefully on the other side of the room. "He doesn't have the look of the ascetic. What do you think? Would he like a woman to keep him warm on such a cold night?"

"Sparthera, have you considered what you're suggesting? My inn's reputation is important to me. If I offer, you'll . . . well. You'd have to *do* it."

"Well?"

"The one time I myself made such a suggestion, you nearly cut my throat."

"That was years ago. I was . . . it had been . . . I'd only just thrown that damned tinker out on his ear. I didn't like men much just then. Besides, this is different. It's business."

Bayram Ali eyed her doubtfully. She was dressed more like a young boy than a woman. Still, the magician was a foreigner. Probably all of the local women looked odd to him. Bayram shrugged and pushed his way across the room.

Sung Ko Ja looked up.

The innkeeper smiled broadly. "The wine was good, eh?"

"Drinkable."

"And the fowl? It was young, tender, was it not? Cooked to a nicety?"

"I ate it. What's on your mind?"

"Oh, noble sir! The night will be cold, and I have a girl. Such a girl! A vision of delight, a morsel of sweetness . . ."

Sung Ko Ja waved an impatient hand. "All right. So she is everything you claim she is. How much?"

"Ten."

"Too much. Six."

Bayram Ali looked stunned, then hurt. "Sir, you insult this princess among women. Why, only last week she was a virgin. Nine."

"Seven."

"Eight and a half."

"Done. And bring me another bottle of wine." Sung tossed down the last few drops in his tankard and paid the innkeeper. Sparthera was waiting for him at the foot of the stairs. He looked her over briefly and then started up the stairs, carrying his fresh bottle of wine. "Well, come on, girl."

He stopped at the door to his room and made a few quick gestures with his left hand before he pushed it open.

"Why did you do that?" Sparthera asked in girlish innocence.

"To raise the spell that protects my room. Otherwise I couldn't let you in, my sweet one." He laughed softly and burped.

Sparthera stopped in the doorway. "If you have a spell on this room, does that mean I'll be locked in?"

"No, no. You're free to come and go—as often as you like." He chuckled. "Until the dawn light comes through that window at the end of the hall and relinks the spell."

She entered. The low bed—hardly more than a pallet—held a straw-filled mattress and bedding woven from the local cotton and wool. There was wood stacked in the small fireplace grate, and flint and steel lay next to a single candle in a holder. The magician's saddlebags were sitting on the floor by the bed.

Sung looked up at the small window where Sparthera had slashed the paper, and frowned. A cold draft was coming through the opening.

"I'll light the fire, shall I?" Sparthera asked.

She hurried to start a small blaze, while Sung, swaying slightly on his feet, considered the open window. Best that he be distracted. She asked, "Is it true that you're a magician?"

He smiled. "There is only one sort of magic I have in mind at the moment."

Sparthera hid her sudden nervousness behind a smile. "Ah, but did you bring your wand?"

The flickering firelight threw their shadows on the wall as Sung guided her to the narrow bed. What followed left Sparthera pleasantly surprised. For all his smooth skin and foreign ways, the stranger proved more than equal to other men she'd known. He was considerate . . . almost as if she were paying, not he. Even if nothing came of this venture, the evening hadn't been wasted.

Two hours later she was beginning to change her mind.

They were sitting up on the straw-filled mattress, sharing the last of the wine. Sparthera was naked; Sung still wore a wide cloth belt. He had opened one of his bags and was showing her a variety of small trinkets. There were birds that chirped when you tightened a spring, a pair of puppets on strings, flowers made of yellow silk, and squares of bright paper that Sung folded to look like bears and fish. He was very drunk, and talkative.

"The immortal Sung and his family rule in the land of the Yellow River, a mountainous land far to the East. I was head of the family for twenty years. Now I have abdicated the throne in favor of my son. But I carried away some magic. Watch: I put a half-twist in this strip of paper, join the ends, and now it has only one side and one edge. . . ."

Sparthera was restless and bored. She had come upstairs expecting to deal with a magician. She had found a cheap toymaker who couldn't hold his wine. She watched his strong, agile fingers twisting a scrap of paper into a bird . . . and wondered. His forehead was high and smooth, his face a little too round for her taste, but undeniably good to look on. It was hard to believe that he could be a complete fool. There must be more to him than cheap toys and bragging and a way with women.

He was rummaging in his bag again and she caught a glimpse of gleaming metal.

"What is that? The box?"

"The pointer. The key to Gar's treasure. A gift to set me on the road."

"Gar's treasure. What's that?" It sounded vaguely familiar.

"It's a secret," Sung said, and he closed that saddlebag and reached across for the other. And while he was turned away from her, Sparthera pulled a twist of paper from her hair, and opened it, and shook white powder into Sung's half-empty goblet.

She didn't use it all, and it probably wasn't needed. Sung was on his back and snoring a few minutes later, long before the drug could have taken effect. Sparthera watched him for a few cautious minutes more before she reached into the saddlebag.

She drew out a silver box. There were pieces of jade and carnelian set in mountings on the lid and sides.

She was half afraid that a spell sealed this, too, but it opened easily enough. The inside was lined with faded crimson velvet, and all it held was an elongated teardrop of tarnished bronze. There were tiny silver runes inlaid along the length of the dark metal.

Sparthera picked it up and turned it this way and that. It was thicker than her forefinger and just about as long. A conical hole had been drilled through its underside.

The box was worth something, but was it worth angering a magician? Probably not, she decided reluctantly. And it certainly wasn't worth killing for, not here. Bayram Ali would never allow such a thing. She would have to flee Tarseny's Rest forever, and Sparthera had none of the tourist urge in her.

The same applied to Sung's cloth belt. She had felt the coins in it when they made the two-backed beast, but it was no fortune.

Sung surely ought to be robbed. It would do him good; make him less gullible. But not tonight. Sparthera dropped the pointer in its box, closed it, and was reaching for the saddlebag when she remembered.

Gar had been Kaythill's magician.

And Kaythill was a bandit chief who had raided the lands around Rynildissen City a hundred years ago. He had lasted some twenty years, until the King's soldiers caught him traveling alone. Under torture Kaythill had steered them to some of his spoils. The rest? A wagonload of gold and jewels had been stolen by Gar the magician. Kaythill and his men had been scouting the countryside for Gar when the soldiers trapped him.

Of course the King's men searched for Gar. Some vital pieces of military magic were among the missing treasure. There had been rewards posted, soldiers everywhere, rumors . . . and Gar's treasure had grown in the telling, had grown into legend, until it reached Sparthera via her father. She had been . . . six? It was a wonder she remembered at all.

And this trinket would point the way to Gar's treasure?

Sparthera dressed hurriedly, snatched up the silver box, and left the room. She hesitated in the hall, looking first at her trophy and then back at the door. What would he do when he woke and found the box missing? She had only seen him drunk. A magician sober and looking for lost property might be an entirely different matter.

She pushed at the door. It opened easily. He hadn't lied, then: She could come and go as she pleased—until dawn.

Sparthera hurried down the stairs and out of the inn. It was nearly midnight and there were only a few jovial souls left in the common room. None saw her leave.

Patrols rarely came to the Thieves' Quarter of Tarseny's Rest, but in the Street of the Metalworkers they were common. Sparthera went warily, waiting until a pair of guards had passed before she began throwing pebbles at a certain upstairs window.

The window came alight. Sparthera stepped out of the shadows, showed herself. Presently Tinx appeared, rubbing his eyes, looking left and right before he pulled her inside.

"Sparthera! What brings you here, little thief? Are the dogs finally at your heels and you need a place to hide?"

"How long would it take you to copy this?" She opened the box and held out the bronze teardrop.

"Hmmm. Not long. The lettering is the hard part, but I do have some silver."

"How long?"

"An hour or two."

"I need it now, tonight."

"Sparthera, I *can't*. I need my sleep."

"Tinx, you owe me."

Tinx owed her twice. Once, for a pair of thieves who had tried to interest Sparthera in robbing Tinx's shop. In Sparthera's opinion, robbing a citizen of Tarseny's Rest was fouling one's own nest. She had informed on them. And once she had worked like a slave in his shop, to finish a lucrative job on time; for Sparthera was not always a thief. But Tinx had had other, more pressing debts, and he still owed Sparthera most of her fee.

The metalworker lifted his hands helplessly and rolled his eyes to heaven. "Will I be rid of you then?"

"Finished and done. All debts paid."

"Oh, all right, then!" He sighed and, still grumbling about his lost night's sleep, went back inside to light some candles and a lantern to work by.

Sparthera prowled restlessly about the tiny shop. She found means to make tea. Afterward she prowled some more, until Tinx glared at her and demanded she stay in one place. Then she sat, while Tinx sawed and filed and hammered until he had a bronze teardrop; gouged grooves on the surface; pounded silver wire into the grooves; polished it, compared it to the original, then held it in tongs over a flame until tarnish dulled the silver. He asked, "Just how good are your client's eyes?"

"I don't really know, but by Khulm we're running out of time!"

"Well, what do you think?" He handed her the copy and the original.

She turned them swiftly in her hands, then dropped the copy into the box and the original into her sleeve. "Has to be good enough. My thanks, Tinx." She was already slipping through the door. "If this works out . . ." She was down the street and out of earshot, leaving Tinx to wonder if she had made him a promise. Probably not.

She stopped inside the front door of the inn. A moment to get her breath, else the whole inn would hear her. Then upstairs, on tiptoe. Third door down. Push. It swung open, and Sparthera swallowed her gasp of relief.

The magician was still asleep and still snoring. He looked charmingly vulnerable, she thought. Sparthera pushed the box into a saddlebag, under a tunic. It cost her a wrench to leave it, but far better to lose a trinket worth a few gold pieces than to face the wrath of an outraged sorcerer. Sparthera had bigger fish to fry. She tiptoed out and shut the door. The first gray glow of morning was showing through the window at the end of the hall.

Sparthera stayed out of sight until she saw Sung mount his odd shaggy horse and start off down the King's Way to Rynildissen. He seemed unsteady in the saddle, and once he clutched at his head. That worried her. "Khulm bear witness, I *did* go easy on that powder," she told herself.

She found Bayram Ali counting money at a table in the common room. He looked up at her expectantly.

"Well? What did you find?"

"A few toys. Some scraps of colored paper, and an old silver box that isn't worth the trouble it would get us."

"No money?"

"Coins in a belt. He never took it off. There wasn't much in it . . . not enough, anyway."

Bayram Ali scowled. "Very intelligent of you, dear. Still, a pity. He left this for you." He tucked two fingers into his wide cummerbund and fished out a pair of silver coins. "Perhaps you've found a new calling. One for you and one for me, hmm?"

Sparthera smiled, letting her strong, even white teeth show. "And how much did he pay you last night?"

"Six pieces of silver," Bayram Ali said happily.

"You sold me so cheaply? You're a liar and your mother was insulted on a garbage heap."

"Well. He offered six. We settled for eight."

"Four for you, four for me, hmm?"

He looked pained. Sparthera took her five pieces of silver, winked, and departed, wondering what Sung Ko Ja had really paid. That was part of the fun of bargaining: wondering who had cheated whom.

But this time Sparthera had the pointer.

On a bald hill east of the village, Sparthera took the bronze teardrop from her sleeve, along with a needle and the cork from one of Sung Ko Ja's bottles of wine. She pushed the base of the needle into the cork, set it down, and balanced the pointer on the needle. "Pointer! Pointer, show me the way to Gar's treasure!" she whispered to it, and nudged it into a spin.

Three times she spun it and marked where it stopped, pointing north, and northwest, and east.

She tried holding it in her hand, turning in a circle with her eyes closed, trying to feel a tug. She tried balancing it on her own fingernail.

She studied the runes, but they meant nothing to her. After two hours she was screaming curses like a Euphrates fishwife. It didn't respond to that either.

Sitting on the bare dusty ground with her chin in her hands and the pointer lying in the dirt in front of her, Sparthera felt almost betrayed. So close! She was so close to wealth that she could almost hear the tinkle of golden coins. She needed advice, and the one person who might help her was the one she had vowed never to see again.

A faint smile crossed her face as she remembered screaming at him, throwing his bags and gear out of the tiny hut they had shared, swearing by the hair on her head that she'd die and rot in hell before she ever went near him again. That damned tinker! Pot-mender, amateur spellcaster, womanizer: his real magic was in his tongue. She'd left her home and family to follow him, and all of his promises had been so much air.

She'd heard that he lived up in the hills now, that he called himself Shubar Khan and practiced magic to earn a living. If he cast spells the way he mended pans, she thought sourly, he wouldn't be of much use to her. But perhaps he'd learned something . . . and there wasn't anyone else she could go to. She stood up, dusted herself off, and bent to pick up the bronze teardrop.

The sky was clouding over and the scent of rain was in the air. It matched her dismal mood.

What about her vow? It had been a general oath, not bound by a particular god, but she had meant it with all her heart. Sometimes vows like that were the most dangerous, for who knew what wandering elemental might be listening? She leaned against Twilight, smoothing his tangled mane and staring out over his back at the rolling foothills and the mountains beyond. Life was too dear and Gar's treasure too important to risk either on a broken vow. She took her knife away from its sheath and started to hack at her own long tawny hair.

Shubar Khan's house, hardly more than a hut, was both small and dirty. Sparthera reined her horse to a halt before the door. She looked distastefully at a hog carcass lying in the center of a diagram scratched in the hard dry ground.

She had sworn never to speak his name, but that name was *Tashubar.*

She called, "Shubar Khan! Come out, Shubar Khan!" She peered into the dark doorway. A faint odor of burning fat was the only sign of habitation.

"Who calls Shubar Khan?" A man appeared in the doorway and blinked out at her. Sparthera swung herself down from Twilight's back and lifted her chin a little arrogantly, staring at him.

"Sparthera?" He rubbed the side of his face and laughed dryly. "Oh-ho. The last time we saw one another you threw things at me. I think I still have a scar somewhere. You wouldn't care to see it, would you? Ah, well, I thought not."

He cocked his head to one side and nodded. "You're still beautiful. Just like you were when I found you in that haystack. Heh, heh, heh. I like you better with hair, though. What happened to it?"

"I swore an oath," she said shortly, wondering a little at what passing time could do to a man. He had been a good thirty years old to her fourteen when they met. Now she was twenty-six, and he was potbellied and sweaty, with a red face and thinning hair and lecherous little eyes. He wore felt slippers with toes that turned up, and five layers of brightly striped woolen robes. He scratched now and then, absentmindedly.

But he still had the big, knowing hands and strong shoulders that sloped up into his neck, and hadn't he always scratched? And he'd never been thin, and his eyes couldn't have shrunk. The change was in her. Suddenly she hungered to get the matter over with and leave Shubar Khan to the past, where he belonged.

"I've come on business. I want you to fix something for me." She held out the piece of bronze. "It's supposed to be a pointer, but it doesn't work."

A small dirty hand reached out for the pointer. "I can fix that!"

Sparthera spun around, reaching for her knife.

"My apprentice," Shubar Khan explained. "How would you fix it, boy?"

"There's a storm coming up." The boy, hardly more than twelve, looked at his master with sparkling eyes. "I can climb a tree and tie the thing to a branch high up. When the lightning strikes—"

"You short-eared offspring of a spavined goat!" Shubar bellowed at him. "That would only make it point to the pole star if it didn't melt first, and if it were iron instead of bronze! Bah!"

The boy cringed back into the gloom of the hut, which was filled with

dry bones, aborted sheep fetuses, and pig bladders stuffed with odd oint-
ments. There was even a two-inch-long unicorn horn prominently displayed
on a small silk pillow.

Shubar Khan peered at the silver runes. He mumbled under his breath,
at length. Was he reading them? "Old Sorcerer's Guild language," he said,
"with some mistakes. What is it supposed to point *at?*"

"I don't know," Sparthera lied. "Something buried, I think."

Shubar Khan unrolled one of the scrolls, weighted it open with a couple of bones, and began to read in a musical foreign tongue. Presently he
stopped. "Nothing. Whatever spell was on it, it seems as dead as the gods."

"Curse my luck and your skill! Can't you do anything?"

"I can put a contagion spell on it for two pieces of silver." He looked her
up and down and grinned. "Or anything else of equal or greater value."

"I'll give you the coins," Sparthera said shortly. "What will the spell do?"

Shubar Khan laughed until his paunch shook. "Not even for old time's
sake? What a pity. As to the spell, it will make this thing seek whatever it was
once bound to. We're probably lucky the original spell wore off. A contagion
spell is almost easy."

Sparthera handed over the money. Gar's treasure had already cost her
far too much. Shubar Khan ushered her and his apprentice—loaded down
with phials, a pair of scrolls, firewood, and a small caldron—to a steep crag
nearby.

"Why do we have to come out here?" Sparthera asked.

"We're just being cautious," Shubar Khan said soothingly. He set up the
caldron, emptied a few things into it, lit the fire the apprentice had set, and
handed the apprentice the bronze teardrop and one of the scrolls. "When
the caldron smokes, just read this passage out loud. And remember to enun-
ciate," he said as he grabbed Sparthera's arm and sprinted down the hill.

Sparthera looked uphill at the boy. "This is dangerous, isn't it? How
dangerous?"

"I don't know. The original spell isn't working, but there may be some
power left in it, and there's no telling what it may do. That's why magicians
have apprentices."

They could hear the boy chanting in his childish treble, speaking gibberish, but rolling his *R*'s and practically spitting the *P*'s. The clouds that

had been gathering overhead took on a harsh, ominous quality. The wind came up and the trees whipped and showered leaves on the ground.

A crack of lightning cast the entire landscape into ghastly brightness. Shubar Khan dived to the ground. Sparthera winced and then strained her eyes into the suddenly smoky air. There was no sign of the boy. Thunder rolled deafeningly across the sky.

Sparthera ran up the hill, heart thumping. The top of the crag was scorched and blackened. The iron caldron was no more than a twisted blob of metal.

"Ooohhh!"

Shubar Khan's apprentice pulled himself to his feet and looked at her with huge eyes. His face was smudged, his hair scorched, and his clothing still smoldered. He held out a blackened fist with the bronze piece in it.

"Did, did . . . did it work?" he asked in a frightened croak.

Shubar Khan retrieved the pointer and laid it on his palm. It slowly rotated to the right and stopped. He grinned broadly and patted the boy heartily on the shoulder.

"Excellent! We'll make a magician of you yet!" He turned to Sparthera and presented the pointer to her with a bow.

She tucked it inside her tunic. "Thank you," she said, feeling a little awkward.

Shubar Khan waved a muscular red hand. "Always pleased to be of service. Spells, enchantments, and glamours at reasonable rates. Maybe someday I can interest you in a love philter."

Sparthera rode back down the mountain trail with the bronze teardrop tucked in her tunic, feeling its weight between her breasts like the touch of a lover's hand. Just above Tarseny's Rest she reined up to watch a small herd of gazelle bound across a nearby hill. Someday she would build a house on that hill. Someday, when she had Gar's treasure, she would build a big house with many rooms and many fireplaces. She would have thick rugs and fine furniture, and there would be servants in white tunics embroidered with red leaves.

She spurred her horse to the crest of the hill. Down below were the river and the town, and across the valley were more hills, leading away to distant mountains.

"I'm going to be rich!" she yelled. "Rich!"

The echoes boomed back—"Rich, rich, rich!"—until they finally whimpered into silence. Twilight nickered and pulled at his reins. Sparthera laughed. She would have many horses when she was rich. Horses and cattle and swine.

She could almost see the hoard trickling through her fingers in a cascade of gold and rainbow colors. Money for the house and the animals and a dowry.

The dowry would buy her a husband: a fine, respectable merchant who would give her fat, beautiful children to inherit the house and the animals. Sparthera took a last lingering look at the countryside before she swung herself back into the saddle. First, find the treasure!

She cantered back into town, put Twilight into the stable behind the lodging house, and went to her room. It was a tiny cubicle with a pallet of cotton-covered straw and some blankets against one wall. Rough colorful embroideries hung on the wattle-and-daub walls: relics of the days at home on her father's farm. Another embroidery was thrown across a large wooden chest painted with flying birds, and a three-legged chair with flowers stenciled on the back stood in one corner.

Sparthera uncovered the chest and threw open the lid. It was packed with odds and ends—relics of her childhood—and down at the bottom was a small pouch with her savings in it.

She opened the pouch and counted the coins slowly, frowning. The search might take weeks or months. She would need provisions, extra clothes, and a pack animal to carry them. There wasn't enough there.

She would have to borrow or beg an animal from her family. She grimaced at the thought, but she had little choice.

It was a four-hour ride to her father's farm. Her mother was out in the barnyard, feeding the chickens, when she rode in. The elder woman looked at her with what might have been resignation.

"Run out of money and come home again, have you?"

"Not this time," Sparthera said, dismounting and placing a dutiful kiss on her mother's cheek. "I need a horse or an ass. I thought maybe Father had one I could borrow."

Her mother looked at her distastefully. "Always you dress like a man. No wonder no decent man ever looks at you. Why don't you give up all those drunkards you hang around with? Why don't you . . ."

"Mother, I need a horse."

"You've got a horse. You don't need another horse."

"Mother, I'm going on a trip and I need a pack horse." Sparthera's eyes lit with suppressed excitement. "When I come back, I'll be rich!"

"Humph. That's what you said when you ran off with that no-good potmender. If your father were here, he'd give you *rich* all right! You're lucky he's in the mountains for a week. I don't know about horses. Ask Bruk. He's in the barn."

Her mother tossed another handful of grain to the chickens, and Sparthera started across the dusty barnyard.

"And get yourself some decent clothes!"

Sparthera sighed and kept moving. Her next-older brother was in the loft, restacking shelves of last season's wheat.

"Bruk? Have you got an extra horse?"

He looked down at her, squinting into the light from the open barn door. "Sparthera? You haven't been here for two months. Did you run out of pockets to pick, or just out of men?"

She grinned. "No more than you ever run out of women. Are you still rolling Mikka in her father's hayricks?"

He climbed down from the loft, looking a little glum. "Her father caught us at it twelve days ago, and now I've got to trade the rick for a marriage bed and everything that goes with it." He was a big man, well muscled, with a shock of corn-colored hair, dark eyes, and full, sensuous lips. "Lost your hair, I see. Well, they say that comes of not enough candlewick. Find yourself a man and we'll make it a double celebration."

Sparthera leaned against a stall and laughed heartily. "Caught at last! Well, it won't do you any harm, and beds aren't as itchy as piles of hay. You ought to be glad. Once you've married, you'll be safe from all the other outraged fathers!"

"Will I, though? They may just come after me with barrel staves. And I hate to cut short a promising career. Oh, the youngest daughter of the family in the hollow has grown up to be—"

"Enough, Bruk. I need a horse. Have you got an extra one?"

He shook his head. "Twilight pull up lame, did he?"

"No. I'm planning a trip and I need a pack animal."

Bruk scratched his head. "Can't you buy one in town? There are always horse dealers in the market square."

"I know too many people in Tarseny's Rest. I don't want them to know I'm planning this trip. Besides," she added candidly, "I don't have enough money."

"What are you up to, little sister? Murder, pillage, or simple theft?"

"Oh, Bruk, it's the chance to make a fortune! A chance to be rich!"

He shook his head disgustedly. "Not again. Remember that crockery merchant? And the rug dealer? And that tink—"

"This time it's different!"

"Oh, sure. Anyway, we haven't got a horse. Why don't you steal one?"

This time it was Sparthera's turn to look disgusted. "You can't just steal a horse on the spur of the moment. It's not like a pair of shoes, you know. You have to do a little planning and I don't have the time. You'd never make a decent thief! You'd just walk in, grab it by the tail, and try to walk out." She pulled at her lower lip. "Now what am I going to do?"

They both stood there, thinking. Bruk finally broke the silence. "Well, if you only want it to carry a pack, you might make do with a wild ass. They break to a packsaddle pretty easy. There are some up in the foothills. I'll even help you catch one."

"I guess it's worth a try."

Bruk found a halter and a long rope and led the way across the cultivated fields and up into the hills. The landscape was scrubby underbrush dotted with small stands of trees. There were knolls of rock, and one small stream that ran cackling down the slope.

Bruk stopped to study a pattern of tracks. "That'll be one. . . . Spends a lot of time here, too. . . . Yup, I'll bet it hides over in that copse. You go left and I'll go right. We'll get it when it comes out of the trees."

They circled cautiously toward a promising stand of small trees. Sure enough, Sparthera could hear something moving within the grove, and even caught a glimpse of brownish hide. A branch cracked under Bruk's boot, something brown exploded from the cover of the brush, and Bruk yelled, swinging the loop of his rope.

"Get the halter! Watch out for its hooves. Yeow, oooof!"

The animal whirled, bounced like a goat on its small sturdy legs, and managed to butt Bruk in the middle. Bruk sat down heavily while Sparthera made a frantic grab for the trailing end of the rope.

The little animal, frantically trying to dodge her groping hands, was braying, whinnying, and making occasional high-pitched whistling noises. It was the size of a small pony and had a long, silky mane that almost dragged to the ground. Its tail was thick, muscular, and held up at an angle. It had two ridiculous little feathery wings, about as long as Sparthera's forearm, growing out of the tops of its shoulders.

Bruk staggered to his feet as Sparthera managed to catch and cling to the rope. He launched himself bodily at the beast, grabbed it around the neck, and threw it off balance. It fell heavily to one side, where it kicked its small feet and fluttered its tiny wings to the accompaniment of an incredible cacophony of hoots, whistles, and brays.

Sparthera clapped her hands over her ears and yelled, "That's no wild ass! What on earth is it? Some sore of magic beast?"

Bruk was busily fitting his halter on their uncooperative captive. "I don't know," he panted. "I think it's half ass and half nightmare. If a sorcerer dreamed it up, he must have been drunk."

He stood back and let it scramble to its feet. It lowered its head, pawed the ground savagely, lifted its tail, and jumped with all four feet. The maneuver carried it forward perhaps two paces, its little wings flapping frantically.

Sparthera burst out laughing, doubled over with mirth. When she recovered enough, she stared at their captive and shook her head. "Do you think it can be broken to carry a pack?"

"Let's get it down to the barn and we'll try it with a packsaddle."

Getting the wingbeast down the hill was a production in its own right. It bolted, tried to roll, then dug its feet in like the most obstinate of jackasses. Finally, tired, irritated, and covered with grime, the three of them made it to the barnyard.

They managed to get the saddle on its back—after Sparthera had been butted and trampled and her brother had been dumped in the watering trough—and stood back to watch.

The small animal bucked. It turned, twisted, flapped its foolish little wings, and rolled in the dust. It tried to bite the saddle girth and scrape the saddle off against the fence. It kicked its heels and brayed. Just when they thought it would never quit, it stopped, sides heaving, and glared at them.

The next day it accepted a ripe apple from Sparthera, bit Bruk in the buttocks, and managed to bolt into the house, where Sparthera's mother hit it on the nose with a crock of pickled cabbage.

Sparthera was losing patience. It was all taking too long. Had Sung Ko Ja discovered her trick? Was he searching Tarseny's Rest for the woman who had stolen his pointer? She had told Bayram Ali that she was visiting her parents. Someone would come to warn her, surely.

But nobody came, that day or the next, and a horrid thought came to her. Sung Ko Ja must have followed the pointer far indeed. Even without the pointer, he must have a good idea where the treasure lay. He might have continued on. At that moment he could be unearthing Sparthera's treasure!

It was three days before the winged beast gave up the fight, trotted docilely at the end of a rope, and accepted the weight of a loaded packsaddle. It even gave up trying to bite, as long as they kept out of its reach. Sparthera named it Eagle.

"It would be better called Vulture!" Bruk said, rubbing at a healing wound. "It's smart, though, I'll grant you that. Only took the beast three days to realize it couldn't get rid of that saddle."

"Three days," Sparthera said wearily. "Bruk, for once you were right. I should have stolen a horse."

She rode back to town, leading the wingbeast along behind. It took her half a day to buy provisions and pack her clothing. In late afternoon she set out on the King's Way, holding the bronze pointer like the relic of some ancient and holy demigod.

She was expecting to ride into the wilderness—into some wild, unpopulated area where a treasure could lie hidden for eighty years. But the pointer was tugging her along the King's Way, straight toward Rynildissen, the ruling city of the biggest state around. That didn't bother her at first.

Rynildissen was four days' hard riding for a King's messenger, a week for a traveler on horseback, two for a caravan. And Gar's band had done their raiding around Rynildissen.

The King's Way was a military road. It ran as wide as a siege engine and as straight as an arrow's flight. It made for easy traveling, but Sparthera worried about sharing her quest with too much traffic. She found extensive litter beside the road: burnt-out campfires, horse droppings, garbage that attracted lynxes. It grew ever fresher. On her third afternoon she was not surprised to spy an extensive dust plume ahead of her. By noon of the next day she had caught up with a large merchant caravan.

She was about to ride up alongside the trailing wagon when she caught a glimpse of an odd shaggy horse with a tail like an ass. There was a figure in bulky eastern robes on its back. Sung!

Sparthera pulled her horse hard to the side and rode far out over the rolling hill and away from the road. She had no desire to trade words with the smooth-faced magician. But what was he doing there? The caravan was protection from beasts and minor thieves, but the caravan was *slow*. He could have been well ahead of Sparthera by now.

He didn't know the pointers had been switched! That *must* be it. The seeking-spell had been nearly dead already. Sung had followed it from far to the East; now he was following his memory, with no idea that anyone was behind him.

Then the important thing was to delay him. She must find the treasure, take it, and be miles away before Sung Ko Ja reached the site.

All day she paced the caravan. At dusk they camped round a spring. Leaving her horse, Sparthera moved down among the wagons, tents, oxen, and camels. She avoided the campfires. Sung Ko Ja had pitched a small red-and-white-striped tent. His unicorn was feeding placidly out of a nosebag.

Stealing a roll of rich brocade was easy. The merchant should have kept a dog. It was heavy stuff, and she might well be spotted moving it out of camp, but she didn't have to do that. After studying Sung's tent for some time, watching how soundly Sung slept, she crept around to the back of the tent and rolled the brocade under the edge. Then away, hugging the shadows, and into the hills before the moon rose. Dawn found her back on the highway, well ahead of the caravan, chuckling as she wondered how Sung would explain his acquisition.

When she dug the pointer out of her sleeve, her sense of humor quite vanished. The pointer was tugging her back. She must have ridden too far.

After a hasty breakfast of dried figs and jerked meat, Sparthera started to retrace her path, paralleling the King's Way. Days of following the pointer had left painful cramping in both hands, but she dared not set it down now. At any moment she expected the bronze teardrop to pull her aside.

She was paying virtually no attention to her path. At the crest of a smooth hill, she looked up to see another horse coming toward her. Its rider was a smooth-faced man with skin the color of old ivory, and his almond eyes were amused. It was too late even to think of hiding.

"Oh-ho! My sweet little friend from two nights ago. What brings you onto the King's Way?"

"My hair," Sparthera improvised. "Cosmetics. There's a witch-woman who lives that way"—she gestured vaguely south and gave him her best effort at a flirtatious smile—"and I find I can afford her fees, thanks to the generosity of a slant-eyed magician."

"Oh, dear, and I had hoped your lips were aching for another kiss." He looked at her critically. "You don't need to visit any witch. Even shorn, you are quite enchanting. You must share my midday meal. I insist. Come, we can rest in the shade of those trees yonder."

Sparthera was afraid to spur her horse and flee. He might suspect nothing at all, else why had he joined the caravan? She turned her horse obediently and rode to the shade of the small grove with him, trailing the wing-beast behind at the end of its halter.

Sung slid easily from his unicorn. He still didn't seem dangerous. She could insist on preparing the food. Wine she could spill while pretending to drink. She swung down from her horse—

Her head hurt. Her eyes wouldn't focus. She tried to roll over and her head pulsed in red pain. Her arms and legs seemed caught in something. Rope? She waited until her head stopped throbbing before she tried to learn more.

Then it was obvious. Her hands were tied behind her; a leather strap secured her ankles to one of the shade trees. Sung Ko Ja was sitting cross-legged on a rug in front of her, flipping a bronze teardrop in the air.

Bastard. He must have hit her on the head while she was dismounting.

"Two nights ago I noticed that someone had cut the paper out of my bedroom window," he said. "I woke yesterday morning with a foul taste in my mouth, but that could have been cheap wine or too much wine. Last night some rogue put a roll of stolen dry goods in my baggage, which caused me no end of embarrassment. I would not ordinarily have thought of you in connection with this. I confess that my memories of our time together are most pleasant. However"—he paused to sip at a bowl of tea, "however, my unicorn, who can whisper strange things when I want him to, and sometimes when I don't—"

"He *speaks?*"

The unicorn was glaring at her. Sparthera glared back. Magician or no, she felt that this was cheating, somehow.

"Such a disappointment," said Sung Ko Ja. "If only you had come to my arms last night, all of this might be different. You sadden me. Here you are, and here is this." He held up the pointer. "Why?"

She looked at the ground, biting her lip.

"Why?"

"Money, of course!" she blurted out. "You said that this was the key to a treasure! Wouldn't you have taken it, too, in my place?"

Sung laughed and rubbed his fingers over his chin. "No, I don't think so. But I am not you. It may be this was my fault. I tempted you."

He got to his feet. He tilted her head back with one hand so he could look into her eyes. "Now, what's to be done? Swear to be my slave and I'll take you along to look for Gar's treasure."

"A slave? Never! My people have always been free. I'd rather die than be a slave!"

Sung looked distressed. "Let's not call it slavery, then, if you dislike it so much. Bondage? Binding? Let's say you will bind yourself to me. For seven years and a day, or until we find treasure to equal your weight in gold."

"And if we find the treasure, what then?"

"Then you're free."

"That's not good enough. I want part of the treasure."

Sung laughed again, this time in pure amusement. "You bargain hard for one who has been pinioned and tied to a tree. All right. Part of the treasure, then."

"How much of it?" she asked warily.

"Hmmm. I take the first and second most valuable items. We split the rest equally."

"Who decides—"

Sung was growing irritated. "I'll split the remaining treasure into two heaps. You choose which heap you want."

That actually sounded fair. "Agreed."

"Ah, but now it is my turn. What are you going to swear by, my little sweetheart? I want your oath that you'll offer me no harm, that you'll stay by my side and obey my commands until the terms of the agreement are met."

Sparthera hesitated. It didn't take a magician to know how to make an oath binding. Even nations kept their oaths . . . to the letter, and that could make diplomacy interesting. . . .

She could be making herself rich. Or she could be throwing away seven years of her life. Would Sung hold still for a better bargain?

Not a chance. "All right. I'll swear by Khulm, the thieves' god who stands in the shrine at Rynildissen. May he break my fingers if I fail."

"You swear, then?"

"I swear."

Sung bent down and kissed her heartily on the lips. Then he set about freeing her. He set out tea while she was rubbing her wrists. There was a lump on her head. The tea seemed to help.

She said, "We must be very near the treasure. The pointer led me back the way we came . . . straight into your arms, in fact."

Sung chuckled. He fished the silver box out of his saddlebag. He opened it, took out Sparthera's counterfeit bronze teardrop, hesitated, then dropped it on the rug. He stood up with the genuine object in his hand.

Sparthera cried, "Stop! That's—" Too late. Sung had flung the genuine pointer into a grove of low trees.

"I'll keep yours," he said. "It's only for the benefit of people who think a box has to contain something. Now watch."

He pressed down on the silver box in two places and twisted four of the small stone ornaments. The box folded out flat into a cross shape with one long arm.

"You see? There never was a spell on the bronze lump. You took it to a spell-caster, didn't you?" Sparthera nodded. "And he put some kind of contagion spell on it, didn't he?" She nodded again. "So the bronze lump sought what it had been a part of: the box. It's been in there too long."

Sung pulled the faded red lining off of the surface. Underneath, the metal was engraved with patterns and lettering. Sung stroked a finger over the odd markings. "It looks like a valuable trinket on the outside. No casual thief would just throw it away. I might have a chance to get it back. But a magician turned robber would take the pointer, just as you did."

She'd had it in her hands! Too late, too late. "When can we start looking for Gar's treasure?"

"Tomorrow morning, if you're so eager. Meanwhile, the afternoon is growing cold. Come here and warm my heart."

"Sung, dear, just how cl . . ." Sparthera's words trailed off in surprise. She had walked straight into Sung's arms. She had behaved like this with no man, not since that damned tinker. Her voice quavered as she said, "I don't act like this. Sung, what magic is on me now?"

He pulled back a little. "Why, it's your own oath!"

"I feel like that puppet you showed me! This isn't what I meant!"

Sung sighed. "Too bad. Well—"

"I don't mean I won't share your bed." Her voice was shrill with near-hysteria. "I just—I want power over my own limbs, damn you, Sung!"

"Yes. I tell you now that binding yourself to me does not involve becoming my concubine."

She pulled away, and turned her back, and found it was possible. "Good. Good. Sung, thank you." Her brow furrowed suddenly and she turned back to face him. "What if you tell me different later?"

She might have guessed that Sung's answer would be a shrug. "All right. What was I trying to say earlier? Oh, I remember. Just how close is the King's Way? We don't want that caravan camping next to us. Somebody might get nosy."

Sung agreed. They moved a good distance down the King's Way before they camped for the night.

* * *

In the morning Sparthera saddled Twilight and loaded Eagle, while Sung packed his gear on the unicorn. The wingbeast caught his attention.

"Where did you get that creature?"

"Near my father's farm. It was running wild. I think it's some sort of magic beast."

Sung shook his head sadly. "No, quite the opposite. In my grandfather's day there were flocks of beautiful horses that sailed across the sky on wings as wide as the King's Way. He rode one when he was a little boy. It couldn't lift him when he grew too big. As time went on, the colts were born with shorter, weaker wings, until all that was left were little beasts like this one. I used to catch them when I was a boy, but never to fly. Enchantment is going out of the world, Sparthera. Soon there will be nothing left."

It was a mystery to Sparthera how her companion read the talisman. It looked the same to her, no matter which way he said it pointed. Sung tried to show her when they set off that morning. He set the flattened-out box on the palm of her hand and said, "Keep reading it as you turn it. The runes don't actually change, but when the long end points right, the message becomes 'Ta netyillo iliq pratht' instead of 'tanetyi lo—"

"Skip it. Just skip it."

In any case, the pointer continued to lead them straight down the King's Way.

They reached an inn about dusk, and Sung paid for their lodging. Sparthera watched him setting the spells against thieves. Sung was not secretive. Quite the contrary: He drilled her in the spells, so that she would be able to set them for him.

Though he had freed her from the obligation, the magician seemed to consider lovemaking as part of their agreement. Sparthera had no complaints. The magician was adept at more than spells. When she told him this, she expected him to preen himself; but Sung merely nodded.

"Keeping the women happy is very necessary in Sung House. How much did I tell you about us, that first night?"

"You were the immortal Sung. You abdicated in favor of your son."

"I was bragging."

"What were you? Not the stable hand, I think."

"Oh, I was the immortal Sung, true enough. We rule a fair-sized farming region, a valley blocked off by mountains and the Yellow River. We know a little magic—we keep a herd of unicorns and sell the horn, or use it ourselves—but that's not what keeps the farmers docile. They think they're being ruled by a sorcerer seven hundred years old."

"The immortal Sung."

"Yes. I became the immortal Sung when I was twenty. My mother had set a spell of *glamour* on me, to make me look exactly like my father. Then I was married to Ma Tay, my cousin, and set on the throne."

"That's . . . I never heard of *glamour* being used to make anyone look older."

"That's a nice trick, isn't it? The spell wears off over twenty years, but of course you're getting older, too, looking more and more like your father, magic aside. When I reached forty my wife put the *glamour* on my eldest son. And here I am, under oath to travel until nobody has ever heard of Sung House. Well, I've done that. Someday maybe I'll meet my father."

"What happens to your wife?"

"She took my mother's place as head of the House. It's actually the women who rule in Sung House. The immortal Sung is just a figurehead."

Sparthera shook her head, smiling. "It still sounds like a nice job . . . and they didn't throw you out naked."

"No. We know all our lives what's going to happen. We think on how we'll leave, what we'll take, where we'll go. We collect tales of other lands, and artifacts that could help us. There's a little treasure room of things a departing Sung may take with him."

He leaned back on the bed and stretched. "When I left, I took the pointer. It always fascinated me, even as a boy. I collected rumors about Gar's treasure. It wasn't just the gold and the jewels that stuck in my mind. There is supposed to be a major magical tool too."

"What is it?"

"It's a levitation device. Haven't you ever wanted to fly?"

Sparthera's lips pursed in a silent O. "What a thief could do with such a thing!"

"Or a military spy."

"Yes . . . and the Regency raised hell trying to find Gar's treasure. But of course you'd keep it yourself."

"Or sell it to one government or another. But I'll fly with it first."

That night, cuddled close in Sung's arms, Sparthera roused herself to ask a question. "Sung? What if I should have a child by you?"

He was silent for a long time. Long enough that she wondered if he'd fallen asleep. When he did answer it was in a very soft voice. "We would ride off into the mountains and build a great hall, and I would put a *glamour* on the child to raise up a new House of Sung."

Satisfied, Sparthera snuggled down into the magician's arms to dream of mountains and gold.

They woke late the next morning, with the dust of the caravan actually in sight. They left it behind them as they rode, still following the King's Way. "This is ridiculous," Sung fretted. "Another day and we'll be in Rynildissen!"

"Is it possible that this Gar actually buried his loot in the King's Way?"

"I wouldn't think he'd have the chance. Still, I suppose nobody would look for it there. Maybe."

Around noon they reached a region of low hills. The King's Way began to weave among them like a snake, but the silver box pointed them steadfastly toward Rynildissen. Sung dithered. "Well, do we follow the road, or do we cut across country wherever the pointer points?"

Sparthera said, "Road, I guess. We'll know if we pass it."

And road it was, until the moment when Sung sucked in his breath with a loud "Ah!"

"What is it?"

"The talisman's pointing that way, south." He turned off, guiding the unicorn uphill. Sparthera followed, pulling the wingbeast along after her. The unicorn seemed to be grumbling just below audibility.

Now the land was rough and wild. There were ravines and dry creekbeds and tumbled heaps of soil and stone. They were crossing the crest of a hill when Sung said, "Stop."

The unicorn stopped. Sparthera reined in her horse. The wingbeast walked into Twilight's haunches, got kicked, and sat down with a dismal bray.

Sung ignored the noise. "Down in that ravine. We'll have to try it on foot."

They had to move on all fours in places. The bottom of the ravine was thick with brush. Sparthera hesitated as Sung plunged into a thorn thicket. When she heard his muttered curses stop suddenly, she followed.

She found him surrounded by scattered bones and recognized the skull of an ass. "The pointer reads right in all directions. We're right on it," he said.

A pair of large stones, brown and cracked, looked a bit too much alike. Sparthera touched one. Old leather. Saddlebags?

The bag was so rotten, it had almost merged with the earth. It tore easily. Within was cloth that fell apart in her hands, and a few metal ornaments that were green with verdigris. Badges of rank, for a soldier of Rynildissen. In the middle of it all, something twinkled, something bright.

Sung had torn the other bag apart. "Nothing. What have you got?"

She turned it in her hand: a bright faceted stone, shaped like a bird and set into a gold ring. "Oh, how pretty!"

"Hardly worth the effort," Sung said. He worked his way backward out of the thicket and stood up. "Diamonds have no color. They're not worth much. You see this kind of trinket in any Shanton jewel bazaar. Give it here."

Sparthera handed it over, feeling forlorn. "Then that's all there is?"

"Oh, I doubt it. We're on the track. This was just the closest piece. It must have been part of the hoard, or the talisman wouldn't have pointed us here. Even so . . . how did it get here? Did Gar lose a pack mule?"

He opened out the pointer. With the bird's beak he traced a looping curve on the silver surface. "There. The talisman is pointing true again. There's still treasure to be found."

They climbed back uphill to their steeds. The King's Way was well behind them now, and lost among the hills. They were picking their way across a nearly dry stream bed when Sung said, "We're passing it."

"Where?"

"I don't know yet." Sung dismounted. "You wait here. Sparthera, come along," and she realized he'd spoken first to the unicorn. He picked his way carefully up a vast sloping spill of shattered boulders: leg-breaker country. At the top, panting heavily, he opened the box and turned in a circle.

"Well?"

Sung turned again. He spoke singsong gibberish in what might have been a lengthy spell; but it sounded like cursing.

"Are you just going to keep spinning?"

"It says all directions are wrong!"

"Uh? Point it down."

Sung stared at her. Then he pointed the talisman at his feet. He said, "'Ta netyillo—' Sparthera, my love, you may be the best thing that ever happened to me."

"I am delighted to hear it. My shovel's still on the horse. Shall I go for it?"

"Yes. No, wait a bit." He started walking, staring at the talisman. "It must be deep. Yards deep. More. Forget the shovel, there must be a cave under us." He grinned savagely at her. "We'll have to find the entrance. We're almost there, love. Come on."

They trudged down the hill, trying to avoid twisted ankles or worse. Sparthera paused to catch her breath and caught a blur of motion out of the corner of her eye. It was headed for the animals. "Sung! What—"

Twilight whinnied in terror. He tossed his head, pulling loose the reins Sparthera had looped over a bush, and bolted downhill. The unicorn had splayed his front feet and lowered his head, as if he thought he still owned a spear. The winged packbeast, filling the air with a bedlam of sound, was bounding rapidly away in two-pace-long jumps, tiny wings beating the air frantically.

Sung let out a yell and charged up to the top of the ravine, swinging a heavy branch he'd snatched up on the way. Sparthera clambered up beside him, swearing as she saw her animals heading off across the landscape. There was a loud wailing sound that put the wingbeast's efforts to shame, and then silence. The thing had vanished.

"What was that?"

"I don't know. I'm more interested in where it went. Keep an eye out, love." Sung pulled his sword from the pack and wandered about the shattered rock.

Sparthera's nose picked up a heavy musky animal odor. She followed it, heart pounding, knife in hand. They were too close to the treasure to stop now.

The odor was wafting out of a black gap in the rocks, less than a yard across. Sung clambered up to look.

"That's it," he said. "It's not big enough, though. If we crawled through that, the thing—whatever it is—would just take our heads as they poked through. We'll have to move some rocks."

Sparthera picked up a heavy boulder, and hurled it away. "I feel an irrational urge to go home."

"I can't go home. Let's move some rocks," said Sung, and she did. The sun had dropped a fair distance toward Rynildissen, and every muscle in her body was screaming, before the dripping, panting Sung said, "Enough. Now we need torches."

"Sung. Did it . . . occur to you . . . to let me rest?"

"Well, why didn't you . . . oh." Sung was disconcerted. "Sparthera, I'm used to giving orders to women, because I'm supposed to be the immortal Sung. But it's just for show. I'm also used to being disobeyed."

"I can't." She was crying.

"I'll be more careful. Shall we rest, have some tea?"

"Good. Offer me a swallow of wine."

"That's not—"

"For Khulm's sake, Sung, do you think I'd go in there *drunk?* It's in there. I know it. I kept waiting for it to jump on me. Don't you have a spell to protect us?"

"No. We don't even know what it is. Here—" He turned her around and began to massage her neck and shoulders, fingers digging in. Sparthera felt tensed muscles unraveling, loosening. It was a wonderful surprise.

She said, "It must have half killed the Sung women to let you go."

"Somehow they managed." She barely heard the bitterness; but it *did* bother him.

It was dark in there. The late afternoon light only reached a dozen paces in. They stepped in, holding the torches high.

There was a rustling flurry of motion and a loud whimpering cry.

If one of them had run, the other would have followed. As it was, they walked slowly forward behind Sung's sword and Sparthera's dagger.

The cave wasn't large. A stream ran through the middle. Sparthera noted two skeletons on either side of the stream, lying faceup as if posed. . . .

Another cry and a scrabbling sound. Something huge and dark moved just outside the perimeter of light. The animal odor had become sickeningly strong. Sung held the light higher.

Off in a corner, something huge was trying to pack itself into a very narrow crevice. It looked at them with absolute panic in its eyes, pulled its long scaly tail closer under its legs, and tried fruitlessly to move away.

"What in the world is it?"

"Nothing from this world, that's certain," Sung said. "It looks like something that was conjured up out of a bad dream. Probably was. Gar's guardian."

The creature was partly furred and partly scaled. It had a long toothed snout and broad paddlelike front paws with thick nails. There was a rusted iron collar around its neck, with a few links of broken chain attached. Now its claws stopped grinding against rock, and its tail came up to cover its eyes.

"What is it trying to do?" Sparthera whispered.

"Well, it seems to be trying to hide in that little crack."

"Oh, for the love of Khulm! You mean it's scared!"

The beast gave a long wailing moan at the sound of her voice. Its claws resumed scratching rock.

"Let it alone," Sung said. He swung the torch around to reveal the rest of the cave. They found a torn and scattered pack, with the remains of weevily flour and some broken boxes nearly collapsed from dry rot. Two skeletons were laid out as for a funeral. They had not died in bed. The rib cage on one seemed to have been torn wide open. The other seemed intact below the neck; but it was still wearing a bronze helmet bearing the crest of a soldier of Rynildissen; and the helmet and skull had been squashed as flat as a miser's sandwich.

Aside from the small stream that ran between them, and assorted gypsum deposits, the cave was otherwise empty.

"I'm afraid the Regent's army got here first," Sung said.

Sparthera bent above one of the skeletons. "Do you think that thing did this? Did it kill them, or just gnaw the bodies? It doesn't seem dangerous now."

"It probably wasn't all that scared in the beginning." Sung was grinning. "Gar must have left it here to guard the treasure, with a chain to keep it from running away. When the Regent's soldiers found the cave, it must have got the first ones in. Then the rest piled in and pounded it into mush. Conjured beasts like that are practically impossible to kill, but did you notice the scars on the muzzle and forelegs? It hasn't forgotten."

"I feel sort of sorry for it," Sparthera said. Then the truth came home for her and she said, "I feel sorry for us! The treasure must have been gone for years. Except—the talisman led us *here!*"

Sung walked forward, following the talisman. He stopped above the skeleton with the flattened skull. "'Ta netyillo—' Yes."

He reached into the rib cage and came up with a mass of color flickering in his hands. Sparthera reached into it and found a large ruby. There were three other besides, and two good-sized emeralds.

Sung laughed long and hard. "So, we have a greedy soldier to thank. He ran in, saw a pile of jewels, snatched up a fistful, and swallowed them. He must have thought it would come out all right in the end. Instead, Gar's pet got him." Sung wiped his eyes with the back of his hand. "Fate is a wonderful thing. Here, give me those."

She did, and Sung began tracing the curve on the talisman, one jewel at a time. She said, "They wouldn't have left a talisman of levitation."

"No, they wouldn't."

"And this stuff isn't worth nearly my weight in gold."

Sung stiffened. "The pointer! It's pointing into the wall itself!" He got up and began moving along the wall.

Sparthera grimaced but said nothing.

Sung called, "Either it's cursed deep in there, or there's another cave, or . . .Why do I bother? It's pointing to Rynildissen."

"Maybe other places too. There was a war with Sarpuree seventy years ago. We lost, so there was tribute to pay. I don't even have to guess where the Regent got the money to pay for it all. He may have sold most of the treasure."

"Humph. Yes. And if there were any decorative items left, they could be spread all through the palace. And some of the soldiers probably hid a few little things like that diamond bird. Even if we were crazy enough to rob the Regent's palace, we'd never get it all. It's the end of our treasure hunt, girl."

"But you said . . . Sung! How can I ever win my freedom if we don't go on?"

"Oh, we'll go on. But not looking for Gar's treasure." Sung scooped the jewels into his pocket and handed her the little diamond bird. "Keep this as a memento. The rest . . . well, I've thought of opening a toy shop. In Rynildissen, maybe."

"A *toy shop?*"

Sung frowned. "You don't like toys, do you?"

"Everybody likes toys. But we're *adults*, Sung!"

"Girl, don't you know that human beings are natural magicians? I think it's hereditary. The magic was always there to be used . . . but now it isn't. And we still want magic. Especially children."

"Those toys aren't—"

"No, of course not, but they're as close as you're likely to get these days, especially in a city. Toys from far places might sell very well."

She was still angry. Sung reached to run his fingers over the tawny stubble on her head. "We'll live well enough. Come kiss me, little thief. Seven years isn't such a long time."

Sparthera kissed him; she couldn't help it. Then she said, "I wondered if a diamond bird could be your talisman of levitation."

Sung's eyes widened. "I wonder . . . it's worth a try. Not in here, though." He took the bird and scrambled up scree toward the cave entrance.

Sparthera started after him. Then, holding her torch high, she looked up. The rock tapered to a high natural vault. It looked unstable, dangerous. Something . . . a bright point?

Compelled, she continued climbing after Sung. But the diamond trinket (she told herself) was no flying spell. She'd been wrong: no soldier would have stolen that. It would be treason. By staying here she would be working in Sung's best interests (she told herself, scrambling up the rocks). There was no point in shouting after him. If she was wrong, at least he wouldn't be disappointed (she told herself, and at last the pull of her oath lost its grip).

Sung was out of sight. Sparthera scrambled back down and set to work.

The soldiers had taken all of their equipment before they turned the cave into a crypt for their brethren by pulling down the entrance. They had taken armor but left the crushed helmet that was part of one corpse. They had taken the metal point from a shaped spear, but a three-pace length of shaft remained.

Sparthera dipped a piece of cloth into the stream, then into some of the moldy flour scattered on the rock floor. She kneaded the cloth until it turned gooey, then wrapped it around the broken tip of the spear. She climbed scree to get closer to the ceiling, and reached up with the spear, toward a bright point on the cave roof.

It stuck. She pulled it down: thin gold filigree carved into a pair of bird's wings, about the size of her two hands. It tugged upward against her fingers.

"Lift me," she whispered. And she rose until her head bumped rock.

"Set me down," she whispered, and drifted back to earth.

No castle in the world held a room so high that she could not rob it, with this. And she waited for the impulse that would send her scrambling out to give it to Sung.

Sung was bounding downhill with his arms flapping, one hand clutching the diamond bauble, looking very like a little boy at play. He turned in fury at the sound of Sparthera's laughter.

"I've found it!" she called, holding the golden talisman high.

And as Sung ran toward her, beaming delight, Sparthera gloated.

For the instant in which she flew, Sparthera's weight in gold had been far less than the value of the paltry treasure they had found.

She might stay with Sung long enough to take back the jewels, or at least the wings. She might even stay longer. If he were right about the toy shop . . . perhaps he need never learn that she was free.

ψ

MANA FROM HEAVEN
by Roger Zelazny

♃

I FELT NOTHING untoward that afternoon, whereas, I suppose, my senses should have been tingling. It was a balmy, sun-filled day with but the lightest of clouds above the ocean horizon. It might have lulled me within the not unpleasant variations of my routine. It was partly distraction, then, of my subliminal, superliminal perceptions, my early-warning system, whatever. . . . This, I suppose, abetted by the fact that there had been no danger for a long while, and that I was certain I was safely hidden. It was a lovely summer day.

There was a wide window at the rear of my office, affording an oblique view of the ocean. The usual clutter lay about—opened cartons oozing packing material, a variety of tools, heaps of rags, bottles of cleaning compounds and restoratives for various surfaces. And of course the acquisitions. Some of them still stood in crates and cartons; others held ragged rank upon my workbench, which ran the length of an entire wall—a rank of ungainly chessmen awaiting my hand. The window was open and the fan purring so that the fumes from my chemicals could escape rapidly. Bird songs entered, and a sound of distant traffic, sometimes the wind.

My styrofoam coffee cup rested unopened upon the small table beside the door, its contents long grown cold and unpalatable to any but an oral masochist. I had set it there that morning and forgotten it until my eyes chanced to light upon it. I had worked through coffee break and lunch, the day had been so rewarding. The really important part had been completed, though the rest of the museum staff would never notice. Time now to rest, to celebrate, to savor all I had found.

I raised the cup of cold coffee. Why not? A few words, a simple gesture . . .

I took a sip of the icy champagne. Wonderful.

I crossed to the telephone then, to call Elaine. This day was worth a bigger celebration than the cup I held. Just as my hand was about to fall upon the instrument, however, the phone rang. Following the startle response, I raised the receiver.

"Hello," I said.

Nothing.

"Hello?"

Nothing again. No . . . Something.

Not some weirdo dialing at random either, as I am an extension. . . .

"Say it or get off the pot," I said.

The words came controlled, from back in the throat, slow, the voice unidentifiable:

"Phoenix—Phoenix—burning—bright," I heard.

"Why warn me, asshole?"

"Tag. You're—it."

The line went dead.

I pushed the button several times, roused the switchboard.

"Elsie," I asked, "the person who just called me—what were the exact words—"

"Huh?" she said. "I haven't put any calls through to you all day, Dave."

"Oh."

"You okay?"

"Short circuit or something," I said. "Thanks."

I cradled it and tossed off the rest of the champagne. It was no longer a pleasure, merely a housecleaning chore. I fingered the tektite pendant I wore, the roughness of my lava-stone belt buckle, the coral in my watch-band. I opened my attaché case and replaced certain items I had been using. I removed a few, also, and dropped them into my pockets.

It didn't make sense, but I knew that it had been for real because of the first words spoken. I thought hard. I still had no answer, after all these years. But I knew that it meant danger. And I knew that it could take any form.

I snapped the case shut. At least it had happened today, rather than, say, yesterday. I was better prepared.

I closed the window and turned off the fan. I wondered whether I should head for my cache. Of course, that could be what someone expected me to do.

I walked up the hall and knocked on my boss's half-open door.

"Come in, Dave. What's up?" he asked.

Mike Thorley, in his late thirties, mustached, well dressed, smiling, put down a sheaf of papers and glanced at a dead pipe in a big ashtray.

"A small complication in my life," I told him. "Is it okay if I punch out early today?"

"Sure. Nothing too serious, I hope?"

I shrugged.

"I hope not, too. If it gets that way, though, I'll probably need a few days."

He moved his lips around a bit, then nodded.

"You'll call in?"

"Of course."

"It's just that I'd like all of that African stuff taken care of pretty soon."

"Right," I said. "Some nice pieces there."

He raised both hands.

"Okay. Do what you have to do."

"Thanks."

I started to turn away. Then, "One thing," I said.

"Yes?"

"Has anybody been asking about me—anything?"

He started to shake his head, then stopped.

"Unless you count that reporter," he said.

"What reporter?"

"The fellow who phoned the other day, doing a piece on our new acquisitions. Your name came up, of course, and he had a few general questions—the usual stuff, like how long you've been with us, where you're from. You know."

"What was his name?"

"Wolfgang or Walford. Something like that."

"What paper?"

"The *Times*."

I nodded.

"Okay. Be seeing you."

"Take care."

I used the pay phone in the lobby to call the paper. No one working there named Wolfgang or Walford or something like that, of course. No article in the works either. I debated calling another paper, just in case Mike was mistaken, when I was distracted by a tap upon the shoulder. I must have turned too quickly, my expression something other than composed, for her smile faded and fear arced across her dark brows, slackened her jaw.

"Elaine!" I said. "You startled me. I didn't expect . . ."

The smile found its way back.

"You're awfully jumpy, Dave. What are you up to?"

"Checking on my dry cleaning," I said. "You're the last person —"

"I know. Nice of me, isn't it? It was such a beautiful day that I decided to knock off early and remind you we had a sort of date."

My mind spun even as I put my arms about her shoulders and turned her toward the door. How much danger might she be in if I spent a few hours with her in full daylight? I was about to go for something to eat anyway, and I could keep alert for observers. Also, her presence might lull anyone watching me into thinking that I had not taken the call seriously, that perhaps I was not the proper person after all. For that matter, I realized that I wanted some company just then. And if my sudden departure became necessary, I also wanted it to be her company this one last time.

"Yes," I said. "Great idea. Let's take my car."

"Don't you have to sign out or something?"

"I already did. I had the same feeling you did about the day. I was going to call you after I got my cleaning.

"It's not ready yet," I added, and my mind kept turning.

A little trickle here, a little there. I did not feel that we were being observed.

"I know a good little restaurant about forty miles down the coast. Lots of atmosphere. Fine sea food," I said as we descended the front stairs. "And it should be a pleasant drive."

We headed for the museum's parking lot, around to the side.

"I've got a beach cottage near there too," I said.

"You never mentioned that."

"I hardly ever use it."

"Why not? It sounds wonderful."

"It's a little out of the way."

"Then why'd you buy it?"

"I inherited it," I said.

I paused about a hundred feet from my car and jammed a hand into my pocket.

"Watch," I told her.

The engine turned over, the car vibrated.

"How . . . ?" she began.

"A little microwave gizmo. I can start it before I get to it."

"You afraid of a bomb?"

I shook my head.

"It has to warm up. You know how I like gadgets."

Of course I wanted to check out the possibility of a bomb. It was a natural reaction for one in my position. Fortunately, I had convinced her of my fondness for gadgets early in our acquaintanceship—to cover any such contingencies as this. Of course, too, there was no microwave gizmo in my pocket. Just some of the stuff.

We continued forward; then I unlocked the doors and we entered it.

I watched carefully as I drove. Nothing, no one, seemed to be trailing us. "Tag. You're it," though. A gambit. Was I supposed to bolt and run? Was I supposed to try to attack? If so, what? Who?

Was I going to bolt and run?

In the rear of my mind I saw that the bolt-and-run pattern had already started taking shape.

How long, how long, had this been going on? Years. Flight. A new identity. A long spell of almost normal existence. An attack. . . . Flee again. Settle again.

If only I had an idea as to which one of them it was, then I could attack. Not knowing, though, I had to avoid the company of all my fellows—the only ones who could give me clues.

"You look sicklied o'er with the pale cast of thought, Dave. It can't be your dry cleaning, can it?"

I smiled at her.

"Just business," I said. "All of the things I wanted to get away from. Thanks for reminding me."

I switched on the radio and found some music. Once we got out of city traffic, I began to relax. When we reached the coast road and it thinned even further, it became obvious that we were not being followed. We climbed for a time, then descended. My palms tingled as I spotted the pocket of fog at the bottom of the next dip. Exhilarated, I drank its essence. Then I began talking about the African pieces, in their mundane aspects. We branched off from there. For a time, I forgot my problem. This lasted for perhaps twenty minutes, until the news broadcast. By then I was projecting goodwill, charm, warmth, and kind feelings. I could see that Elaine had begun enjoying herself. There was feedback. I felt even better. There—

". . . new eruptions which began this morning," came over the speaker. "The sudden activity on the part of El Chinchonal spurred immediate evacuation of the area about—"

I reached over and turned up the volume, stopping in the middle of my story about hiking in the Alps.

"What—?" she said.

I raised a finger to my lips.

"The volcano," I explained.

"What of it?"

"They fascinate me," I said.

"Oh."

As I memorized all of the facts about the eruption I began to build feelings concerning my situation. My having received the call today had been a matter of timing. . . .

"There were some good pictures of it on the tube this morning," she said as the newsbrief ended.

"I wasn't watching. But I've seen it do it before, when I was down there."

"You visit volcanos?"

"When they're active, yes."

"Here you have this really oddball hobby and you've never mentioned it," she observed. "How many active volcanos have you visited?"

"Most of them," I said, no longer listening, the lines of the challenge becoming visible—the first time it had ever been put on this basis. I realized in that instant that this time I was not going to run.

"Most of them?" she said. "I read somewhere that there are hundreds, some of them in really out-of-the-way places. Like Erebus—"

"I've been in Erebus," I said, "back when—" And then I realized what I was saying. "—back in some dream," I finished. "Little joke there."

I laughed, but she only smiled a bit.

It didn't matter, though. She couldn't hurt me. Very few mundanes could. I was just about finished with her anyway. After tonight I would forget her. We would never meet again. I am by nature polite, though; it is a thing I value above sentiment. I would not hurt her either: It might be easiest simply to make her forget.

"Seriously, I do find certain aspects of geophysics fascinating."

"I've been an amateur astronomer for some time," she volunteered. "I can understand."

"Really? Astronomy? You never told me."

"Well?" she said.

I began to work it out, small talk flowing reflexively. After we parted tonight or tomorrow morning, I would leave. I would go to Villahermosa. My enemy would be waiting—of this I felt certain. "Tag. You're it." "This is your chance. Come and get me if you're not afraid."

Of course, I was afraid.

But I'd run for too long. I would have to go, to settle this for good. Who knew when I'd have another opportunity? I had reached the point where it was worth any risk to find out who it was, to have a chance to retaliate. I would take care of all the preliminaries later, at the cottage, after she was asleep. Yes.

"You've got beach?" she asked.

"Yes."

"How isolated?"

"Very. Why?"

"It would be nice to swim before dinner."

So we stopped by the restaurant, made reservations for later and went off and did that. The water was fine.

The day turned into a fine evening. I'd gotten us my favorite table, on the patio, out back, sequestered by colorful shrubbery, touched by flower scents, in the view of mountains. The breezes came just right. So did the lobster and champagne. Within the restaurant, a pleasant music stirred softly. During coffee, I found her hand beneath my own. I smiled. She smiled back.

Then, "How'd you do it, Dave?" she asked.

"What?"

"Hypnotize me."

"Native charm, I guess," I replied, laughing.

"That is not what I mean."

"What, then?" I said, all chuckles fled.

"You haven't even noticed that I'm not smoking anymore."

"Hey, you're right! Congratulations. How long's it been?"

"A couple of weeks," she replied. "I've been seeing a hypnotist."

"Oh, really?"

"Mm-hm. I was such a docile subject that he couldn't believe I'd never been under before. So he poked around a little, and he came up with a description of you, telling me to forget something."

"Really?"

"Yes, really. You want to know what I remember now that I didn't before?"

"Tell me."

"An almost-accident, late one night, about a month ago. The other car didn't even slow down for the stop sign. Yours levitated. Then I remember us parked by the side of the road, and you were telling me to forget. I did."

I snorted.

"Any hypnotist with much experience will tell you that a trance state is no guarantee against fantasy—and a hallucination recalled under hypnosis seems just as real the second time around. Either way—"

"I remember the *ping* as the car's antenna struck your right rear fender and snapped off."

"They can be vivid fantasies too."

"I looked, Dave. The mark is there on the fender. It looks just as if someone had swatted it with an antenna."

Damn! I'd meant to get that filled in and touched up. Hadn't gotten around to it, though.

"I got that in a parking lot," I said.

"Come on, Dave."

Should I put her under now and make her forget having remembered? I wondered. Maybe that would be easiest.

"I don't care," she said then. "Look, I really don't care. Strange things sometimes happen. If you're connected with some of them, that's okay. What bothers me is that it means you don't trust me . . ."

Trust? That is something that positions you as a target. Like Proteus, when Amazon and Priest got finished with him. Not that he didn't have it coming. . . .

". . . and I've trusted you for a long time."

I removed my hand from hers. I took a drink of coffee. Not here. I'd give her mind a little twist later. Implant something to make her stay away from hypnotists in the future too.

"Okay," I said. "I guess you're right. But it's a long story. I'll tell you after we get back to the cottage."

Her hand found my own, and I met her eyes.

"Thanks," she said.

We drove back beneath a moonless sky clotted with stars. It was an unpaved road, dipping, rising, twisting amid heavy shrubbery. Insect noises came in through our open windows, along with the salt smell of the sea. For a moment, just for a moment, I thought that I felt a strange tingling, but it could have been the night and the champagne. And it did not come again.

Later, we pulled up in front of the place, parked and got out. Silently, I deactivated my invisible warden. We advanced, I unlocked the door, I turned on the light.

"You never have any trouble here, huh?" she asked.

"What do you mean?"

"People breaking in, messing the place up, ripping you off?"

"No," I answered.

"Why not?"

"Lucky, I guess."

"Really?"

"Well . . . it's protected, in a very special way. That's part of the story too. Wait till I get some coffee going."

I went out to the kitchen, rinsed out the pot, put things together and set it over a flame. I moved to open a window, to catch a little breeze.

Suddenly, my shadow was intense upon the wall.

I spun about.

The flame had departed the stove, hovered in the air and begun to grow. Elaine screamed just as I turned, and the thing swelled to fill the room. I saw that it bore the shifting features of a fire elemental, just before it burst apart to swirl tornadolike through the cottage. In a moment, the place was blazing and I heard its crackling laughter.

"Elaine!" I called, rushing forward, for I had seen her transformed into a torch.

All of the objects in my pockets plus my belt buckle, I calculated quickly, probably represented a sufficient accumulation of power to banish the thing. Of course the energies were invested, tied up, waiting to be used in different ways. I spoke the words that would rape the power-objects and free the forces. Then I performed the banishment.

The flames were gone in an instant. But not the smoke, not the smell.

. . . And Elaine lay there sobbing, clothing and flesh charred, limbs jerking convulsively. All of her exposed areas were dark and scaly, and blood was beginning to ooze from the cracks in her flesh.

I cursed as I reset the warden. I had created it to protect the place in my absence. I had never bothered to use it once I was inside. I should have.

Whoever had done this was still probably near. My cache was located in a vault about twenty feet beneath the cottage—near enough for me to use a number of the power things without even going after them. I could draw out their *mana* as I just had with those about my person. I could use it against my enemy. Yes. This was the chance I had been waiting for.

I rushed to my attaché case and opened it. I would need power to reach the power and manipulate it. And the *mana* from the artifacts I had drained was tied up in my own devices. I reached for the rod and the sphere. At last, my enemy, you've had it! You should have known better than to attack me here!

Elaine moaned. . . .

I cursed myself for a weakling. If my enemy were testing me to see whether I had grown soft, he would have his answer in the affirmative. She was no stranger, and she had said that she trusted me. I had to do it. I began the spell that would drain most of my power-objects to work her healing.

It took most of an hour. I put her to sleep. I stopped the bleeding. I watched new tissues form. I bathed her and dressed her in a sport shirt and rolled-up pair of slacks from the bedroom closet, a place the flames had not reached. I left her sleeping a little longer then while I cleaned up, opened the windows and got on with making the coffee.

At last, I stood beside the old chair—now covered with a blanket—into which I had placed her. If I had just done something decent and noble, why did I feel so stupid about it? Probably because it was out of character. I was reassured, at least, that I had not been totally corrupted to virtue by reason of my feeling resentment at having to use all of that *mana* on her behalf.

Well . . . Put a good face on it now the deed was done.

How?

Good question. I could proceed to erase her memories of the event and implant some substitute story—a gas leak, perhaps—as to what had occurred, along with the suggestion that she accept it. I could do that. Probably the easiest course for me.

My resentment suddenly faded, to be replaced by something else, as I realized that I did not want to do it that way. What I did want was an end to my loneliness. She trusted me. I felt that I could trust her. I wanted someone I could really talk with.

When she opened her eyes, I put a cup of coffee into her hands.

"Cheerio," I said.

She stared at me, then turned her head slowly and regarded the still-visible ravages about the room. Her hands began to shake. But she put the cup down herself, on the small side table, rather than letting me take it back. She examined her hands and arms. She felt her face.

"You're all right," I said.

"How?" she asked.

"That's the story," I said. "You've got it coming."

"What was that thing?"

"That's a part of it."

"Okay," she said then, raising the cup more steadily and taking a sip. "Let's hear it."

"Well, I'm a sorcerer," I said, "a direct descendant of the ancient sorcerers of Atlantis."

I paused. I waited for the sigh or the rejoinder. There was none.

"I learned the business from my parents," I went on, "a long time ago. The basis of the whole thing is *mana*, a kind of energy found in various things and places. Once the world was lousy with it. It was the basis of an entire culture. But it was like other natural resources. One day it ran out. Then the magic went away. Most of it. Atlantis sank. The creatures of magic faded, died. The structure of the world itself was altered, causing it to appear much older than it really is. The old gods passed. The sorcerers, the ones who manipulated the *mana* to produce magic, were pretty much out of business. There followed the real dark ages, before the beginning of civilization as we know it from the history books."

"This mighty civilization left no record of itself?" she asked.

"With the passing of the magic, there were transformations. The record was rewritten into natural-seeming stone and fossil-bed, was dissipated, underwent a sea change."

"Granting all that for a moment," she said, sipping the coffee, "if the power is gone, if there's nothing left to do it with, how can you be a sorcerer?"

"Well, it's not *all* gone," I said. "There are small surviving sources, there are some new sources, and—"

"—and you fight over them? Those of you who remain?"

"No . . . not exactly," I said. "You see, there are not that many of us. We intentionally keep our numbers small, so that no one goes hungry."

"Hungry?"

"A figure of speech we use. Meaning to get enough *mana* to keep body and soul together, to stave off aging, keep healthy and enjoy the good things."

"You can rejuvenate yourselves with it? How old are you?"

"Don't ask embarrassing questions. If my spells ran out and there was no more *mana*, I'd go fast. But we can trap the stuff, lock it up, hold it, whenever we come across a power-source. It can be stored in certain objects—or, better yet, tied up in partial spells, like dialing all but the final digit in a phone number. The spells that maintain one's existence always get primary consideration."

She smiled.

"You must have used a lot of it on me."

I looked away.

"Yes," I said.

"So you couldn't just drop out and be a normal person and continue to live?"

"No."

"So what was that thing?" she asked. "What happened here?"

"An enemy attacked me. We survived."

She took a big gulp of the coffee and leaned back and closed her eyes.

Then, "Will it happen again?" she asked.

"Probably. If I let it."

"What do you mean?"

"This was more of a challenge than an all-out attack. My enemy is finally getting tired of playing games and wants to finish things off."

"And you are going to accept the challenge?"

"I have no choice. Unless you'd consider waiting around for something like this to happen again, with more finality."

She shuddered slightly.

"I'm sorry," I said.

"I've a feeling I may be too," she stated, finishing her coffee and rising, crossing to the window, looking out, "before this is over.

"What do we do next?" she asked, turning and staring at me.

"I'm going to take you to a safe place and go away," I said, "for a time." It seemed a decent thing to add those last words, though I doubted I would ever see her again.

"The hell you are," she said.

"Huh? What do you mean? You want to be safe, don't you?"

"If your enemy thinks I mean something to you, I'm vulnerable—the way I see it," she told me.

"Maybe . . ."

The answer, of course, was to put her into a week-long trance and secure her down in the vault, with strong wards and the door openable from the inside. Since my magic had not all gone away, I raised one hand and sought her eyes with my own.

What tipped her off, I'm not certain. She looked away, though, and suddenly lunged for the bookcase. When she turned again she held an old bone flute that had long lain there.

I restrained myself in mid-mutter. It was a power-object that she held, one of several lying about the room, and one of the few that had not been drained during my recent workings. I couldn't really think of much that a nonsorcerer could do with it, but my curiosity restrained me.

"What are you doing?" I asked.

"I'm not sure," she said. "But I'm not going to let you put me away with one of your spells."

"Who said anything about doing that?"

"I can tell."

"How?"

"Just a feeling."

"Well, damn it, you're right. We've been together too long. You can psych me. Okay, put it down and I won't do anything to you."

"Is that a promise, Dave?"

"Yeah. I guess it is."

"I suppose you could rat on it and erase my memory."

"I keep my promises."

"Okay." She put it back on the shelf. "What are we going to do now?"

"I'd still like to put you someplace safe."

"No way."

I sighed.

"I have to go where that volcano is blowing."

"Buy two tickets," she said.

It wasn't really necessary. I have my own plane and I'm licensed to fly the thing. In fact, I have several located in different parts of the world. Boats, too.

"There is *mana* in clouds and in fogbanks," I explained to her. "In a real pinch, I use my vehicle to go chasing after them."

We moved slowly through the clouds. I had detoured a good distance, but it was necessary. Even after we had driven up to my apartment and collected everything I'd had on hand, I was still too *mana*-impoverished for the necessary initial shielding and a few strikes. I needed to collect a little more for this. After that it wouldn't matter, the way I saw things. My enemy and I would be plugged into the same source. All we had to do was reach it.

So I circled in the fog for a long while, collecting. It was a protection spell into which I concentrated the *mana*.

"What happens when it's all gone?" she asked, as I banked and climbed for a final pass before continuing to the southeast.

"What?" I said.

"The *mana*. Will you all fade away?"

I chuckled.

"It can't," I said. "Not with so few of us using it. How many tons of meteoritic material do you think have fallen to earth today? They raise the background level almost imperceptibly—constantly. And much of it falls into the oceans. The beaches are thereby enriched. That's why I like to be near the sea. Mist-shrouded mountaintops gradually accumulate it. They're good places for collecting too. And new clouds are always forming. Our grand plan is more than simple survival. We're waiting for the day when it reaches a level where it will react and establish fields over large areas. Then we won't have to rely on accumulators and partial spells for its containment. The magic will be available everywhere again."

"Then you will exhaust it all and be back where you started again."

"Maybe," I said. "If we've learned nothing, that may be the case. We'll enter a new golden age, become dependent on it, forget our other skills, exhaust it again and head for another dark age. Unless . . ."

"Unless what?"

"Unless those of us who have been living with it have also learned something. We'd need to figure the rate of *mana* exhaustion and budget ourselves. We'd need to preserve technology for those things on which *mana* had been used the last time around. Our experience in this century with physical resources may be useful. Also, there is the hope that some areas of space may be richer in cosmic dust or possess some other factor that will increase the accumulation. Then, too, we are waiting for the full development of the space program—to reach other worlds rich in what we need."

"Sounds as if you have it all worked out."

"We've had a lot of time to think about it."

"But what would be your relationship with those of us who are not versed in magic?"

"Beneficent. We all stand to benefit that way."

"Are you speaking for yourself or for the lot of you?"

"Well, most of the others must feel the same way. I just want to putter around museums. . . ."

"You said that you had been out of touch with the others for some time."

"Yes, but—"

She shook her head and turned to look out at the fog.

"Something else to worry about," she said.

I couldn't get a landing clearance, so I just found a flat place and put it down and left it. I could deal later with any problems this caused.

I unstowed our gear; we hefted it and began walking toward that ragged, smoky quarter of the horizon.

"We'll never reach it on foot," she said.

"You're right," I answered. "I wasn't planning to, though. When the time is right something else will present itself."

"What do you mean?"

"Wait and see."

We hiked for several miles, encountering no one. The way was warm and dusty, with occasional tremors of the earth. Shortly, I felt the rush of *mana*, and I drew upon it.

"Take my hand," I said.

I spoke the words necessary to levitate us a few feet above the rocky terrain. We glided forward then, and the power about us increased as we advanced upon our goal. I worked with more of it, spelling to increase our pace, to work protective shields around us, guarding us from the heat, from flying debris.

The sky grew darker, from ash, from smoke, long before we commenced the ascent. The rise was gradual at first but steepened steadily as we raced onward. I worked a variety of partial spells, offensive and defensive, tying up quantities of *mana* just a word, just a fingertip gesture away.

"Reach out, reach out and touch someone," I hummed as the visible world came and went with the passage of roiling clouds.

We sped into a belt where we would probably have been asphyxiated but for the shield. The noises had grown louder by then. It must have been pretty hot out there too. When we finally reached the rim, dark shapes fled upward past us and lightning stalked the clouds. Forward and below, a glowing, seething mass shifted constantly amid explosions.

"All right!" I shouted. "I'm going to charge up everything I brought with me and tie up some more *mana* in a whole library of spells! Make yourself comfortable!"

"Yeah," she said, licking her lips and staring downward. "I'll do that. But what about your enemy?"

"Haven't seen anybody so far—and there's too much free *mana* around for me to pick up vibes. I'm going to keep an eye peeled and take advantage of the situation. You watch too."

"Right," she said. "This is perfectly safe, huh?"

"As safe as L.A. traffic."

"Great. Real comforting," she observed as a huge rocky mass flew past us.

We separated later. I left her within her own protective spell, leaning against a craggy prominence, and I moved off to the right to perform a ritual that required greater freedom of movement.

Then a shower of sparks rose into the air before me. Nothing especially untoward about that, until I realized that it was hovering for an unusually long while. After a time, it seemed that it should have begun dispersing. . . .

"Phoenix, Phoenix, burning bright!" The words boomed about me, rising above the noises of the inferno itself.

"Who calls me?" I asked.

"Who has the strongest reason to do you harm?"

"If I knew that, I wouldn't ask."

"Then seek the answer in hell!"

A wall of flame rushed toward me. I spoke the words that strengthened my shield. Even so, I was rocked within my protective bubble when it hit. Striking back was going to be tricky, I could see, with my enemy in a less-than-material form.

"All right, to the death!" I cried, calling for a lightning stroke through the space where the sparks spun.

I turned away and covered my eyes against the brilliance, but I still felt its presence through my skin.

My bubble of forces continued to rock as I blinked and looked forward. The air before me had momentarily cleared, but everything seemed somehow darker, and—

A being—a crudely man-shaped form of semisolid lava—had wrapped its arms as far as they would go about me and was squeezing. My spell held, but I was raised above the crater's rim.

"It won't work!" I said, trying to dissolve the being.

"The hell you say!" came a voice from high overhead.

I learned quickly that the lava-thing was protected against the simple workings I threw at it. All right, then hurl me down. I would levitate out. The Phoenix would rise again. I—

I passed over the rim and was falling. But there was a problem. A heavy one.

The molten creature was clinging to my force-bubble. Magic is magic and science is science, but there are correspondences. The more mass you want to move, the more *mana* you have to expend. So, taken off guard, I was dropping into the fiery pit despite a levitation spell that would have borne me on high in a less encumbered state. I immediately began a spell to provide me with additional buoyancy.

But when I had finished, I saw that something was countering me—another spell, a spell that kept increasing the mass of my creature-burden by absorption as we fell. Save for an area between my feet through which I saw the roiling lake of fire, I was enclosed by the flowing mass of the thing. I could think of only one possible escape, and I didn't know whether I had time for it.

I began the spell that would transform me into a spark-filled vortex similar to that my confronter had worn. When I achieved it, I released my protective spell and flowed.

Out through the nether opening then, so close to that bubbling surface I would have panicked had not my mind itself been altered by the transformation, into something static and poised.

Skimming the heat-distorted surface of the magma, I swarmed past the heavily weighted being of animated rock and was already rising at a rapid rate, buffeted, borne aloft by heat waves, when it hit a rising swell and was gone. I added my own energy to the rising and fled upward, through alleys of smoke and steam, past flashes of lava bullets.

I laid the bird-shape upon my glowing swirls, I sucked in *mana*, I issued a long, drawn-out rising scream. I spread my wings along expanding lines of energy, seeking my swirling adversary as I reached the rim.

Nothing. I darted back and forth, I circled. He/she/it was nowhere in sight.

"I am here!" I cried. "Face me now!"

But there was no reply, save for the catastrophe beneath me from which fresh explosions issued.

"Come!" I cried. "I am waiting!"

So I sought Elaine, but she was not where I had left her. My enemy had either destroyed her or taken her away.

I cursed then like thunder and spun myself into a large vortex, a rising tower of lights. I drove myself upward then, leaving the earth and that burning pimple far beneath me.

For how long I rode the jet streams, raging, I cannot say. I know that I circled the world several times before any semblance of rational thinking returned to me, before I calmed sufficiently to formulate anything resembling a plan.

It was obviously one of my fellows who had tried to kill me, who had taken Elaine from me. I had avoided contact with my own kind for too long. Now I knew that I must seek them out, whatever the risk, to obtain the knowledge I needed for self-preservation, for revenge.

I began my downward drift as I neared the Middle East. Arabia. Yes. Oil fields, places of rich, expensive pollutants, gushing *mana*-filled from the earth. Home of the one called Dervish.

Retaining my Phoenix-form, I fled from field to field, beelike, tasting, using the power to reinforce the spell under which I was operating. Seeking . . .

For three days I sought, sweeping across bleak landscapes, visiting field after field. It was like a series of smorgasbords. It would be so easy to use the *mana* to transform the countryside. But of course that would be a giveaway, in many respects.

Then, gliding in low over shimmering sands as evening mounted in the East, I realized that this was the one I was seeking. There was no physical distinction to the oil field I approached and then cruised. But it stood in the realm of my sensitivity as if a sign had been posted. The *mana* level was much lower than at any of the others I had scanned. And where this was the case, one of us had to be operating.

I spread myself into even more tenuous patterns. I sought altitude. I began circling.

Yes, there was a pattern. It became clearer as I studied the area. The low-*mana* section described a rough circle near the northwest corner of the field, its center near a range of hills.

He could be working in some official capacity there at the field. If so, his duties would be minimal and the job would be a cover. He always had been pretty lazy.

I spiraled in and dropped toward the center of the circle as toward the eye of a target. As I rushed to it, I became aware of the small, crumbling adobe structure that occupied that area, blending almost perfectly with its surroundings. A maintenance or storage house, a watchman's quarters. . . . It did not matter what it seemed to be. I knew what it had to be.

I dived to a landing before it. I reversed my spell, taking on human form once again. I pushed open the weather-worn, unlatched door and walked inside.

The place was empty, save for a few sticks of beaten furniture and a lot of dust. I swore softly. This had to be it.

I walked slowly about the room, looking for some clue.

It was nothing that I saw, or even felt, at first. It was memory—of an obscure variant of an old spell, and of Dervish's character—that led me to turn and step back outside.

I closed the door. I felt around for the proper words. It was hard to remember exactly how this one would go. Finally, they came flowing forth and I could feel them falling into place, mortise and tenon, key and lock. Yes, there was a response. The subtle back-pressure was there. I had been right.

When I had finished, I knew that things were different. I reached toward the door, then hesitated. I had probably tripped some alarm. Best to have a couple of spells at my fingertips, awaiting merely guide-words. I muttered them into readiness, then opened the door.

A marble stairway as wide as the building itself led downward, creamy jewels gleaming like hundred-watt bulbs high at either hand.

I moved forward, began the descent. Odors of jasmine, saffron and sandalwood came to me. As I continued I heard the sounds of stringed instruments and a flute in the distance. By then I could see part of a tiled floor below and ahead—and a portion of an elaborate design upon it. I laid a spell of invisibility over myself and kept going.

Before I reached the bottom, I saw him, across the long, pillared hall.

He was at the far end, reclined in a nest of cushions and bright patterned rugs. An elaborate repast was spread before him. A narghile bubbled at his side. A young woman was doing a belly dance nearby.

I halted at the foot of the stair and studied the layout. Archways to both the right and the left appeared to lead off to other chambers. Behind him was a pair of wide windows, looking upon high mountain peaks beneath very blue skies—representing either a very good illusion or the expenditure of a lot of *mana* on a powerful space-bridging spell. Of course, he had a lot of *mana* to play around with. Still, it seemed kind of wasteful.

I studied the man himself. His appearance was pretty much unchanged—sharp-featured, dark-skinned, tall, husky running to fat.

I advanced slowly, the keys to half a dozen spells ready for utterance or gesture.

When I was about thirty feet away he stirred uneasily. Then he kept glancing in my direction. His power-sense was still apparently in good shape.

So I spoke two words, one of which put a less-than-material but very potent magical dart into my hand, the other casting aside my veil of invisibility.

"Phoenix!" he exclaimed, sitting upright and staring. "I thought you were dead!"

I smiled.

"How recently did that thought pass through your mind?" I asked him.

"I'm afraid I don't understand. . . ."

"One of us just tried to kill me, down in Mexico."

He shook his head.

"I haven't been in that part of the world for some time."

"Prove it," I said.

"I can't," he replied. "You know that my people here would say whatever I want them to—so that's no help. I didn't do it, but I can't think of any way to prove it. That's the trouble with trying to demonstrate a negative. Why do you suspect me, anyway?"

I sighed.

"That's just it. I don't—or, rather, I have to suspect everyone. I just chose you at random. I'm going down the list."

"Then at least I have statistics on my side."

"I suppose you're right, damn it."

He rose, turned his palms upward.

"We've never been particularly close," he said. "But then, we've never been enemies either. I have no reason at all for wishing you harm."

He eyed the dart in my hand. He raised his right hand, still holding a bottle.

"So you intend to do us all in by way of insurance?"

"No, I was hoping that you would attack me and thereby prove your guilt. It would have made life easier."

I sent the dart away as a sign of good faith.

"I believe you," I said.

He leaned and placed the bottle he held upon a cushion.

"Had you slain me that bottle would have fallen and broken," he said. "Or perhaps I could have beaten you on an attack and drawn the cork. It contains an attack djinn."

"Neat trick."

"Come join me for dinner," he suggested. "I want to hear your story. One who would attack you for no reason might well attack me one day."

"All right," I said.

The dancer had been dismissed. The meal was finished. We sipped coffee. I had spoken without interruption for nearly an hour. I was tired, but I had a spell for that.

"More than a little strange," he said at length. "And you have no recollection, from back when all of this started, of having hurt, insulted or cheated any of the others?"

"No."

I sipped my coffee.

"So it could be any of them," I said after a time. "Priest, Amazon, Gnome, Siren, Werewolf, Lamia, Lady, Sprite, Cowboy . . ."

"Well, scratch Lamia," he said. "I believe she's dead."

"How?"

He shrugged, looked away.

"Not sure," he said slowly. Then, "Well, the talk at first was that you and she had run off together. Then, later, it seemed to be that you'd died together . . . somehow."

"Lamia and me? That's silly. There was never anything between us."

He nodded.

"Then it looks now as if something simply happened to her."

"Talk . . ." I said. "Who was doing the talking?"

"You know. Stories just get started. You never know exactly where they come from."

"Where'd you first hear it?"

He lowered his eyelids, stared off into the distance.

"Gnome. Yes. It was Gnome mentioned the matter to me at Starfall that year."

"Did he say where he'd heard it?"

"Not that I can recall."

"Okay," I said. "I guess I'll have to go talk to Gnome. He still in South Africa?"

He shook his head, refilled my cup from the tall, elegantly incised pot.

"Cornwall," he said. "Still a lot of juice down those old shafts."

I shuddered slightly.

"He can have it. I get claustrophobia just thinking about it. But if he can tell me who—"

"There is no enemy like a former friend," Dervish said. "If you dropped your friends as well as everyone else when you went into hiding, it means you've already considered that. . . ."

"Yes, as much as I disliked the notion. I rationalized it by saying that I didn't want to expose them to danger, but—"

"Exactly."

"Cowboy and Werewolf were buddies of mine. . . ."

". . . And you had a thing going with Siren for a long while, didn't you?"

"Yes, but—"

"A woman scorned?"

"Hardly. We parted amicably."

He shook his head and raised his cup.

"I've exhausted my thinking on the matter."

We finished our coffee. I rose then.

"Well, thanks. I guess I'd better be going. Glad I came to you first."

He raised the bottle.

"Want to take the djinn along?"

"I don't even know how to use one."

"The commands are simple. All the work's already been done."

"Okay. Why not?"

He instructed me briefly, and I took my leave. Soaring above the great oil field, I looked back upon the tiny, ruined building. Then I moved my wings and rose to suck the juice from a cloud before turning west.

Starfall, I mused, as earth and water unrolled like a scroll beneath me. Starfall—The big August meteor shower accompanied by the wave of *mana* called Starwind, the one time of year we all got together. Yes, that was when gossip was exchanged. It had been only a week after a Starfall that I had first been attacked, almost slain, had gone to ground. . . . By the following year the stories were circulating. Had it been something at that earlier Starfall— something I had said or done to someone—that had made me an enemy with that finality of purpose, that quickness of retaliation?

I tried hard to recall what had occurred at that last Starfall I had attend-ed. It had been the heaviest rush of Starwind in memory. I remembered that. "*Mana* from heaven," Priest had joked. Everyone had been in a good mood. We had talked shop, swapped a few spells, wondered what the height-ened Starwind portended, argued politics—all of the usual things. That business Elaine talked about had come up. . . .

Elaine. . . . Alive now? I wondered. Someone's prisoner? Someone's insurance in case I did exactly what I was doing? Or were her ashes long since scattered about the globe? Either way, someone would pay.

I voiced my shrill cry against the rushing winds. It was fled in an instant, echoless. I caught up with the night, passed into its canyons. The stars came on again, grew bright.

The detailed instructions Dervish had given me proved exactly accurate. There was a mineshaft at the point he had indicated on a map hastily sketched in fiery lines upon the floor. There was no way I would enter the thing in human form, though. A version of my Phoenix-aspect would at least defend me against claustrophobia. I cannot feel completely pent when I am not totally material.

Shrinking, shrinking, as I descended. I called in my tenuous wings and tail, gaining solidity as I grew smaller. Then I bled off mass-energy, retaining my new dimensions, growing ethereal again.

Like a ghost-bird, I entered the adit, dropping, dropping. The place was dead. There was no *mana* anywhere about me. This, of course, was to be expected. The upper levels would have been the first to be exhausted.

I continued to drop into dampness and darkness for a long while before I felt the first faint touch of the power. It increased only slowly as I moved, but it did begin to rise.

Finally, it began to fall off again and I retraced my route. Yes, that side passage . . . Its source. I entered and followed.

As I worked my way farther and farther, back and down, it continued to increase in intensity. I wondered briefly whether I should be seeking the weaker area or the stronger. But this was not the same sort of setup as Dervish enjoyed. Dervish's power source was renewable, so he could remain stationary. Gnome would have to move on once he had exhausted a local *mana* supply.

I spun around a corner into a side tunnel and was halted. Frozen. Damn.

It was a web of forces holding me like a butterfly. I ceased struggling almost immediately, seeing that it was fruitless in this aspect.

I transformed myself back into human form. But the damned web merely shifted to accommodate the alteration and continued to hold me tightly.

I tried a fire spell, to no avail. I tried sucking the *mana* loose from the web's own spell, but all I got was a headache. It's a dangerous measure, only effective against sloppy workmanship—and then you get hit with a backlash of forces when it comes loose. The spell held perfectly against my effort, however. I had had to try it, though, because I was feeling desperate, with a touch of claustrophobia tossed in. Also, I thought I'd heard a stone rattle farther up the tunnel.

Next I heard a chuckle, and I recognized the voice as Gnome's.

Then a light rounded a corner, followed by a vaguely human form.

The light drifted in front of him and just off to his left—a globe, casting an orange illumination—touching his hunched, twisted shape with a flame-like glow as he limped toward me. He chuckled again.

"Looks as if I've snared a Phoenix," he finally said.

"Very funny. How about unsnaring me now?" I asked.

"Of course, of course," he muttered, already beginning to gesture.

The trap fell apart. I stepped forward.

"I've been asking around," I told him. "What's this story about Lamia and me?"

He continued gesturing. I was about to invoke an assault or shielding spell when he stopped, though. I felt none the worse and I assumed it was a final cleanup of his web.

"Lamia? You?" he said. "Oh. Yes. I'd heard you'd run off together. Yes. That was it."

"Where'd you hear it?"

He fixed me with his large, pale eyes.

"Where'd you hear it?" I repeated.

"I don't remember."

"Try."

"Sorry."

"'Sorry' hell!" I said, taking a step forward. "Somebody's been trying to kill me and—"

He spoke the word that froze me in mid-step. Good spell, that.

"—and he's been regrettably inept," Gnome finished.

"Let me go, damn it!" I said.

"You came into my home and assaulted me."

"Okay, I apologize. Now—"

"Come this way."

He turned his back on me and began walking. Against my will, my body made the necessary movements. I followed.

I opened my mouth to speak a spell of my own. No words came out. I wanted to make a gesture. I was unable to begin it.

"Where are you taking me?" I tried.

The words came perfectly clear. But he didn't bother answering me for a time. The light moved over glistening seams of some metallic material within the sweating walls.

Then, "To a waiting place," he finally said, turning into a corridor to the right where we splashed through puddles for a time.

"Why?" I asked him. "What are we waiting for?"

He chuckled again. The light danced. He did not reply.

We walked for several minutes. I began finding the thought of all those tons of rock and earth above me very oppressive. A trapped feeling came over me. But I could not even panic properly within the confines of that spell. I began to perspire profusely, despite a cooling draft from ahead.

Then Gnome turned suddenly and was gone, sidling into a narrow cleft I would not even have noticed had I been coming this way alone.

"Come," I heard him say.

My feet followed the light, moved to drift between us here. Automatically, I turned my body. I sidled after him for a good distance before the way widened. The ground dropped roughly, abruptly, and the walls retracted and the light shot on ahead, gaining altitude.

Gnome raised a broad hand and halted me. We were in a small, irregularly shaped chamber—natural, I guessed. The weak light filled it. I looked about. I had no idea why we had stopped here. Gnome's hand moved and he pointed.

I followed the gesture but still could not tell what it was that he was trying to indicate. The light drifted forward then, hovered near a shelflike niche.

Angles altered, shadows shifted. I saw it.

It was a statue of a reclining woman, carved out of coal.

I moved a step nearer. It was extremely well executed and very familiar.

"I didn't know you were an artist . . ." I began, and the realization struck me even as he laughed.

"It is *our* art," he said. "Not the mundane kind."

I had reached forward to touch the dark cheek. I dropped my hand, deciding against it.

"It's Lamia, isn't it?" I asked. "It's really her. . . ."

"Of course."

"Why?"

"She has to be someplace, doesn't she?"

"I'm afraid I don't understand."

He chuckled again.

"You're a dead man, Phoenix, and she's the reason. I never thought I'd have the good fortune to have you walk in this way. But now that you have, all of my problems are over. You will rest a few corridors away from here, in a chamber totally devoid of *mana*. You will wait, while I send for Werewolf to come and kill you. He was in love with Lamia, you know. He is convinced that you ran off with her. Some friend you are. I've been waiting for him to get you for some time now, but either he's clumsy or you're lucky. Perhaps both."

"So it's been Werewolf all along."

"Yes."

"Why? Why do you want him to kill me?"

"It would look badly if I did it myself. I'll be sure that some of the others are here when it happens. To keep my name clean. In fact, I'll dispatch Werewolf personally as soon as he's finished with you. A perfect final touch."

"Whatever I've done to you, I'm willing to set it right."

Gnome shook his head.

"What you did was to set up an irreducible conflict between us," he said. "There is no way to set it right."

"Would you mind telling me what it is that I did?" I asked.

He made a gesture, and I felt a compulsion to turn and make my way back toward the corridor. He followed, both of us preceded by his light.

As we moved, he asked me, "Were you aware that at each Starfall ceremony for the past ten or twelve years the *mana* content of the Starwind has been a bit higher?"

"It was ten or twelve years ago that I stopped attending them," I answered. "I recall that it was very high that year. Since then, when I've thought to check at the proper time, it has seemed high, yes."

"The general feeling is that the increase will continue. We seem to be entering a new area of space, richer in the stuff."

"That's great," I said, coming into the corridor again. "But what's that got to do with your wanting me out of the way, with your kidnapping Lamia and turning her to coal, with your sicking Werewolf on me?"

"Everything," he said, conducting me down a slanting shaft where the *mana* diminished with every step. "Even before that, those of us who had been doing careful studies had found indications that the background level of *mana* is rising."

"So you decided to kill me?"

He led me to a jagged opening in the wall and indicated that I should enter there. I had no choice. My body obeyed him. The light remained outside with him.

"Yes," he said then, motioning me to the rear of the place. "Years ago it would not have mattered—everyone entitled to any sort of opinion they felt like holding. But now it does. The magic is beginning to return, you fool. I am going to be around long enough to see it happen, to take advantage of it. I could have put up with your democratic sentiments when such a thing seemed only a daydream—"

And then I remembered our argument, on the same matter Elaine had brought up during our ride down the coast.

"—but knowing what I knew and seeing how strongly you felt, I saw you as one who would oppose our inevitable leadership in that new world. Werewolf was another. That is why I set it up for him to destroy you, to be destroyed in return by myself."

"Do all of the others feel as you do?" I asked.

"No, only a few—just as there were only a few like you, Cowboy and the Wolf. The rest will follow whoever takes the lead, as people always do."

"Who are the others?"

He snorted.

"None of your business now," he said.

He began a familiar gesture and muttered something. I felt free of whatever compulsion he had laid upon me, and I lunged forward. The entrance had not changed its appearance, but I slammed up against something—as if the way were blocked by an invisible door.

"I'll see you at the party," he said, inches away, beyond my reach. "In the meantime, try to get some rest."

I felt my consciousness ebbing. I managed to lean and cover my face with my arms before I lost all control. I do not remember hitting the floor.

How long I lay entranced I do not know. Long enough for some of the others to respond to an invitation, it would seem. Whatever reason he gave them for a party, it was sufficient to bring Knight, Druid, Amazon, Priest, Siren and Snowman to a large hall somewhere beneath the Cornish hills. I became aware of this by suddenly returning to full consciousness at the end of a long, black corridor without pictures. I pushed myself into a seated position, rubbed my eyes and squinted, trying to penetrate my cell's gloom. Moments later, this was taken care of for me. So I knew that my awakening and the happening that followed were of one piece.

The lighting problem was taken care of for me by the wall's beginning to glow, turning glassy, then becoming a full-color 3-D screen, complete with stereo. That's where I saw Knight, Druid, Amazon, etc. That's how I knew it was a party: There were food and a sound track, arrivals and departures. Gnome passed through it all, putting his clammy hands on everybody, twisting his face into a smile and being a perfect host.

Mana, mana, mana. Weapon, weapon, weapon. Nothing. Shit.

I watched for a long while, waiting. There had to be a reason for his bringing me around and showing me what was going on. I searched all of those familiar faces, overheard snatches of conversation, watched their movements. Nothing special. Why then was I awake and witnessing this? It had to be Gnome's doing, yet . . .

When I saw Gnome glance toward the high archway of the hall's major entrance for the third time in as many minutes, I realized that he, too, was waiting.

I searched my cell. Predictably, I found nothing of any benefit to me. While I was looking, though, I heard the noise level rise and I turned back to the images on the wall.

Magics were in progress. The hall must have been *mana*-rich. My colleagues were indulging themselves in some beautiful spellwork—flowers and faces and colors and vast, exotic, shifting vistas filled the screen now—

just as such things must have run in ancient times. Ah! One drop! One drop of *mana* and I'd be out of here! To run and return? Or to seek immediate retaliation? I could not tell. If there were only some way I could draw it from the vision itself . . .

But Gnome had wrought too well. I could find no weak spot in the working before me. I stopped looking after a few moments, for another reason as well. Gnome was announcing the arrival of another guest.

The sound died and the picture faded at that point. The corridor beyond my cell seemed to grow slightly brighter. I moved toward it. This time my way was not barred, and I continued out into the lighter area. What had happened? Had some obscure force somehow broken Gnome's finely wrought spells?

At any rate, I felt normal now and I would be a fool to remain where he had left me. It occurred to me that this could be part of some higher trap or torture, but still—I had several choices now, which is always an improvement.

I decided to start back in the direction from which we had come earlier, rather than risk blundering into that gathering. Even if there was a lot of *mana* about there. Better to work my way back, I decided, tie up any *mana* I could find along the way in the form of protective spells and get the hell out.

I had proceeded perhaps twenty paces while formulating this resolution. Then the tunnel went through an odd twisting that I couldn't recall. I was still positive we had come this way, though, so I followed it. It grew a bit brighter as I moved along, too, but that seemed all for the better. It allowed me to hurry.

Suddenly, there was a sharp turning that I did not remember at all. I took it and I ran into a screen of pulsing white light, and then I couldn't stop. I was propelled forward, as if squeezed from behind. There was no way that I could halt. I was temporarily blinded by the light. There came a roaring in my ears.

And then it was past, and I was standing in the great hall where the party was being held, having emerged from some side entrance, in time to hear Gnome say, ". . . And the surprise guest is our long-lost brother Phoenix!"

I stepped backward, to retreat into the tunnel from which I had emerged, and I encountered something hard. Turning, I beheld only a blank wall of rock.

"Don't be shy, Phoenix. Come and say hello to your friends," Gnome was saying.

There was a curious babble, but above it from across the way came an animallike snarl and I beheld my old buddy Werewolf, lean and swarthy, eyes blazing, doubtless the guest who was just arriving when the picture had faded.

I felt panic. I also felt *mana*. But what could I work in only a few seconds' time?

My eyes were pulled by the strange movement in a birdcage on the table beside which Werewolf stood. The others' attitudes showed that many of them had just turned from regarding it.

It registered in an instant.

Within the cage, a nude female figure no more than a hand high was dancing. I recognized it as a spell of torment: The dancer could not stop. The dancing would continue until death, after which the body would still jerk about for some time.

And even from that distance I could recognize the small creature as Elaine.

The dancing part of the spell was simple. So was its undoing. Three words and a gesture. I managed them. By then Werewolf was moving toward me. He was not bothering with a shapeshift to his more fearsome form. I sidestepped as fast as I could and sought for a hold involving his arm and shoulder. He shook it off. He always was stronger and faster than me.

He turned and threw a punch, and I managed to duck and counterpunch to his midsection. He grunted and hit me on the jaw with a weak left. I was already backing away by then. I stopped and tried a kick and he batted it aside, sending me spinning to the floor. I could feel the *mana* all about me, but there was no time to use it.

"I just learned the story," I said, "and I had nothing to do with Lamia—"

He threw himself upon me. I managed to catch him in the stomach with my knee as he came down.

"Gnome took her. . . ." I got out, getting in two kidney punches before his hands found my throat and began to tighten. "She's coal—"

I caught him once, high on the cheek, before he got his head down.

"Gnome—damn it!" I gurgled.

"It's a lie!" I heard Gnome respond from somewhere nearby, not missing a thing.

The room began to swim about me. The voices became a roaring, as of the ocean. Then a peculiar thing happened to my vision as well: Werewolf's head appeared to be haloed by a coarse mesh. Then it dropped forward, and I realized that his grip had relaxed.

I tore his hands from my throat and struck him once, on the jaw. He rolled away. I tried to also, in the other direction, but settled for struggling into a seated, then a kneeling, then a crouched, position.

I beheld Gnome, raising his hands in my direction, beginning an all-too-familiar and lethal spell. I beheld Werewolf, slowly removing a smashed birdcage from his head and beginning to rise again. I beheld the nude, full-size form of Elaine rushing toward us, her face twisted. . . .

The problem of what to do next was settled by Werewolf's lunge.

It was a glancing blow to the midsection because I was turning when it connected. A dark form came out of my shirt, hovered a moment and dropped floorward: It was the small bottle of djinn Dervish had given me.

Then, just before Werewolf's fist exploded in my face, I saw something slim and white floating toward the back of his neck. I had forgotten that Elaine was second *kyu* in Kyokushinkai—

Werewolf and I both hit the floor at about the same time, I'd guess.

. . . Black to gray to full-color; bumblebee hum to shrieks. I could not have been out for too long. During that time, however, considerable change had occurred.

For one, Elaine was slapping my face.

"Dave! Wake up!" she was saying. "You've got to stop it!"

"What?" I managed.

"That thing from the bottle!"

I propped myself on an elbow—jaw aching, side splitting—and I stared.

There were smears of blood on the nearest wall and table. The party had broken into knots of people, all of whom appeared to be in retreat in various stages of fear or anger. Some were working spells; some were simply fleeing. Amazon had drawn a blade and was holding it before her while gnawing her lower lip. Priest stood at her side, muttering a death spell, which I knew was not going to prove effective. Gnome's head was on the floor near the large archway, eyes open and unblinking. Peals of thunderlike laughter rang through the hall.

Standing before Amazon and Priest was a naked male figure almost ten feet in height, wisps of smoke rising from its dark skin, blood upon its upraised right fist.

"Do something!" Elaine said.

I levered myself a little higher and spoke the words Dervish had taught me, to put the djinn under my control. The fist halted, slowly came unclenched. The great bald head turned toward me, the dark eyes met my own.

"Master. . . ?" it said softly.

I spoke the next words, of acknowledgment. Then I climbed to my feet and stood, wavering.

"Back into the bottle now—my command."

Those eyes left my own, their gaze shifting to the floor.

"The bottle is shattered, master," it said.

"So it is. Very well . . ."

I moved to the bar. I found a bottle of Cutty Sark with just a little left in the bottom. I drank it.

"Use this one, then," I said, and I added the words of compulsion.

"As you command," it replied, beginning to dissolve.

I watched the djinn flow into the Scotch bottle and then I corked it.

I turned to face my old colleagues.

"Sorry for the interruption," I said. "Go ahead with your party."

I turned again.

"Elaine," I said. "You okay?"

She smiled.

"Call me Dancer," she said. "I'm your new apprentice."

"A sorcerer needs a feeling for *mana* and a natural sensitivity to the way spells function," I said.

"How the hell do you think I got my size back?" she asked. "I felt the power in this place, and once you turned off the dancing spell I was able to figure how to—"

"I'll be damned," I said. "I should have guessed your aptitude back at the cottage, when you grabbed that bone flute."

"See, you need an apprentice to keep you on your toes."

Werewolf moaned, began to stir. Priest and Amazon and Druid approached us. The party did not seem to be resuming. I touched my finger to my lips in Elaine's direction.

"Give me a hand with Werewolf," I said to Amazon. "He's going to need some restraining until I can tell him a few things."

The next time we splashed through the Perseids we sat on a hilltop in northern New Mexico, my apprentice and I, regarding the crisp, postmidnight sky and the occasional bright cloud-chamber effect within it. Most of the others were below us in a cleared area, the ceremonies concluded now. Werewolf was still beneath the Cornish hills, working with Druid, who recalled something of the ancient flesh-to-coal spell. Another month or so, he'd said, in the message he'd sent.

"'Flash of uncertainty in sky of precision,'" she said.

"What?"

"I'm composing a poem."

"Oh." Then, after a time, I added, "What about?"

"On the occasion of my first Starfall," she replied, "with the *mana* gain apparently headed for another record."

"There's good and there's bad in that."

". . . And the magic is returning and I'm learning the Art."

"Learn faster," I said.

". . . And you and Werewolf are friends again."

"There's that."

". . . You and the whole group, actually."

"No."

"What do you mean?"

"Well, think about it. There are others. We just don't know which of them were in Gnome's corner. They won't want the rest of us around when the magic comes back. Newer, nastier spells—ones it would be hard to imagine now—will become possible when the power rises. We must be ready. This blessing is a very mixed thing. Look at them down there—the ones we were singing with—and see whether you can guess which of them will one day try to kill you. There will be a struggle, and the winners can make the outcome stick for a long time."

She was silent for a while.

"That's about the size of it," I added.

Then she raised her arm and pointed to where a line of fire was traced across the sky. "There's one!" she said. "And another! And another!"

Later, "We can count on Werewolf now," she suggested, "and maybe Lamia, if they can bring her back. Druid, too, I'd guess."

"And Cowboy."

"Dervish?"

"Yeah, I'd say. Dervish."

". . . And I'd be ready."

"Good. We might manage a happy ending at that."

We put our arms about each other and watched the fire fall from the sky.

Printed in the United States
99909LV00005B/82-198/A